CRUEL
DELIGHTS

SIENNE VEGA

Cover Design by Steamy Designs

First paperback edition October 2023

Content Warning

Hello!

So, I just want to make it clear that this book is **FICTION**. It is written purely from a fictional standpoint. I **do not** condone any of the situations or content as it applies to real life.

This is a dark romance that features a stalker and serial killer plot line. It will feature content that some readers may find upsetting. The relationship between the MMC and FMC, Kaden and Lyra, is what I would categorize as "toxic". **Kaden as an MMC will NOT be redeemed**. As in, he will remain unapologetic, there will be no groveling and no changing into the "good guy". Likewise, with Lyra. These characters are who they are and they accept this about themselves. That's part of what makes them the only match for each other (in my view). If you are looking for more of a traditional romance story, then this is NOT the book for you.

Below is a more specific list of some of the content that will be included:

- Graphic gore and violence
- Graphic nonconsensual sexual violence
- Graphic dubious consent sexual situations/nonconsensual sexual situations
- Graphic depictions of somnophilia
- Graphic depictions of BDSM
- Graphic depictions of mental health struggles, including suicide
- Brief depictions of substance abuse
- Brief depictions of child abuse
- Brief mentions of human trafficking
- Other controversial subject matter, including brief depictions of racism, "slut-shaming", eating disorders and derogatory language about drug users

This book **is not** suitable for readers under the age of 18.

Now that that's out of the way, buckle up, and dive into this dark journey with Kaden and Lyra!

Don't forget to join my reader group HERE where you can discuss the book. 🖤

Sienne

1. LYRA

HIGH ALONE - ŞEVDALIZA

There's only one place I go when I'm trying to clear my head. It's my favorite spot in the city. Maybe the quietest too.

It's a hike up a grassy incline as good as any leg day in the gym. A huge elm tree greets you once you reach the top, from where you can look out and see thousands of people.

I plop down in the shade and unpack my things. I set up my laptop, peer out at the calming view, and then get to work.

Some find it depressing that I *choose* to spend time here. Some even call it morbid.

What they don't realize is that they're proving just why I like it here. Just why I don't like it down *there*.

In the city. With the rest of civilization.

Dead people don't judge. Dead people don't call you weird. They *definitely* don't give a damn that I sit atop the hill at the cemetery and telework.

You'd think the living wouldn't care either—it's not like they sign my paychecks.

I cross my legs, my laptop perched on my thighs, and I peer out at my loyal audience.

Gravestones stretch on for miles. Thousands upon thousands of once-alive people, now six-feet-under.

And it's *my* job to write about them.

My loyal audience.

Without them, I'd be stuck writing classifieds, or worse, horoscopes. Now *that* would be depressing.

As a warm, late-summer breeze feathers across my skin, I catch the eye of a mother at the bottom of the grassy knoll. She stands peering up at me, the hand of her small boy wrapped in hers.

If looks could kill, I'd be dead on the spot.

Yep, people definitely find it strange I hang out here. It's a good thing I don't give a fuck what they think.

I stopped caring what others thought a long time ago—*including* my family that barely remembers my name.

But it doesn't matter what they think anymore. I've survived long enough on my own to stop wondering about what my family would think. Any jobs I take up have managed to get me by, from my gig teaching piano lessons to writing obituaries for the local newspaper. Even my other source of income, the one some might consider less than appropriate, helps me make ends meet.

I smile to myself and bring up my banking app on my phone when I realize it's payday. Twelve-hundred bucks to spend as I please. Never mind that eighty percent of it's already spent. Six for the rent, two for my meds, one for my weed guy, the rest split between frivolous bills and the hope I'll one day build up the pennies that are my savings.

Except, I'm not happy as I open my banking app and see no deposit. Just the sad, pitiful double-digit numbers available in my checking account.

Where the fuck is my money, Winston?!

As if he's magically attuned to my thoughts, my phone

vibrates in my hand. An incoming call takes over my screen, his name popping up.

Naturally, since I want him to run me my money, I press accept.

"Lyra," he says in greeting. He sounds breathless. "I'm glad I could get a hold of you."

"Winston, I sent the latest obituaries through. I met my deadline."

"I saw."

Pause. Cue awkward silence.

He says nothing and I say nothing, and for a moment, we listen to each other breathe. Him, heavily. Me, seething and almost soundless.

"Um," I say finally, "it's Friday."

"Right. It is."

I blink. "Today's... payday."

"Right. It is," Winston repeats. Then he sighs. "About that, Lyra. You're not going to like this."

"That's what my Granny Opal said when she gave me up to the foster system."

"Listen, we value you. We really do. But..." he gulps down some air and I swear I hear another voice in the background— a low, sultry female voice. "We have to let you go, Lyra. It's just not working out. Your obituaries, they're pretty good. Well written."

"Isn't that what you wanted?"

"I've had five complaints just this week. You've gotten too tongue-in-cheek. People want their loved ones respected. Not belittled."

My jaw drops open. "I don't belittle anyone!"

"You called Mr. Herald Singleton a racist and sexist dinosaur of his time."

"I'm... not seeing the issue."

"Obituaries are an announcement of the dead—they're paying respects publicly."

"Cut the crap, Winston," I snap, jamming my things into my book bag. First my decade-old laptop, held together by duct tape and gum. Second, my sweater and crumpled up gum wrappers. "This isn't about my 'tongue-in-cheek' blurbs."

"Alright, Lyra, I'll keep it real with you. It's funding. The newspaper is making some cuts... and you happen to be one of the things on the chopping block. Turns out, nobody gives a damn about obituaries. Nobody even reads them."

"Baby, come back to bed," coos a voice in the background.

I sit up straighter against the elm tree, my spine rigid. "Who was that?"

"Nothing. Nobody. Point is, sorry. We're not able to keep you—"

"Is that Claudia from Astrology? Winston, that better not be fucking Claudia from Astrology!"

Claudia must hear me shriek on the phone, because she answers back, "Can't you just... hang up on that girl?"

Winston clears his throat a split second too late to conceal the comment. "Anyway, Lyra, I've got to go. I appreciate the work you've done. But, unfortunately, this is the end of the road with the *Easton Times*. Feel free to use me as a reference. We'll try to get you your final check in the next week or two."

"Winston, no! Don't hang up on me—is this because I wouldn't sleep with you at the holiday party—WINSTON!"

The line clicks, going dead.

My jaw's still hanging open. I stare at my phone, half shocked, half pissed as hell. I'm about to dial him back and tell him off when the groundskeeper approaches me wringing his hands. An unnatural, almost pained smile stretches across his lips.

"You've been disturbing the cemetery guests again with

your presence," he says. "We're going to have to ask you to leave."

"I'm sorry... but what? This is a cemetery! It's a public space."

"We've had complaints."

"It's the lady with the little boy, right? She had Karen written all over her."

I'm too pissed about my phone call with Winston to bother battling for my right to chill at the cemetery. I snatch my book bag off the grass and stomp toward the uncompromisingly tall and foreboding iron gates.

Winston doesn't answer the angry texts I send him. My calls go straight to voice mail. At the beep, I give him a piece of my mind.

"This is because I wouldn't fuck you, right?" I ask. "You had to make some cuts and a few sections were on the chopping block. Hmmm, I wonder who would go between fucking Horoscopes and Obituaries? One opened their legs, the other didn't! Fuck you, Winston—I petsit for your iguana when you were in the hospital getting your gout in check!"

After leaving two more messages just like that one, I reach the conclusion he's blocked me. I know because I test the theory using Google Voice and his number *rings*.

To think, I'd probably still have a job if I just let him hit at the office Christmas party. He was drunk off spiked eggnog; he probably would've given new meaning to the term minute man.

My job at the newspaper is my main source of income. What am I going to do?! It's not like decent paying jobs around the city are eager to hire some Black girl with zero professional experience, a music degree, and a nose ring.

"Fuck," I sigh. Then I pull up the calendar on my app to check my upcoming piano schedule. I have four clients booked for lessons this month. Not the most lucrative, but it'll keep the cash flowing in.

And then there's the other job. The less than appropriate one.

I was supposed to log on tonight anyway. I could put in an extra couple hours. Offer some exclusive deals. Maybe a bonus two-for-one pack. I'm mulling over the idea the whole time on the subway ride home.

Rent is due next week, and I refuse to ask for help. Not that I have many options. Granny Opal would hang up on me. Grady would tell me to work for it. Jael would try to recruit me into her line of work. And Imani's as broke as I am, meaning I could never take from her.

I dial up my clients. It's a short list, but a few have outstanding balances.

"Hello, Mr. Lee," I say brightly, putting on the fake happy voice I use to appear pleasant when interacting with clients. "Hi, it's Lyra. I was calling because I noticed you haven't paid your latest invoice. I can resend it if you'd like—hello? *Hello?!* Motherfucker!"

The asshole hung up on me. Three other clients do the same.

I become familiar with the dial tone by the time the subway pulls to my stop. Two go so far as to block me. Which also means I've probably lost them as clients.

I almost miss getting off at my stop because I bury my face in my hands and have a mini meltdown on the subway (something everyone riding ignores since mental breaks are depressingly common on public transpo).

At the last second, I get off, squeezing through the closing subway car doors.

Fuck. Fuck. Fuck.

It's not supposed to be like this. Then again, when has my life ever gone as I'd hoped it would?

Nobody gives a fuck about the piano. Even my clients,

most school-aged, don't care if they learn. It's their parents forcing them to learn how to play for *cachet*.

When I majored in music at Easton U, I'd been so hopeful. Stupidly so.

The idea was I'd be some brilliant talent discovered months into post-graduation. I'd play some concert as a newcomer on the scene and an agent scouting for talent would be amazed enough to offer me representation on the spot. As a professional concert pianist (how fancy does that sound), I'd be living the life—making money *and* pursuing my dream.

That's right. Obituaries are *not* my passion.

Granny Opal used to say if it's too good to be true, then it definitely is.

I found that out the hard way, when I graduated Easton U and found myself typing up paragraphs about somebody who died by choking on a chicken bone.

Not the most prestigious occupation.

Nobody grows up wanting to write about death... and do the other things I do.

A sigh blows from my lungs as I drag my feet.

How the hell am I going to explain this to Taviar and Jael?!

Thankfully, Taviar's pretty lax about the rent. He's the high-earner of the three of us—some sort of online seller that operates a digital shop. The finer details he keeps ambiguous.

As I turn the key in the door and enter our place, I'm reminded just how little I know about what he does.

Boxes fill up the wide, open spaced apartment. It's reminiscent of a warehouse in its construction. Chipped brick walls and exposed metal piping. Lightbulbs that go uncovered, bright and fluorescent, yet still a permanent shadow hovers along the edges of the room.

Our living room is basically his shipping center. More often than not, it's full of stacks and stacks of boxes. Boxes he does not want Jael and I to ever touch. His biggest stipulation for us living here, in an apartment where only his name's on the lease.

Other than that, Taviar is pretty chill, considering he pays half the rent. Jael and I split the other fifty percent. Her, twenty-five. Me, twenty-five.

Neither of us bother pretending we're as successful as Taviar apparently is. While I work odd jobs to make ends meet, Jael's no different.

A party girl hot on the social scene, Jael strives to model professionally. Sometimes, not-so-subtly, she winds up as a pretty wannabe model on the arms of wealthy men.

I don't ask *what else* she's doing to make her part of the rent.

It's not like I'm in any position to judge.

A line of sweat has broken out on my forehead as I drop my keys on the kitchen counter and rush to pour myself some cold water.

That's the other thing about my situation—I'm not in the best health.

My hand shakes as I pour the pitcher and chug a cool glass of water. I stop just before I take my horse pills. I've got sixty bucks to my name and can't afford to take regular doses. I can't even have a full meal with the dose. The only food that's mine in the pantry is a moldy loaf of bread and a bottle of Sriracha sauce.

My stomach gurgles in protest. A 'don't-you-fucking-try-it-unless-you-want-to-end-up-on-the-toilet' warning.

I'll have to ration the pills I do have left. Which means I need to skip this dose.

Instead, I shuffle to my room and do the only thing that'll calm my nerves instead.

I light up.

Kicking off my shoes and throwing my jean jacket into the growing pile of clothes at the foot of my bed, I grab a joint from my stash and welcome the relaxing calm that settles over me within minutes.

Tension deflates from my body. Stress vacates every nook and cranny it inhabited. My mind empties of stressful thoughts about bills and jobs, and fills with silly, faux deep thoughts.

I roll over on my bed and swing upside down, hanging halfway off the edge. My long, thick box braids spread out over the floor.

This is what I've needed.

Fuck Winston and those dumb ass horoscopes Claudia writes.

Fuck my piano clients who refuse to pay their invoices.

And fuck that groundskeeper and the Karen who complained about me at the cemetery.

They can all go to hell.

I'm indignant, yet somehow still calm on a kumbaya type of wave. I inhale, exhale, breathe in and out, stare around my messy room, feeling like my body's weightless and my mind's free.

Totally free.

I hum happily.

The paranoia crashes down on me out of nowhere.

SHIT!

I was fired! My main source of income is gone. What the hell am I going to do for money? How am I going to pay for my meds? How am I going to pay for this weed? Will Winston take me back if I agree to a hand job?!

That's meeting in the middle, right?

My gaze wanders, my body still hanging upside down on the bed, my heartbeat frantic.

I land on the far corner of my cramped, messy room.

It's where I do my other job. My dingy laptop rests on the top of the table, adorned by the different, fading stickers I've slapped across the case. Beside my trusty duct-taped laptop rests a leather cat mask.

Tonight.

The thing about pot is, you lose concept of time. I don't know how long I dangle upside down off my bed and stare absently at my desk. It must be minutes though. At some point, there's a sharp, insistent knock.

Immediately following, the door busts open.

Jael struts inside, placing her hands on her slim hips. How the hell does she manage to make entering a room look like a fashion show?

Legs impossibly long. Her waist basically nonexistent. Her face camera ready at all times.

She appears almost like a figment of my imagination. I blink several times to make sure she's real. Though Jael and I have been roommates for almost a year, we're not close. She's too cool and sociable for me.

The girl looks like Naomi Campbell. I'm her vertically challenged, baby-faced, less glamorous cousin, twice removed. The one you keep locked in the basement (at least in my head).

"Jael?"

"Get up, Lyra. We're going out."

"We... are?"

"You good to go or are you too high? Your eyes are pink."

I squint and sit up, my thick braids hanging down my shoulders. "I'm too high. You're kinda spinning right now."

"Girl, stop. Come with me. I'll fix you up."

"But... why?"

She shrugs. "I heard you got fired."

"How did you—"

"I've got some things you can try on. You've got a cute little figure. *Somebody'll* be interested."

"Wait... what... I'm not..."

"I'll sober you up."

"I've taken off my bra."

As far as I'm concerned, that's a definitive end to any discussion. No ifs, ands, or buts about it.

Once it comes off, it's not going back on.

Jael disagrees. She hacks out a sharp laugh. "Lyra, your tits are B at best. You don't need no fucking bra. Besides, it might work better if you don't wear one. It's provocative. Are you interested?"

"But where? I'm confused." I rub my temples, my mind muddled. "What kind of party is this?"

"Very upscale. Very highbrow and elite. Invite only."

"How'd you…"

"I snagged one thanks to Paulo, the guy I've been… seeing. I can bring one guest. Preferably a young and attractive female for his friend."

"No, I don't think—"

"When was the last time you had a dick in your pussy, girl?" She snatches hold of my hand and yanks me off my bed so suddenly, I trip over my own feet. "What I mean is—when was the last time you were on a date?"

"I'm not sleeping with some friend of your fuckbuddy, Jael."

"You don't have to sleep with him. Just be fun and flirty for a night. It'll be fun. I do it all the time. How do you think I met Paulo? You might like this, getting dressed up, made to feel beautiful and adored by rich men! Who knows? You might meet somebody you really *do* like.

"There's going to be doctors, lawyers, bankers, CEOs, celebrities. If you still can't find a man then, girl, it's you," she explains, leading me into the hall outside my room. Her long legs prove their use as she strides down the passageway and toward the last door on the right. Her room. "I'll loan you something. You're petite, but we'll make it work. It's official. No going back, Lyra."

I try and fight her for a couple footsteps. We pass Taviar in the hall. He frowns at me and says, "Lyra, where are you going?"

"Jael's taking me to a party?" I answer in question form.

His frown only deepens more in confusion before Jael pulls me away.

We disappear into her room. Over the next hour, I sway in a pot-induced mellow mood, Jael fussing over me like I'm a doll.

It doesn't fully register until we hit the building elevator and I catch my reflection in the glass.

I've been done up in a sexy, deep-plunging mini dress that shows plenty of thigh and hugs my ass. Sky-high heels I can barely walk in are strapped to my feet, and I'm caked in more make up than I've ever worn in my life.

I barely recognize myself.

Jael seems to love it, smirking as she spies me admiring myself. "You're a ten in that dress, Lyra. Tonight'll be good for you. You'll see."

I sure hope so.

2. LYRA

GET INTO IT (YUH) - DOJA CAT

"You're an asset," Jael says in the Uber ride to the party. "If you remember one thing from tonight, remember that. You've got value."

Night has fallen, filling the backseat of the car with shadows. In contrast, the streets couldn't glitter more. I sit as a shapeless figure in the dark, peering out the window like a tourist.

Never mind that I've lived in Easton my whole life. But the Easton I know—*that I'm familiar with*—is nothing like this.

From either side, I'm inundated with the dizzying spectacle of the rich and famous. Luxury hotels, designer boutiques, swanky bars and restaurants that look too expensive to breathe the air of, let alone set foot inside. Massive fountains and marble statues backlit by LED lights and wide sidewalks where spoiled passersby lazily stroll. Men in tailored suits stepping out of their million-dollar sports cars. The gazelle-like models on their arms fling their long hair over their shoulders and strut as if photographed on a runway in Paris.

They just might be. A gaggle of photographers flock

toward the entrance of a restaurant called Arcadia—apparently, some A-List starlet just arrived with her handlers in tow.

Everything seems to sparkle here. The personification of opulence. I can taste the money in the air, practically see the endless void of bank accounts stacked with millions. *Billions.*

What am I doing here?!

"Did you hear me, Lyra?" Jael asks.

"Hmmm?"

"You realize this could be your big break?"

"Value? Big break? Huh?"

Jael laughs with a roll of her eyes. "Let me break it down. Real short and simple for your high ass. Nobody gives a fuck if you can play the piano like Van Gogh or whatever."

That snaps me out of my reverie.

"Van Gogh? Van Gogh didn't play the piano. He literally cut off his own ear. Which would be the worst thing a musician could do."

"Whatever! You get my point. Nobody gives a fuck about you playing the piano like some famous dead guy. All the talent in the world doesn't mean squat unless you've got the right connections. Get it?"

I don't answer her. I've once again become taken with the sights and sounds outside the cramped backseat of the Uber. We've turned down Somerset Boulevard, one of the most famous streets in the state. If not country.

My gaze snaps to the Easton Opera House, and my jaw drops open in slow-motion fashion. Chills capture me, making me shudder in my seat.

The moment's surreal. The historic building comes to life before my eyes. Timeless stone columns and baroque facades with so much detail it'd take hours to study. All crowned by the massive glass dome. A skylight if there ever was one.

Dozens of men and women in black-tie dress make their way up the cascading steps leading into the renowned theater.

Tonight they're in for the operatic beauty that's *La Boheme*.

A sense of deep longing pulls at me. I've never wanted to belong somewhere more...

Even as we finish driving by, I twist in my seat and crane my neck for one last view.

Jael snaps her fingers for my attention. "*Do not* make me regret bringing you. Do not act all weird and doped out. Follow my lead. Tonight could be the night."

She primps in the rearview mirror despite the fact that the Uber driver openly leers at us. Pushing her tits up and smacking her lips together to make sure her lipstick's good and her mouth looks extra pouty, she's satisfied.

We pull up outside the Winchester. The most expensive hotel in the city.

There's a line of limos and town cars passing through. The routine is the same. The valet opens the rear doors and helps the next wealthy businessman or famous public figure step out. They're escorted into the hotel by the staff.

Everyone's in sweeping gowns and tailored tuxedos. Everyone's in masks.

I turn my head to Jael. "This is the party? We're not dressed right—"

"Sure we are."

"We don't have masks."

"Sure we do. Stop talking."

It's a command I become familiar with. I've still got a high going, though it's quickly fading. Jael steps out of the Uber half a block down. With her mile-long legs and sleek, torso-length hair, she looks like one of the models on the arms of the businessmen we saw earlier.

I'm not full of as much aplomb and instant sex appeal as she is.

I do my best, standing tall in my heels, popping a hand to

my hip. Jael shakes her head and then starts a fast stride down the street. I rush to keep up.

We're doing this. We're headed for the Winchester.

"What are we doing when they turn us away?"

"They won't."

"How do you know?"

"This is a Midnight Society party. A club full of some of the richest, most elite people in the country. Ever heard of them?"

"I've heard *of* them—not sure I buy it's a real thing. Sounds a little too illuminati for my tastes."

"We won't be turned away, Lyra. Girls like us are their bread and butter."

"But—"

"Here, our invitation. Give it to the security guard."

I take the little black card and wobble forward as she stands back and strikes a pose like a true model.

The man reads the card, looks up at us, and then gives an overt once over. He's deciding if we're attractive enough.

"Follow me."

We set off at another fast pace behind the man. He leads us through an alternate entrance that's not quite as extravagant as the plush-carpeted main door, but still stunning with glittering chandelier lights and thick-veined marble.

"Here."

He presents me with a mask—a much different, less ornate mask than many of the others donned by the privileged party-goers who used the main entrance.

It's made of delicate black lace with cut-outs for my eyes, only covering the upper half of my face. Barely a disguise at all.

Jael pulls hers out of her purse. At my raised brow, she says, "I kept mine from last time."

"Your phone," says the security.

I look away from Jael, then to him, before looking back at her. She shrugs.

"I don't bother bringing mine. They're not allowed here. You have to turn it in here and it's kept in a lockbox 'til the night's over."

"Oh... um... okay."

After another hesitant pause, I present the security guy my phone.

"You may wait here," he says, escorting us into another room.

We're not alone. The room is occupied with a handful of others waiting around, wearing the same masks we do. Mostly women, with a couple of men sprinkled in.

Everyone's beautiful. It's like I've walked into a casting room full of models.

What am I doing here?!

I glance at Jael. "What's going on? Why do we have to wait here?"

"Because we're *guests*. We don't have a real invite. Paolo should be coming down any second to get us."

"This isn't my kind of thing," I say, pulling my short dress further down my thighs. "I'm going to go."

Jael grabs my elbow. Her long nails pinch at my skin. "You're not going anywhere. You *need* this!"

I'm not sure what 'this' Jael is referencing, but a second later, a man with waxy hair that's slicked down to his scalp appears. He smiles in familiarity, wearing a cream suit and a popped collar, darting straight for me.

"*Buonasera, Lyra.*"

With no other pretense, he steps forward and kisses either of my cheeks.

"I'm sorry... who are you?"

"That's Francesco. Paolo must've sent him down to come get us. Let's go."

I'm herded along with the other two into a glass elevator. Francesco presses the fourth floor, then casts a polite smile at me.

"You are very exquisite," he says in a thick Italian accent.

My face warms. "Oh, err, thanks. You're, um, very exquisite too. I like your shoes."

There's a beat of awkward silence as the elevator cranks and we're being carried up several stories.

"He's very taken with you," Jael whispers. "Do your thing and flirt with him. His suit cost more than everything you own."

I glower at her and then turn back to Francesco. He hasn't stopped eying me—actually, it's more of a leer, like I'm a piece of meat to be devoured. I shift uncertainly and search my brain for topics I'd have in common with an Italian businessman who barely speaks a word of English.

"It's been really warm lately," I say conversationally.

His brow creases. "*Scusi?*"

"Hot," I say again, only louder. "It's been warm for September."

Jael tries to hide her giggle behind a polite cough.

I've never been more grateful for the ding of an elevator as its doors roll open. We walk out to an open-spaced atrium with a vaulted ceiling, full of people in fanciful gowns and tuxedos. They wear their even fancier masks over their faces and socialize to the backdrop of Chopin's Nocturne op. 9, no. 2.

I close my eyes, immediately swept away by the calming tempo and fluid composition.

My fingers ache to play along. They twitch at my sides, fluttering as if I'm at the keys, playing myself.

To any casual observer, I probably look odd as hell. But I don't care—I'm lost in the melody of the timeless piece.

Jael finally snaps me out of it. "Why don't you give Lyra a tour of the banquet hall, Francesco?"

My eyes pop open. "Huh? Wha?"

"Francesco's going to give you a tour. Paolo and I will be on the terrace. He's waiting for me out there."

She slips straight into the masked crowd socializing about their latest Teslas. Francesco offers me his arm. I almost rush after Jael, but she's disappeared among the sparkling gowns and waitstaff wandering around with trays of hors d'oeuvres, so I don't bother.

I should've known this would happen. Last year I attended some rooftop bar party with her, and she did the same thing; she disappeared with the first guy who made her see dollar signs.

With a sigh, I resign myself to keeping Francesco company. That's obviously what Jael wanted—me to keep him away from Paolo long enough for her to sink her hooks in him. I'll give her half an hour, then I'm out.

Francesco is nice enough, but unsettling nerves swim inside me. There's an element of assumption in his stare that makes me feel like he's started some kind of countdown in his head.

He shows me the large fountain at the center of the atrium, dipped in gold and shooting perfect arcs of water through the air. Though he tries his best as he speaks, I can barely understand a word. I resort to polite nods and vacant smiles.

It's too late by the time I realize one of these nods is answering a question—do I want to see more?

Francesco tucks my hand under his arm and leads me toward the glass elevator.

"I'd rather stay here than go."

"Yes, we go. Fifth floor," he answers, patting my hand.

"No, I meant I don't want to go."

"Yes, we are going."

As we step into the elevator, I'm beginning to think he's mishearing me on purpose. I wrench my arm from his and step back.

"We don't go. You go. Bye."

"Lyra—" his lips move as he speaks, but the elevator doors shut and silence him for me.

I huff out a deep breath, feeling like I've unloaded unpleasant weight. No offense to Francesco. He seemed okay... at times. I just had no interest in being his entertainment for the night.

Turning back around, I survey my surroundings. The classical music has continued to play in the background and the party attendees carry on socializing amongst themselves. Lively chatter and poised sips of champagne. They're all so rich, yet so boring.

This was the elite party Jael made a big deal about?

I scoff and move in the direction that'll take me to the exit. The only problem is, I step into a man. Another staff member of some kind. Unlike many of the others, who don a modest white jacket and black pants combo, this man is dressed in all-black with an earpiece.

"Are you one of the players?" he asks.

My left brow ticks up and I let out a confused laugh. "Players? As in for a live band? Is there one? I play the piano."

He seems to find my answer amusing... or at least his lips curl.

But it's not the kind of curl that makes me feel flattered.

"Come with me." His arm comes around my back. It doesn't touch me, but hovers close, meant to signal I'm supposed to walk with him.

I do, curious about what he wants. Jael's words echo back to me.

Nobody gives a fuck about you playing the piano like some

famous dead guy. All the talent in the world doesn't mean squat unless you've got the right connections? Get it?

What if there are connections at this party? What if I can impress someone with my skills and parlay that into a new opportunity?

The party is filled with sickeningly wealthy people. One of them has to have some kind of hookup.

If the party needs someone to play piano, I can do that. I'm still slightly high, but I'll *force* myself to sober up.

3. LYRA
BITING DOWN - LORDE

The man leads me up a wide staircase that gradually curves into an S shape. We come up on the next floor and I gasp at the Steinway in the open parlor. It's arranged in the center, between some tasteful accent chairs and artwork.

Not just any Steinway. It's the Red Parlor Grand Piano. Priced at over a million dollars. Made of more than thirty different types of wood.

It's like seeing Beyoncé in person. I'm so enamored I don't notice the man mentioning something about waiting there.

But I gladly do. I edge closer to the beautiful piano with its carved inlays and sleek polish and my mouth almost waters. What I wouldn't give to sit on this bench for five minutes and play...

Maybe I will. Maybe that's what they brought me up here for.

In the distant background, more chatter buzzes in the air. More party-guests wander down the hall. In my periphery, a handful of men in Venetian masks and long cloaks stride by.

I only have eyes for Red.

If I'm going to play, I need to be on my best behavior. I

need to bring my A-game. Digging around in my wristlet, I pop my next dose of meds. The horse pill catches in my throat, but I swallow a few more times and force it down.

The last thing I need is for my health issues to mess up this opportunity.

"Who do we have here?"

The voice is unfamiliar. Female. Shrill, with a side dose of patronization.

I look up to a woman swaying toward me, wearing a sneer on her pale face and a deep-plunging, emerald dress on her svelte frame. She almost looks like someone from an era gone by, like she's time-traveled to the present just to be a snobby bitch.

And I *know* she's a snobby bitch even at a glance.

Her blood-red lips stretch to reveal teeth, her eyes that are the same color of her dress rake over me. "You? You're who they've gotten to fill in?"

My brows squish together, and I'm about to answer her when I notice she's not alone. There's a man several feet behind her. He stands still and stares, his hands in his tuxedo pockets, giving no indication either way if he knows her or just happened by.

He's what most would call tall, dark and handsome. Handsome, because even despite the steel mask he wears covering half his face, it's clear his features are perfectly symmetrical. Between his strong jaw, straight nose and sharp cheekbones, he must have no short supply of women after him.

Tall, because he's several inches past six feet. His stature reads as masculine and powerful. The type that's commanding and confident and allows him to dominate any space with his size.

Dark, because his eyes might be darker than my own—two deep pools where no emotion, no spark lives. His hair is no less dark—the scruff decorating his angular jawline reveals he didn't bother shaving, and the rest of his hair frames his face in earthy brown locks pushed back by his ears. It's been months since his last cut.

If I didn't know any better, I'd say he threw on a tuxedo last minute and didn't give a damn about looking as debonair as everyone else.

Yet, that's what makes him look so fine. The effortlessness of his appearance. He's like a male model who wandered into a masquerade and slipped on a steel-molded mask in disguise.

But I see right through him—he's fine as hell, and judging by his cold indifference, he *knows* it.

My attention is forced back to the woman when she speaks. "Where'd they drudge you up from? Some slum in the inner city? Or was it Northam?"

"Excuse me?! An inter city slum?!"

"No need to be offended. I know what you are."

"And that would be?"

"Celeste," hisses the man. Though he's standing composed, his tone betrays him. It's chiding, like he's scolding a child.

The woman named Celeste rolls her eyes from behind her sparkling silver mask before she obeys. The mystery man's already started walking away in strides far too fast for her and her heels.

"Baby, slow down!" she pants.

As equally perturbed as I am perplexed, I return to my study of the Steinway—or *try* to for a few seconds.

The guy who brought me up here comes to collect me. I seize my chance, launching into questions about the player they're seeking, and listing my musical qualifications. My words make no difference. He remains nonplussed.

We start down the same hall Celeste and the mystery man went down. They disappeared through double gold-plated doors. Instead, we stop at a smaller, less ornate door halfway down. I'm following the man inside when I catch a glimpse of another door opening and shutting.

And a scandalous peek of what's inside.

A pudgy, liver-spotted man naked as the day he was born many decades ago, and an equally nude, much younger woman strutting toward him. A second nude woman slips out of the room as the door shuts. She walks the rest of the way down the hall in her tiny lace mask as if she's wearing everything she needs.

Nothing at all.

My eyes have widened. I can't help staring. What in the hell is going on? Is this one of those weird sex parties or are those women simply nudists?!

I'm still reeling. The guy jerks my arm and pulls me the rest of the way into the room.

It's as luxurious as every other space in this hotel. Gold trim and furnishings made of the most expensive woods. Lush wallpaper and carpeting and glittering lights. In the far corner, there's a vanity mirror and a foldable divider screen that seems to be dipped in as much gold as everything else.

"Is this a dressing room?"

"Wait here."

"I'm done waiting. What's going on?"

"The show begins in five minutes. Freshen up."

He walks out. I'm left alone. When I dart toward the door, it's locked from the outside. I back away as panic flutters to life inside my chest. I'm done with this strange party. I don't give a damn if Jael doesn't want me to go, or if she'll dismiss me as some boring cornball.

Better than what is going on here.

I pound on the door and wrench at the knob. I yell for someone to send help. Even go for my wristlet to grab my phone, then remember it was confiscated at the start of the party.

Shit.

I'm screwed. Job prospect or no job prospect, it doesn't matter anymore. I just want to go home, get high in the privacy of my room, and do my little show for my fans like I normally do on a Friday night at 11 p.m.

This isn't what I asked for.

The five minutes must end. The door flies open, and the guy grabs me despite my protests. He's with another guy this time, someone even brawnier than he is, who can probably crush me in the palm of his hand if he wanted.

"Let go of me!" I scream.

But no number of protests seem to do anything. I'm dragged through the last door next to the gold-plated double doors Celeste went into.

The second I'm forced inside, the excited buzz of chatter vibrates in the air. Dozens, maybe hundreds of voices. All behind what seems to be a massive curtain that stretches wall to wall. A split second too late, it dawns on me this is a stage.

I'm on stage.

The curtain lifts. Blinding stage lights make my eyes water. Rows upon rows of masked partygoers sit obediently in their seats. Many with curious, knitted brows. Many with wide smiles. Others with the flare of judgment and disgust to their nostrils.

I look to my left.

There's a bed. A bed sitting in the middle of the stage.

My heart explodes. It beats so fast it's a wonder it doesn't beat its way out of my chest. I take a horrified step back. The guys who have brought me out here, push me forward.

I fall to the ground. My knees bang against the wood flooring and my palms fly out to catch myself from sliding.

The audience *laughs*. Apparently, me falling is hilarious. My head tilts up as I cast them a glare.

What the hell is so funny about me skinning up my knee?

Several of them intake audible breaths. I follow where their attention has gone, and my insides go ice-cold.

A man walks up the stairs to the stage. He's in the proper party guest uniform, a designer tux and steel-molded mask that hides half his face. Unfortunately, his bottom half is still visible—the sick grin he's aiming at me.

All the pieces click together. This *is* a performance of some kind.

These people are here to watch the show. Watch me perform.

On that bed.

I scramble to my feet, but the man reaches me first. He grabs me by my elbow and wrenches me toward him.

"Not bad," he says, and a few more members chuckle. "Get on your knees and open that pretty mouth."

I'm horrified. I'm guided down by him and his hand clamped on my shoulder. My sore knees touch the ground for a second time and my ice-cold insides feel like they're so frozen they'll snap in half. If I take a breath too deep, if I move too suddenly, my ribcage will crack and my lungs will implode.

My gaze swings from the man standing above me, unzipping his pants, to several hoots and hollers from the audience, to the two security guards blocking my exit.

The man whips out his penis—average in size and girth, uncircumcised—and he tells me to get started.

"You know what to do."

I glance out at the audience. Despite their masks, their faces teem with anticipation.

The man scrabbles at my hair to force my attention back to him. His dick is inches away from my face, half hard.

"Please," I gasp. My brain has gone blank. Either from

horror, fear, panic, or all three. I can't think and my body feels incapable of moving as fast as I'd like. "Please don't make me."

The audience *roars* with laughter. As I look back out at them, I realize they believe this is role-play. That I'm acting.

He does too. His grin grows nastier and his fingers twist deeper into my thick braids. "Naughty girl," he says. "Do you really think those sad eyes will make me feel sorry for you? Suck my fucking cock."

"AHHH!" I scream.

He yanks me onto him so hard, my scalp prickles from the rough tug. My mouth fills with his penis 'til I'm pressed against his pelvis and wiry pubic hair, and he's hit the back of my throat. I flail and push at him. My hands slap onto his thighs and I fight against him. He's trying to choke me on his dick and I'm trying to push myself up off it.

A moment that feels like an eternity passes where we're locked into this struggle. Me trying to fight his dick out of my mouth and him squashing me back down onto it.

I can't breathe. A wave of dizziness washes over me. I begin screaming around his dick. The muffled sounds fill the theater and more members of the audience laugh, hoot, applaud.

The man who's shoved his dick into my mouth seems to be realizing I'm not role-playing. I actually don't want to suck him off. But he's going to force me anyway. His aura darkens, his teeth gritting. He digs his fingers tighter than ever into my hair and barks at me.

"You're going to suck this fucking cock and if you dare to use teeth, then—ARGH! *ARGHHHHH*!"

In my panic, as my lungs run out of air and my screams go ignored, I'm left no choice. I go to my last resort. His warning about teeth comes at the same time I use them. I bite down as hard as I can on his dick.

Through his silken flesh. Straight into the hardened tissue. So deep, my teeth sink down and blood fills my mouth.

The man hasn't stopped screaming. Loud, obscene, sonorous with torment.

I've bit his dick off—or as close to biting it off as possible. He's so shocked, so frozen and encapsulated in abject pain, that he hasn't let go of my hair. He hasn't even moved. He's stuck screaming out to no one but the sea of spectators in the audience.

Finally, I'm free. I pull myself off him and fall backward onto my ass. The man collapses. The security guards rush toward me, likely to apprehend me. Punish me somehow.

I don't want to find out.

As they launch at me, I anticipate them and roll to my right. My body tumbles across the stage 'til I'm able to get back on my feet. Ditching my heels, I take off barefoot. Not toward the door we came through, but a different door.

The emergency exit door that's glowing from the right side of the stage. My only chance at freedom. Chaos is breaking out behind me. I don't glance over my shoulder to check. The cacophony of sound tells me all I need to know.

Between shocked gasps and murmurs from the audience, the angry growls of the security guards, and the pained screams from the guy whose dick I bit off, I've left a huge mess.

But I couldn't care less. I keep running. I shove the emergency exit doors open and tear off into the night.

4. KADEN
MOTH TO A FLAME - THE WEEKND & SWEDISH HOUSE MAFIA

"**W**ell," says Mr. Vanderson, grinning broadly, "that was quite the show, wasn't it? A bit gorier than usual, but *very* entertaining."

His wife purses her lips and pulls her shawl tighter about her shoulders. "They've certainly gone for shock value."

"That couldn't have been real," says Talia Weinberg. She blinks around the table with big cow eyes and long lashes. "Klein didn't really get his... *appendage* bitten off, did he?"

From where he's seated, Nolan snorts sipping his whiskey sour. "No, Talia, the gallon of blood he lost was simulated. It was ketchup."

"Really—"

"No, really, you twit." Nolan shakes his head and swills the rest of his drink. Ignoring the hurt flickering onto Talia's face, he turns to everyone else at the table. "I spoke with him a few minutes ago. He's got to have forty stitches on his schlong just to *maybe* get it reattached the right way."

Mr. Vanderson strokes his grizzled, grayed beard. "I do wonder... getting your Johnson bitten off like that? What will it be like in the aftermath? Will it ever function?"

"Harold," hisses his wife.

"What, June? I'm simply wondering. As all men at the table are."

Several men nod their heads. One or two's faces turn green with nausea. Nolan interjects again.

"You know it won't be. I'd be surprised if he ever gets a hard-on again. His dick is forever broken thanks to that bitch."

"Who was she, anyhow?" asks Mr. Newton, pushing his glasses up his round nose. "I've never seen her at the Market here or the Mill in Northam. She's certainly never been to any of the prior shows."

Mrs. Vanderson's expression goes tart. "She was one of *your* kind. Wouldn't you know?"

When her husband shoots her a pointed look, she falls silent. However, her tart countenance remains. Mr. Newton gives nothing away. He sits, cool and levelheaded, picking up his Scotch to nurse in hand.

"This might surprise you, June," he says. "But, no, we don't all know each other. And it would do you well to refrain from your prejudice. It speeds up the aging process."

"Well!" she gasps, tossing her dinner napkin.

The table erupts into dramatics. Mrs. Vanderson cries out for an apology. Mr. Vanderson tries his best to shush and sedate her. Mr. Newton stands his ground and goes on to remind Mrs. Vanderson about her husband's many affairs. Talia and Nolan break out into an argument about the sky being blue... or some other juvenile topic.

I sit and watch from my seat at the end of the table.

Two shows in one night. Both uninteresting. Both a chore as I sit and wait them out.

What's being discussed only interests those prone to gossip. People easily drawn into useless discussions about scandal and what will or won't happen next. They pass judgment and then crow when judgment is passed on them.

Mrs. Vanderson being a prime example.

She springs out of her chair and then waddles away with distressed wails that echo in her wake. Left no choice except to follow, Mr. Vanderson gives the rest of us an apologetic smile and then falls into line. He disappears from the dining room in search of his wife.

Mr. Newton sits taller, his round shoulders straighter. He cuts into his lamb chops with extra zeal.

Nolan turns to me. "You've been extra quiet. Even for you."

I sip from my brandy. "I'm simply enjoying the atmosphere."

"Give it a rest, K," Nolan laughs. "You're bored as hell, and you know it. I can't blame you. I'm bored as hell too. You'd think Klein getting his dick munched off would be more epic than it was. That's what he gets for volunteering to participate in the show. You never do the Market's live show. Buy your products in private like a normal guy seeking to get his rocks off. Now he's without a working dick."

Every last word Nolan utters goes unheard and ignored. My attention has moved to Talia. She sits directly across from me.

Her features are too pinched, and the plastic surgery she's had has become distracting, but her cheeks are still flushed from her argument with Nolan. The way the pink creeps along her pale complexion is distracting.

It conjures up what many would say is the wrong kind of imagery.

Imagery like the pooling of blood over time. What she'd look like losing air, her airway constricted and cut off entirely as she sputters to do something as simple as breathe. Then the inevitable vacancy in her eyes once she loses the fight and can no longer hold on. The color that once filled her cheeks gone. Never to return...

Clanging silverware forces me out of my fantasy.

I return to the present to Nolan prattling on. He hasn't noticed my inattentiveness. Though Talia has moved on from sitting poised in her chair and picking at the greens on her plate to engaging Mr. Kimura in conversation.

Talia Weinberg is the daughter of a movie producer. She's a former beauty queen and failed actress, which means she has scrambled eggs for brains. However, because she's so stupid and useless, it wouldn't be fair to pursue her. She poses no threat. She's done no wrong. She has hurt no one... except for herself by going under the knife so many times to carve up her face.

Simply put: she doesn't meet my criteria.

I bring my glass to my lips for another taste of brandy. I'll have to keep looking.

Tonight will make three weeks and five days. Three weeks and five days too long.

After so long, the urge intensifies. It mutates into a hunger that's ravenous. That's desperate.

I prefer never to reach such hunger. Such desperation. Carelessness is the end result.

My mortal enemy when I pride myself on composure. At all times, I am in control of what, when, who, how.

Why.

The why is always the most integral piece of the act. The reason always has to be justified.

However, when I'm desperate—*when I'm hungry*—I'm careless, and the why ceases to matter.

I will have to sate myself soon. Before I ever reach careless desperation.

Celeste appears in the dining room doorway. Her dark red

lips stretch into a lascivious smile. Then she wanders away. Back out of sight, going off to who knows where.

Because she knows I'll follow.

"Excuse me," I say. I toss my dinner napkin onto my plate and leave Nolan chatting with no one. He doesn't notice the difference.

I leave the formal dining room behind. It's one of many.

Soirees like tonight draw almost every self-important member of the Society. It's an excuse to dress up and show off, two of their favorite things in life.

One of my favorite things in life, I'm pursuing right this moment.

I stalk the hall, slow and silent, passing by the other formal dining rooms filled with zealous chatter about tonight's show.

Everyone is so scandalized a prostitute bit off Klein's dick. If they'd seen a tenth of the dismembered parts I have, they wouldn't be so impressed...

I keep up the hunt. I track her down the rest of the hall and find her in the room I knew she'd be.

My hunger for flesh might be growing, but the other kind of hunger for flesh will have to do.

For now.

I barge into the room and slam shut the door.

Celeste spins around from the vanity mirror with feigned shock on her face. This is the moment she's been fantasizing about all night. The next time I'd have her. Despite the fact that I discard her after every use.

In Celeste's head, I'm merely playing... *hard to get*.

She comes to me, meeting me halfway across the room. Her talon-fingers glide up my chest, and she leans closer in hopes for a kiss.

"There you are," she purrs. "Baby, I've missed you. Let's be naughty—come with me and we'll sneak onto the stage. No one has to—*ouch*!"

I've gripped Celeste's arm with crushing force and tossed her over the armrest of the sofa in the room. Her waif-like form is almost airborne for a moment. Weighing no more than a hundred, maybe a hundred and ten pounds, she's all sharp bones from years of casual bulimia.

I am not attracted to Celeste in the slightest.

Her cheeks are hollowed out, and the rest of her face, from her heavy brow to her square chin, vaguely resembles Klein, her cousin. Her body is an unsightly mix of scars and bruises. There's little to grab onto. Little softness, fewer curves, mostly bones.

At one point in time, she may have looked better. Healthier, with more color and less of an aura of self-loathing.

However, she's an easy, quick, desperate lay. So her cunt will have to do.

She purrs some more as I shove up her dress and tear away her panties. I've pulled out my cock and rolled on a condom.

"Baby," she says, trying to adjust her position.

My hand clamps down on her shoulder and I push her back down. Then I slam into her. Her purr turns into a throaty groan. It could be from pleasure, though I suspect it's more so from pain. I'm well-endowed and she's barely wet—always an issue with her, prompting her to carry lube for her many casual hookups.

Unfortunately, I'm impatient and I'm already inside of her. Meaning, I don't care to stop, and she'll have to deal.

Celeste takes what she can get. She knows if she protests, I'm gone. The fantasy she's dreamed up will evaporate, and she'll be left alone and sober. Her worst living nightmare.

I'm quick to get myself off. I pump away as she squirms beneath me and murmurs baby into the sofa cushion. Once or twice she winces when I go too hard, too deep, and she's too dry. Not once does she protest, knowing this is what she wanted.

This is how I treat her. This is what scrap from me she'll take.

Any small, insignificant scrap.

I come and promptly remove myself from her. The condom gets tossed into the nearest bin. She remains bent over the sofa armrest for a moment longer, her bare, flat ass still presented to me as if in hopes I'll come back for more.

I tuck myself away and zip up.

"You're pathetic," I say. "We're done. Move on."

"Baby." She sinks to the floor, looking every bit a disheveled mess. Her dress hangs loosely, her hair's started falling out of its pinned updo. Sweat gleams on her pale skin and the marks on her arms are fully visible, no longer covered by makeup. She holds out a hand to me. "We should do it. Perform at the Market's live show. I'd do it... I'd suck your cock in front of everyone. I'd fuck you in front of them. Wouldn't it be naughty?"

"Get one of the other men you fuck to do it."

"But—"

I slam shut the door as abruptly as I reeled it open.

After that quick tryst with Celeste, I should be fine. My appetite should be somewhat calmed. Instead, as I walk down the hall, I feel more predatory than before. It's alive in my veins, the craving for the hunt.

The real thing.

"Kaden, there you are," says Nolan. He approaches clutching his drink. "The Owner is looking for you. He's joined us in our dining room. He says it's very important."

I grit my teeth, though I oblige. I am a member of the club out of obligation and tradition. Not of my own volition. If it were up to me, this club would be disbanded, and everyone belonging to it would spontaneously combust into flames.

The world would be better off.

On my way following Nolan, we pass by a distraught Mrs.

Vanderson and her husband. She's weeping into her handker-chief as he rubs her shoulders and tells her it's okay.

"You were right, m'dear," he shushes. "But you shouldn't say that type of thing out loud. You know how they get."

"H-he attacked me, and y-you did nothing."

My gritted teeth grind together. No one notices. It's subtle enough that it doesn't reflect on my face.

On the outside, I look bored and indifferent. On the inside, I'm making a mental note to return to the Vandersons. They just may be the why I'm looking for. Two people toxic enough they cause harm with their irrational prejudice based off characteristics as natural-born as something like skin tone.

There are far more valid reasons to hate someone than a hue of color. The stupidity astounds me.

The Owner waits for me at the head of the table. He sits in his majestic robe and gold-plated bauta mask in the shape of an owl. The mask conceals his entire face from view. He wouldn't have it any other way. The rest of the table has been cleared. Others, like Talia and Mr. Newton have presumably been dismissed.

Nolan and I stop at the opposite end.

"You wanted a word," I say.

He sips from a goblet plated in gold. The liquid slips under the opening of his mask where his mouth is, and he gives a slow nod.

"Yes," he says in a voice many would call deep and mysteri-ous. "Nolan was just reminding me of your after hour proclivities."

Nolan nods too. His nod is faster, more eager. The pride on his face vanishes when he glances at me.

"What about them?" I ask with restraint.

"The woman who escaped tonight," he says. "She was not a player. She was some guest brought illegally into our club."

"Yes, and...?"

Nolan sucks in air. The Owner stills.

Both are surprised by the impatience in my tone. My lack of deference to him. I remain indifferent.

"And we do not allow outsiders to escape once they've been invited inside," he explains. "Your *hobby* will be of use."

"You want me to capture her and return her to you."

"I want her eliminated. She cannot be allowed to get away under any circumstances. Is this something you are willing to undertake?"

A moment of silence passes. Nolan's stopped breathing at my side. The Owner peers at me from behind his gold, molded mask with his gold-plated goblet. I consider my options and his offer.

However, it's the urge that rises up. That senses the opportunity at my fingertips. It climbs up inside me like a monster buried within.

My expression remains the same while my eyes tell a different story. They flash with hunger.

"Yes, it's something I'm willing to undertake."

5. KADEN
INERTIA CREEPS - MASSIVE ATTACK

Lyra Nicole Hendrix is twenty-four-years-old. She is one of two children. She grew up in lower Harrisburg, one of Easton's poorer boroughs. She graduated from Easton University with a Bachelor of Arts in Music and a minor in American History.

According to the state identification card she registered a year and a half ago (she has no license and can't drive), she's five foot three, a hundred and thirty-three pounds. Her employment history reflects many young adults in her tax bracket—a depressing ballad of struggle and poverty that seems never-ending. Thirteen jobs in five years. All minimum wage. None she worked longer than six or seven months. Several she worked at once, in between classes, running the gamut between cliché waitress positions and novelty gigs like Christmas elf at the local shopping mall.

She has seventy-five dollars and eleven cents in her checking account and a buck-thirty in her savings. In comparison, she's sixty-nine thousand dollars in debt from the myriad of loans she took out to pay for her college education. Loan payments she's since gone delinquent on.

No children. Darker complected. African American. Mid-back length hair she keeps in some sort of braided style (note to research at a later date). She has few friends and spends an inordinate amount of time online, tapping away on the keyboard of her decade-old laptop (so old the manufacturer no longer makes it, and she holds together with duct tape).

There isn't a single detail about Lyra Hendrix that doesn't inspire pity—*or* agitation, depending how I view the situation.

The girl was given an unfair hand from birth. She was born into an environment that left little room for success, let alone real wealth. Due to no college savings on the part of her ill-prepared family, she was forced to take out loan after loan. Forced to work menial jobs that were either insufferable or degrading (sometimes both). She graduated with thousands upon thousands of dollars in debt, and zero career prospects to her name.

Coming from a lower class family put her at a severe disadvantage from the start. Being both Black and female did not help matters. In the reality of the world we live in, she was already working against a strong current that pushed back against her at every turn. Doors were always unfairly closed for her that never would've been for someone like me—a Caucasian male born into a family that has a decades-long legacy in terms of wealth and power.

However, there's many choices she's made that have made her situation worse, demonstrating a lack of rationale on her part. She majored in one of the most useless degrees imaginable—*music*. She was an average student in most subjects, earning Bs and Cs and the occasional D. Her appearance likely turns away employers in professional environments. In particular, the nose ring she insists on wearing to job interviews and the dark lipstick she won't let go of. The state of dress she's often found in doesn't help matters—tight-fitted t-shirts baring her midriff and worn tennis shoes or distressed-anything.

The girl lacks sense. She lacks logic and ambition. Worst of all, *discipline*.

It's no wonder her life is a chaotic dumpster fire.

I dedicate a day to learning about my newest prey and am bored before noon. The fact that she wakes up a quarter after ten makes it that much more pathetic.

Two hours spent observing the girl, and I'm questioning if I've been subjected to some undiscovered form of human torture—following around a clueless, irresponsible young woman who eats Hot Cheetos for breakfast and has little more than ten cents to her name.

I heave an exasperated sigh as Lyra strolls down the street engrossed in her cell phone. I will give kudos where kudos is owed—one skill she's mastered is the ability to walk down a busy city street with her eyes glued to her phone screen.

Other pedestrians come the opposite way and she dodges each one. She steps left to avoid the door of a dry cleaner's swinging open, and she pauses just in time as the crosswalk light turns red and a slew of cars drive by.

Not once does her gaze leave the phone.

The stereotype is dauntingly true: "Generation Z" as they're affectionately called by the greater society, are obsessed with their personal devices.

It's their ultimate form of communication and socialization.

She's texting. Her fingers fly over the screen as she waits for the light at the crosswalk. Instinctively, when the light blinks from red to white and others around her begin moving, she does too.

The girl *crosses the street* still with her attention on her phone.

Either she's a master at feigning obliviousness, or she's a kidnapper's nocturnal emission in the flesh.

Replace kidnapper with mugger. Rapist. Escaped convict on a killing spree.

Or *me*.

Common sense would dictate that, after an ordeal like Lyra suffered mere days ago, she'd be traumatized. Perhaps paranoid the secret ultra-rich club she escaped Friday night would be after her. An assumption that would be correct.

They are after her.

And though I do not, and will never, consider myself *one of them*, I am also after her. More so for my own selfish motivations than any other why, but it still seemed to fit my usual set of principles.

Prostitutes are fair game. So are any other dregs on society.

The problem is, upon further research, it appears Lyra Hendrix isn't a prostitute. If she is, then she's a relatively new one with no traceable history I could find (and I am meticulously thorough when conducting research).

This means she no longer fits my criteria. Beyond being tasked to eliminate her by the Society and as pitiful as her life is, she does not appear to meet my *why*.

I force my observation to continue anyway.

Lyra walks another three blocks to the headquarters of the *Easton Times*. The newspaper's reputation hovers between gutter-level and rancid piss water. Its readership has fallen by more than sixty percent in the last five years, and they've gone through a revolving door of head editors. Most of the articles they publish are rubbish you can find on any quack website online.

It's no wonder they employed Lyra.

She disappears inside. I may no longer be able to see her, but I won't be losing her whereabouts anytime soon. I've linked our phones with a useful tracking app that provides me

Lyra's exact coordinates at all times. Assuming she has her phone on her. Which she does. The device often accompanies her to the *toilet*.

I wait it out.

In the meantime, I call the office. Rebecca answers formally, as if it's a patient calling and not her fucking boss.

"What are you doing?"

"Doctor Raskova, I was hoping you would call in. Eunice Mitchell called earlier to reschedule her pre-op consultation. I told her I would check with you before settling on a new date."

"I couldn't give less of a damn about rescheduling her. Pick a date that doesn't conflict with any of my other patients."

"Any preference as to day of the week? Time?"

"It would be wonderful if you would make a decision for once, Rebecca. Without consulting me over every trivial detail. I didn't call you about Eunice Mitchell and her atherosclerosis. I called so that you could clear out my calendar for the rest of today."

"But you just said you don't care when you're scheduled—"

"Something has come up. I am preoccupied. Clear out my schedule. Do you understand?"

She sounds more confused as she answers with, "I guess so."

I provide no further clarification before hanging up. I don't have the time nor patience to coddle Rebecca and her inability to follow simple directions. She lacks decisiveness and is thoroughly unable to adapt to my workflow.

One more fuck up, and she will be at the unemployment line like the others.

It's no surprise I go through medical secretaries and assistants like Celeste cycles through random men on Easton's nightclub scene.

I require perfection from those I employ because I demand it of myself. I didn't become a vascular surgeon because I needed to, or even wanted to out of some selfless desire to help mankind.

As the son of the third richest Russian man on the earth, I didn't have to do anything with my life beyond exist as my father's heir. I chose the field I did because of my superior intellect and abilities. I save humans from themselves—as their weak, fragile, failing anatomies collapse, I am there to save the day.

Play God.

Soak in the blood as I cut them open and peer inside their souls. With their life in my hands, I am all-powerful. I am capable of giving life *and* taking it away.

My hunger often lurks inside me as a hidden creature demanding to be let out. Demanding that I give in and take the life away. It would be so simple to do so and pass it off as natural causes.

If Lyra does not fit my why, perhaps Eunice Mitchell will on my operating table. The woman has always been unpleasant; she was once charged with animal cruelty after refusing to slow down for a stray dog in the road (when I say I am a thorough researcher, I mean it).

She deserves to die more than Lyra, who may be pathetic but seems harmless.

The thought is at the forefront of my mind when the doors to the *Easton Times* office open. Lyra wanders out looking distressed.

It's the first time I've seen her without her phone in hand. She wraps her arms around herself as if cold on this humid September afternoon and tucks her head down. She's still refusing to pay attention to where she's going, walking fast down the block with her gaze on her beat-up shoes. Does this girl realize how easy it would be to come up behind her and pull her into the nearest alleyway? Make her disappear *forever*?

Agitation prickles the back of my neck.

Perhaps Lyra deserves to die, after all. She's so irritatingly clueless and defenseless. She doesn't even *try* not to be.

I might need a new why category—*too pathetic to go on*.

These would be the people who would be best put out of their misery. A complete and total waste of life.

I tail her the entire way home. From the many blocks on the street she rushes down to the subway underground, where she plops into a seat and remains sullen-faced and silent for the duration of the ride.

A sad, innocent little lamb that's being led to slaughter without even knowing it.

What is it that's gotten you so down in the dumps, little lamb?

The question lingers at the forefront of my mind as I stand on the opposite side of the train car, holding on to the metal bar above.

She doesn't notice a thing. She's completely unaware that, as she jumps to her feet and gets off at her subway stop, I do the same from two doors down. She has no clue a predatory man who could devour her as an afternoon snack trails behind her every step of the way home.

Such easy, easy game. Too easy, too unearned.

Lyra lives in an apartment building that was once a sheet metal warehouse. The building still possesses many qualities of a warehouse—squat in shape, cold floors and unsightly brick walls, a permanent draft that surfs the air, with structural issues that likely wouldn't pass modern building code.

The rent per apartment is well out of her income bracket; however, she's been lucky enough to latch onto a man willing to pay most of the rent. She contributes a measly six hundred for her single bedroom while the rest of the space seems to be his.

As she retreats into the warehouse building, I invite myself to the second floor of a corner store across the street from her. The entire floor is comprised of an office, though judging by the cobwebs I find when I pick the lock and enter, it's not often used. If someone happens by, I'll lie and pretend I'm interested in purchasing the property.

With the salary I make and inheritance I have, I easily could. If I truly wanted to, I could buy the whole damn block Lyra lives on.

I make it to the office window at the same time the door pops open to her bedroom. She tosses her book bag on the floor and then flops backward onto her bed.

No surprise that she keeps an incredibly messy room. It's borderline unsightly.

Clothes scattered everywhere. Stacks of books wedged onto a small bookshelf and even used as a prop for an old can of soda and an assortment of other crumpled up snacks she's only half eaten. She's papered the walls with collages and mood boards known as "lifestyle inspo."

For a while, she lays around in her unmade bed, staring up at the ceiling. Occasionally, her lips move as she presumably talks to herself.

I need a means of listening in. I make a mental note to bug her room at my first opportunity. In the trunk of my Tesla I keep a duffle bag of camera and mic equipment for instances like these, where I may need to track my prey.

Eventually, she sits up and digs around inside the drawer of her bedside table. She pulls out a lighter and what looks vaguely like a cigarette. Squinting my eyes from behind the pair of binoculars I've brought with me, I stare at the tiny rolled up item in her hand and realize it's no cigarette.

It's a joint.

Lyra Hendrix is a pothead.

Of course she is.

Perhaps the most unsurprising piece of information I've learned about her.

She lays back amongst her many pillows and wrinkled sheets and inhales a deep puff from her joint. Whatever was troubling her only moments ago seems to melt away as she closes her eyes and lets her limbs spread out at her sides.

You'd think she was on vacation at some luxury resort the way she's lounging. The calm sense of satisfaction that comes over her face.

No wonder she's a loser.

When she's not feeling sorry for herself like earlier, all she does is lay around and get high.

I grit my teeth and glare at her from behind my binoculars. Perhaps I really *do* need to add a new why to my list of requirements—a waste of life deserving to have it taken away.

That category perfectly fits someone like Lyra Hendrix. If she won't fight for herself, then she deserves to be put out of her misery.

6. KADEN
CYBER SEX - DOJA CAT

Hours pass by before I realize it. I have a tendency to immerse myself in my surveillance when pursuing new prey. Those in my life, like Rebecca, my secretary at the medical office, are aware I have a habit of disappearing at random.

Usually when I do, it's for a reason like this. However, I've never lost track for *hours* before.

The sun is setting by the time I blink and Lyra's springing up in her bed. She's spent the afternoon high as a kite, rolling around every so often. At some point, she grew too hot and stripped off her pants, settling in her tank top and panties.

She's still high getting up off the bed. The only difference is she's realized she's running late for something. She rushes about her room, tossing aside wrinkled blouses and denim shorts. Finally, she resorts to her closet, disappearing inside for a brief second.

I step closer to the window, peering unblinkingly at the open door. I can't see inside, but she must be changing behind it. Her tank top and panties fly through the air and join the growing pile of clothes on the floor.

When she emerges, she's in one of those summer dresses women wear when they pretend they don't realize it drives men insane—though, admittedly, most men are like neanderthals the second an attractive woman reveals even a sliver of skin. Neither party is innocent.

Where is she going dressed like that? A date? A meet up with friends?

As far as my research revealed, Lyra Hendrix is a loner with few friends and no family she keeps in regular contact with.

It has to be some kind of meet up with someone. She wouldn't dress like this otherwise.

The dress is tight at the bust with thin straps and stops at midthigh. The light, breezy fabric might as well be alive; every time she moves, it flicks along with her, teasing another inch of thigh. At one point, as she spins around and faces the oval-shaped mirror hanging on her wall, the dress flips at such an angle, I catch a peek at the underside of her ass cheeks.

Definitely a date.

This is the dress a woman wears to do this: play innocent and tease the hell out of some man.

Is she even wearing panties? She never went to the dresser to grab any...

My grip on the binoculars tightens. Though I may have only been following Lyra Hendrix's every move for a few hours, her poor choices have already begun to breed deep irritation. I'm not sure why the pathetic girl is able to get under my skin so easily.

It must indeed be a sign she deserves to be my next kill. No one unworthy would inspire such a reaction out of me.

She applies some make up at the mirror—nothing off-putting like the dark lipstick she seems keen on. In fact, she puts on some kind of pink shade and then messes with that wand women use to apply mascara.

Grabbing her phone and a purse, she rushes out the bedroom door.

Two minutes later, she's doing the same out the building's front door. I've already gone downstairs to meet her from across the street. As she lightly jogs down the block, I'm using my long stride to my advantage, walking only a few paces behind to keep up.

We ride the subway together. We walk down several more blocks, heading deeper into the heart of the city. She's going to one of the most popular streets in town, well known for its nightlife.

Vale Street is a long stretch of different bars and clubs. It starts off innocuously enough. A few bars and lounges that provide a mellow atmosphere for those simply wanting a drink or two as they spend time with friends. By the midpoint, the street takes a dive into seedier and seedier territory, transforming into a line full of dance clubs and pubs where people go to party and drink and do drugs until sunup.

I've always been above such weak human impulses. Even during early adulthood, when many of my college peers were binge-drinking until they blacked out or vomited their insides.

Thankfully, Lyra doesn't go far down Vale Street. She stops at one of the first establishments on the block—The Velvet Piano.

My interest is piqued as I wander inside the crowded bar a couple minutes after her. I stop footsteps inside and scan the sea of patrons. Ambient lighting tints everything and everyone inside the bar a neon purple.

The setup couldn't be more chaotic. Seats and tables outline the edges of the bar on all sides except the narrow hall leading to the back of the establishment. In the center of the room is the bar counter and then a platform where two grand pianos are perched.

Patrons erupt into cheers as an announcer comes on stage and informs them of their next performers.

"You got a reservation?" a snotty-toned young woman asks. In the purple-tinted lighting, she looks like a member of the undead—pale skin and black lipstick with her hair messily pulled into a ponytail. She's wearing a tight-fitted t-shirt with the words 'Velvet Piano' over her right breast as she clutches a tablet and stylus.

"No reservation," I answer, looking beyond her.

"Sorry, then you'll have to sit at the bar. We're a full house," she snaps.

My cold gaze finally falls onto her. "Then move the hell out of my way."

A simple direction spoken in an authoritative tone. Most people are cowards and will buckle the second you challenge them with confident authority.

She's no different. Her bad attitude vanishes, and she shifts one step to the side. I walk past her without dignifying her any further.

Lyra's nowhere in sight.

I search the crowd and then search again for any sight of her. Did she stop by the restroom? Is someone already seated waiting on her?

I pick out the men who are by themselves.

One sits at a table in the corner, studying the drinks menu. Though I know little about her love life, he doesn't appear to be her type—or what I imagine it would be. He's too clean cut, too strait-laced, with a short crop of hair and a polo shirt. She likely gravitates toward the alternative types. The ones who seem in need of some grooming and make their earnings from playing guitar on subway platforms.

I glower at the thought. Her bad choices seem never ending.

I wedge myself in the last open space at the bar counter

and order a brandy and coke. The incompetent bartender has no clue how to make drinks; I'm handed back a watery monstrosity that tastes like piss.

The piano players on stage have begun playing. At first, they play along with each other, and then, as they hit the climax of the song, it turns adversarial. The man on the left begins slamming his fingers on the keys to cheers from the audience. He plays fast, showing off with finesse to more applause. Soon, the woman on the right takes over and plays with as much gamesmanship, even swaying along to the notes she strikes.

By the end of the song, they've synced once more, playing out the finale in unison.

The crowd loses any decorum. I sit still and unaffected as everyone around me erupts into a massive round of applause. Some whistle, and others turn to their friends to rave about the performance.

My threshold for public outings like this is short. Most people annoy me; most human beings wandering this planet are extremely useless. To the point that, sometimes in moments like these, as I sit, a composed statue in comparison to every other breathing creature, I give into dark, violent thoughts.

I imagine what they'd do if I shut them up myself. If they would be so loud and obnoxious with an axe to the skull.

I blink out of my murderous trance at the sound of the announcer's voice.

"Now for our next matchup! We have six-time dueling piano champion, Maximillion Keys and his challenger, newcomer Lara Hendrix!"

The crowd goes into idiotic overdrive, thundering applause at Maximillion's name. Little to no one adds any applause for Lyra (aside from the fact the announcer butchered her name). The pair on my left turn to each other and voice their confusion.

"Lara who?"

My grip clenches on my piss-water brandy and coke, half a second away from correcting the idiots.

Maximillion and Lyra walk out onto stage before I can. They're polar opposites in how they handle the moment.

Maximillion grins ear-to-ear and waves out at the crowd—he's a fragile-looking man otherwise, barely scraping five-six or five-seven at most, with corduroy jeans that are too tight and a button down white shirt that's supposed to resemble the keyboard of a piano. His hair's trimmed on the sides with an odd swoop of bangs that fall partially into his eyes. He has what Nolan would jokingly call a punchable face.

The more people cheer him on, the more he eats it up. He waves and winks, doing a mock victory dance like an imbecile.

And then there's Lyra.

She couldn't reek of more insecurity. She appears like a pathetic mouse. She scurries across the stage and throws a nervous smile out at the crowd before beelining for her piano.

The woman has a master's degree in music and has been playing the piano for much of her life. Yet she moves as if she'll projectile vomit her lunch of PopTarts and Ramen any second.

However, I'm unable to take my gaze off her on the stage.

Most uncultured, simple-minded people of today do not appreciate true art. They prefer to rot their brains with slap-stick-humored movies and mind-numbing video games. They listen to crass music with dumb, often linguistically incorrect lyrics, the instruments replaced by some digitized beat created in a studio.

I hold an appreciation for quality art—beautiful pieces of classical music. Though I won't find that in a lowbrow place like the Velvet Piano, I can't lie and pretend I'm not somewhat curious to find out how Lyra plays. If she *actually* possesses talent to create such art.

The song they're playing starts off at a jarring pace. The crowd recognizes it as Great Balls of Fire and cheers.

Right away, Maximillion establishes himself as the dominant player. He shows off for the audience, even chancing a quick wink at them. His fingers race across the keys, and he adds flair to his movements and the bounce of his knee.

Lyra tries to keep up, though more than once her nimble fingers slip and she flubs a key. The first one, she's able to quickly recover and disguise. The second, she struggles to recapture her composure. Maximillion goes for the solo and she pauses, her face a blank canvas of what can only be imposter syndrome.

I recognize the knitted brows and shift of her glassy eyes. She's inside her head, fretting over her mistakes and the solo that's to come.

Where Maximillion drops off, she's supposed to pick up. She misses by half a second, struggling to strike the proper keys in tune with the place in the song. A few mutters break out in the crowd.

Her terrible performance snowballs. She hits another wrong key and sets off a dissonant cord throughout the bar. One tipsy woman in the back boos. Others laugh.

Maximillion swoops in with the save. His hands move fast over the keys and his arms lift high and dramatically as he plays out the rest of the fast-paced song.

The bar explodes into minute-long adulation. People give standing ovations and thunderous applause. The same tipsy woman who booed Lyra jumps up and screams out, "I love you, Max!"

He laughs and bows.

I look to the right side of the stage. Lyra's quietly gotten up from her bench at the piano and snuck off the side of the stage.

No one but me notices.

Not a single person pays enough attention to notice Maximillion is alone on the stage—or if they do, perhaps they don't care.

Humans can be cruel and callous for as self-righteous and morally superior as they like to pretend to be.

At least I'm honest. At least I don't lie about what I am and what I do.

My dark, violent desires.

They lie to themselves and pretend they're actually good people. All while they ignore anyone they deem unworthy. In this case, someone like Lyra.

I get up from the bar and force my way through the crowd. She's disappeared to the back of the bar. Possibly to the restroom or some lounge for employees and performers. Either way, I need to find out where she's gone.

The tracking app on my phone beeps. She's leaving the premises.

I push open the Velvet Piano's front door as she speeds by from the side of the building. She's upset again—her arms wrap around her torso, and she rushes down the block, weaving in between the people on the sidewalk.

Even I'm taken aback. It takes more effort than I expect to keep up with her. She's even more upset than she was earlier. That much is clear.

Thirty minutes later, we've ridden the subway, and she's making the last block home. I mirror her by diving into the building across the street. I'm coming up on the window of the decrepit, cobwebbed office as she slams shut the door to her bedroom.

Suddenly, there's a furious energy about her. She pays no

mind to her partially open blinds, far too focused on what's bothering her.

Her purse is tossed across the room. Her sandals kicked away. She strips off her dress and lets it fall to the ground in a bundled up ball.

I step closer to the window, the binoculars pressed into my eyes.

She's *naked*.

Though I only catch a quick glimpse before she's turning away and grabbing the top drawer of her dresser.

What I saw will be imprinted in my mind's eye forever— Lyra Hendrix has a very visually appealing body. Dark brown skin that looks smooth and supple covering a female shape that's enticing and womanly. Breasts that are just enough. A handful, almost pointed in shape, with distinct nipples I could make out even at a glance. Her stomach is a flat valley that then spreads out into feminine hips and thighs.

She's clean-shaven.

I work the tension from my jaw, my mind polluted with imaginative thoughts about what her cunt looks like.

Perhaps before I make her my next victim, I will make a point of finding out.

She returns from the bathroom donning a satiny robe that hangs open—she's put on some kind of bra and panty set that resembles what you'd see in a lingerie advertisement.

What the hell are you doing, Lyra?! A second ago, you were feeling sorry for yourself.

She picks up her laptop from her desk and, curiously enough, a mask of some kind. After she walks both to her bed, she goes to the window, and finally thinks to shut the blinds the rest of the way.

Just like that, Lyra Hendrix's partially open view into her bedroom is taken away.

Damn it!

A current of frustration beats through me. I toss the binoculars and swear out loud. Glaring around the dusty old office shrouded in shadows, I rack my brain for another means of spying on her in this moment.

I can't walk away. I've committed the entire day and most of the evening to surveilling her.

This doesn't end until *I'm* satisfied enough to walk away.

What was she about to do? She changed into what looked like lingerie, grabbed her laptop, and then a mask...

The idea materializes in the next second.

I wrench my phone from out of my pocket and do another internet search of Lyra Hendrix. During my earlier perusal, I had only come across an Instapix and MyFace account she's barely updated since graduating college.

Come to think of it, I had only used her birth name. She wouldn't do what she's doing using her birth name.

My fingers tap at my screen, typing in the different email address and username handles I know she's created on other sites.

Most turn up nothing... until I reach KuteKittty96. A Cyber Fans profile is at the top of the results page. I quickly click on it, my heart rate speeding up.

I don't have a Cyber Fans account. Before this moment, I never would've been so pathetic to pay money to watch women who are strangers post photos and videos online. The only reason I know of Cyber Fans even as the page loads is because Nolan and Klein *are* that pathetic—both have a subscription to a few models who have started selling content on the lurid site.

It takes me another minute to throw together an account. I use one of my aliases for the profile information, along with the credit card I'm forced to put down. Then I click subscribe to KuteKitty96's page (she has a few hundred subscribers).

From what I've gathered, that's a smaller scale channel... but surely she makes some income off what she's doing.

A small icon glows next to her profile picture—a teasing photo of her in a mask with her breasts pushed up in a bra. She's live camming right now, available for her subscribers to tune in if they want to. I promptly log into the chatroom, for once ignoring how I'd otherwise find such an action to be embarrassing and stupid.

Sure enough, Lyra comes up on my screen. She's disguised behind her leather cat mask, sitting on her bed. Though she's technically clothed in her robe, she's left it untied, intentionally revealing to her subscribers that she's in a lacy bra and panties.

My pulse is beating so fast, I can *hear* it. It's almost louder than Lyra on my screen.

She lets out a fake giggle as a subscriber tells her a joke. The joke is unfunny and would likely garner an eye roll if he ever told a woman in person. Online is a different story; she's pretending he's funny and that she's into it.

It becomes evident she pretends she's into everything her subscribers say.

The many creeps who keep typing things like, "ur so sexy" and "hey beautiful" to the more forward, outright aggressive comments like, "show us ur tits" and "play w/ urself".

The truly bad ones she seems to ignore, pretending they don't exist. If it bothers her, she doesn't show that it does. However, a user named mrsteel820, begins filling up the chat box with increasingly degrading comments.

I scowl at my phone watching him make demands she stops stalling and begins taking her clothes off. He threatens to take his money elsewhere if she doesn't.

Two other users jump in and offer an additional tip if she takes her bra off.

Lyra's mask conceals any distinguishable expression until

cracks begin forming. The pervert losers watching her live might not pick up on it, but I do—the subtle flicker in her eyes and tightening roll of her lips. Her smile dulls, even faker than it already was.

"I have to go," she says a few minutes later. "Thanks for spending the night with me. Miss you. Bye."

The video screen where she's displayed goes dark. The small icon glowing green next to her picture grays out. She's logged off.

I can no longer see her, however, in the next fifteen minutes, the light in her window flicks off. She's going to bed.

For a moment that drags on, I stand among the deep shadows of the old, unused office. I'm considering what to do. If I've finally had enough surveilling of my next victim, or if I'm not yet ready to move on. My pulse has not slowed and the drum of frustration beating inside me has gone nowhere.

A range of different, perplexing sensibilities spike through me, like a volatile bolt of electricity. I don't know what to do or how to proceed.

Perhaps a first.

I make my decision in a state of disassociation. I leave the office behind and cross the barren street. I climb up the fire escape along the side of the brick warehouse building, and then cross over to the window in the uttermost corner that's Lyra's.

It's unlocked, the latch undone.

She lays in bed, barely covered by the sheets and blanket. Still in her robe, bra, and panties, she must've fallen asleep minutes after logging off. Her laptop sits on her bedside table. She's a deep sleeper.

As I ease the window open, she doesn't stir. She remains as is, completely clueless that she's no longer alone.

There's a predator in the midst.

I stand up straight and feel cramped in her small, overcrowded room, where at every turn there's a heap of clothes or her furniture crammed inside. This sets off my tendency for organization and order. Even glancing around the chaotic mess makes me itch.

For the time being, I ignore my disgust and press on. I move through her room like a deadly shadow, placing the cameras and mics I've retrieved from the trunk of my Tesla. Necessary if I'm to keep a close surveil of her.

She moans and then rolls onto her back. Her robe slips further open.

I stop when I take notice. My gaze slides over her form. Dark as it may be in the room, I can still make out every tempting curve of hers. Every naked inch of skin. I step toward her bed, my violent urges awakened, and I stand over her.

Her worst nightmare has come into her life.

She just doesn't know it yet.

7. LYRA
NOBODY GETS ME - SZA

I had expected Jael to ditch me at the party she took me to, I didn't expect for it to be the last time I saw her. Her absence the morning after is a given. But, in the days that follow what turned out to be the worst party I've ever been to, she doesn't return home.

The first morning, as I woke sweaty in my bed, questioning if my night at the Winchester was a fever dream, Jael was nowhere to be found.

She must have spent the night with Paolo.

I tried to wait out her return—she must've known the party organizers so I could attempt to get my phone back.

On the second morning, I give in and resort to my old cracked phone I've held onto and keep stuffed in my drawer. Jael must be spending the weekend with him. She's mentioned he has a super yacht that he frequently takes for sails along the Atlantic coast whenever he's in the country. It makes sense he'd suggest she come with him, especially if their time together at the Midnight Society party went well.

I half consider being bold enough to reach out to the club itself, but when I do an internet search for contact info, nothing comes up. Almost as if the club doesn't exist in the light of day.

After a week goes by and still no Jael, a pang of worry hits me. We're not the closest, but I care if she's disappeared into thin air. I check in by texting her several times. When that produces no results, I break her cardinal rule of texts only and call her.

"We're sorry, but the number you are trying to reach is not in service. Please hang up and try again."

I frown at my phone and then redial her number. The same automated woman answers and tells me the number's no longer in service.

Jael, please tell me you didn't do anything crazy?! Please tell me you're not... at the bottom of the ocean with cinderblocks tied to your ankles! Do murderers do that in real life?

My panicked thoughts spiral from there. I send off several more text messages despite knowing the number's apparently not working. Then I resort to pulling up social media to message her privately.

Only, every account of hers that I know about is gone.

Her Instapix. Her MyFace.

Her Cyber Fans.

Jael makes double the money I do on Cyber Fans.

There's no way she would delete her account unless she had a damn good reason to. Unless Paolo had asked her to marry him and have twenty of his babies (no prenup included).

"Jael, what the fuck?" I mutter, typing her email address in the 'to' box. I'll have to resort to sending an email and hope she sees it.

Her absence only fuels my confusion about the night at the Winchester. I had been herded off by some member of security to the second floor, where I was essentially forced into performing in a sex show.

Where I bit a guy's dick off.

I went running into the night. I was crazed and hysterical upon escaping.

Barefoot, breathless, my dress torn, I ran for at least a mile before I stopped and hid away in a coffee shop open late into the night. The waitress took one pitying look at me and gave me a free coffee on the house.

I don't remember making my way home. Just that she lent me some old sneakers she claimed were left behind by a waitress who had recently quit, and that I sat catatonic in an empty subway car.

Dozens of people watched on as some creep stuffed his dick in my mouth. They *laughed* while I screamed.

The security guards came at me like I'd done something wrong.

For days, I'm wondering if it's the last I'll hear of it. If maybe I should get ahead of the curve and file a police report.

After giving it some thought, I decide against it. The police have never been helpful when I have gone to them, and I was some broke Black girl in a slutty dress crashing a party full of elites I shouldn't have been at. I chose to go with the guy upstairs to attend the *sex performance*.

No one held a gun to my head.

There's at least a hundred witnesses to what happened. But they're the rich and powerful one percent of society. None of them are on my side.

I decided to let it go, like I've let many bad things that have happened to me go.

It wouldn't be the first time. Probably won't be the last...

What hurts more is Winston playing me for a fool. He promised he'd send me my final check for the *Easton Times*. He owes me a full paycheck plus the obituaries I wrote the day he fired me. Every last penny matters, and I expect to be fairly compensated.

Instead, when I turn up at the newspaper's headquarters, he sends the receptionist out to turn me away. I'm ready to stand my ground until they call security and I'm escorted out the front door.

That's not even touching my disaster at the Velvet Piano. My mind won't allow me to relive that nightmare.

I did a surprise cam session with my Cyber Fan subscribers *just* to distract myself. Even that went wrong when one of the creeps in the chatroom began demanding I show more skin or he was unsubscribing.

With the luck I'm having, I can't afford to lose any more money.

I sigh when waking up in the morning.

It's half past ten o' clock by the time I work up the energy to get out of bed and wash my face and brush my teeth. I'm supposed to be job hunting today. The Velvet Piano, the latest odd job I've taken on, probably won't keep me much longer.

Imani texts me and asks me to lunch.

My treat 😊

Guilt anchors inside me accepting her invite. Imani's about as broke as I am. Rather than living in an old warehouse sharing an apartment with two other people, she lives in a narrow townhouse with five roommates. One of which she shares an actual room with.

But at least her job at Strictly Pleasures is more stable than any I've had over the years.

I get dressed and shut the door to my room. I've been told I'm not the most observant person when it comes to noticing my surroundings, but as I pass by the open door of Jael's room, I stop on the spot.

It's empty.

Her bed's gone. The rest of the furniture is gone. Every tube of lipstick and pair of shoes. The lush feminine artwork she'd put up on the walls has been taken down.

I stand and stare for several seconds. Has she moved out and not told me? Does this mean she's seen my texts, calls, and emails and decided to ignore me? Has Paolo put a ring on it?

I'm flummoxed the whole trip to meet Imani. She notices the second she sees me. A curious smile lights up her face and she laughs.

Some say we could be sisters... except Imani embraces the girl-next-door aesthetic. No piercings, no tattoos, she's sweet and unassuming on the surface, with cinnamon brown skin and a short bob haircut.

But it's when you get to know her that the inner freak comes out. That's what I love about her.

"You look like you've had a day... and it's not even noon," she says. "Spill, Ly. What bad luck have you had now?"

I drop into the seat across from her. We're eating at Urban Greenery, the vegan spot across from her work.

It takes me another moment to piece together what I even want to say.

"My roommate's missing."

Imani laughs again, slurping on her soda. "Jael? Jael's not missing."

"She's not?"

"*Jael?*" she repeats. "I've never met the girl... but after everything you've told me, you do know what she does, right? She's probably with whomever her latest sugar daddy is."

"Paolo."

"Yeah, him. Whoever he is, she's with him."

"I haven't seen her in over a week."

"And? Girls like Jael, they go where the money goes. She's probably in Italy on his yacht or holed up in whatever resort he's got her in."

"He has a yacht here in America. Along the coast of Montbec."

"Of course he does. They always do. And you're worried why?"

"Her stuff has been cleared out of her room."

"She probably came back when you weren't around and moved out. Especially if she owes Taviar some rent."

Imani has an answer for everything. Maybe I'm over-reacting.

I grip the laminated menu detailing the day's special, a chickpea curry packed with spices and herbs, and pretend I'm possibly going to order it for lunch.

What I'm *really* doing is thinking over how to tell Imani what's on my mind. If I'll sound crazy as hell telling her about what happened at the Winchester. Imani works at an adult shop and isn't a stranger to the world of kink, but secret sex party thrown by powerful elites sounds like every nutty conspiracy theorist out there.

I can hear the ring of her laughter now. *Especially* when I go into detail about the guy whose dick I chomped into.

There's also the chance Imani might take me seriously and insist I go to the authorities. Back when we worked together as Christmas elves (the odd job where we'd met), she was the one who led the charge against the pervy Santa Claus who was groping the female elves. She takes things like consent very seriously.

A sexual assault on a performance stage would be a crusade for her.

Meanwhile, I just want to forget it happened and for my roommate to remember where she lives.

"What are you doing the rest of the day?" Imani asks once we've ordered and our food has been delivered.

I wound up ordering the chickpea curry.

"Job hunting."

"I thought you just got the thing at the Velvet Piano?"

"That won't last."

Imani tilts her head. "Isn't it your first week?"

"There's a good chance I might beat my record. I was fired in a week and a half waitressing at Steinman's Bar and Grill. It's looking like I won't even last a week at Velvet."

"But you're an excellent piano player! Is it the nerves again? Ly, what have I told you? You've gotta get over that!"

I cringe in my seat, stirring my spoon in my curry. "I know, I know. It's easier said than done. Something comes over me the second I look out at the audience and walk on stage."

"Then don't look at them. Look at your piano."

"My eyes have a mind of their own. They dart straight to the audience. I can feel their stares."

Imani sighs. "I thought you couldn't care less about what people think."

"I don't... usually. It's different with my piano. I... I want to be good."

"You *are* good, Ly. One of the best."

"You're my only friend. You're obligated to say that."

"What about Grady? How's that *friend* doing?"

A sound of disgust hacks out of me. "Grady and me... we're... just friends. Not the kind of friends you're implying. Not... not anymore."

"Mmhmm," she hums, grabbing the bottle of hot sauce on the table. "Said every person in a situation like yours ever. You need to cut him loose."

"I have."

"Then why does he keep coming around?"

I roll my eyes. "We've known each other since high school."

"Girl, high school was forever ago at this point. Block his number."

"How do you know I haven't?"

"He told me he's video called you. He was at the store the other day."

Another sound of disgust sticks in my throat. I make a promise to Imani I'll block Grady's number for good. Honestly, with everything that's happened over the last week and a half, I haven't given him much thought.

Our arrangement had soured recently, and I've been distracted by my job situation.

Before our lunch date is up, Imani makes me promise yet again I'll cut Grady loose. She leaves me on parting words of encouragement, reminding me to fight my stage fright and go easy on myself.

"I'll ask DJ if he'll have any openings at the store," she says on her walk out. "It'd be fun to work together again."

I stay behind and sit stirring my spoon in my half eaten chickpea curry. Where food is concerned, I have to be strategic. I need to eat for my medication, but I also need to pace my meals and stretch them as long as possible due to my financial situation. The same can be said for my meds.

Every pill counts.

As the staff wipes down tables during their afternoon lull, I'm one of the few who remain.

"Would you like to take that to go?" a waitress asks.

I take it as her hint that I've been here too long and need to leave. She packs up my curry into a carton and slips it into a bag. I'm so broke, I can barely afford to leave two dollars let alone a real tip.

This curry will have to last me a while. So will my meds... I skipped today's dose. I'm so caught up in my head that I don't see the man passing by. I step into him as he steps into me. We crash into each other in a rough collision that forces me backward and makes me lose my hold on the container of curry.

The bag slips out of my hand and then explodes on the ground. The curry sauce splatters onto me, staining my blouse, marking up my denim shorts. Some of it even gets into my mouth as my jaw drops open in surprise.

Almost none of it gets on the man.

I gape at him, wide-eyed and speechless, trying to figure out if our collision was my fault or his.

He appears just as shocked.

He's... *perfect*.

A man that looks too good to be true. He's tall and broad-shouldered, dressed in a neat white button-down and slate gray slacks. His hair manages to look both tousled and combed at the same time—it's longer, reaching his ears in waves that are naturally pushed back from his face.

His face that's a blend of classic handsome features and stoic masculinity. Things like a strong jaw and nose, lips that are nice and full for a man, and defined cheekbones that could probably land him a modeling gig.

He's gentle and intimidating all at once.

A tall, dark, handsome, Prince Charming in real life... and then he *smiles*.

Right at me.

His dark eyes twinkle and my insides flutter.

I'm even more taken aback at his reaction.

"Let me help you," he says as the restaurant staff come by to clean up. They wave him off and slap down the sopping wet mop over the mess. He turns to me still wearing his sheepish smile that almost makes me smile. Even if I'm covered in curry sauce. He steps toward me. "I sincerely apologize. I should have been paying better attention."

"No... no... it's okay. I should've been too. I just got up without looking."

"But I'm the one who almost knocked you down. I've ruined your blouse. I hope you had nowhere important to be."

"I was... um... actually, going on a job interview."

"That makes the situation even more embarrassing. Please allow me to make it up to you somehow."

My cheeks warm. "Really, it's okay. I'll go home and change."

"I owe you dinner... or lunch, I suppose."

"Oh, no," I say, shaking my head. "It's really fine."

"I insist. It's the least I can do." His eyes soften with kindness. Never once do they stray from mine.

The collision was an accident and was probably both our faults. But how can I turn him down?

He's kind, handsome, and well-mannered. Besides, I'm poor, destitute, and often starving. Am I really in the position to turn down a free meal? Particularly when the leftovers I'd been hoping to stretch for several days have been knocked to the ground?

"Sure," I say with a slow, almost hesitant smile. "But we haven't even really introduced ourselves. I'm Lyra."

He engulfs my hand with his firmer, larger hand. "Lyra is such a beautiful name. Very fitting if that's not too inappropriate to say. It's nice to meet you. I'm Kaden."

8. Kaden
Atmosphere - Joy Division

"**A**re you enjoying yourself?" I ask, secretly amused.

Lyra sits up straighter and rushes to swallow the rice she has in her mouth. We are the only two seated at the Korean BBQ restaurant on Fifty-Eighth Street. Normally, the family owned and operated establishment closes in the hours between lunch and dinner. An obstacle I overcame by slipping Mr. Yeun an extra hundred dollar bill. He opened up just for me and my guest.

It helped that I'm already a regular and have made a point to come by for their lunch special at least once a week for years.

I am a man of routine and well aware of it.

Since bringing her here, she's tried to act nonchalant, as if she isn't very hungry. Every so often she slips and shovels an extra spoonful of her bean paste soup into her mouth or reaches for more pork belly.

Sensing her insecurity, I flash her a bright smile. The kind of smile I've been using from the moment I purposely knocked into her at the disgusting vegan restaurant (the food has nothing on the Yeuns). She'd stumbled back and gawked at me like an innocent small lamb lost on its way. She assumed I'd snarl at her or disparage her for bumping into me.

Little did she know it was by design.

The second I smiled at her, however, she'd lowered her defenses. The tension dissipated from her hunched shoulders and her lips spread to return my friendly gesture.

I come in peace, mine said.

I mean you no harm.

So she thinks.

"I'm not normally this hungry," she says, pushing her plate away. "I took my meds, and they make me nauseous. I try to balance it out with food, but that doesn't help much either."

Interesting.

I've already reviewed Lyra's medical history—or as much of it as I could find. She's far from the healthiest person, though I am not sure what medication she could possibly be on that would cause regular nausea.

...unless she's lying to save face.

"Have you spoken to your physician about that?" I ask noncommittally, sipping from my ginger tea. I haven't touched any of the platters of food on the table. I had some stuffed shiitake mushrooms and now I'm indulging in my usual afternoon tea.

Lyra shakes her head. "No... not really..."

"Any particular reason?"

"It's not important."

"I would say nausea is important. It can be disruptive to your daily life. I'm sure there are better medications he can prescribe you."

"I guess... but, um, I don't have health insurance."

My left brow arches. "Meaning you don't have a primary physician."

"Not really... no..."

Then where the hell do you get your meds from? Some dealer off a street corner?

I refrain from asking. Pressing her further would cross into much more personal territory, and as it is, we're still on polite, barely acquainted terms.

Instead, I gesture to the tiny tattoo on the inside of her forearm. Simplistic piano keys inked onto her brown skin.

"You play?"

Her eyes light up for the briefest second before dimming.

Her favorite topic...

Until she remembers her recent performances at the Velvet Piano. I have no way of knowing with certainty that these are her thoughts, however, I am confident in saying so. In only a matter of days, I've become an expert at reading her.

"I do," she answers mildly. "I've been playing since I was four."

"That's extremely young. Younger than most pianists."

Her gaze dips to her forearm, her brows knitting. "Yeah, it is. I've always enjoyed it..."

"*But,*" I supply.

"But?"

"But, what? You trailed off, Lyra. If I didn't know any better, something's happened that makes you enjoy it less."

"Good thing you said you don't know any better, because you don't," she snaps. A sudden defensive air develops about her. A spark I've yet to see from her.

Little Lamb Lyra, do you have fire inside you yet? Not as pitiful and defenseless as you seem?

I could terrify her by revealing the true form of the monster she's tried to challenge. I could resort to skewering her with sharp condescension and make her feel small like I do many in my social circles and in my private life.

However, I do neither—as far as Lyra Hendrix is

concerned, I'm mild-mannered Kaden Raskova, who is friendly, charming, and simply trying to get to know her.

As she snaps, I feign concern. I frown and give a reassuring motion of my hand, letting her know it's okay.

"You're right," I say. "I overstepped my place. I shouldn't have tried to analyze you like some amateur armchair psychiatrist. It was presumptuous of me. I guess that's what I get for listening to one too many psychiatry podcasts."

I end my non-apology apology with a self-depreciating laugh that sounds as sincere as my words.

Though neither are.

Lyra melts. Her spark extinguishes. She gives a laugh like mine, soft and unassuming. "We're even. I'm sorry I went from zero to sixty out of nowhere. That happens when I take my meds. I can get cranky."

It sounds like these meds are no good for you. Mental note: research more about her off-the-street prescriptions.

"It's quite alright," I say. "I'd love to hear you play. If you're open to that."

She scratches her neck and then slides her hand around to rub at her nape. "I don't play often... not anymore. The only place I've been playing lately is at the Velvet Piano, and I doubt I'll be there much longer. I haven't won a duel yet."

"The Velvet Piano? I love that place."

Lies. LIES.

"I must've come by on the nights you're off. When do you duel?"

"Well... tonight, actually. But don't come. I suck."

I laugh. "I'm sure you're amazing. You have a piano tattoo and you've been playing since you were a small child. I bet you're being modest."

"Really not. But if you want to check it out, then that's on you. Just don't expect me to do well," she says, reaching for her phone. "I was supposed to be job hunting today for a reason."

"I won't make any promises, but if I'm in the area, I'll drop by. That way it's no pressure. We should exchange numbers."

Her eyes pop up from the phone she holds in her hands and onto me. Surprise lights up in her gaze. She wasn't expecting me to ask for her number.

"Is that okay?" I ask, tilting my head to the side. "I've really enjoyed our impromptu late-afternoon lunch date, and you're pretty interesting. I'd like to keep in touch."

She licks her lips, and her full mouth seems to be on the cusp of asking something.

Why?!

It almost makes me laugh in a patronizing way Lyra Hendrix can tell we're from different worlds. I exist in an entirely different universe than she does... and she's right to think so. However, it's not often people take an interest in her. It's not often she takes an interest in people either. Despite this, an inkling tells me she'd like to keep in touch too.

I really can read her like a book. What's more, I've begun to *understand* her, and the way her brain works.

She's a loner at heart. Meaning, new connections startle her. New connections are a big deal.

"Sure," she says finally. "Yeah, okay. But I mostly text. No calls."

"Sounds perfect. I'm usually too busy with work for calls."

We part ways with me intentionally noncommittal about showing up tonight for her performance (though, of course, I'll be there). I insist Lyra take the platters of uneaten food on our table home. She pretends she doesn't want to before ultimately obliging. I stand outside the restaurant and watch her walk in the opposite direction clutching a small grocery of takeout bags.

Now she'll have the food she was worrying about.

Whoever said I was a bad man?

At least I feed my prey before devouring them.

————

Celeste is waiting for me in my penthouse. I know she's in my home before even seeing her.

From the moment I walk through the door, the heady scent of her perfume permeates the air. I clench my teeth and toss my keys on the credenza along the wall.

My penthouse is located on West King Street in the Primark Tower. One of the most affluent neighborhoods and buildings in the entire city standing at seventy floors high, the piece of real estate is owned by my father. It's a space I've been given free reign over, which means the entire building is devoted to my use as I see fit.

Windows make up the majority of my wall space, affording me an almost 360 degree view of the city from the seventieth floor on which I live.

I keep my penthouse as neat and minimalist as possible. All-white color scheme with touches of black. Sleek, modern furniture and the vast open space that only makes my place seem five times larger than it already is. Considering it's eight thousand square feet, that's a bold yet entirely accurate statement.

Dusk reflects in the sky. The dying natural light pours into the many windows as the sun glows a golden hue and then sinks minute by minute.

I cross the wide open space, letting my designer oxfords thud against the obsidian flooring. I want Celeste to know I'm home. I want her to *hear me* approaching.

She's in the bathroom, soaking in the tub. The air stinks of her perfume mixed with artificial vanilla and caramel, or whatever frivolous bath bomb type product she's used.

Candles flicker, perched on top of the nook in the shower wall; candles I've never seen a day in my life. That she must've purchased and brought along just for her fantasy of a spa-like evening in my penthouse.

Her eyes flit to mine in the doorway, and she smirks. "Evening, baby. I knew you'd be tense and worked up from a day in the operating room, so I ran us a nice, hot bath. Get in."

"Get out. Now."

"Don't be a sourpuss," she purrs, sitting up in the tub. No longer is she disguised by the suds. Her bare breasts and the rest of her naked torso are on display as if to entice me.

Letting me know she's right here if I so choose to have her.

I push my hands into my trouser pockets and give a dry blink. "Celeste, I'd be more attracted if you put things *on* rather than take them *off*. Including a burlap sack over your head."

She scowls. "You are such a jerk."

"Thank you."

"Here I am, trying to be sexy and romantic. My love goes unappreciated," she sighs, grabbing a loofah I've also never seen before, and soaping up her chest area.

"There is no love between us. Nothing sexy or romantic. Only hate and hate fucking. Get it through your drug-addled brain."

Her bottom lip pokes out. "You won't even give me a chance."

"You're high. I can see the fresh track marks on your arms. Get the hell out of my bathtub. I'll need to disinfect it now. I have no clue where you've been or who you've fucked. You likely don't either."

She splashes water at me, making a mess on the floor. "You're going to let me leave with nothing? I'll blow you."

"The idea of your lips on my cock makes me nauseous, Celeste."

"I'll let you fuck my ass."

"The answer is no. You have sixty seconds."

"Have you killed her yet?" she asks in an airy tone, running a soapy hand along her arm. Her blood-red talon nails drag across her skin in a slow motion I'm sure she believes is erotic and enticing. "I heard about your assignment. The Owner himself asked you. He wants her dead."

"I want *you* dead. Forty-two seconds."

"You haven't killed in so long. Is that your way of flirting with me? Mmm, I'm into it."

"Thirty."

"Why haven't you?" she asks, rising up from the bathtub to step out. She stands before me without making an attempt to reach for a towel.

Part of me is grateful. I do not want her talons touching my linens.

"I will eliminate her when I am ready to do so. You have less than twenty seconds, or you will be the one I eliminate."

She giggles, brushing past me in the nude. "Is my baby seeing another woman? Are you smitten with her? Some cheap hooker from the slums? Some Black bitch who bit Klein's dick off? You know he's still in the—*AHHHHH*!"

Celeste screams bloody murder as I grab her by the back of the neck and drag her across my penthouse. She stumbles backward with no choice but to come along. Her long arms and legs flail in her struggle to regain her balance, or to free herself somehow.

Though I never let her.

I drag her to the penthouse door, wrenching it open and shoving her into the hall. The door slams shut in her face.

It's not until I make it to the bathroom that I remember her clothes. She's still standing on the doormat outside, shivering with a sick gleam in her gaze, waiting for me. I toss the clothes at her and tell her to never show her fucking face in my penthouse again.

Or next time I *will* end her.

The threat falls on deaf ears, like so many others. One day, I will make good on it.

Celeste might be the only person more fucked in the head than I am. She'll find her way back, discover another means to worm herself into my life.

I'll have to change the locks again. And fire my housekeeper and security team. The only possible people who could've let her in.

I set to cleaning up and disinfecting my bathroom. I am not only a neat freak, I'm a clean freak as well.

Celeste had her bare pussy and ass in my thirty thousand dollar roman tub. Who knows where it's been?

For the next hour, I scrub the bathroom down. I air out the room to rid it of the foul stench from the bath bombs she used and candles she burned.

My cleanliness has been a part of me since I was a small child. I didn't like being dirty; I didn't like *mess*. Even as I stayed up late and watched the gory horror movies playing on the television screen, the messy disregard annoyed me. My fascination was more for the violence being enacted.

Even when I wandered down the echoing hall of my father's castle and stumbled upon the blood and gore that was real... it was a thought on my mind.

Cleanliness.

I conduct myself this way even during my urges. My special dungeon sparkles by the time I'm through.

The bathroom is no less pristine when I tear off my rubber gloves and toss them in the trash. The urge to light every belonging Celeste has left behind on fire strikes me. From her

shoes to her make up bag and the box of chocolate straw-
berries.

Instead, I hurl it down the trash shoot.

Dusting my hands off, I return to the penthouse in time to
see my phone lighting up.

The alarm I set for myself.

At half past eight, it's almost time for the dueling to begin
at the Velvet Piano. My plan is to show up conspicuously late
and behave as casual and noncommittal as possible. Lyra is so
skittish around new people in her life that if I show up with
too much enthusiasm, it'll turn her off.

I open the latest spy app I'm using to monitor her.

Today at the Korean BBQ spot, I used a small opportunity
to my advantage. Lyra got up to ask the server for another
spoon and left her phone on the table. In the minute and
fifteen seconds she was gone, I linked her phone with mine
using an impressive, albeit unsettling, spy app that records
people.

Now I'll be able to not only track her movements and
watch her in her bedroom, I'll be with her everywhere she
takes her phone.

For instance, right now, Lyra's backstage at the Velvet
Piano. I turn up the volume as Maximillion walks up to speak
with her.

"Hey, Butterfingers, you ready for tonight?" he asks.

Lyra looks up from where she sits with her phone in her
hand (offering me a view of her from below).

"I'd call you a dick, but when it's that small, does it really
count?"

I can hear the fake pleasantness in his tone, even without
seeing him. "That doesn't change that you're a loser. I was
telling Francine I'm not sure why Erma even hired you. You
can't play piano. You can barely walk and talk at the same
time."

She glares, though another retort seems to elude her. At least in the two seconds Maximillion gives her to respond.

"See you on the stage, Butterfingers. Don't fuck up again."

He hacks out a loud laugh and the sound of his footsteps die out.

Lyra sits still for seconds to come. I recognize the look—the self-critical, overthinking, deep dive she does that sabotages her performance.

I scowl miles away watching it happen live. She's let him get to her. She's going to mess up on stage.

Maximillion is the type of arrogant blowhard that I can't stand. That ignites my bloodlust to an irrational level. He believes he's above others due to his talent. His overinflated ego gives him the courage to demean someone already down in the dumps like Lyra.

I snatch my keys off the credenza and storm out the door.

Lyra Hendrix is supposed to be my next kill. But I can't guarantee I won't make some detours along the way.

9. Lyra

STRANGE EFFECT - UNLOVED & RAVEN
VIOLET

"**Y**ou can do this," I repeat for the fiftieth time. I'm staring in the mirror of the single stall bathroom of the Velvet Piano. I roll back my shoulders and stretch out my arms and then transition into my piano exercises.

It consists of lots of finger and hand motions to warm both up.

I'm splaying my fingers on a five count when the bathroom door swings open and the bar manager, Erma walks in.

A sheepish smile comes to my face, and I pretend I'm running my fingers down my thick braids instead of doing silly exercises in the mirror. She meets my embarrassed smile with a polite one, stepping up to the sink next to mine.

"Are those your piano stretches?" she asks, twisting on the faucet. She might as well be a kindergarten teacher asking her five-year-old student if the scribbles on her paper are a drawing. Her polite smile widens. "I wouldn't bother tonight. I've made some changes to the line up. Rooney is going to play tonight. And since Chantal called out sick, you'll be hostess."

"But Rooney doesn't work tonight."

"I called him in."

I stare at her in the mirror. My smile has slid off my face, but hers remains—as patronizing and polite as ever. More so the longer time goes on.

A tingling sensation sweeps over me, down the back of my neck and then spine. It leaves me dizzy with a sudden hyper-awareness of myself.

My hot face. My awkward arms. My summer dress I'd hoped would make a good impression on the crowd. *I painted my fucking nails.*

Champagne pearl.

"Yeah... okay," I say finally. "Hostess. Right."

"Just to make things easy. You won't have to stress. And we won't have to deal with the crowd booing your perfor-mance. A win-win for everyone." She finishes up washing her hands and then yanks at the paper towel dispenser. "See you out there."

I don't bother answering as the door swings shut.

Damn, I wish I had some weed right about now. I'd walk out so high I wouldn't give a fuck what task I've been given to do tonight.

Anything is better than being forced to agonize over the truth.

Erma chose to call Rooney in on a night off just to have him play. She took the opportunity of Chantal calling out to switch me to hostess.

It wouldn't surprise me if I'm fired next.

The role of hostess is hectic on a normal night, but nothing compares to Friday. I'm slammed from the moment I set up at the door.

Regulars and new patrons alike flood in, requesting tables and spots at the bar. I do my best to keep up with the crowd, seating those with reservations, and sending a steady flow of guests to the bar area.

After a while, the many faces blur and everyone becomes a

twin. Everyone looks like somebody else and somebody else looks like everyone.

The bar feels stuffy and the music blares louder as Maximillion duels Rooney to enthusiastic cheers.

I grit my teeth, force a smile, and greet more patrons. I'm so swamped, so disillusioned by how the night's turned out, I don't even recognize faces that aren't supposed to look like everybody.

Including the familiar face of a man I had lunch with only a few hours ago.

"Busy?" Kaden asks when I gesture for him to follow me to a table.

I do a double take and then smack a hand to my cheek. "I'm so sorry. I didn't even... *ugh*. Tonight's crazy. As you can tell."

He glances around the rowdy bar stuffed with a lively audience and equally lively dueling pianists. "Definitely crazy. Between the two of us, I don't like crowds this big."

My lips almost quirk into a small smile. "Me neither."

"Have a seat. Take your break."

"I wish. But I can't. Too busy."

"By law, they're required to give you a break every four hours," he recites. His eyes narrow, momentarily losing their kind gleam. "Have they not been giving you your breaks?"

"No. I mean, yes. Well, actually, no. It's... complicated. Have you ever worked in a bar or restaurant? It usually depends on the crowds."

But as I pose the question, I know the answer—Kaden's never worked a minimum wage job a day in his life. Much less at a bar or restaurant on Friday night.

I'm not sure *how* I know this with such certainty, but I *do*. Maybe it's the model-like pose he naturally strikes when at a standstill—his shoulders masculine and wide but relaxed, like he's beyond normal stressors, with his hair in easy, loose waves

behind his ears, and one hand in the pocket of his well-tailored pants. He wears another white cotton button-up shirt with the top button undone and the sleeves rolled up to his elbow, and though it looks exactly like the perfect, wrinkle-free shirt I saw him in earlier, something tells me this is a different one.

A different shirt of the same exact design.

He probably has a closet full of them. Several of each color. How much does one cost?

Probably my whole paycheck.

"You're owed a break regardless of how busy it gets," he says, dodging my question. "Would you like me to speak to your manager? I have a knack for reasoning with people."

"Erma? No, no, no. Don't do that. I'm already this close to being fired." I hold my thumb and forefinger so close together they almost touch. "Anyway, I better get back to the door. A line's formed again."

Kaden's about to protest, though I don't give him enough of an opening. I return to my station at the door. Once again, I'm in hostess mode, offering the couple at the front of the line an apology for the wait. I'm losing track of specifics and details.

Everyone melts together.

To such a degree it takes me five seconds before recognizing the grungy man standing in front of me is Grady.

He's got a backward ball cap on and a beard that has tripled in fuzz since the last time I saw him. His shirt looks like something he might've run through a food processor—holes puncture the thin fabric, some tiny and others gaping, like the one under his armpit. If I didn't know any better, I'd say he either just rolled out of bed, or just got done smoking.

Possibly both.

"Grady... what are you...?"

"You work here now?" he mumbles, stuffing his hands in the pockets of his jeans.

"Yeah."

"Since when?"

"A week ago? Who told you?"

"Who was that guy?"

My brows knit. "What... guy?"

"The guy." Grady juts his chin to a point beyond my shoulder.

I toss a quick glance and my gaze lands on the table in the far corner, where Kaden sits. He's *already* staring—with that same narrow-eyed look he'd had earlier about my breaks. It's an alarming stoniness that's the opposite of the easy-going kindness he's otherwise shown.

A strange shiver racks down my spine and I pull my attention away. Back to facing Grady, I shrug. "He's a customer. He was asking about the specials."

"We should talk. When's your break?"

Why the hell does everyone think I get a break!? Apparently, I'm the only one who has ever worked a service job!

"Not sure. You want a seat at the bar? I didn't see your name on the reservation list."

"I've been trying to get a hold of you."

"I've been busy."

"You blocked me."

I did.

"I didn't," I say. "Just been busy. Do you want a seat or not?"

"You're real wishy washy, Ly. After all the times I've been there for you."

"Grady, I'm at work."

"I left the car shop the time you collapsed and they had to take you to the ER to pump your stomach. I dropped everything and came by."

"That was different."

"I pushed you to do piano lessons. You wanted to give up."

"Actually, that was Imani—"

"You've always used me," he interrupts. "Every fucking time you want something, I'm there. Then when I need you, you're dropping me. It's real fucked up."

My brain feels sluggish. The stuffiness in the air, the earsplitting music making my ears ache, the lightheadedness from inconsistent doses of my meds. I can't properly defend myself when I'm like this. I reach out and rest a hand on my podium for leverage.

"Grady, now's not the time," I grit out.

"You want me to feel sorry for you when you never feel sorry for me?"

"All I've done is try to be your friend."

"Blocking me is what you call being my friend? You're a user, Lyra."

"Grady, stop. Don't make a scene."

"I'll stop if you stop playing the victim."

"She asked you to stop. You *will* stop."

Grady and I freeze at the sound of the paralyzing voice. It's cool and calm, yet unsettling at the same time.

I look up and find myself standing only a few feet away from Kaden. When did he get up and come over?

And so fast...

For a long, drawn out moment, tension cinches the air we're breathing. It becomes a feeling, the instant animosity between Kaden and Grady. Both men share in a reproachful glare 'til Grady blinks and then scoffs.

"Whatever, man. I'm done here." He walks off with a shake of his head.

Kaden's chilling gaze follows him every step of the way.

I wave a hand in front of his face to bring him back. "What was that about?"

At last, he remembers normal human beings blink, and he does too, the scary calm vanishing. His easy-going, friendly vibe returns. "I'm sorry. I just don't like when men give women a hard time, and it sounded like he was harassing you."

I fold my arms. "I didn't need you to get in. I had Grady under control."

"Of course. I didn't mean to presume—"

"You do that a lot. *Presuming*. We barely know each other, Kaden. I only met you a few hours ago, and already you're taking me to lunch, showing up at my work, trying to scare off my ex."

"That was your ex?"

"No... sort of. It's complicated. Anyway, chill, okay? You're starting to scare me."

"Of course," he repeats. For the first time, I sense uncertainty about him, like he's a robot about to malfunction. He sticks both hands in his pants pockets and forces on a grin. "It's getting late. I should go. I have an early morning. Enjoy your evening, Lyra."

A minute ago, I was in the middle of a surprising standoff between two polar opposite men. As Kaden excuses himself from the Velvet Piano, I find myself the last one standing out of the three.

In a crowded bar yet somehow completely alone.

———

My spirits don't pick up. Closing time arrives and the duelers walk out well before everybody else on staff. Maximillion winks at me and wishes me a good night in the fakest, most taunting tone imaginable. I scowl and consider spraying him in the back of the head with my bottle of all-purpose cleaner.

I'm stuck cleaning up alongside Erma, the bartender, and the servers on shift. We make quick work of the compact, purple-tinted bar by dividing and conquering. The bartender wipes down the bar area. The servers clean the tables and stack the chairs. I'm on the go, locking the front door and mopping the floors.

Erma supervises, which is really standing around and fussing with her phone.

When everyone's satisfied, they migrate to the backroom to collect their things out of their cubbies. I'm not as eager to leave.

After such a shitty week and a half, and an even shittier night, I need something to take the edge off.

My gaze swings from the fully stocked bar counter to the stage. Both pianos sit obediently and untouched under the hue from the neon purple lighting.

I can't explain it. I can't begin to put it into words or make sense of it.

But my feet move. I fall under a trance.

In a matter of seconds, I'm seated at the bench of the piano to the right and my fingers hover over the keys. I inhale a careful breath, a bundle of nerves fluttering inside, and then I let go.

I let my fingers take over.

The empty bar fills with the soothing, trilling melody of Chopin's Nocturne in C-minor.

My eyes close. My body sways. My fingers *dance*.

I'm swept up in a kaleidoscope of rich notes and fluid composition. I'm soaring among the stratosphere. Free as a bird. High as the sky.

Beauty becomes a sound as I play with romantic abandon, feeling every stroke of the keys in my soul.

It's a moment.

One I haven't had in a very long time. One that ends with a satisfied beat of my heart as I play the last note and strike the last key.

Musical perfection.

I sigh contently. That felt wonderful. Even if it was fleeting...

I look up only to realize I'm being watched. Erma's jaw hangs open.

"I didn't expect that out of you! That was concert pianist worthy. You need to play like that all the time," she says.

And just like that... reality comes crashing down. I remember where I am and what transpired tonight. My mood tanks, and I give a stiff nod as she wishes me good night.

If only it were so simple...

———

When I make it to my apartment building, Grady sits on the top stair leading to my floor. A resigned sigh blows from my lungs, and I scratch my brow in exhaustion.

Why am I even surprised to find him here?

He always does this, turns up late at night like this.

"Grady, go home."

"You don't mean that. We need a moment. I've got stuff to say."

"I'm exhausted."

"Then let's chill. I waited out here for over an hour."

"That's not my problem," I say, bypassing him on the stairs. He follows me down the hall like a living shadow and doesn't give up even as I reach my apartment door, keys in hand. "I don't want to chill. Go home."

"Can't."

"Don't tell me your uncle kicked you out again."

He gives a hapless shrug. "Told you I'm going through things. Thought you'd care enough to be there for me."

I sigh again, overcome by guilt. "Come in."

It's a mistake.

A huge mistake. Even as I unlock the door and let him follow me inside, the tiny rational half of my brain screams at me. It tells me to stop right now and think straight before I relapse and do something I'll regret.

Before I let things get complicated and messy again.

You'd think I'd listen... but I don't.

We go to my room and sit around. I light up a joint and we pass it between us, inhaling, savoring the high it gives us. Grady tells me all about his problems—his difficult time finding a job, his depressive episodes, and his family troubles that are almost as messy as my own.

None of it is new to me. I've known Grady since I was fourteen.

He's probably the only person still in my life who *truly* knows me.

The good, bad, and hideously ugly sides.

And maybe that's why I *choose* to relapse, why I let it happen while knowing I'll regret it. His venting turns into us on my bed undressing. Some kisses sprinkled between the impatience and frustration.

Grady doesn't bother taking off my dress. But he does slide off my panties. He groans and pumps away, moving above me with his eyes closed. I lay under him and try to tune into the moment in any way I can.

I try to enjoy the feel of him inside me. I try to move my hips in tune with his. I try to get off, my fingers finding my clit.

Sex with Grady has been frequent and infrequent through the years, but one thing it's always been is disconnected. Like we're two separate people getting off on our own despite using the other's body.

Just as I'm toying with myself and finding a motion that makes me shudder with the beginnings of pleasure, it's over.

Grady groans, pumps a couple more times, and then

comes in the condom. He wipes his brow with a satisfied breath and then drops beside me.

He's out within minutes.

It's nothing new. In fact, it's *déjà vu*.

The ending to most of our encounters. As Grady snores at my side, I spend a few minutes getting myself off.

My orgasm is a small blip on the radar. My body gives a tremor and a feeble wave of pleasure passes over me, and then it's over.

A fitting end to a crappy, disappointing night. Sighing, I roll over onto my side, facing away from Grady, and urge myself to go to sleep.

Better luck tomorrow.

10. KADEN
KILL OF THE NIGHT - GIN WIGMORE

Lyra was more upset with me than she was her junkie loser of an ex-boyfriend. The image of her folding her arms and glaring up at me, the purple hue of the bar tinted in her eyes, is something I replay in my head several times.

She'd looked at me as though *I* were the problem.

Not the junkie loser harassing her.

The best course of action was to back off. She felt I had come on too strong in too short an amount of time. She's the type to need space.

I said I was leaving, though I never did.

I've sat half a block down from the Velvet Piano the entire time.

As Lyra and the others closed up, I lurked from within the confines of my Tesla and watched her walk toward the subway. The thought crossed my mind to follow her, do as I've done before, and ride with her.

Walk behind her the entire way home. Unbeknownst to her. I'd be an unseen shadow in the night.

The urges are too strong. My bloodlust is leaking into my external facade in such a manner I'm not sure I can control myself much longer. It's in the tension twined inside my body and the hunger aching in my stomach. My tongue itching for a taste of violence.

The monster clawing to be set free.

It's for the best I didn't follow Lyra home tonight. I may have done something reckless.

I wouldn't be the only one. Recklessness is a running theme of the night.

As I sit in the dark shadows of my Tesla, I decide to open up the app for the spy cameras I've set up in her bedroom.

Lyra's foolishly allowed that junkie loser into the apartment. She's invited him into her room, sitting beside him as he prattles on and on about his stupid problems. I grit my teeth glaring at my phone screen.

How can she not see where this will lead? Does she know and simply not care?

He's hardly subtle. He leeches off her marijuana and then waits until he can catch her by surprise.

My grip on my phone tightens and I sit up straighter, half a second away from starting the car and speeding over. From busting down her bedroom door and wrenching him off her.

Then she goes with it.

She lets him kiss her and push her back against the pillows. She allows the useless loser to undo his pants and slide off her panties. I'm seething, shaking with near-blinding rage by the time he's inside her.

A few times she tries to engage him with a kiss, but he's lost in his own world of weak pumps and throaty groans. He has no clue what the fuck he's doing. He touches her all wrong; I know this without ever having touched her myself.

His clumsy hand grips her hip and thighs and he stabs away at her with poor, rhythmic thrusts. I'm watching through video and yet it's evident she's barely wet, if wet at all.

Who the hell taught you how to fuck, micro penis?!

Another brilliant male of this generation raised off porn.

My teeth are grinding to the point of pain by the time he comes. He pulls out and falls asleep in what must be a minute, two at most. Completely oblivious to the fact that he's satisfied and Lyra is left hanging.

The girl seems resigned to this outcome.

With a deep sigh, she rubs herself to the soundtrack of the junkie loser's snores. She comes with a faint tremble and then rolls the opposite way he is, facing the window with her gaze on the inky sky.

Slowly, she nods off...

The disappointment drips from my phone screen.

So you're not being fucked properly, little lamb. How about I do you a favour?

Before I'm compelled to do what I must do and end you.

I drum my fingers on my steering wheel and watch Lyra sleep. I've taken to this habit the past few nights. Ever since setting up the cameras in her bedroom.

The sight of her asleep fascinates me. So still, so peaceful, so inexplicably erotic in a way.

Perhaps it has to do with how she sleeps half naked. She lays wonderfully still with the sensual curves of her body on display. The steep dip of her waist rises into the swell of her hips and then fills out into thighs I bet are achingly soft.

Sometimes, her tank top slips down and her breasts peek out. Pointed tips that beg to be suckled.

Lyra Hendrix has never been fucked properly. That much is clear. The girl deserves at least one explosive orgasm before she dies.

Earlier she demonstrated what I suspected about her talent; she played the piano flawlessly. I sat in awe as Lyra's delicate fingers soared across the keys and played a breathtaking rendition of Chopin's Nocturne in C-minor.

Even her bitch of a manager admitted she was impressive.

My view momentarily shifted. Her gift wasn't the kind that came along often. It was to be treasured in a decaying society like Easton.

Then she had to go and ruin my piqued curiosity, my possibly changing opinion, and allow that grubby-handed junkie to touch her.

Fuck her.

I stow away my phone with a dissatisfied scowl and ragged breath. I can't even savor the view of her sleeping tonight when all I can think about is how she let that loser touch her.

It can't happen again.

A dark, impulsive idea blooms to life in my twisted frame of mind.

Grady as she'd called him, can't fuck her again if he's met an unfortunate ending. Have I just stumbled upon my next true kill?

He meets my criteria as a loser male leeching off society and providing nothing of value. At best he's a pothead. At worst, he's into much harder drugs.

Something tells me it's the latter.

It doesn't matter regardless. I can plant quite the murder scene. Because of my profession, I have an unfettered access to medications and prescription drugs.

Grady will be found dead by overdose. No one will question it. Barely anyone will care.

The murder plot takes form as I go to push the ignition start button. I'll wait outside Lyra's apartment and then catch him on his way out tomorrow morning. He'll be found in two days in some alleyway after a presumed bender...

A man strolls down the block toward the Velvet Piano and interrupts my sinister thoughts. It takes me half a moment to recognize him; however, once he passes under a lamp post and light illuminates his face, I do.

Maximillion Keys saunters down the sidewalk like it's a

stage. Despite the fact that the only people around this late at night are drunk college kids bar-hopping and junkies that are even bigger losers than Grady, Maximillion acts with an air of self-imagined celebrity.

Why is he heading to the Velvet Piano more than an hour after it's closed?

He stops at the front door and lets himself in with his set of keys.

Bad news for Maximillion. My attention's now on him.

Mere hours ago he'd been an absolute ass to Lyra. He called her Butterfingers. After hearing Lyra *truly* play, they're nowhere near the same stratosphere in terms of talent. Lyra plays with a striking balance of grace and vulnerability juxtaposed against a hint of wild passion and freedom. I can't help wondering how well she'd play if she tapped into her full potential.

In comparison, Keys is cheap, store-bought tofu. Manic energy he puts on for the crowd that's hammy and artificial. He's a caricature in how he presents himself. All gimmicks and flashy behavior. I bet he's never properly mastered a Chopin or Stravinsky piece.

Lyra, however...

———

Maximillion forgot his wallet. He lets himself into the dim bar and uses his senses to chart a blind path past the tables and toward the back room. He pulls open his cubby and digs around inside.

In the loud silence of the empty bar, he hears a door snicking shut. He looks up with his manicured brows raised and then goes to peek his head around at the bar floor.

No one is there.

The chairs remain stacked on the tables, and the grand pianos resemble museum relics on the stage.

Realizing it was a figment of his imagination—or a drunken college idiot making noise outside—he returns to his cubby. His wallet goes in the back pocket of his jeans, and he grabs a pack of cigarettes he's stashed away as well.

He's heading onto the bar floor when it happens again.

Snick.

Quiet. Gentle. Almost hushed.

He freezes and surveys the bar area.

Nothing. Not a single thing out of place, or person around.

However, this time, he finds it impossible to shake his bad feeling. He sneaks a peek over his shoulder at the back room where the collection of cubbies is, and then turns his head forward.

He screams.

I'm standing in front of him. So close I can touch him.

My face is stoic. My expression an empty void. My eyes are on him in silent appraisal as he shrieks and stumbles several steps back.

"Who the... what the... where'd you come from?!"

I don't move. I remain perfectly still except for my mouth as I answer. "I was here to watch the dueling."

He's unnerved.

Everything about me unsettles him. From my unending stare and flat, monotone voice to my looming presence over him.

He takes another step back and tugs on the hem of his shirt. "Oh. Well... the bar closed an hour ago. How'd you get in anyway?"

"I want to hear you play."

His shock flickers out when my request sinks in. He grins. "That explains it. So you're a fan. I shouldn't be surprised. I get it a lot. I once had some girl throw her panties at me. Poor girl didn't realize I bat for the other team. But don't worry. I'll sign a napkin square for you, okay?"

I take a step closer. "I said I want to hear you play."

He gives off a dismissive laugh. "Listen, I'm exhausted. I've been playing all night. Rooney and I had to pick up the slack from Butterfingers. The girl couldn't play her way through Twinkle Twinkle Little Star. Worst player I've ever— *OOMPH!*"

I swipe my blade across his throat in a swift motion. His blood spurts everywhere as his jugular severs and his hands clap to his gaping wound in an ill fated attempt to slow his bleeding. His mouth opens and closes, then opens and hangs that way.

Hideous and shocked with bulging eyes.

He almost resembles a goldfish.

I pocket my specially designed scalpel and stare at him as if I'm far removed from the bloody sight before me.

In the next second, he drops to the floor. He squirms and gurgles. A slow, morbid pool of blood forms around him. It's gotten everywhere. All over his clothes and dyed onto his skin. A few specks have even splattered onto my designer loafers.

I'll have to buy another pair.

In the meantime, as Maximillion Keys bleeds out and dies, I start on my new task for the night.

Setting the most gruesomely undetectable crime scene.

11. Lyra
Love Language - SZA

The ping from my phone wakes me up. I groan as I roll over and scrabble for it off my nightstand.

Kaden has texted me good morning. Squinting at the short message on my screen, my brain's still warming up. I won't be fully awake for another thirty minutes. Maybe an hour.

"Fuck, Ly. Do you have to make so much noise?"

I freeze at the familiar voice. Then the weight lying beside me in my bed dawns on me.

I'm not alone. I'm lying in bed with Grady because...

...we had sex last night!

Suddenly, I'm awake. I spring up in my bed with my eyes wide and my thick braids heavy on my shoulder. Every pitiful moment from the night before flashes through my mind, playing like a movie I'm watching on the screen inside my head.

Last night was terrible.

I was put on hostess duty. Belittled by Maximillion and Erma. Treated like crap by patrons. Accosted by Grady and then stuck in the middle of a male pissing content between him and Kaden.

To top the night off, as I finally made it home, Grady was waiting for me. What else can I say but that I fell for his manipulative tactics?

It wouldn't be the first time. Show up on my door with a seemingly innocent intent to vent, then, as time goes by and I'm comforting him, he makes a move.

For some reason, I go along with it. As always. In the back of my mind, I'm thinking about our past.

Grady knows me better than maybe anyone...

"You need to go," I mutter, rubbing my hands over my face. "Get up and get out."

"There you go being Dr. Jekyll, Missus Hyde again. It's not even eight yet—"

"Go! And don't ever tell me not to make noise in my own room again! Get the hell out, Grady."

Kicking him out of my room feels like chasing a mouse with a broom. I have to shadow him down the hall and to the door as he complains about dressing on the move.

"Don't do this again. Don't show up like you did last night," I warn. "This was the last time."

He scoffs. "That's what you said last time."

I slam the door in his face. While he might be right, the fact that he's bold enough to say it tells me I have to prove him wrong.

For real this time. Last night was the last time Grady will *ever* touch me.

I pivot from the door and stomp my way into the kitchen with what must be a moody expression. Taviar stands at the counter pouring creamer in his coffee mug.

"You're up early. For you," he adds.

"Gee, thanks. I'd wake up early if I had a real job to go to. Turns out, nobody wants to hire me."

"You'll find something. You always do."

I grunt my thank you as Taviar hands me his coffee and then sets to making a second cup.

"Grady spend the night again?"

"You saw me kicking him out?"

Taviar nods, tearing into a sugar packet. "You need to stop inviting him over."

"He tends to... invite himself over."

"That's when you put your foot down, Ly. Stop falling for his game."

I sigh and hold up the coffee mug for a sip. "It's so hard. Grady... he helped me *a lot* when I was younger."

"It doesn't matter. You've repaid your debt to him five times over. Just say no. Like that drug campaign. DARE or some shit?"

"None of us said no to that. Not even you."

A glimmer of humor passes over Taviar's face. "Careful, Ly. I'm still successful."

"True. How's the business going?"

"You know better than to ask. You got your rent money? It's due today."

My stomach flutters with an abrupt case of nerves. "I'll get it to you this afternoon. I wanted to ask you... now that Jael's all but disappeared... what does this mean for the rent? I can't afford more than the twenty-five percent, Taviar."

"Jael who?" he asks before he walks off with an air of dismissiveness.

"That's not funny! You know who and you know what I mean. Now that she's gone, how much do I owe you?"

I follow him out of the kitchen and halfway down the hall before finally he stops and turns around.

"We're doing what we always do. Waiting 'til we get a third roommate. I have the room up on social media and the room-mate rental sites. Somebody'll bite eventually."

That's the most I'm getting out of Taviar for the time being. He returns to his room, and I return to mine. He'll likely be busy with his online shop, and I shut the door to my room with my gaze falling on my phone.

Kaden texted me and I never responded. I set down the coffee Taviar made me and pick up my phone. My fingers hover over my keyboard, torn between my temptation to respond and my urge to delete his number.

He's just some guy I met at a vegan spot.

He seemed nice and he was cool enough when we had lunch, but there's something about him I don't trust; something *off* about him.

I do neither—I don't respond but I don't delete his number. I simply... leave him on read.

I have enough issues going on without dealing with what to do about a guy like Kaden.

———

For the next two days, I focus on job hunting. For the next two mornings, Kaden texts me early. I ignore him and press on about my day. In forty-eight hours, I go on six job interviews. I receive zero call backs.

The restaurants, pet shop, and music studio are all a bust.

I'm so depressed, I return to my 'spot' at the cemetery, where I once spent so many afternoons typing up obituaries for the *Easton Times*. It's almost as if I believe hanging out under the huge elm tree will take me weeks back in time, where I had my steady little crappy job working for Winston (who still hasn't paid me).

On the fourth morning, a Wednesday, Kaden texts me yet again. I've already decided I'm taking it off from job interviews. Instead, I wind up at Strictly Pleasures standing among a shelf of bottles of flavored lube and an assortment of anal plugs.

I pick up an acorn-shaped metal plug with a purple crystal on the handle. "I like this one."

"Take it. On the house. You need it."

I choke on my next breath. "Excuse me? Speak for yourself. I don't *need* it."

Imani grins. "Just in case. For the next guy named Not Grady."

"You're never going to let me forget I had a backslide, are you?"

"I'm hoping maybe the humiliation will finally make you stop," she answers from behind the register. "What about the other guy? The one who spilled your lunch on you at Urban Greenery?"

"Hmmm?"

My interest shifts to the purple crystal anal plug, fiddling with its smooth, cold metal shape.

"Don't hmmm me. You mentioned he was texting you?"

"I haven't answered."

"It's been three days."

Shrugging, I return the plug to its rightful spot among its brothers and cousins. "He seems like a decent guy... but I don't know. We're not compatible."

"How do you know unless you get to know him more? See where it goes."

"Something's off about him."

"Like?"

I rack my brain to articulate the feeling, yet I can't come up with anything better than another shrug. Imani raises her brows and then shakes her head.

"You're never gonna get out of your funk, Ly," she says. "You insist on going in circles. Isn't it time you did something different? Step away from the Grady's and crap minimum wage jobs you hate. Pursue what you really love and give a different kind of guy a chance."

"It makes a lot of sense when you say it that way."

"Gimme your phone." Imani snatches it up before I can stop her. "Passcode?"

"Ugh. No. You're not going to text him for me, are you?"

"That's exactly what I'm going to do. Passcode. Now."

"898718."

"That's a lot of eights."

I watch with an eruption of nerves in my stomach. Imani hardly gives what she types any thought. Within seconds she's sending off the text, and then within another minute, we're gasping at the response that comes through.

"He's inviting you to lunch. Yes?"

I chew on the inside of my cheek in hesitation. "Okay... one more lunch. But that's all!"

"Done. He wants to meet you at the Wharf House. You're welcome."

Imani's smugness can't even be argued with—I leave Strictly Pleasures with her reminding me to update her about my lunch date later.

Kaden and I agreed to meet at the Wharf House for a light seafood lunch. I'm not really dressed for a so-called lunch date, especially with a guy who routinely looks like he belongs on the cover of GQ, but there's nothing I can do about my crop top and leggings now.

On the subway ride to the Wharf House, I luck out and land a seat in the corner. At first, I'm preoccupied with thoughts about my lunch with Kaden—and vague considerations of backing out last minute—but then I pull out my phone to distract myself.

A news alert pops up on my screen. The headline is so shocking and morbid, I gasp and garner several looks from other passengers.

. . .

POPULAR VELVET PIANO PERFORMER FOUND
MUTILATED AND MURDERED

My heart races in my chest and my throat feels like I've
swallowed chalk. After the first few seconds of shock pass, I
read the article start to finish.

This can't be true... this can't be real... who could've been
attacked?

"Maximillion Keys," I mutter to myself as if saying it
aloud will help me process the bombshell easier. "He's dead."

12. KADEN
CAREFUL - LUCKY DAYE

Lyra shows up dressed inappropriately for the Wharf House. Several guests stare with open umbrage from their tables. I rise as the skeptical maître d' approaches with Lyra closely behind.

"Sir, I apologize for disturbing your lunch experience. However, this woman claims she's here to meet you. I didn't see her name listed on the reservation and I did my absolute best to turn her away. Unfortunately, she *insisted* I bring her to you," he explains in a tone leaking of disapproval.

I raise a brow at him, my demeanor icy. "Perhaps she *insisted* because that is the case. She is here meeting me for lunch. Now go be useful and retrieve us a bottle of Slvenbaldi sparkling water. Two glasses. And bring Ms. Hendrix a proper menu."

The dismissive air surrounding the maître d' evaporates. He blinks, dumbfounded for a couple amusing seconds, and then stutters out, "Yes... of... of course. I will return in a moment."

A second passes in which he shuffles off and Lyra turns to me. I move around to pull out her chair. As she lowers herself into the seat and I scoot her in, I bend low enough to speak next to her ear.

"He tried to turn you away because of how you're dressed."

"I've never been here before. How would I know what to wear?" she asks. Then with a glance around, her expression shifts to its own form of flat disapproval. "I'm not sure I've ever eaten somewhere where there was a dress code for *lunch*."

"Baring your midriff and wearing tights for pants is generally frowned upon at most restaurants of the Wharf House's caliber."

"So if I walked in wearing a thousand dollar dress, he would've let me in no problem?"

Aware of what she's insinuating, I don't shy away from her probing gaze. I meet it with unblinking honesty. "Possibly not. He may have turned you away for... other reasons."

"So, then, why should I change the way I dress for people like him when there's nothing I can do about how he feels?"

"That is true," I admit. "However, sometimes in order to navigate certain circles, you have to be strategic. Despite how you may detest the rules."

I should know. I do so every moment I present myself as a well-adjusted man who doesn't have an unending appetite for violence.

But Lyra isn't satisfied with my answer. The maître d' returns to deliver us the bottle of Slvenbaldi water—priced at two hundred dollars each—and pours us our glass. She's rolling her lips together as I pick mine up and take a sip.

"What?" I ask. "What is it? What's on your mind?"

"I don't want to have to navigate these circles. Circles *you* seem to belong to. Which is why I think this lunch is a mistake."

"I do not belong to any circles. I am my own person."

"Then why would you invite me here?"

"Because I wanted to treat you to a nice lunch to apologize for the other night—"

"Even if everyone stares? Look around you."

I do and find myself on the receiving end of several curious, pointed stares from idiots at other tables. I recognize Ms. Diane Sutter, the dean of the boys school I attended over a decade ago, eying Lyra and I as though we're soaked in blood. When I glare back, she quickly returns her attention to the acquaintances she's with and keeps chatting.

"I don't feel comfortable here," Lyra says.

"You should. You belong here as much as anyone else. These people around you they're some of the most useless people on the planet. And yet they lap in luxury and wear the most ridiculous prejudices as a badge of honor. They don't realize they're fooling themselves. They're no better than anyone. Most of all you. I'd say it's the opposite."

My words are meant to uplift her; judging by the small smile she gives they do. But her uncertainty about the situation still remains.

"I don't know what you want with me."

My gaze is pulled back to her. "I want to get to know you."

"*Why?*"

"Because..." I pause, thinking fast. "You interest me. I think you're smart, and I find you witty. You're a breath of fresh air."

"But you said it yourself. You don't know me."

"So, let me find out. What is the worst that can happen? Do you think I'm going to do something wrong?" I ask reasonably. "Have I ever made you feel unsafe? Have I ever given any indication I don't respect your wishes? Did I not immediately leave the other night?"

Her brows shift closer. "You did... I... I just..."

"What is it, Lyra?"

"I don't know," she answers, and then sighs and reaches

for her water. "I'm so sorry if I seem like I'm flip flopping every other second. It's a really difficult period in my life. I don't want to unload on you, but I'm just focusing on setting myself straight. The last thing I'm looking for is any new men in my life."

"What about a friend?" I ask.

She blinks long and slow from across the table. "We... we could do friends. Maybe. It depends."

"On...?"

The corners of her lips tip up in a vague smile. "If you pass the vibe check."

The answer is so unexpected, my next sip of water almost slips down the wrong pipe. I swallow harder than usual and set down my water glass, letting the humor of the moment reflect in my expression.

"Vibe check? Alright. Go ahead. Give me your best shot."

"What do you like to do for fun?"

You don't want the real answer, little lamb. You couldn't handle it.

"I read. Often," I answer. "Usually medical journals and scientific research papers. But I'm thinking that's not cool enough to pass the vibe test."

She cringes as a laugh plays from her lips. I have my answer without a single word. "It's vibe *check*, by the way," she adds.

"I'm guessing calling it a test kills 'the vibe'," I tease good-naturedly. "What about hiking and rock climbing? Are those better?"

"Eh, marginally." She holds up her hand and tips it left to right as if it's become a scale.

"I was once a violinist. I was only third chair and quit by the time I was a fourteen. But I was once a musician like you."

Now I have her attention. Her dark brown eyes glimmer and she sits up straighter with sudden perky interest.

"You play the violin?"

"*Played*. I haven't touched one in almost twenty years."

"Why did you stop?"

"Did you hear the part about the third chair? I wasn't very good." We pause briefly to place our orders and hand off the menus to the waiter who has arrived at our table. Once he's promised he'll return with the fresh garlic oysters we've ordered as a starter, I pick up our conversation as if it was never interrupted. "I bet you, however, are a very good pianist."

She almost chokes on her water, thumping a hand to her chest. "Me?! You wouldn't know."

"I can tell you are."

I also spied and watched you play the other night...

"You're flattering me for no reason. You've never heard me play."

"Tell you what. I will play the violin for you, if you play the piano for me."

The wary look she gives me, complete with an arched brow, is amusing. "That sounds more like it'll work in your favor. You've already said you're bad. All you have to do is show up, bomb a quick etude, and then I'm forced to let you hear me play."

"You underestimate the level of humiliation bombing a quick etude will cause me."

For a moment that stretches on, she regards me with narrowed eyes, twisted lips, and a scrunched up nose. The expression is unexpected and what some in my world would call unladylike, however, I'm amused.

"Fine," she sighs eventually. "I guess I should get used to playing again. With Maximillion gone, she's asked me to fill in."

I keep my reaction tempered. "Maximillion's gone? Remind me which one he is?"

...the same one whose throat I slit.

"Maximillion Keys," she clarifies. "He's basically the star of the Velvet Piano—or was, anyway. He was murdered the other night. You haven't heard about it? The police are investigating."

...and they'll never trace it back to me.

"I'm afraid not. I've been preoccupied with three aortic aneurysms this week. Do they have any idea who could've done it? Did he have any known enemies?"

She shakes her head. "The police are stumped. Apparently, the killer didn't leave much in terms of evidence aside from his dead body... almost as if they were taunting authorities."

That's exactly what I was doing.

"Such a shame," I say, forcing a solemn frown. "He seemed so talented."

"Yeah, I wasn't a fan of the guy—he was kind of an asshole, actually—but I didn't want him dead. It's even weirder now my manager seems to want me to play. She put me on the door the other night because she didn't want me to."

"Then you shouldn't."

Her brows jump. "Shouldn't... play? You can't be serious."

"Lyra, you are better than some dive piano bar where half the patrons are belligerently drunk," I explain matter-of-factly. I dig into the pocket on the inside of my blazer and retrieve a business card I've intentionally brought along to this lunch. "Here," I say, pushing the card into her hand. "This is the direct line to a friend of mine, Fyodor Kreed. He is on the hiring board at the Easton Opera House. They are always searching for new talent, particularly as the holiday shows are currently being put together. However, you have to have an impressive resume—or an insider connection—in order to land an audition. Tell him Kaden gave you his number and recommends you."

Lyra stares. She stares and stares, holding the business card as though it's a foreign object she's never seen before. Then she looks up and pierces me with the same awestricken, speechless type of stare.

I settle back in my seat and wait out her shock.

She might not realize it, but in this moment, she's quite an exquisite sight—long, natural lashes that flutter as her curious, almond-shaped eyes stare back at me, and she holds her mouth with her full lips slightly parted. Youthful cheeks curve into a delicate jawline and a round-tipped nose punctuated by a tiny silver loop that's strangely... *her*.

That perplexingly adds to the uniqueness of her.

From where she sits, the sunlight filters in from the glass ceiling and leaves her smooth, dark brown complexion with a radiance that's almost entrancing.

My mind jumps back to the other night, watching her play so eloquently, and I can't resist melding the two instances—visualizing her like this, in a sunlit room where she'll sit in front of the piano and play for me. The look of soft surprise that would linger on her face when I make my request and then attentively pose as her sole audience member.

Does she realize how talented she is? How striking she looks when she plays?

I force myself to clear my throat. "Well, are you going to call him?"

She nods out of her dazed look and then blinks the last of it away. "Yes... yeah... I'll definitely call him. But are you sure?"

"Call him Sunday morning. Around nine a.m. Mention my name. That I heard you play and knew you would be a good fit for his holiday orchestra. Tell him your educational background and that you are presently a piano teacher. Leave out the rest."

"Kaden—"

"When he brings you in for an audition, dress conservatively. A simple black dress will do. Sleeveless if possible. Wear your hair up. Fyodor has a thing for female players who show their neck and shoulders. Be polite and agreeable, and he will hire you. Do you understand?"

"Why are you doing this? You haven't even heard me play..."

"I've told you. I can tell you have talent. Now take my help and tell me how it goes."

Lyra gives a sharp nod as it seems to sink in. Her mood lightens considerably, and she checks and then rechecks the business card several times.

When our lunch is over and we part ways, she apologizes for ignoring me for several days. I wave it off and tell her I understand. That she was correct to be wary of me—and she was.

She still should be.

As we part ways and I loiter an extra moment to watch her walk away, I stick my hands in my pockets, and wonder *why*.

Why am I helping this girl? Why did I feel the need to better her job situation? Why did I kill Maximillion?

In the moment, I believed I understood—he was a grating, pompous idiot, and he deserved to be put in his place.

But did he really? Did he meet my why, or was I reacting out of some other subconscious motive?

Finally turning away and walking off, I'm not sure of the answer.

————

One a.m., I sit in the dark across the street from Lyra's apartment building. Her bedroom light is off and she's not home. After our lunch, she went out and ran some errands (I know because I was with her almost the entire time).

Then she came home to shower and change for her shift at the Velvet Piano. Part of me was tempted to go sit outside the bar; however, I decided against it. Since I have several methods to monitor her movements at all times, I didn't want to risk the chance she'd happen by and catch me.

She was right about her manager at the Velvet Piano. Erma had her duel against a player named Rooney. Lyra's nerves bested her, and she lost... though not nearly as devastatingly as the last time.

Perhaps a sign she's overcoming her nerves.

She kept her phone in her pocket as she played, which meant I couldn't see the performance. I could only listen to it using the spy app I've used to link her phone to mine.

The duels ended and the bar closed for the night.

I check the time with an impatient glower. She should be home by now. If she's decided to make any stops along the way, particularly to see that junkie loser ex of hers...

I grit my teeth and glare at the numbers on the clock.

Despite the fact that I haven't consciously stopped to think about my newfound obsession in Lyra, I'm distantly aware of it. I'm cognizant of the fact that I've begun to dedicate an increasing amount of time to monitoring her. I've devoted entire segments of my day to observing her and following her.

She's begun to invade my thoughts at all hours.

There's something about her that draws me.

It wouldn't be the first time I've formed an obsessive attachment.

My father would sneer and remind me of how I behaved around my mother as a young boy. Before I could make sense of the world around me and the violence I had been born into, I often sought her out to hide. Hear her play beautiful melodies for me. She was a form of comfort and peace against an ever-darkening urge. At least I believe it the comforting music was coming from her...

It was her beautiful music that often called to me in the dark halls of our home.

I followed the sound, always so ensnared from the first breathtaking note.

I wander for what feels like miles. At first, I did so quietly, hoping to remain quiet and unseen, then I'd pick up the pace. I'd trot down the hall with a heart pounding in anticipation.

She was supposed to look up and smile sweetly at me. Invite me inside so I could sit and listen, like a private concert just for me.

...instead there was blood. Everywhere.

Seeping into the floors. Spreading far and wide 'til it reached my feet.

And tears. Sobbing.

I didn't give any thought to what I did. I stepped into the puddle of blood, and I was never the same...

The psychiatrists that would later treat me would claim it's what altered my behaviors for the duration of my adolescence into adulthood. I would say it is an accurate assessment.

At any given point in time, I range from fully detached and far removed to deeply obsessed.

I can feel it taking over me. Even more powerful than my bloodlust. Urges I don't know what to do with or how to process.

I didn't know then. I don't know now.

Lyra returns home. I'm pulled from my dark headspace by the beep of my tracker app. I look up and see the light blink on in her bedroom. She doesn't immediately close the curtains. Only after she takes off her earrings and pulls open her dresser drawer does she remember to pull them shut.

I resort to the cameras I've installed in her room and the breath stalls in my lungs. She's taken off the blood-red velvet crop top she was wearing and roams her private space topless.

Clueless that as she grabs her toiletry items and moves into her bathroom, I'm watching.

The sound of streaming water echoes through my phone, though the angle from which the camera films only catches a distant shot of her.

I bite down hard on my jaw and shut out the dark impulse begging to be freed.

I'm not sure how much longer I can go on.

How much more I can resist before introducing my little lamb to the monster inside the man...

13. KADEN
Bad Guy - Billie Eilish

After her shower, Lyra emerges in her bedroom in a towel. Steam clouds around her and her dark complexion glistens with beads of water.

If only the camera could zoom in further. If only it could capture each bead as it trickles down the cleft of her cleavage.

It should feel wrong that I'm watching her. Invading her privacy and trust in this way. On a fundamental human basis, I can acknowledge that it *is* wrong. I'm sure it's something she'd consider a violation.

However, right and wrong has never mattered to me. At least in the traditional sense.

Much of human belief lacks nuance. Their morals are stringent and impractical. So much so, they often prove themselves to be hypocrites in due time, stating they believe one thing and later doing something that directly contradicts their said belief.

I skip all of that.

I have no true moral code fleshed out. I have no care for anyone else but myself and what I want in the moment.

Everyone in my life is either to be used for my own selfish

means, disregarded and ignored entirely, or disposed of if I see fit.

Good, evil, right, wrong—it's all subjective. All meaningless drivel.

Lyra may believe it is a violation that I'm watching the towel fall from her svelte, delectable, naked body, but *I* would argue it's in her favor I've taken such an interest in her. If I hadn't, she'd already be dead...

Two weeks going strong. She's not only managed to hold my interest, she's managed to *grow* my interest.

My insides burn hot. My dick swells and my pants become uncomfortably tight. I husk out a rough breath and attempt to readjust myself. Calm myself down.

The view on my phone screen doesn't help.

Lyra stands directly in front of the camera, completely nude.

Her body leaves me speechless. She's on the petite side, barely a few inches over five feet, yet she has a curviness to her form that couldn't be more womanly—pointed breasts with puffy nipples and a flat stomach I bet I can cinch within my hands. Subtly rounded hips and thighs that look silken, and a mons pubis that draws my attention.

She's shaven, offering me a sneak peek of the plump, beautiful v-shape that is her vulva.

"Damn it," I grunt, unable to resist rubbing the front of my pants.

Lyra might as well be modeling for me. She reaches into her dresser drawer and then shimmies into a pair of panties. The kind that hugs her hips but covers her up well. The female version of briefs.

Some men would be disappointed. They would hope for a sexy bikini cut or some type of thong.

However, I find it *sexier* that she's wandering around her

room in briefs, like she's comfortable in her skin as she unknowingly teases me.

I won't deny myself another second. As Lyra attempts to tidy up in her room, picking up piles of clothes, I pull out my dick. My hand wraps around my length and I stroke myself. Perhaps the oddest, most mundane jerking I've ever done— I'm getting myself off to the sight of a woman walking around in her panties and a cartoon t-shirt.

But it's the *details* that do me in.

The way her puffy nipples poke through the flimsy, faded fabric of her t-shirt and how her ass moves as she steps around.

I close my eyes and imagine myself in the room with her. I imagine what she'd do if I showed up. If I did what Grady did and invited myself into her room, kissed her on the mouth, let my hand explore the curves of her body...

My strokes grow faster as I attempt to get myself off. I'm tuned into Lyra's room and out of the physical environment that surrounds me. The abandoned office with its dust laced in the air and stale smell couldn't affect me less.

My dick throbs in anticipation. I tighten my grip and fist it even faster.

So close. So fucking close.

If only it were Lyra's hands on my cock. If only it were Lyra's mouth wrapped around it. Her pussy clenching my girth as I buried myself inside her.

I'm breathing heavily, stroking fast, on the precipice of coming when... I lose it. The climax I'm working toward vanishes, my chest sputtering its next breath.

I lose it because of what I'm seeing on my phone screen. Lyra's finished tidying up and has sat down at her desk. She's logged onto her laptop. She's put on that fucking mask of hers.

The leather cat mask she wears when she's talking to *them*. She knows what she's doing—though technically they can't see that she's in her panties, I'm sure they're able to see her nipples poke through the fabric of her shirt.

It's just the right level of tease for her. For her to sexualize herself and garner their interest just enough without offering too much. Without crossing an invisible, unspoken line it seems she has.

Anger surges through me watching her cam show. It goes on for almost an hour.

I log onto the Cyber Fans account I created purely for her and clench my fists at the deluge of crude messages filling up her chatroom.

Men asking her to strip. Men speaking to her like a whore. Men demanding she offer more explicit content.

There are the ones who speak sweetly, pathetically, to her as though she's their real girlfriend and not a woman who simply wants their subscription money. In some ways, these creeps are almost worse. They're delusional enough to believe they have a real chance with her.

The entire show is a form of torture I was unaware existed.

By the time Lyra logs off, I'm glaring at her through the phone screen. How *dare* she cam with dozens of strange men mere hours after a lunch date with me!?

Admittedly, she agreed to lunch under the pretense of friendship; however, it feels like a betrayal. I've given her a job opportunity she'd never have earned on her own.

Fyodor would slam the door in her face without my recommendation.

I'm torn between staying put and spying some more and giving up my endeavor altogether. Sensibility would dictate I do the latter. I collect my dignity and leave her be. At least for the night. Enough is enough.

This proves more difficult than my staunch ego would like.

I'm still scowling as I stay where I am and watch Lyra

ready herself for bed. She disappears to the bathroom to wash her face and brush her teeth and then emerges with her hair wrapped up in a scarf to pull back the covers on her bed. She drops onto her many pillows and wraps an arm around a ratty teddy bear she seems to keep on her bed as some homage to her childhood.

Minutes pass with her laying still, her gaze up on the ceiling.

What's on your mind, little lamb? Tell me.

I begin wondering if she'll get high. A habit of hers when she's in contemplative moments like this. She surprises me with a turn of events that evokes the same tight, constrained feeling in my pants as earlier.

She slides a hand down the front of her panties and starts playing with herself. I groan even though I can't see the explicit details of what she's doing to her pussy. Seeing the outline of her hand in her panties is enough.

I do the same. I reach into my pants and pull my dick out again. As Lyra tilts her head back and moans, I grip my cock and grunt my approval. My hand jerks up and down my length while her fingers rub her clit.

"Yes," I breathe, my motions fast and aggressive. "Yes, little lamb. Rub yourself. Play with your pussy. It deserves better than to be fucked by that loser ex of yours. It deserves to be fucked by my thick cock. You have no idea how I'd fuck you 'til you're crying tears from all the pleasure I've given you. I'll fuck you so good, you'll be sore for days."

The moment becomes a union between us. Some sort of mirrored team effort. Lyra getting herself off and me getting myself off to the sight of her doing so.

Just as the moment builds, a crescendo rising to its peak, it's gone.

Again.

For the second time in the same night, I lose it.

Lyra makes me lose it.

Because she loses hers.

As her fingers seem to move faster within her panties and she writhes in bed, suddenly her orgasm seems to elude her. Her eyes pop open and she falls still. The hot, flushed look about her fades away as she sits up and releases a low sigh.

What the hell happened!?

It occurs to me, as I hold my softening dick, I can't come 'til she does. I've built up this moment as a joint effort between the two of us so much that when she calls it quits, I'm going flaccid in my grasp.

Lyra rolls onto her side and switches off the lamp on her nightstand. Darkness engulfs her cramped bedroom and for the seventeen minutes it takes her to fall asleep, she lays still, seeming in deep thought.

Something's bothering her. Something's on her mind.

To such an extent she was unable to finish her session.

"What is it, little lamb?" I whisper, regretfully tucking myself back into my pants. "What is it that's bothering you? How can I help?"

———

A stillness falls over the street of Lyra's apartment building. The night reaches such a late hour that even those who routinely stay up begin turning in. Almost every light in every window on the block goes dark. No cars pass through. No pedestrians.

Loud silence except for the distant and occasional sounds from other parts of the city.

Lyra long ago fell asleep.

I did too. After our anticlimactic masturbatory session, I watched her drift off, and then did so myself. I wake in the sunken leather office chair I've taken up camp in, with a crick in my neck and flakes of dust tickling my nose.

It would make sense to go home. End my obsessive surveillance of Lyra and pick up where I've left off another time.

My compulsions run too deep. Both the violent urges which are a daily struggle to hide, and the intensifying urges I have for Lyra.

An idea floats to mind staring at her dark window from across the street. If surveilling her via the hidden camera was a violation of trust, this would be a demolition of it.

Assuming Lyra trusts me in the first place. I still sense a wariness on her part.

Regardless, once I have the idea, once my sick and twisted mind grabs hold of it and refuses to let it go, there's no turning back.

I'm leaving the office behind. I'm crossing the empty street and using the fire escape to once more make my way up to Lyra's room. I'm letting myself inside.

Thankfully, she's quite the heavy sleeper.

As I slip through the window and stand up, she lets out a soft breath and clutches a throw pillow against her chest.

So peaceful, so beautiful in her sleep.

It's not the first time I take notice. I move around to the front of her bed and then stop for a chance to observe her longer.

Being this close up, I can pick up her scent. The smell of whatever products she puts in her hair and on her skin—light traces of what I recognize as coconut. I inhale a deep breath as my dick wakes from another disgruntled and unsatisfied slumber.

The hardness has become uncomfortable. I've let my orgasm escape me twice tonight.

But now it will be a different story.

Lyra shifts again, rolling from her side to her back.

The perfect position. A slight grin twists onto my face, disguised by the deep shadows in the room. I move closer until my body grazes the edges of her bed and then I extend my arms. Using their long length, I reach over her with slow and measured movements, and carefully hook my fingers into the hem of her panties.

I go completely still when Lyra makes another soft sound and her hips tilt partially sideways. Almost as if, even from her deep sleep, she senses something—or someone—has touched her. I wait until she's fallen still again before continuing. Lowering her panties inch by inch.

It's a slow, delicate task. Being gentle and cautious enough that I slide the pair past her hips and then down her thighs and legs. At the halfway mark, I stop altogether, with my gaze intensely focused on her cunt.

I'm so close I could touch her. I could bury my face in it and taste her. I lick my lips and my adrenaline races at the sheer magnitude of my opportunity.

Though I'm so damn hard and turned on I could come in my pants right now, I have to be rational. I have to be careful about this moment.

Lyra could wake at any second. She'd scream in horror, and I'd have no choice but to end her. A dark deed I'm not yet ready for if I can avoid it.

Waiting for another moment where I'm sure she's deeply entrenched in her dreams, I lean closer. My hand glides along her silky, bare thighs and then dips between them. I have to bite down on my cheek to keep from releasing a groan of pleasure at the feel of her.

Soft and moist. Warm flesh that feels incredible to the touch. That would feel even more incredible squeezing my cock.

I find her clit and run my thumb over the little nub.

Lyra's head falls to the side and a breathless moan escapes her lips. Her eyes never open.

I do it again. My thumb rubs her clit in steady, slow motions that build. Her pussy becomes wetter as I do. Slickness builds along her lips, and I help myself to the taste of her. Curling two of my digits inside of her, I savor the tight and slick clench she gives as if distantly aware, even miles away in dreamland, that I'm finger-fucking her.

By the sounds she makes, the soft soughing breathes she gives, she's loving it. On some level, she's aroused and content to finally get off.

It's okay, little lamb. I'll relieve you. I'll make you feel so good.

I suck on my two fingers and then return them to Lyra's tight channel. Her pussy pulses around me and her body begins to squirm.

Every one of my senses is on high alert. Acutely aware as my dick stiffens in my pants, that she can snap and wake up at any second.

It should make me more cautious. More reserved.

Yet I take more liberties. I rub Lyra harder and pump my fingers inside her. I lean over her body and stare into her sleeping beauty of a face and watch the pleasure flicker across her features. Her brows knit, and her lips part. One of her hands finds her breast and she cups it out of instinct.

"Yes, little lamb," I whisper. "You feel so good, don't you? Come for me. Come on my fingers. Next time, it'll be my tongue. My fucking cock."

Lyra obeys. She does as I say and comes.

It's a glorious moment for us both. As she writhes in place in bed and creams herself, I'm finally letting go too. My rock hard dick gives a violent jerk and comes. The first time I've come in my pants in years, and yet I feel no shame.

Quite the opposite. A beat of triumph pulses through me.

I reluctantly pull my hand from between Lyra's lush thighs, licking my fingers of her taste, and then I set to righting her panties. I drag them back over her hips and smirk thinking of the mess she'll find a few hours from now.

"Good night, little lamb."

————

Day breaks into the sky in a burst of golden light that chases away the night's deep blues and purples.

I've spent the night in the abandoned office across the street from Lyra's apartment. The crick in my neck has worsened and my eyes are bloodshot.

However, it'll be worth it. I can sense it will be as I wait out what I'm hoping will happen.

Hour by hour, as the morning arrives, the street becomes alive. People bustle out of their front doors with travel mugs full of coffee and city buses pass through. The birds twitter out grating morning songs and the late-summer warmth makes itself known.

It's half past eight by the time Lyra wakes in a state of confusion. She sits up and immediately seems to realize something's off.

Her panties are damp.

I crack a small smirk watching the surprise on her face and her hand between her legs, feeling the crotch of her panties. Her fingers linger a second longer than they should, as though she's deep in her mind recollecting a memory.

Then she snaps out of it, jumps off her bed, and beelines straight for the restroom.

"You remember, don't you?" I ask no one. I peer at my phone and wait for her return. "Some part of you sensed I was there last night, didn't you?"

A flush of the toilet and rinse of the sink later, she emerges in a bathrobe clutching the used pair of panties. I watch as she drops them in a pile of other dirty clothes before moving to collect new garments from her dresser drawer.

She seems to be getting ready for another shower.

Are you embarrassed by your wet dream, little lamb? Don't be. It was my pleasure.

At the last second, on her walk toward the bathroom, she changes her mind. Doubling back, she goes to her nightstand instead. She picks up her phone and pauses in another silent deliberation. Her fingers gradually begin to move.

What happens next is better than I could've anticipated.

My phone *rings*.

Lyra's name appears on the Caller ID. The same level of high-intensity adrenaline from last night floods me, and I force myself to wait a few rings before I answer.

"Hello?" I make my voice sound as preoccupied as possible.

"Hey," she says in a breezy tone. Little does she know I'm watching her from across the street as she paces her room.

"Hey. I didn't expect a call from you."

"Too soon?"

"Not too soon. Just a nice surprise."

She gives a shrug she doesn't realize I see. "You were on my mind."

"You mean what I told you about Fyodor Kreed?" I grin to myself at my feigned innocence.

"Not exactly," she mutters. A breathiness develops about her voice, though she seems to catch herself a second later. "I think I had a dream about you."

"Good dream or bad dream?"

She *smiles*. She smiles and bites down on her lip while considering how to answer. "It left me feeling like I had to call you."

"That doesn't answer my question, Lyra."

"Would you like to do coffee this morning?"

I glance down at my clothes. I'm dressed in the same outfit as yesterday. I begin collecting my things and rushing for the door. "Sure," I answer. "But in an hour. I'm handling some business right now."

"An hour works."

"The Java King on Thirty-Fourth?"

"I'll be there," she says. Then as if sensing I'm about to hang up, she adds, "and Kaden?"

"Yes?"

"It was a very good dream."

Halfway down the old building's stairwell, my grin widens. "I bet."

14. LYRA

I had no plans to date anyone new. I'm equally as surprised as Imani when, after two lunch outings and a coffee meetup, I find myself not only dating but dating a man I never thought I would.

Kaden Raskova, polished and kind-hearted vascular surgeon who drives a luxury vehicle and wears designer threads. He's impossibly good looking and earns double takes from women wherever we go. And yet he only has eyes for me.

He's gone so far as to give me a hookup for a potential job at the *Easton Opera House*.

It's like some freakish dream I'm not waking up from.

The first week flies by in a whirlwind of careful coffee meetups, casual lunches, and an evening where we order pizza.

The latter is when I finally agree to call what we're doing *dating*. Up until that point, we've hidden behind the "platonic friends" excuse despite the fact that each time I see him the chemistry between us grows.

It becomes undeniable that he's checking me out when he thinks I'm not looking (but really, I am), and that I'm flustered and flirty whenever around him. Considering I'm not the flirty type, it's *kind of* a big deal.

"You mean to tell me you haven't fucked him yet?" Imani asks over smoothies. "That man is too fine and available for you to be dragging your feet."

I slurp down another mouthful of my peanut butter smoothie and shrug. "Not just that. I haven't even kissed him yet."

Imani nearly chokes on her mixed berries. She coughs and then smacks a hand to her chest. "Ly, what?! What are you doing?"

"We haven't kissed yet. I've only known him for two weeks. And most of our time spent together was as friends. It wasn't 'til pizza gate where we agreed... we'll go out."

"Are you sure he's into you?"

"I've caught him checking out my ass, like, ten times. He's into me." We walk down the side of the street at a lazy pace, the sun following us wherever we go. "I might not know much, Mani. But trust me. I know when a guy is into me. He's started finding any reason to touch me."

"Has he done the hand on the small of your back thing?"

My nod is my answer, my lips returning to my straw.

"He *is* basically hooking you up with a job. All signs do point toward interested. Which brings me back to my original question—why haven't you fucked him yet?"

"We're taking things slow. He's been respectful. He didn't get pushy last night when it ran late, and I mentioned I was tired. Grady would've insisted on spending the night."

"Ly, we've established Grady's an asshole."

"Who is blocked for real this time. You know he showed up at the Velvet Piano again?"

He hadn't had as much luck accessing me. Since Maximillion's death and the spontaneous performance Erma saw of mine, she's made me into a regular dueler. Something I wouldn't mind so much if it didn't feel like I were the new Maximillion.

Business is cutthroat. Though the investigation into Maximillion's murder is still very much active, Erma's carried on at the bar like nothing happened. One tribute night later, she's coaxed grieving regulars to return with half-priced drinks and finger foods.

I've even been given my own cubby. *Finally.*

It just so happens to be Maximillion's old cubby. Another aspect that creeps me out.

Between my missing roommate and my dead coworker, it seems there's still a dark cloud hanging over me.

Even as I do make good on Kaden's suggestion and give Fyodor Kreed a call. He answers in a Russian accent so severe it's difficult to understand at first.

"Hi," I say, my insides doing backflips. "I'm... I'm..."

"Who is this?" he growls, interrupting me. "Do you believe it is a joke to call this number?"

"Oh. No, it's not a joke! I'm... I'm Lyra Hendrix. I play the piano."

"Why should I care? That means nothing to me! Do not phone this number again!"

My throat tightens at the sound of anger in his voice. "Kaden Raskova told me to call you. He... he said to mention his name. He said that you're... uh, looking for talent for the shows this holiday season."

Silence.

More silence.

Even more silence.

Sooo much silence I think we've been disconnected. Just as I'm pulling the phone away from my ear to check on the screen, he speaks.

"You are a friend of Mr. Raskova?"

"Yes."

"You play the piano?"

"I do. Since I was four."

A few more seconds of silence, and then...

"I will need to hear you play for myself."

My heart thumps in excitement. I stand up from my bed. "Yes, of course. I would be happy to play for you."

"I expect to see you next Sunday. Noon. Arrive to the opera house and wait on the steps outside."

I'm opening my mouth to gush out a thank you when he hangs up before I'm able to. I'd be insulted if I hadn't essentially been offered what could potentially be the most amazing job opportunity of my life.

I don't even care that Fyodor Kreed has hung up on me. My phone drops from my hands and I release a loud squeal that might alarm Taviar if he's home.

In no time, I'm blasting my music app and dancing like a fool around my room.

Finally, some good news! Something that feels like a win!

Never mind that I still have to audition. That's a stressor for tomorrow. Right now, I'm celebrating.

I'm so excited, smiling wide to myself, I almost forget to let Kaden know. I shoot him off a text telling him about my phone call with Fyodor. He answers within seconds.

Good. I knew you could do it.

I send back a heart smiley emoji and thank him for the connect. He answers almost as quickly as my text goes through.

You can thank me by allowing me to take
you out to dinner tonight.

My celebratory high is too disorienting. I respond without
thinking. Before I know it, Kaden's telling me he'll be by at six
to pick me up and to wear a nice dinner dress. I'm scrambling
around my room to see if I have any clothes nice enough for
where he'll be taking me.

Times like this I wish Jael was still around to offer me
access to her closet.

I dig around and find a figure-hugging velvet dress I've
only worn once, months ago. The thin straps and low cut
expose plenty of neck, shoulder, and cleavage while the
midnight purple shade complements my dark complexion.

Considering the dress stops mid-thigh and is also backless,
some might say it's too sexy. It could be inappropriate for
whatever restaurant Kaden's taking me to.

But everything else I own is too casual, which means the
velvet dress wins by default.

I spend the rest of the afternoon getting ready. I shave—
including a fresh shave of my nether regions—and video call
Imani twice for makeup advice. My braids are gathered in a
half down, half up style with a bun on top and I decide on a
bold berry-toned lip.

Kaden turns up on my doorstep right on time. He buzzes
the door and sticks both hands in the pockets of his tailored
all-black suit. Upon answering, I'm inundated with a flashback
to a night earlier this month. The night I'd love nothing more
than to put behind me.

"Who do we have here?"

*The voice is unfamiliar. Female. Shrill with a side dose of
patronization.*

I look up to a woman swaying toward me, wearing a sneer on her pale face and a deep-plunging, emerald dress on her svelte frame. She almost looks like someone from an era gone by, like she's time-traveled to the present just to be a snobby bitch.

And I know she's a snobby bitch even at a glance.

Her blood-red lips stretch to reveal teeth, her dark eyes raking over me. "You? You're who they've gotten to fill in?"

My brows squish together, and I'm about to answer her when I notice she's not alone. There's a man several feet behind her. He stands still and stares, his hands in his tuxedo pockets, giving no indication either way if he knows her or just happened by.

I blink, realizing I'm staring. Kaden's head tilts to the side.

"Are you alright? I told you you look amazing, and you developed this faraway look."

"Oh. Yes, thank you. You look... very handsome."

He offers me his arm and I accept. He walks me the rest of the way to his car.

The Tesla costs more than all the money I've earned in my life, with a dark and sleek interior that's both futuristic and sexy. I look at the panel on the dashboard with a screen larger than my laptop and listen to the cool, female automated voice feeling like I'm in a spaceship instead of a car.

Kaden casts me an amused glance. "Something wrong?"

"No," I say with a slow shake of my head. "I've just never ridden in a spaceship before."

"Buckle up. Once in a lifetime opportunity."

He's speaking in jest, however, I can't help thinking that it probably is. I live in a room the size of a tin can and often scrape together loose change to buy ramen and stuff to make peanut butter and jelly sandwiches.

Growing up, it was no different.

Mom played her saxophone brilliantly. But there was no money to be made. Once she was let go of her gig at the jazz club, she was forced to return to bussing tables and playing her instrument on street corners and subway platforms. The kind people dropped a quarter or two. The crueler ones tossed buttons or balls of lint. The worst ones knocked her down and stole her sax.

She didn't ever get a chance to buy another.

In this way, Grady and I understand each other. His family and mine were on the same footing.

I can't relate to Kaden.

As he drives us into the ritzier side of Easton, I'm struck by the rich splendor surrounding us. The boulevards of designer boutiques and luxury hotels. The glimmering lights and speckless streets. The people are better dressed, better looking. It's like the evening of the party I attended with Jael all over again.

Except even *more* extravagant from the stylish interior of Kaden's half a million dollar car.

We drive by the Easton Opera House with the full moon haloing its glass dome ceiling in light, and my heart skips several extra beats.

Soon I could be there; soon I could live my dream.

Kaden catches me staring, then grins. "We're almost there."

We pull up outside of the Arcadia, one of the most well-known, Michelin-starred restaurants in the country. *Celebrities* regularly dine here.

My jaw drops open, though I don't move. I stay cemented where I am.

"C'mon."

Kaden presses the button, and my car door swings open. I'm on his arm again on the approach to the front entrance, which might as well be the fine dining version of a red carpet. Paparazzi stay camped out on either side, snapping away photos and shouting at guests about various celebrities and famous members of the elite.

I bow my head and pretend I'm invisible as we're escorted inside. Is this what it feels like being famous?

We're seated in a private section, cordoned off by a half wall and frosted partition. The section is cozier and candlelit, carrying a sweet, warm scent I can't place.

Kaden once again demonstrates a side of him I've rarely seen—the wealthy, privileged man of means used to the finer things in life. Upon taking our seats at our table, he orders our server to retrieve the bottled water he prefers as well as a four hundred dollar bottle of Cabernet.

My eyes bulge. I could buy two months' worth of my meds for that amount... or a few months' worth of weed...

"You get this look on your face," he says, unfurling his dinner napkin. "It's very funny."

I loosen up by rolling back my shoulders. "I forget how the other half lives."

"You'd be surprised to know we're insecure, boring people. Look around you. Every last person sitting in this room is worrying about whether or not they're perceived as good enough. A bunch of vapid idiots wearing gold watches and silk threads, hoping it impresses their friends. They're stuck in the mentality of fifteen-year-olds trying to belong. Like I said, it's all very boring."

I offer a polite smile to the waiter as he returns with our bottles. "But you're a part of this world."

"I am."

"Then are you talking about yourself?"

"No. I have never tried to impress anyone."

I raise a brow. "Never? Ever? Not once?"

"Not in the manner of which I am speaking. No. You don't seem to grasp that I can't stand these people, Lyra," he says plainly. He gestures to my glass of wine. "Something tells me you'd feel the same if you spent enough time around them."

A shudder captures me, thinking of the night of the party. "Oh, trust me. I already do."

"Tell me about Fyodor. What exactly did he say?"

"I stuttered a lot. He sounds very aggressive. I almost hung up. But then I introduced myself and he was the one about to hang up. He assumed it was a prank call."

"You mentioned my name."

I nod. "And after some silence, he told me he wanted to hear me play."

"That's what I presumed. This is your chance. If you play for him, and he enjoys it, he will make an offer. Have you been practicing?"

"With what piano? The only time I get to play these days is when I have lessons with a client or dueling at the Velvet.

Kaden makes a humming noise as he sips from his Cabernet and stares narrow-eyed past my shoulder.

A beat of uncertainty strikes me, and I follow his lead. I twist in my seat to check out what he's staring at—a somewhat distant table of three men enjoying drinks over lukewarm conversation. Normally, I'd think nothing of it except their gazes are on us.

They're watching us with interest. Kaden must know them.

I sigh, my skin warming up. "Will we always get stares wherever we go?"

Kaden's gaze tears away from their table and returns to me. "What about stares?"

"It seems like whenever you bring me somewhere, like *here*, we get stares."

"I know the men seated at that table. That is why they're staring."

I remain unconvinced. I pick up my glass of wine and

sample its dark, fruity flavor, working up the courage to voice how I feel. The wine gives me a tiny boost in the right direction.

"Have you ever dated a Black woman before?"

For a second, Kaden's brows draw together as if confused. Then dawning seems to wash over his face and the way he's eying me changes.

It grows more... understanding.

"Is it a deal breaker for you if I haven't?"

"Maybe. Have you?"

"No," he answers simply. "I never have."

"That's what I figured."

"I have slept with Black women before."

"Also what I figured."

He surveys me under a creased brow. "Have I mentioned I don't have relationships? Most women I've seen are just women I've slept with. The Black women have been no different."

"No girlfriends ever?"

"I didn't say that either. I have had girlfriends. A couple, that is. No one worth mentioning."

"Cold-blooded. If I were your ex, I'd be insulted."

"It is traditional in my world to be coupled at early ages. Betrothed in the case of some families. It is treated as a business deal of sorts. Two powerful families seeking to maintain that power. Each with a son or a daughter they can pair off."

"So you were fixed up with your girlfriends?"

"In a manner of speaking, yes."

"And what about now?"

"I couldn't give less of a damn. I have come to do what I want, when I want," he says with a thread of selfish satisfaction in his tone.

Impressive in a way I can't articulate. I just know I'd love to reach the same level of indifference.

While I've never cared about fitting in, I can't *truly* do what I want. I have to fight hard to stay afloat and not drown. If I were as wealthy as Kaden, I wouldn't need to. I'd have "fuck you" money as it's called.

Kaden's observing these thoughts flitter through my head. I know he is because as I blink out of my self-induced trance, I'm on the receiving end of his full attention. He sits across the candlelit table in his expensive suit with his head of loose chocolatey locks pushed back behind his ears.

The light hits him at all the right angles, emphasizing the perfect dimensions of his face—chiseled jawline and cheeks anchored by a straight, aquiline nose and thick, masculine brows. But it's his eyes that capture me.

Dark and searching.

Piercing straight through me as though he's reading my mind.

I blink again and drop my gaze to my wine glass in some clumsy attempt to fight off whatever mind-meldy trick he's pulling.

"You want to do it too," he says in a hushed tone. "You'd like to be set free from playing by the rules. The lesson to keep in mind is to know what you need to do to get there—before you can break free of the rules, you have to play by the rules. You have to play so well, you manipulate the game pieces in your favor. You win the game altogether and then you change the game. You can change the *rules*."

I hack out a sound between a laugh and cough. "But I don't play by the rules, Kaden. Aren't you always scolding me for being dressed inappropriately?"

"What I'm talking about encompasses far more than your manner of dress."

"How am I doing, by the way? Is this dress too much? Too little?"

I regret asking for his input. Being on the receiving end of a once-over from Kaden Raskova is unlike anything I've ever experienced.

His mysterious deep-set eyes possess the power to make my heart go still. They make me hyperaware of myself and my body as they flit over me.

Heat and tension thicken between us in the seconds it takes. I sit obediently in my chair and wait out his intent study. Those dark orbs dipping from every inch of my face, down my throat, past my shoulders, and for a final appreciative gander at my breasts.

He openly eye fucks me.

That's what's happening. What I basically asked for.

My face warms up and my throat feels parched. I reach for my glass of way-too-expensive sparkling water.

"Is it a dress appropriate for the Arcadia?" he says. "No."

I swallow down my water and then frown.

"Is it a dress that I quite enjoy seeing on that figure of yours?" he asks before a momentary pause. "Abso-fucking-lutely."

I laugh so abruptly, the stuffy woman at the table nearest ours throws me a dirty look. Answering her look of offense with a stink eye, I return to my amusement with Kaden.

"I think that's the first time I've heard you cuss. You're so perfect, I assumed it was beneath you."

"There's much you don't know about me. My occasional crass language is just one thing."

"Okay then, tell me. How do you break the rules? In what ways do you do what you want when you want?"

The subtlest smirk pulls at the left side of his mouth. He doesn't let it win though. In another millisecond, it's gone.

"I don't think you can handle knowing, Lyra. That very real side of me can be... a lot to handle."

"Try me. Tell me more."

"I'll do more than tell you. I'll show you. Let's go."

"What, but dinner—okay, okay!"

Kaden's up on his feet and he's whisking me away. We're speed walking through the extravagant candlelit dining room of the Arcadia, garnering pointed stares as we go. Several staff members attempt to stop Kaden with furrowed brows and worry imbued in their tones. They think something about the Arcadia has displeased him and they're desperate to fix it.

He waves them off without a care.

I'm scrambling into my seat in his Tesla. We shoot out from the valet lane and merge into oncoming traffic with high speeds.

Several times I attempt to ask where we're going, but Kaden merely ignores me and hits the accelerator even harder.

I'm disoriented by what's going on, surrounded by the headlights of traffic and the many ritzy buildings whipping by.

Until Kaden stomps on the brake and we stop outside the Easton Opera House.

Tonight it's closed. Meaning no shows, no performances, no anything.

Kaden parks. He creates his own parking space on the curb of a busy street despite the fact that there are giant white letters painted into the tarmac stating 'NO PARKING' and the sign posted on the sidewalk warning the same.

I try to protest, but he grabs my hand and leads me two at a time up the cascading stone steps.

"Are you crazy?" I mumble as we go. "We're not about to do what I think we're about to do... are we? Kaden, it's closed. The opera house is closed. We can't break in—oh my god, we're breaking in! I'm too sober for this."

"Shhh."

Kaden stops in front of the grand doors leading into the famed opera house and then taps his knuckles on the glass.

Taps. His. Knuckles. On. The. Glass.

At this point, I'm gaping at him. My eyes are wide and my

mouth hangs partially open and I've wrenched my hand from his in case I need to run for it. The last thing I need is to get arrested for trespassing, and he seems hell bent on forcing our way inside.

The security guard standing in the polished marble lobby startles at the sudden noise. He's standing against a marble column with his arms folded over his pigeon-shaped chest but jerks forward once he hears Kaden's tapping.

Thankfully, he seems as confused as I am. His brow creases and he glances around, like he's checking if anyone else sees what he's seeing. Since he appears to be alone in the lobby, no one does. He walks toward us from the opposite side of the door with stilted movements.

More than once, I spy his hand hovering near the walkie and baton clipped to his belt.

"Can I help you?" he asks upon unlocking and cracking open the door.

Kaden is unfazed. "I need access to the Grande Stadio."

The security guard double-blinks. "It's closed. The entire opera house is closed. You'll have to visit the box-office when it's open if you'd like tickets—what the hell are you doing?!"

Kaden's pried the door open, catching the guard by surprise. He breezes through the now-open doorway, snatching hold of me by the wrist as he does.

"Stop! Stop right there!" the guard cries out, fumbling for any of the tools on his belt. "I have a stun gun and I will use it!"

Kaden stops on a dime. He spins around with a dark, venomous look on his face. Similar to the one he wore the night he and Grady got into it.

The expression sends chills down my spine now like it did then.

"I am Kaden Raskova," he snarls. "And I am authorized

access to this building at any hour I wish. I am here exercising that right. Is that understood?"

The security guard snaps into a military-like stance, rigid and straight, with his chin lifted. "Y-yes, sir. Yes, it's understood. Mr. Raskova, of course. Please, s-stay as long as you'd like."

Kaden doesn't dignify him with an answer. He simply drags me along the rest of the way through the long, tunneled lobby comprised of polished marble. I've lost my voice for the moment as we go, too busy studying every detail of the place.

I've been dreaming of seeing the Easton Opera House since I was a little girl.

"Can't you behave yourself for five seconds? How many times do I have to tell you to sit straight?" Mom snarls. She pinches my elbow between her fingers to force a yelp of pain out of me. "You wonder why your posture is so awful. Look at you. You better not act up on the plane."

I bow my head and keep my gaze in my lap.

I want so badly to look out the car window. To see the Easton Opera House.

But I'm so small, I need to climb up on the seat and press my face to the glass.

The car lurches as we reach the next stoplight. I sneak a look over at Mom.

She's smiling at him. The man who makes my life even more miserable than she does.

He pats her on the thigh but remains as composed as ever. Mom's lovey dovey eyes go unreturned.

I twist in my seat for another look at the Opera House. I'll be scolded for it... but the pretty domed building feels like something out of my dreams.

Maybe... someday...

Kaden pushes open the doors to the largest theater, the Grande Stadio. The doors fall open and we step inside. My heart flutters and a dreamy, surreal wave washes over me at the wondrous sight.

The ceiling of the opera house might be curved into a glass dome overhead, but the theater itself is a large bell shape. The stage is at the center, with gorgeously lush red curtains canopied on either side. Before that is the pit where the orchestra traditionally sits, and though it's currently empty, it's still mesmerizing to see the many seats.

The same can be said for the rest of the theater—the hundreds of seats fan out across the cavernous space, rising up into tiered loges built of wood and lined with beautifully hand-painted canvases. I follow the artwork with my eyes, my mouth dropping open as I do, admiring the cherubic angels and the vivid floral patterns.

Gold is the finishing touch wherever I look. It's in the molding and the facades, wrapped around the columns at the entrance.

But it's the piano on stage that holds my attention the longest—it steals my breath away and makes my feet move on their own. Hesitantly, but locked into a trance from the second I set eyes on it.

The piano is handcrafted. The dark wood unspeakably expensive. I know this even walking up at a distance. If I had to guess, I'd say ebony. Though it's one of the largest I've ever seen, there's a delicate beauty about it; something about the way the dark wood has been carved and curved that's perfect geometric harmony.

So smooth, so polished, I can see myself reflected in it.

I stop in front of it, admiring the untouched ivory keys and gold inlay, and a deep ache starts up inside me.

Longing.

I've never wanted something so much...

I blink and find I have tears in my eyes.

"Go on," Kaden says, standing back, both hands in his

trouser pockets. He inclines his head in the direction of the Steinway. "Play for me."

"You can't be serious?"

He takes a step closer, his mysterious eyes like endless dark pools. "I said play for me, Lyra. I want to hear you."

His tone has changed. His demeanor has changed. *Everything* about him has shifted.

There's a new vibe circling us that I can't place. It's like he's taken the heat and tension from our candlelit dinner and dialed it up another hundred notches.

Something deep and sexy drips from the commanding tone he uses with me. The hawkish way he watches me as I stand uncertainly tells me I'm not imagining things. He's demonstrating he's in control and I'm to do as he says.

...or else. Or else what? I'm not sure.

I swallow, my heartbeat pounding in my chest, and then I walk toward the Steinway. I'm fidgeting and my heels strike the hard wooden flooring of the stage. In the empty theater capable of seating a thousand, it sounds loud and sonorous.

I take my seat at the bench and inhale a deep breath. Then I quickly stretch my fingers and get into position. I tell myself this isn't real.

This doesn't mean anything. There's no crowd and no judges.

Except Kaden.

I tune him out for the moment. I tune every last shred of doubt and crippling imposter syndrome out, and I play what first comes to mind.

Sergei Prokofiev's *Suggestion Diabolique, Op. 4 No 4.*

My fingers become my form of expression. They take me to a place where my mind was only moments ago.

From the first key stroke, I set the mood.

Tension fills the air. Kaden's gaze sharpens. But mine

closes. I let go and give in to the dark growling note my touch produces.

The sound of warning of what's to come.

I explode in a frenzy of fast fingers and violent key strokes. There is no composure, no grace, as I'm lost in a whirlwind of intense emotion and moody undertones.

The piece matches me. The tempo speeds up almost like it's driven not by the composition but my fast-working fingers. They slam down and produce the angry, chaotic sound that echoes throughout the theater.

You'd think I was playing for Mom. I was playing for my childhood instructor.

Subconsciously, my eyes clenched shut, I am. I'm playing for them both.

But Kaden needs to see this too. He needs to hear it. He needs to understand.

I'm so often a ball of self-doubt and uncertainty when all I want to do is explode.

Let everything bottled up out.

This is my moment. The one time I have centerstage. Maybe the only chance I'll ever get to play a piano as magnificent as this in a place as opulent and beautiful.

The final deep melodic note plays, vanishing as suddenly as it began.

I'm breathless, with a feeling of relief bubbling to the surface. I open my eyes and allow a slow-spreading smile to come to my lips.

A single pair of hands fills up the vacant theater with their applause.

Kaden's applause. I twist in my seat on the bench to find him ten feet behind me with a tantalizing dark shine in his gaze.

My spine vibrates once I understand what it means. My insides flutter and my pussy clenches.

"That was..." he pauses to consider his words. "Unexpected... but intense. You continue to impress me."

He starts toward me with a patient, lazy kind of stroll that reveals his confidence and utter certainty.

I'm going nowhere. He knows this. I know this.

There's no escape, and even if I were to try, he would catch me. He would hunt me down and catch me.

Because I'm his prey.

In this moment, as this realization strikes me, I've never been more certain about anything in my life.

Yet, I stay rooted on the bench, watching him approach. I can't find it in myself to react. I've fallen under his spell.

When he's an arm's length away, he stops. He issues his next command. One I'd never expect in a million years.

Not here. Not *right now*.

"Take off your dress."

15. LYRA

I WANT IT ALL - CAMERON GREY

"My dress off?" I repeat, then I do what the security guard did earlier.

I glance around the empty theater in search of an invisible person to corroborate if I've heard him correctly. Like earlier, no one's around to back me up.

It's just the two of us.

Kaden raises a brow. "I believe you heard me, Lyra. But do you dare give in?"

"G-give in?" I stutter back, feeling lost.

He sets off at a slow stride, pacing around the gorgeous Steinway on the stage, and in turn, circling around me too. I try my best to keep him within my line of sight. Something easier said than done as I rotate in place and follow him with my gaze, but he still eludes me. He winds up behind me, coming up close enough that his body heat radiates off him. I can almost feel his hard body pressed against mine.

I swallow thickly and choke out his name, "Kaden..."

One of his hands grips my waist. The other slides up my body in achingly slow fashion, making my heart pound in my chest, stopping only once it encloses around my throat.

"We established tonight we would break the rules, Lyra. Which means it's time to come clean—I have behaved myself every moment I've been around you. Despite the fact that all I'd like to do is strip you bare and fuck you in every way imaginable."

I lose my breath listening to his words. The calm filthiness of them as he grips my hip and gives a squeeze to my throat.

Desire lights me up. It throbs in my sex, making me aware of an intense want and need deep inside.

I've been left unsatisfied for *so* long...

"And you know what?" he asks, lowering his head so our cheeks almost touch. His whisper's dark and silky yet authoritative. "I think you feel the same. I think you've been neglected and overlooked for so long, you crave to be appreciated. You crave to let go and be worshipped."

I close my eyes and bite my lip, trying to steady my racing heartbeat.

His words resonate. They feel like my truth being spoken aloud to me.

Kaden nips at my ear, such passion in that small gesture, I'm dizzy. "You have no idea the things I could do to you. All the ways I can make you come. The question is, can you handle it?"

"Yes," I whisper in answer. "Yes, I can."

I can feel his smirk. No longer does it possess the same kindness or easygoing vibe that it once had. It's morphed into its truest form—subtle with a slight curl of his lip and undercurrent of darkness.

"Something tells me you might not realize what you've just agreed to," he says, giving my throat a final squeeze, then stepping back. Suddenly, his hands are gone. His heat's no longer radiating around me. "You're quite exquisite, Lyra. I've been mesmerized from the first time I saw you. From the first time I heard you play so beautifully. But just know my interest in you isn't to be taken lightly. My interest is the kind that will be so intense you may not be able to handle it. You may only realize you're a lamb that's been led astray once you're about to be devoured. Once it's too late. It already *is* too late. Now, take off your fucking dress."

The command echoes in the loud silence of the theater.

I lick my lips, acutely aware of the pulse between my thighs.

Though Kaden's warnings are cause for concern, I can't deny my growing curiosity. A jolt of excitement tremors through me.

My hands shake reaching for the straps of my dress. The fabric slides down my body 'til it pools on the ground at my feet.

"Turn around."

I do as I'm told, naked except for my pair of panties.

My heart's never beat so fast. I turn around to find Kaden's intense gaze already trained on me.

"Take off your panties."

I bend doing so. My panties are left discarded on the ground beside my dress. Once I'm standing upright, I await his next set of instructions with the terrifying and exciting feeling of the unknown.

The power dynamic couldn't be less equal in this moment.

Yet I've never been more turned on. My sex throbs away, hot and slick with arousal.

Kaden's still fully dressed in his expensive suit. I'm naked and on display for him in the middle of the Easton Opera House's stage. If anyone were to walk in...

He steps toward me without warning. His hands cinch on my waist and he hoists me off my feet. I'm deposited onto the lid of the piano. He leans in to press his lips to my throat and kiss the pulse point he finds.

I swallow against the feel of his warm lips, so on edge my body's tightly wound.

"You have no idea how good you look displayed on this piano, little lamb," he says, his breath hot on my skin. "I just may make you play like this from now on."

Air sputters out of my lungs as he drops more kisses along the hollow of my throat. My nipples have gone noticeably stiff and I'm drenched.

Dripping on the smooth ebony finishing of the Steinway I'm perched on.

He's got me so turned on, I can't think straight. It's a level of desire I've never known was possible. One I've never even begun to experience with guys like Grady.

"Spread your legs," he orders, cupping my breasts in his large hands. His touch feels so unbearably good, I shudder straightaway. "Play with yourself, little lamb."

I feel drunk with lust as he steps back and I do as he says— I spread my legs wide, my feet flush on the lid of the piano, offering him an obscene view of myself. My hand snakes in between and I begin touching my pussy.

His eyes darken watching me, his jaw clenching. When it becomes too much and I try to close my eyes, he barks at me to keep them open.

"Look at me as you touch yourself," he snaps. "I want you to show me how good you can make yourself feel."

I moan as his silkily dark words slide over me, emboldening me to keep going. My fingers trace my folds before I dip two inside and pleasure immediately builds. I touch myself just the way I like.

In all the ways I've always wished someone like Grady would.

I pump my fingers in and out in varying speeds, then switch it up, circling my swollen clit.

My skin's warm and flushed. My body tingles on the edge of an impending orgasm.

It's so close, I can feel it creeping up.

I forget all about Kaden standing back a few feet away and watching me pleasure myself.

Adding a third finger, I gyrate and rock my body at a faster, more frenzied pace. One of my legs slips, the heel of my foot crashing down on the black and white piano keys. A dissonant chord reverberates across the stage that reflects the intense orgasm that's rushing toward me.

My expression's almost pained as I let go. I ride my fingers to an eruption so strong and powerful, I cry out, pleasure sparking from my pussy, like a wildfire razing everything in its path and burning its way up my spine.

For seconds to come, I'm left racked by aftershocks. It takes me time to realize I'm shaking, my legs still spread wide and lewd, my fingers still inside me.

Kaden closes the gap between us, grabbing my wrist to pry my fingers from myself. They're shiny and slick with my juices. He holds my gaze as he brings them to his lips and sucks them into his mouth.

Tasting me.

I'm dazed watching him suck the slick evidence of my orgasm from my fingers.

Then he brings them to my lips. I take the cue and part my lips for a taste of myself and him.

Tangy and sweet.

He pries my fingers away and then yanks me toward him in a desperate kiss.

As if I could be more lost to the moment.

Kaden kisses me.

Vaguely, in the recesses of my mind as he claims my mouth in a deep kiss, I realize this is our *first* time.

We've never even kissed before, much less done anything else.

And here I am, naked as the day I was born, having bared myself to him, *pleasured* myself for him.

The unusualness of the situation turns me on more.

Kaden's a puzzling mix of aggression and sensuality. His mouth plunders mine in dominating fashion. His arm hooks around me, his fingertips tracing the length of my spine. The grazing touch forces a shudder out of me as he sucks my tongue and makes my head spin.

"Your cunt tastes so fucking good," he tells me as we break apart. "I bet it'll feel even better squeezing my cock."

He eases back enough to allow me a front-row view of his hands falling to his belt buckle to undo his pants.

I'm so flushed and breathless, still dazed from my orgasm, I can't even move from where I'm positioned.

I sit and watch him as he never wavers under my stare.

Kaden undresses with a few quick movements. His suit jacket's tossed, his pants unbuckled and kicked away. His fingers make easy work of his crisp button-up shirt, and he lowers his plain black boxer briefs to reveal what I've known he has—a dick as gorgeous and perfect as he is.

It's fat and long, a silky hard rod that stands erect and drips with precum.

I lick my lips, my pussy aching to feel him.

He strides toward me, hooking his arms under my thighs and dragging me toward the edge of the piano lid.

I hardly have time to process what's happening before he's impaling me and I'm arching my back and crying out.

To say it's intense from the moment he enters me would be an understatement.

My mind reels as my body pulsates and my pussy clenches around him.

A thick growl rumbles from him. He holds my thighs far apart and begins working his hips in punishing thrusts.

Every stroke of his dick brings him deeper into me. Then he's withdrawing, pulling back to the head before slamming into me all over again.

At some point, I can't hold myself up anymore. I lower myself into a sprawl on the lid of the piano and ride the euphoric waves washing over me.

Kaden flips me over and spears back into me to the hilt. I scream at how deep he goes, the sound breathless and hoarse, echoing around the empty theater.

He squeezes my hips and half collapses on top of me. His long, fat dick reaches parts of my pussy I wasn't aware of. Parts Grady never even *began* to pleasure.

He's relentless and dominating, pinning me down with his clenching grip and muscled weight. My body bucks back against him only to be pushed down. My pussy rubs into the smooth wooden lid of the piano, and I groan at the unbearable friction it creates.

I realize I can reach the piano keys and stretch my arms out over my head.

For every deep thrust of Kaden's hips, I strike a key and produce an even deeper, resonating sound.

We create our own performance. Our own music as we grunt and fuck 'til my pussy's tingling and I'm floating.

The theater's only the beginning.

Less than an hour later, I'm walked through the dark open space of Kaden's posh penthouse, and then tossed onto his enormous bed. My dress is shredded off me, and I'm devoured all over again.

I'm screaming out, my pussy walls unbearably tight around his dick, as he fucks into me from behind. I know it's unbearable for him, because he's starts grunting out a string of swear words. He slams a hand into my ass and tells me he's going to fuck me so hard I won't be able to walk come morning.

I shudder and squeeze my eyes shut, so slick and hot I can't think. I definitely can't react beyond the screams ripping from my throat.

The night blurs into a string of intense orgasms. Kaden takes me so many times, I lose count. My pussy's sore and swollen and dawn's lighting up the sky outside by the time he buries himself deep one last time. His warm seed spills into me before he pulls out, dripping with sweat and husking out ragged breaths.

I'm half conscious. *Beyond* spent.

But I recognize I've never seen him like this before—unrestrained and untamed in a way I suspect few have.

He's lost all composure. He's as gone as I am, his dark eyes bleary and unfocused.

I'm vaguely wondering what's next when he bends over me and kisses me on the mouth.

He's still panting as he pulls away. "Shower. Then bed."

I don't question it.

Kaden's clearly particular. He has his idiosyncrasies he abides by, and if I'm in his home, I'll have to as well.

As though aware I'm as solid as jelly, he picks me up off the bed and takes me into his large, clinically sanitized bathroom.

We shower in silence.

...until we have *another* quickie. Kaden can't resist and cages me in against the tiled shower wall. His fingers work my clit fast and my hand wraps around his long dick. We get each other off this way 'til we're coming again.

Then we start our shower from the top.

By the time we're returning to his bedroom, I'm exhausted enough to sleep standing up.

Kaden slips a plain white t-shirt over my head—it smells of him, notes of cedar and soap—and tells me to get in his bed.

"You are the first woman to sleep here," he says. His composed tone is back. So is his demeanor. "Consider it the most special exception, little lamb. But you are *not* to go wandering anywhere in my home. Is that understood?"

I yawn. "I just want to sleep for an hour... or twelve."

The left side of his mouth quirks. "Make yourself comfortable. Just don't snore."

"Women don't snore. We purrr."

"You're pushing your luck, Lyra."

I smile at him, then crawl onto the side of the bed that seems designated as mine. He joins me at my side, lying on his back.

We're out for hours.

So long the next time I wake, it feels like a whole season has gone by. I glance to my side where Kaden's still fast asleep.

I'm thirsty, hungry and I need to pee. He said not to go wandering in his penthouse, but he looks too comfortable to wake him up. I'll make a quick stop to the restroom and kitchen for a glass of water and then wait for him to wake up.

With my mind made up, I slink from the bed and out of the room. His penthouse feels even more luxurious and intimidating when exploring alone. It almost feels like I'll get caught red-handed any moment and then put on timeout like a child.

It's as I enter his bathroom that I notice there's no hand towel for use. He must've forgotten to put one out. I double back into the hallway where the laundry room door hangs half open.

I'll just grab a quick one and then put it out for him.

I sneak a peek over my shoulder, double checking I'm alone. The deep silence projects far across every square foot of the luxury penthouse.

So silent, my thoughts become noise, like my brain's desperate attempt to fill the void.

I press on. My bare feet pad against the dark wood flooring, down the hall, past several closed doors. I stop in front of the laundry room and then ease it open. When I'm certain I'm quiet enough and still alone, I slip inside.

Kaden has enough of an inventory to rival any linens shop. His selection rises feet above me, folded neatly by shade and fabric on each shelf. Ten versions of white bedsheets in increasingly higher thread counts and towels of every size in cotton-white, pearl-white, and who can forget off-white?

I shake away the smirk that teases my lips and reach for the first hand towels in reach. It doesn't matter to me whether the towel is Turkish or Egyptian so long as it's clean and absorbent.

I'm about to turn away to flee the scene of the crime but freeze before I can. My gaze happens to fall on the hampers arranged in a neat row along the wall. There's four. One for colors, another for whites, another for towels, and the last for what is labeled as other.

It's the other that holds my attention. That produces a spine-tingling ripple of shock shooting through me. I step closer and peer into the hamper.

I stare for so long you'd think I've never seen a shirt in need of a wash before.

But it's not just any shirt needing a wash—it's a shirt stained with *blood*.

Lots of it.

I gulp down the nausea rising up. I took my meds and haven't eaten anything. On a good day I'm slightly nauseous; on a day where I'm looking at the blood-soaked shirt of the guy I'm dating, I'm bound to spew bile.

The last thing I want to do is be nosy. I don't want to grow uneasy or make assumptions.

Even as my heartbeat leaps into overdrive inside my chest, I rationalize it away. Kaden's a vascular surgeon—I'm sure he's covered in blood all the time. He deals with blood vessels and the human circulatory system.

This is probably a Tuesday for him.

But why would he have a shirt that's not part of his scrub uniform like this? In what scenario would he have been performing surgery in a white button-down shirt? Did he recently get hurt, or help someone off the street who was injured?

My nausea roils inside me, a warning I've got to get to the toilet soon, or wolf down some heavy enough food like bread.

I force away my shock and tell myself there's a reasonable explanation. I escape the laundry room and start rushing down the hall. Still as stealthy as I can be, but with my footsteps significantly faster.

The only thing is, I'm no longer alone. As I flee down the hall, beelining for the bathroom, I feel a change in the air. I *feel* Kaden's presence.

It looms over me, invading the hall, cloaking everything it touches with an unmistakable dark aura.

I stumble trying to stop. My breath's caught in my lungs.

He's behind me.

"I didn't want to wake you," I choke out. "I was... I was looking for a hand towel."

Silence answers me, and then... the first measured pad of a footstep. Then another. And another, until he's closing in and his aura's so stifling, I feel dizzy.

But I still don't turn around.

It doesn't matter. Kaden stops directly behind me and leans in. His lips brush my ear. His voice is cool and controlled, eliciting an icy shiver from me.

"I thought I told you not to go wandering in places you shouldn't be."

16. KADEN
OBSESSED - ZANDROS & LIMI

"I was grabbing a towel to wash my hands," Lyra sputters. "Just really quick. I didn't... see... anything..."

She trails off in a manner that reveals she hasn't even convinced herself. She *did* see something. It's reflected in every stilted bone of her body and stiff breath she tries to drag into her lungs. Her words may be in denial, however, her voice drips of confession.

Lyra disobeyed my wishes. She went wandering in my penthouse when I explicitly forbade her to do so.

I've ended people's existence for less. A viable option considering the task I've been given by the Owner. I was supposed to finish the job days ago—ensure Lyra was dealt with so what happened on stage would never be tracked back to the Society.

For now, Lyra will suffer a different kind of punishment.

My hands enclose around her upper arms, and I steer her down the path in the hall from which she came. Initially, for the first few steps, she resists me, trying to bear down with her feet and refrain from moving.

There is no choice in the matter.

I simply *make* her move, driving her forward despite her protests. Though I can't see her face, I know where she thinks we're going—she believes I'm returning her to the laundry room where she'd wandered off to against my wishes.

Instead, I catch her by surprise, and steer her to the second to last door on the left. I reach in front of her, and pry open the door. We enter a room that's often hidden away. It's a dungeon of sorts—filled with instruments that I use to derive both pleasure and pain. There are shelves with toys and devices Lyra's probably never imagined. In the center is a leather bench that I've found great use in. That Lyra will soon discover can make her toes curl from euphoric highs or make her scream out in pleas of mercy.

My personal play room.

Few women have earned the privilege of venturing inside.

"What is...?" she begins, half turning.

I tighten my hold on her upper arms and keep her in place. "Take a guess. Look around you."

Her uncertainty lives in how she follows my instruction; she glances from wall to wall and surveys the various devices on display. She's standing still enough that I can sense her heart pounding in her chest.

"You said you're into certain things," she says in a quiet tone. "I'm guessing the things in this room."

"Good guess. Now, can you tell me why I've brought you in here?"

"Kaden, I don't... this isn't my—"

I squeeze her arms in my viselike grip to emphasize my point. "You wandered off. I explicitly told you not to do so. Which means this can end in one of two ways. You atone for breaking my rule, or I will show you the door, and we're done."

"But—"

"I will call up Kreed and tell him to call off your audition."

Cruel? Yes. Coercive? Also, yes.

However, she needs to understand there are consequences to her actions. If she breaks my rules, she'll suffer like everyone else. Possibly a different kind of suffering than what I usually reserve for the people I punish. Nevertheless, *still* a punishment.

Besides, it's not as though Lyra's innocent. She takes money from lonely, pathetic men so starved for female attention, they sit obediently in front of their computer screens with the futile hope that they'll catch a nip slip.

Lyra doesn't know I know about her Cyber Fans account. She doesn't know I've watched her cam shows.

There's a lot Lyra doesn't know. There's a lot I do know, like the fact that she likely let me fuck her last night to officially secure her audition with Fyodor.

Almost all women are the same in this regard. Always subconsciously calculating what they can and will receive in exchange for sex.

I am indifferent about it. Men are often willing to barter for it.

In Lyra's case, I'm no exception. My growing appetite for her has kept her alive.

Her swallow is audible. "What do you want me to do?"

"Select two items. Just two. Choose wisely."

Her hesitation stretches on for another moment before she obeys. She steps forward and I release her. The items she selects will reveal more than she realizes about her desired proclivities and hidden appetites.

She stops in front of the selection of blindfolds.

I grin.

Tame. *Very* tame.

But foolish. She doesn't realize how she's just informed me of what she desires on a deeper, subconscious level.

Lyra wants the unpredictable; she wants to be in the dark,

giving up control. Her sight taken away, she wants to feel what's being done to her rather than see it coming.

The second item amuses me.

She chooses a vibrator. The smallest one I have, a little silver egg that packs much more power than she probably realizes it does.

"Good choices," I say calmly, walking up behind her. "Take off your shirt."

"Kaden—"

"Take it off. Or I will rip it off for you. And you will not like what happens next."

She gasps, then promptly does it. She pulls the shirt I'd given her to sleep in over her head and lets it drop to the floor. My gaze flits over her mostly naked form. An urge I can't squash even though I've seen her a number of times.

Only her panties remain. I step closer from behind and ease away the blindfold she's chosen—a silky cherry-red that is otherwise safe.

"What will you do?" she asks, nerves trembling in her tone.

"I hate to be cliché, Lyra, but that's for me to know and you to find out," I tease. I brush my lips against her cheek before laying the blindfold flush across her eyes. "If you wanted to know, then perhaps the blindfold was a foolish choice."

"Then I change my—"

"My turn," I interrupt. "Two items of my choosing."

I stroll along the many shelves and display cases showing off my impressive collection. You'd think I were out for a shopping trip on Somerset Boulevard the way I peruse my offerings, pausing here and there as I make up my mind. At last, I select the two items that will pair well with what I have planned.

Lyra has remained where she is, obediently still, albeit

anxious. She's worrying her bottom lip, and her brows have formed into a solitary line.

Her nipples have *hardened*.

My blood heats up, like a canine catching the scent he's been on the hunt for. Though I remain perfectly composed, my body temperature dials up. My skin's warmer, flushed by the prospect that Lyra's a naughty, nasty little liar.

For all her protests, she's excited. Nervous, but *excited* just the same.

Last night revealed her hand. She came five times. Her desperate gasps for air and impassioned moans told me she has an undiscovered thirst for the dark thrills I enjoy. In the back of my mind, I've begun wondering if I'll be able to let go of my new obsession anytime soon.

Thus far, I've found pleasure in the ways I have invaded her life. How soon am I willing to end it?

These are thoughts I leave behind for the time being. The matter of Lyra's punishment must be handled.

"I advise you to stand still."

"Kaden," she mumbles. "I don't... like this. What are you —ow!"

I've come around to face her and unscrewed the first nipple clamp. The metal teeth enclose around the puffy bead, tighter and sharper until I decide to stop the screw. Lyra shakes as I do, her ribcage sputtering and her breasts heaving. I grip her shoulder and forcefully hold her still.

"Stop that... or I will select a third item."

Her teeth rake over her bottom lip. "You try standing still when it feels like your nipples are being bitten off."

"I can always tighten the screw. Your choice."

She lets out a soft whiny noise that couldn't be more amusing if she tried. I set to applying the second clamp, undoing the screws and then placing the metal clamp around her nipple. It's one of my more attractive, feminine clamps—

the metal curves in the shape of a flower with the screws along the side.

Both clamps are linked by a single, delicate chain. I stand back and admire my work once I'm done, and she shudders. The end result is sensuous and erotic. If only she could see how beautiful she looks. Blindfolded, completely bare except her panties, the stunning metal jewelry clamped to her nipples, and the chain decorating her breasts.

I can't resist. I tip her chin toward me and kiss her on the lips. A rarity for me, and I make the most of it—my tongue massages her and I explore her mouth, turning the kiss deeper' and more passionate.

She's startled by it.

Since we've started seeing each other, we've barely kissed. Even last night, as I fucked her senseless, I refrained from doing so often.

If Celeste could see me in this moment, she'd burst into tears... or flames from murderous envy.

I have never once kissed her vile lips. How could I when they've been sealed over the cocks of half the city?

Drawing away from Lyra's lips, I only grip her chin tighter. "How does it feel, little lamb?"

"Intense," she mutters. "Like they're being squeezed."

"Do you like it?"

"I... don't know."

I walk around her, returning to my position directly behind her. My hands fill with her breasts, caressing her mounds in light, teasing touches.

"It doesn't really matter if you do," I say, dropping a kiss to the side of her neck. "This is a punishment. Which means it's supposed to hurt. Though I can make you feel good too."

The egg-shaped vibrator has been held limply in her hand this entire time. I take it from her and then slide my hand down the front of her panties. It buzzes when I flick the tiny 'on' switch and begins vibrating faster than a hummingbird.

I strategically place it right under her clitoral hood.

"Maybe you'll enjoy this more. Touch it, and you will regret it."

"Oh. Oh!" she gasps at the feel of the metal egg against her clit. "That feels... mmmm."

"One more caveat. You're not allowed to come. You come, and you will regret it. Do you understand?"

Her lips part, her skin warming. She's caught between the pinch of her nipple clamps and the deep, pleasing vibration of the egg.

I grab her by the chin, though she cannot see me. "Do. You. Understand?"

"Yes. Yes!"

"Good. Now, for my other item. Come here."

My hand encloses on her elbow, and I bring her along with me to the middle of the room, where my play bench stands ready for use.

"On your hands and knees."

"What if I don't want to play anymore?"

"You should've thought about that before you broke a rule. Get down on your knees."

She doesn't move. Her nerves are returning despite the sensations she's feeling. I can tell by the air she expels, her naked torso shuddering out a deep breath.

"I am not asking. I am telling you. Hands and knees."

My hand clamps down on her shoulder and I force her down. Because she's blindfolded, I angle her arms and legs into the correct position. She's before me, propped up on her hands and knees on my leather play bench. Her blindfold is still secured over her eyes and her tits hang, connected by the metal chain.

I walk around to the back and admire her round backside

and the dampened patch in the gusset of her panties. Her thighs shake from the strong vibrations of the egg.

I grin. My dick throbs. My blood's on fire. I'm insanely turned on right now. And this is only the beginning—only the first game we'll play. The first punishment I'll give.

"If only you could see yourself right now, little lamb," I say, forcing my tone to remain even. It's a challenge given how incredibly erect I am. My dick pushes against the front of my sweatpants, formed into a giant and insistent tent. "You are quite a sight the way you are. I must say, I am loving this punishment game."

"Yeah..." she chokes out, breathless sounding. "I can only imagine what's next."

"What do you *think* is next?"

"You probably have some kind of... of... whip. Some kind of... of paddle. I'm about to be spanked, aren't I?"

I hum along, circling the bench. A predator about to devour his prey. She's offered up to me on what might as well be a silver platter.

"Good guess," I answer. I withdraw the device I've had tucked under my arm since making my selection. "But you'd be wrong, little lamb. At least, this time."

"Then what are you going to—OW!"

She yelps at the shock of it. The electric zap that jolts her bare skin. The first of many. I started off simple. On the underside of her thigh, where she has more flesh and meat than other parts of her body.

"What was that!?!" she cries out. "Was that... did you just *electrocute* me?"

"Yes."

I do it again. The second time on her other thigh. She trembles in her hands and knees position, almost losing her balance. I place a hand on her spine to recenter her.

"You broke a rule. Therefore, I will make you understand never to do it again."

"Believe me, I've learned my lesson!"

"I'm unconvinced."

I press the wand to the side of her torso and send another small jolt of electricity through her. Just enough of a zap that she shudders and heaves a difficult breath. It's remarkable that just as she's made peace with the nipple clamps, the electric wand seems to be the new bane of her existence.

I toy with her. I pace the circumference of the bench. Along the way, she's asked questions, and I decide whether I like her answer. If I do, she's spared. If I don't, she's zapped.

"What did you see in the laundry room?"

"N-nothing. I told you... ahhh!"

I zap her round backside. The left cheek, before smoothing a hand over its curve. "Are you sure about that or are you lying?"

"I'm not lying!"

Zap!

On her breast. Near the clamp. That one had to hurt.

"Argh!" she grinds out, her arms shaky. "Okay, fine. Fine! I... I saw a shirt. It had blood on it."

I know. I saw you.

"Do you think it was fair that you went snooping around my penthouse?"

"No. I'm sorry."

"Are you?"

"Yes."

I drag the wand along her spine. Slow and taunting. She arches, her body going rigid, her ass deliciously round and pushed back. She's anticipating the next zap, waiting for the spark that'll jolt through her. Exactly why I *don't* do it. Then I walk to the back of the bench and spot the soaked fabric of her panties.

Even wetter than earlier.

The egg still buzzes along, it's droning background noise. I stare at her panties with a renewed taste for punishment.

"Lyra?"

"Y-yes?"

"Did you come?"

She hangs her head and releases another sound that's a whine. That's a *yes*.

"What did I say about coming?"

"It wasn't allowed."

"And what did you do?"

"I... I came. Kaden, that bullet vibrator thing has made my clit numb. What the hell do you—AHHH!"

In a swift motion, I snatch away her panties. The cheap cotton tears and her pussy is on display. Sure enough, glistening with her juices. I point the wand at the soft skin of her pussy lips and give her the most startling shock yet.

She keens in what must be some fucked up blend of pleasure and pain. Yet her body doesn't shirk away. She remains in place, firmly on her hands and knees, even as she pants and bows her head.

I step closer, slipping the wand into my back pocket. My hands glide over the round curves of her backside and then her wet, overstimulated cunt.

I need to be inside her.

"I'd say you've learned your lesson for now. Would you agree?"

"Yes," she breathes. "Kaden, please."

"One more thing, little lamb. My cock."

I lower my sweatpants and free myself. I've deprived my throbbing dick for minutes as I've tormented Lyra and punished her for her mistake. She got off when she was explicitly told not to.

My fucking turn.

I grip her hips and slam into her. We lose our breath at the same time. Me from how incredible her pussy feels. Her from the shock of my brutal thrust into her.

The moment has transformed from her punishment to my pleasure. Last night, I made her come five times, I let her sleep in my bed, in my t-shirt. I've kissed her and spoiled her with fancy dates and a fucking job at the Easton Opera House.

And she repays me by snooping around.

A burst of rage surges through me as I fuck her. As I use her pussy for my benefit.

Lyra whines and pants and sways on the bench. Her body feels fragile against my dominant, muscular one the harder, more savagely I pump into her. She's determined to learn the hard way—I have no feelings, no consideration for anyone.

I couldn't care less if she's apologetic, or if her pussy's sore and she's tired.

I intend to fuck her until *I'm* ready to stop. Until I've exerted every ounce of rage and resentment beating through me at what feels like a betrayal. The more I think about it, in my foggy, aroused state of mind, the angrier I become.

I was composed earlier. Calm. Cool. Even *amused* as I punished her and she whined about things like the nipple clamps.

However, in this moment of pure aggression, my thrusts unrelenting and my dick spearing into her, I realize how foolish I've been.

I let my guard down. I fell asleep with a woman I barely know in my bed. My short sightedness gave her free rein to wander my penthouse and discover the bloody shirt from the night I murdered Maximillion Keys.

A man I murdered, in a way, *for* her.

In recent days, I've been so preoccupied, so obsessed with all things Lyra, I hadn't bothered to properly dispose of it, like I usually would.

My teeth grit and I drill into Lyra even harder. She's collapsed from holding herself up on her hands and resorted to laying flush against the bench. Her cheek pressed into the leather, she's tilted upward at an angle, her hips and ass in the air. Dazed and spent, she occasionally gives a tiny moan as I fuck her.

Her walls spasm around my dick. If I had to guess, she's come again. Despite the fact that she's already far too over-stimulated and likely sore.

My release racks through me a few pumps later. I snap forward in a series of deep thrusts, greedily experiencing every inch of her pussy before I wrench myself from her. Stroking my dick with a furious grip, I spill onto her lower back and round ass.

Pleasure blinds me. It bursts through my tense, muscled body and strips me of all decorum. I'm heaving ragged breaths and jerking my dick to spurt out every last drop.

Satisfaction comes in the aftermath. It's a steady, fulfilling sensation that makes me grin at the scene before me.

Lyra collapsed on the bench. Her round ass in the air. My cum dripping from her ass cheeks. Her cum dripping from her pussy lips. The blindfold still snug over her eyes, though something tells me they're closed. However, her lips hang open and her body quivers.

The nipple clamps remain intact, smashed into the leather cushion from the position she's in. She's so spent, she's not capable of moving even if she wanted to, and I'm certain she likely does.

First, I collect myself. My dick's tucked back into my sweatpants, and I smooth my hair behind my ears. Then I step toward her and raise her up. I take away the blindfold and stroke her cheek.

"I'm going to take the clamps off," I warn.

Dazed, she nods.

I'm careful loosening the screws and removing the metal teeth from her sensitive peaks. She winces as I do.

"Sore?"

Again, she nods.

My hands cup her breasts in a leisurely massage. I do it before it registers with me that I am. Though I do not regret what has transpired—it gave me the most powerful orgasm I've had in months—the petty anger I felt moments ago has evaporated.

Lyra has been punished. I have recognized I let my guard down last night. The atmosphere between us reverts to more sensible territory.

I help her up from the bench. Her legs wobble as she walks.

"Take a hot bath. Relax," I say. "I have Epsom salt and plenty of soaps to choose from. Do *not* wander elsewhere."

Her third head nod is her most fervent yet.

I deliver her to the bathroom, armed with the supplies she'll need—Epsom salt, soaps and bath bombs, my finest type of Turkish bath towel, and another t-shirt of mine she can wear.

The sound of running water follows me the rest of the walk down the hall and to my bedroom. The punishment game Lyra and I played took well over an hour. In the time I've been gone, I've missed four calls.

Two from Rebecca at the office. Another from Nolan. The last from an unknown number.

I call Rebecca first. She answers in a stressed ramble about my schedule and missed appointments. I've cut my hours in half over the past two weeks, rescheduled with several clients, and even pushed back Eunice Mitchell's surgery a second time.

"Figure it out," I snap. "Pencil in Horschman to cover for me on the bypass surgery. Call Mitchell back and tell her we will proceed forward with the sixteenth. Yes, for certain this time. And Rebecca?"

"Yes, Dr. Raskova?" she warbles out.

"Don't ever call me in a ditzy panic again, or I will fire you. Do you understand?"

I hang up on her before she gives me an answer. It doesn't matter whether she understands. That's what will happen regardless.

Typically, it disturbs the perfectionist inside me to let my work go with such little care. However, current circumstances have muted my professional obsession. The recent interest I've developed in Lyra takes precedence for the time being

On a number of occasions in the past, I covered for my partner, Doctor Titus Horschman. It's more than time he returns the favor.

I go through the other alerts on my phone. Nolan's call gets ignored. The unknown number holds my attention for a split second before I move on to email.

Halfway through reading the first one, my phone rings. It's the same unknown number calling.

"What do you want?"

"Kaden," comes the deep, rumbling voice of the Owner. "You have been avoiding the club."

My grip tightens on my phone, and I rise from the side of my bed. "I have been busy. There's a difference."

"You are never too busy for the Society. You would do well to remember."

I glare at the generous open space of my bedroom as if the Owner has materialized in front of me. "Duly noted. But it would also be beneficial if you'll tell me what it is that you want. I doubt someone as important as you has called me just to tell me to attend club events. I have missed plenty before with no objection."

"Your task," the Owner says simply. "Is it complete?"

A second passes in the time it takes me to answer.

"No, not yet."

"For what reason?"

"Some minor... complications," I answer. "But it will get done. And soon. I keep my word."

"A week. Or I will reassign your task to someone more dependable, and you will have many things to answer for. You choose how this goes."

He hangs up. Which is more than fine with me considering I didn't want to talk to the insufferable bastard in the first place.

A door in another part of the penthouse opens and closes. My head lifts up as I listen for other sounds.

Lyra couldn't possibly be foolish enough to go wandering again... could she?

I scowl and pocket my phone. If today's not proving to be one fire after another, I don't know what is. I stride down the hall, following the echo of what is female voices.

Not one. But two.

Emerging from the hall, I'm greeted by an unexpected sight in my gourmet kitchen.

Lyra stands in the t-shirt I've given her to wear, looking almost as flabbergasted as I am. Standing opposite her is Celeste, with a nasty smirk and glint in her eye. Before I can think up a response that's as scathing as the situation calls for, Lyra breaks the silent stand off between the three of us.

She turns to me and says, "I thought I recognized you. The Midnight Society Party. Kaden, you were there."

17. Lyra

Eyes Don't Lie - Isabel LaRosa

"Get out of my fucking penthouse, Celeste," Kaden snarls in a flash of immediate rage.

"Baby," the waif answers with a coddling smile. "Why aren't you happy to see me? Though I should be the one upset. You have this prostitute girl in your penthouse wearing your clothes. Are you cheating on me or is this your way of telling me you want a threesome? I am very open minded and always willing to fulfill your fantasies. Even with the likes of *her*."

"Prostitute?" I choke out. My brows knit and I take a step toward her. "Who the hell are you calling a prost—"

"I said get the fuck out!" Kaden bellows. His outburst drowns out my offended words. He rushes past me, cutting me off, and snatches the woman named Celeste up by the arm. She winces and shrieks that he's hurting her, but he presses on.

I distantly trail behind, lost as to what is happening.

This started with a noise I heard from the bathroom. I had been drying off after a nice soak in the bath when it sounded like someone other than Kaden was rummaging in his kitchen. Celeste stood by the galley cabinets, digging inside. She mistook me for Kaden and spun around clutching a skillet, asking if I'd like her to cook breakfast.

When she saw me, it was like her world shattered. The crazed smile fell off her face and her forest-green eyes lost their zeal. Her features morphed into pure loathing, and she sneered at me like I was roadkill.

"*You*," she spat. "Of course. It makes sense."

I had no clue what she was talking about, but I did recognize her—it was the bitch in the emerald dress and silver mask from the night of the party. All of a sudden, I was transported back to that night; a night I've largely tried to put behind me.

She had confronted me as I stood by the redwood Steinway. An unspeakably handsome man was behind her. He, too, wore a mask, but I knew he was good-looking by what little I could see of him. His hair fell in loose waves he tucked behind his ears. Effortless confidence like a sexy male model in an ad.

Kaden.

It was Kaden.

Does that mean Kaden saw me on stage? That he knows what happened to me? What I did to the man who shoved his dick in my mouth? Why hasn't he said anything?!

Celeste seemed to pick up on my realization. Her sneer deepened. "I can see the gears turning in that skull of yours. Yes, you have it right, sweetie. Kaden saw it all. The man whose dick you bit off—*my* cousin, Klein Fairchild—is out of the hospital, and he's pissed."

Kaden had interrupted us. I was still making sense of what she said when he appeared and discovered Celeste had somehow let herself inside his penthouse.

As he drags her to the door, I stand back and watch.

"But, baby... baby, please!"

"You are pushing me," he grits out, shoving her past the threshold. "I told you what would happen if you did this again—"

Her sweet act vanishes, and she scoffs. "Are you sure you want your little prostitute girlfriend to find out about your bad habits—"

"*ARGH*!" Kaden roars like a murderous beast. He slams shut the door with such force, it reverberates against the frame.

His anger pulses through him and exists in the space between us. I hover uncertainly, staring at the rippled muscle on his back, wondering if I should grab my things and go.

He breathes out a ragged breath that would produce fire if humanly possible.

Yeah... he's pissed.

I should go.

As I turn to do just that, I remember why I shouldn't. Kaden owes me answers.

"What was that about?"

"She's a stupid, drug-addicted bitch that lives in a fantasy nine times out of ten. Take anything she says with a grain of salt," he spits, turning away from the door.

"How did she get in your place? Does she have a key?"

"Do you think I'd give someone like that a key to my penthouse? I thought she was getting the keys through my housekeepers or security team, so I fired the last group and rehired new ones. I have no idea how the hell she got in just now."

"She was from the party. The... the Midnight Society party."

His expression darkens. He strides past me, but I'm not giving up that easily. I follow him back into the gourmet galley kitchen.

"And so were you," I tell him. "You were with her that night."

"So what, Lyra?"

"You were in the audience, weren't you? You saw me. You saw what happened on stage."

He's unsure how to react. For the first time since I've known him, Kaden loses his decisive, self-assured air. He plants both hands on his kitchen countertop and peers at me with his dark, brooding eyes vacant of direction. He doesn't know how to answer or where to lead the conversation.

"Tell me the truth. You've known all along. You saw me bite off that guy's dick and you pretended like you had no idea who I was! Suddenly, our meeting at Urban Greenery doesn't feel so unplanned. It feels a lot more orchestrated."

He sighs, his handsome face flat with exhaustion. "Lyra..."

"No, Kaden, you knew! You bumped into me on purpose, didn't you? You tracked me down!"

I don't expect him to fess up. Why would he? If he's been orchestrating some grand scheme on behalf of the weird elite club he belongs to, his loyalty is to them. He owes me no allegiance. Every interaction we've had up until this point has been by design.

My arms wrap around myself as a protective shield. I feel used and confused. I feel empty. Once again let down by someone I had begun to let into my life.

Turns out, Kaden's more of the same.

I turn to go.

"Lyra," he says slowly. "I did track you down. I knew who you were from our first encounter. That's true."

A disgusted sound escapes from my throat. "Why would you do that to me? Why lie?"

"I... was intrigued. I saw you the night of the party and knew you weren't a member."

"How would you know that?"

"I know all the members. And you were obviously not one."

My chin quivers as I stare at him in disbelief. "You saw what happened to me on stage... and you thought you'd find me to do what? Fuck me when your pal failed?"

"I wanted to get to know you. You were so different than every other person at that party, you held my attention. For the record, Klein deserved to have his penis torn off."

"You wanted to get to know me after you saw me bite a guy's dick? So you tracked me down and then pretended not to know who I was? You think that's okay?"

I turn away from him and start down the hall. I don't care that I don't have any clean panties. I'll throw on my dress from last night and make do on the trek home.

One thing is clear: I need to get the hell away from Kaden. He's doing the following thing now. He dogs my footsteps into his bedroom and tosses shut his door to barricade me inside.

"Kaden, you're not stopping me—"

"You're not listening to what I'm saying."

"It doesn't matter. We're done."

"You're not done. We're not done. We're just getting started—"

"You don't get to decide that for me!" I yell with indignance swelling in my voice. "I can't trust you, and I don't want to do this anymore. It's gotten too weird, too fucked up."

Kaden steps in front of me and walks me several steps back. His gaze is trained on my face, piercing and unnerving, but in a way that stirs a sense of thrill inside me. "You're weird. You're fucked up. You've said it yourself."

"What's your point?! Let me go!"

"My point is, you wouldn't know normal if it bit you on the nose, Lyra Hendrix, and neither would I. There's a reason you can't resist me, why you've dreamed of me, why your body trembles at the mere thought of me touching you. Despite the fact that every rational piece of you screams at you to run far, far away. Isn't that correct?"

Yes. Oh, yes.

Very.

I steel myself under his knowing gaze. My face becomes unreadable, or so I hope. "You don't know me. Do yourself a favor and stop pretending that you do!"

"On the contrary, I know you very well, Lyra. Which is why I know you've sensed the truth all along. You subconsciously recognized me. That's why you were so hesitant to give me a chance."

"I was hesitant because I didn't understand why you were interested."

"For the same reason you are. There's a reason I can't resist you. I've found myself thinking about you at all hours of the day and night. Thoughts about wanting to pleasure you in every way humanly possible and imaginable. Despite the rational side of me demanding I let you go. Are you noticing a pattern? We're inevitable."

Kaden kisses me. We've gravitated close enough that he grabs me by the shoulders and plants a hard kiss on my lips.

My hands come up to his chest and push against him. I try to force him off me.

No. No. No. So wrong!

Yet, his kiss fogs up my brain. His lips on mine make it harder to think by the second. My palms on his muscled chest go from pushing against him to marveling at the erratic beat of his heart. His tongue grazes the seam of my lips and I let his tongue brush mine 'til we're locked into a deep, air-depriving dance of passion.

His large hands cup my face, and he draws away to peer down at me for a second that feels like he's surprised. Even though he's the one who kissed me.

We hover in one last moment of uncertainty before we give in completely. Kaden sweeps me up and tosses me on his bed. We meet again in another hot, passionate kiss, and attack each other's clothes. His sweatpants and my long t-shirt that belongs to him.

In no time, we're naked, fucking, and lost in the throes of our mind-numbing orgasms.

———

It's noon by the time we have breakfast. Things between us are still uncertain. The latest turn of events have made our relationship, or lack thereof, feel stranger.

Which says a lot considering it already felt weird to begin with.

I take back some control. I insist we go to a place where *I* feel comfortable. The grease spot known as Mama's Hot Cakes may not be much. It's located in Bainbridge and has stuffing coming out of the cushioned booths, but their burnt coffee is surprisingly decent, and they have the best pancakes in Easton.

Kaden glances around the shabby diner. He tries to stay neutral, though I can read him well enough to pick up his judgments.

I smirk. "So I'm learning you as well as you've learned me. What's grossing you out about Mama's?"

"An easier question would be what's not disgusting about the place. I believe I just saw a rat scurrying near the glass display of pies."

I roll my eyes. "You are so dramatic. They fumigated weeks ago. No more mice."

Kaden's ivory complexion *almost* morphs into a sickly green. I hold up the laminated menu and grin to myself from behind it. I'll have to find out little ways to exact revenge for his deception. Disgusting him with Mama's seems like a great place to start.

"Hey, babies," Mama says, walking up with her size double G breasts and a bright smile. "What can I get ya?"

"Just a coffee. Black," Kaden answers, sliding the menu toward her.

I slap down my menu over his and return her smile. "We'll both have the Mama's Triple Cake special. Can I have blueberry? Kaden likes chocolate chips in his. Hash on the side. Jam with the toast, please. Oh, and orange juice for two. Charge it to his card. His treat."

Mama's quizzical glance between us tells me all I need to know; she's confused as hell. She winks at me and then says, "Coming right up. Sit tight, babies."

Kaden waits 'til she's waltzed off before he glares at me. "What the hell was that? Do you plan on eating two orders worth of pancakes?"

"One is for you, Kaden."

His dark eyes narrow. "I know what you're doing Lyra, and I'm not amused."

"You made some decisions for me. I'm making some decisions for you. It's only fair, right?" I ask. He doesn't refute me, but the ever-increasing narrowing of his eyes tells me how he feels on the matter. A rebellious smirk tugs at my lips and I fold my hands, leaning partially over the table. "I can see it in your gaze. What are you thinking, Kaden? How much you want to punish me? Play another round of nipple clamps and electric zapper? Guess what? I *liked* it."

So I may or may not be pushing my luck.

I'm taunting him, openly challenging him as I sit back in the booth and watch in amusement as he restrains himself. A difficult feat for him considering he has little ground to stand on—I caught him red-handed orchestrating what's happened between us. How can he punish me when he's the one who fucked up?

Though I'm not so sure that'll stop him. He seems to stand firm in his rules once they're established.

Still, as Mama delivers our food, setting down large plates

of pancakes in front us, Kaden swallows down his urge for payback. He unfurls his knife and fork from the paper napkin on the table and slices into his hot cakes.

"Chocolate chips," he says dryly. "Delicious."

"Aren't they?"

"Yes, almost as enjoyable as other things I'm thinking of. But those will come later."

I bring my fork to my smirking lips. "You should probably finish your pancakes first, before talking a big game."

I'm not imagining things. As I swallow my first bite of blueberry hot cakes, Kaden watches me, and for the briefest blink of an eye, he smirks too.

———

My ass is sore by the end of the afternoon. Kaden held up his end of the bargain. He finished every bite of Mama's triple stack chocolate chip pancakes—and then he promptly exacted revenge the second we returned to his penthouse.

He brought out a different pair of clamps and bent me over the bench, but he didn't use the electric zapper. This time, I was paddled. I was made to count aloud with him as he alternated between stroking my ass and playing with my pussy and slamming down the wooden paddle on various parts of my backside.

I came twice, though I'm certain I won't sit down normally for a week.

I regret nothing—Grady's never made me come, and Kaden practically hands out orgasms like Oprah did cars that one time.

The issues between us aren't resolved. I'm still not sold on trusting him. I'm not sure how I feel about his deception. He's lied to me for two weeks, letting me believe he happened to bump into me when he planned it in advance.

But I rationalize it by telling myself our relationship's not serious. We're not even officially exclusive. Whatever we've developed is more like some thrilling, explosive sex arrangement, where we occasionally act more coupley and do coupley things.

I can ride the orgasm train around the block a few times and then end it once I'm ready to close this chapter of my life.

His association with the Midnight Society is still cause for concern. He didn't give his input about the incident on stage other than to say the guy deserved for his dick to be bit off.

Then there's the matter of Celeste.

The lady has a few screws loose, and that's putting it mildly. She seems obsessed with Kaden. And she mentioned the guy whose penis I chewed up was her cousin and he's pissed.

Does that mean he knows who I am? Where I am?

I throw a paranoid look over my shoulder on my subway ride home. Kaden had offered to drive me, but I insisted on going by myself. I needed the time amid the repugnant stench of BO and the sticky wads of gum on the metal poles to think on everything.

Could it be possible I'm missing a piece of the puzzle? Did Kaden tell me the truth when he said I was interesting and he pursued me for that reason?

Celeste had mentioned something about bad habits—

"Lyra!"

I'm pulled from my thoughts at the sound of my name. I turn around to find a slim, red-eyed man jogging toward me. It takes me a second to recognize him, because his normal pompadour hair lays flat and lifeless, and he's in a dowdy sweatsuit.

"Hey, Rodrigo. How're you holding up? Sorry for your loss."

He sniffles and withdraws a crumpled tissue from the pocket of his sweatpants. "I can't believe Max is gone."

"Right. Me neither. It happened so... suddenly."

"You didn't see anything that night, did you?" he asks, his eyes widening with hope. "The investigators are at an impasse. All their leads have gone nowhere."

"Rodrigo, I've already told them everything I know."

"Keep thinking. It could be any small detail. An unusual customer. A tense interaction. You were working the door that night."

"We had hundreds of customers..."

"You have to do your part, Lyla," he says, sniffling. "Maximillion deserves justice! Do... do you know what it's been like having to box up his things? All his piano memorabilia. You know he asked me to marry him over a solo piano rendition of All of Me by John Legend?"

"That sounds sweet."

"He was such a great player. A real natural. I heard you've taken his spot at Velvet."

Sudden suspicion narrows Rodrigo's gaze. I take half a step back.

"Erma sets the schedule—"

"You take his spot. You don't remember anything about that night. Max said you never got along and were always making disrespectful comments. You don't see how that looks?"

"Excuse me," I say coldly. "I have to go."

I leave Rodrigo and his accusations behind. Though I know I'm innocent, a thread of guilt loops inside of me and pulls tight in my chest. I don't know how Maximillion ended up dead, or who killed him, but something tells me this won't be the last time I hear such an accusation.

18. KADEN
SWEET DREAMS (ARE MADE OF THIS) - EMILY BROWNING

I used to carry out my workday with effortless precision. Down to the minute, my day was mapped out in a revolving door of patients, procedures, and tedious paperwork. Often, I'd forgo my lunch hour altogether to spend my time doing one of two things: poring over medical documentation and ensuring our practice dotted our i's and crossed our t's.

I have the medical history of most of my patients memorized down to the letter.

I work on weekends. On holidays. Late into the evening. I'm obsessed with my work, and I demand the same of those I employ.

Some of my receptionists, assistants, nurses, and other members on the staff thought I micromanaged. I was a bad, rude, horrible boss.

Horschman has always been their preferred doctor in the office.

I've always delighted in the idea they hate me. I've never cared about being liked or valued. Ask me a thousand times which I prefer, and I'd choose respect over being liked each and every time.

However, in recent weeks, things have changed. Lyra has blown through my life like a destructive tornado. The difference being she has a tight, warm cunt I can't resist and a musical gift that I'm increasingly ensnared by.

I've not only recorded her in the privacy of her bedroom, I recorded her musical performance too (I've been making her play for me).

As I'm in the surgery room operating on Eunice Mitchell's artery, I'm engrossed in the sprawling notes of Italian Concerto in F Major, BWV 971. Lyra's prowess reveals itself as she masters each run with ease and then jarring passion and power for every allegro. My hands work separately from my mind.

My mind recaptures the image of her seated at the piano, her body swaying on the bench. Her delicate, nimble fingers precise and quick on the keys. She was a goddess-like virtuoso before my very eyes.

I had to have her. So I made her strip off her dress. I treated myself to a taste of her sweet pussy and came in my pants without shame.

Lyra creates art with her hands. We're alike in this way.

As I operate on Eunice Mitchell, blood on my latex gloves and the front of my surgical gown, I'm creating art too.

My scalpel and forceps are my tools.

My hands.

The incision scar that will remain on Mitchell's body will be the proof to the world of my masterpiece.

I wash up, coming out of my reverie. The Hibiclens soap cleans my skin and kills germs on contact. The surgery is over, and I have no recollection of it.

My preoccupation with Lyra runs that deep.

In an effort to give myself space—and Lyra asked for it as

she works a late shift at the Velvet Piano—I meet up with Nolan and Klein for drinks. On the drive there I listen to more of my recordings of Lyra's music. I check my phone more than once. The apps show me what she's doing at the moment.

She relaxes on her laptop enjoying an edible until it's time to get ready for work and she takes a shower. Over the past couple days, she's learned a mild high takes the edge off her performances at the Velvet Piano. For the first time, she won a duel and earned the crowd's applause.

Nolan grins at me as I enter the Mint Room. The upscale lounge has walls papered a deep forest green and lacquered wood that's polished and attractive to the human eye. The Mint Room would settle for no less, designed to entertain a rogue's gallery of clientele willing to spend sixty dollars per cocktail. Clients like big bankers and corporate lawyers out for a location where they can lounge in tufted leather armchairs and wax poetic about how important and wealthy they are.

Walking into the moodily lit den of insipid vultures, I'm tempted to turn around and go. I meet Nolan's Cheshire Cat grin with the growing homicidal urge to swipe a knife off a table and lodge it into his throat. Would he scream like a terrified schoolgirl like Klein had when Lyra bit his dick off?

A smirk comes to my face at the thought.

She'd boldly done so in front of a sea of masked spectators worth infinitely more millions than she was. His blood had filled her *mouth*. She simply spat it out and made her escape.

A thick pulse of arousal awakens inside me, though I stamp it down just as quickly.

Nolan extends his hand and gives mine a shake. "I didn't think you'd make it. Klein was saying you'd stand us up."

Klein doesn't shake my hand. He remains seated, his Bourbon Sour in hand, his pale eyes studying me.

I glance down at his groin area and take my seat. "How are you holding up? Are your parts sewn back together?"

Nolan snorts. "They're back together alright. Klein, show him the photo."

Klein's weak chin clenches hard. He sips more of his Bourbon Sour in response.

Unfortunately for him, Nolan's rarely one to let anything go. He nudges his pal with the same grin he's greeted me with. "Kleiny boy, don't be shy now. Show our resident medical professional the Frankensteinian hack job that was done to your toy soldier."

When Klein still doesn't bite, Nolan shifts his attention onto me. He's buzzing with the excitement of a teenage girl fresh on the hot gossip. Something he should be ashamed of, though he thrives on chaos too much to be.

"Klein tried to fuck Talia Weinberg last weekend. It was when they got sloshed at the Vanderson soiree. An event you didn't turn up to, by the way. I suspect Talia was feeling sorry for him—that, and she's a stupid pageant queen with air for brains. She'll open her legs so long as you're nice to her for five minutes. Turns out, he couldn't get it up! We were right—his dick's broken!"

Uninterested in what he has to say, I motion for the server. Nothing Nolan says surprises me. Everyone knows Talia Weinberg is an empty-headed bimbo, and I don't care to hear about any sexual encounter she had with Klein.

If I'm honest, Klein's very existence has begun to bother me. Significantly more than usual.

Time passes and Nolan blathers on. The server delivers my Old Fashioned. I try my best to be unbothered and indifferent, however, irritation uncoils inside me. It slithers through me as I'm forced to sit across from Klein and his stabbable face.

He stuffed his dick inside Lyra's mouth. Despite her protests to the contrary. My grip on my glass cinches and red-tinted fantasies of Klein's murder play before my eyes. What would he do—what would any of them do—if I leapt over our table and shattered my glass over his face? If I used its sharpest shard to puncture his organs?

I could have him bleeding out on the floor.

In revenge for Lyra...

"Kaden?"

"Yes?" I turn a glaring eye on Nolan for interrupting my violent runaway imagination.

"Klein asked you a question. About the prostitute."

I'm about to snap what prostitute when it occurs to me who he speaks of. Focusing across the table on Klein, I'm already under his intent study. The glint in his gaze tells me what I need to know—Celeste informed him of what she found the last time she came over to my penthouse.

He knows I've fucked Lyra; he knows I'm involved with her in some capacity.

His frostiness makes sense.

Though I give nothing away. My face a blank canvas of composure, I drain the last of my Old Fashioned and push my chair back. "It's in progress," I answer vaguely. "You'd do better to worry about your appendage problems."

I leave them gaping after me. The heavy wooden door of the Mint Room swings shut behind me, and I'm steeped in the late evening roar of the big city.

Honked horns and screeching brakes. The white-noise rush of traffic speeding by. Lively chatter firing off from all cylinders around me. People going places and streetlights twinkling on.

I set off down the busy street and pull my phone out.

Lyra answers with a distracted tone. It doesn't impede me from what's on my mind.

"How about I come by the Velvet and fuck you in the bathroom?"

Though said half in jest, I can hear her frown. "Kaden, I'm up in five minutes. And I told you I'm exhausted. I haven't been sleeping well. I'm going straight to bed when I get home."

"That's what we call a joke, Lyra. However, if I can't be inside you, then I'll settle for watching you perform."

"Weren't you having drinks with friends?"

I scowl. "Yes. Is that what you'd prefer I'd do?"

"I didn't say that. I was asking—"

"Something's come up. Goodbye."

I hang up before she can make sense of my sudden bad mood. Some might say my reaction was juvenile. Frankly, if it were Klein or Nolan reacting the same way to a woman who didn't want to see them, I'd say it was.

This is different.

As irrational as that sounds, it simply is. I grit my teeth and storm down the rest of the block.

Lyra didn't want to see me as desperately as I wanted to see her. At my suggestion I drop by the bar, she sounded borderline reluctant. The nature of our relationship overwhelms her —I often overwhelm her with the intensity of the games we play when I fuck her.

She's spent much of her life ignored. Disowned by family with a small number of friends. Losers like Grady who couldn't even fuck her properly. Her special gift unnurtured and unnoticed.

No wonder she's running scared from the intensity of what my obsession entails.

I pocket my phone and calm determination settles over me. I'll simply have to... get creative.

————

I lurk in wait for when Lyra's off work and returns home. She won't know that's the case. My workaround would likely upset her. However, what Lyra Hendrix doesn't know won't hurt her—and if it pleasures me in the process, even better.

In the hours she's been at the Velvet Piano, I've snuck into her room. I couldn't resist tidying up (unlikely she'll notice). I stopped at the bedside table where she keeps her pill case for her medications and I swapped out her melatonin for a 15 mg dose of Proxamil, a sleeping aid only available by prescription. It's often given to chronic insomniacs. The pill resembles her melatonin to the letter.

She won't be able to tell the difference.

Although I haven't been able to determine what medications she's currently taking, it's unlikely any of them would trigger an adverse reaction if Proxamil was added to her system. I simply used my unmonitored access as a medical professional to sign them out of the pharmacy at the local hospital.

My plan is seamless—Lyra and I will both get what we want. She'll have one of the best night sleeps she's had in a very long time, and I'll get to be with her like my insatiable urges demand.

Lyra trudges through her bedroom door with an exhausted sigh and droop of her shoulders. Her crossbody purse flops to the floor and she kicks off her ankle boots. She goes straight into undressing. Her arms twist behind her back to unhook her bra and she steps out of the miniskirt she's wearing.

This is the riskiest part—the moment in which she changes.

I'm tucked away into the farthest recesses of her closet, hidden by deep shadows and an old rack of clothes and boxes. My most daring move yet in terms of stalking and surveilling her.

The closet door pops open and she appears at the front.

Her exhaustion is written all over her face. Heavy-lidded

eyes and a constant yawn stretching her mouth. She barely pays any mind to what she's digging out of her closet, grabbing the first sleep shirt on a hanger within reach.

For the next thirty minutes, I wait in the dark, listening to the sounds of running water in her bathroom. Her nighttime routine consists of a long, hot shower and some pampering skincare. The last thing she does is moisturize her scalp with some kind of hair oil before she wraps up her thick braids at the top of her head and secures them with a silky scarf.

I watch on my phone as she emerges from the bathroom in a baggy sleep shirt and another yawn escapes her. Most nights she'll browse the internet on her laptop for twenty, thirty minutes before bed. Tonight she doesn't bother.

She crawls into bed, swallows down her assortment of pills, and then twists off her bedside lamp.

Lights out.

My excitement pulses in my veins. It heightens to such a degree it's like I'm experiencing a pre-high before the high. That high being the indescribable pleasure I'll soon feel. I'm an addict in search of my next fix, and that fix happens to be fucking Lyra Hendrix in any way I see fit.

It's not long before she dozes off. The Proxamil works its medicinal magic.

She's out, so deeply asleep it'll be difficult to disturb her. She'll wake naturally eight to nine hours from now, completely well-rested—*and pleasured.*

I open the closet door and step out with hardly any of the stealth I've used in the past.

Stopping in front of her bed, I savor the sinfully sweet sight before me.

Lyra asleep with the sheets barely slung over her hips. She was so tired she didn't even grab the raggedy bear she usually sleeps next to.

I fling the sheets off her and then slip an arm under her to roll her onto her back. Even with the change in position, she doesn't stir.

She's a real life version of sleeping beauty. Her body lays loose and relaxed, with the sleep shirt she's wearing having ridden up her thighs.

My dick throbs as I reach out and feel how soft and supple her skin is.

I pry her legs the rest of the way open and then lean over her. My body being longer and taller than hers, I easily cover her with my length. I hover above her and drop a kiss on her lips. She turns her head and her eyes flutter beneath her closed lids.

However, she doesn't wake up. Her dreams have taken hold of her and refused to let go.

I stand up enough to unbuckle my pants and pull out my dick. After waiting so long for her, I'm already hard as humanly possible. My shaft aches as I stroke myself and admire the sleeping goddess lying in bed.

I have to be inside her.

The intensity to which I feel this compulsion is enough to drive me borderline insane.

If I don't have Lyra right now, I *will* go mad—or homicidal and kill the next living being I come into contact with.

I tug her panties off, pausing long enough to enjoy the view, before I ease myself onto her bed. The mattress shifts with my added weight, though still she doesn't stir.

My dick grazes her entrance. My gaze watchful of the erotic moment I enter her.

"Holy fuck," I grind out, watching myself disappear inside her pussy. My desperate lungs drag more air into them.

I have to stop myself for a moment.

Recollect myself. Center myself.

If I don't, I'll lose it. I'll become a brainless savage whose sole goal is to the fuck the hell out of her.

The muscles of my body ache from how tense I've become. I'm holding myself off as long as possible. I'm seeking to retain some semblance of human thought before I give in and descend into madness.

But then Lyra's pussy clenches around me, and it's over.

A deep groan leaves me, and my hips move of their own accord. I draw back and then sink deep. My movements slower, still contained, though no less urgent and rough. I watch Lyra's beautiful sleeping face and grope her unconscious body as I see fit.

Her breasts bounce along with me and my deep strokes. Neither the dark room nor her sleep shirt hide their shape or softness. My palm slides over them and I give them an appreciative squeeze. Her nipple a light twist.

She squirms and her head tips. Her lips part and a breathy noise leaves her.

I concentrate on her face, watching it for any sign of recognition.

The faintest, smallest sign she's waking up. I haven't the slightest idea what the hell I'd do if she did—what I'd even say, or how I could possibly explain what's happening.

Only that I needed to be inside her. I needed to experience her.

Her pussy agrees. I'm drowning in her slick wetness and the mess we're making. My dick sinks deep and her tight walls close in. Our parts fit perfectly together, our bodies working in perfect harmony to achieve a shared goal.

Even if it's one Lyra doesn't consciously realize she wants in this moment.

She moans and I sweep my arms under her thighs. I come in closer, our pelvises aligned. I've bottomed out inside her, gone as deep into her as I can go, and her pussy rewards me with another tight squeeze.

The pleasure's rising. It's building upon itself. It expands throughout my body until I'm a careless animal rutting away. A beast seeking release in the most primal, dominant way imaginable—in the suffocating clench of a warm, wet hole.

I'm teetering on the edge. I'm *falling* over the edge. Warmth envelopes me whole and my balls tingle and tighten.

At the last possible moment, I wrench myself free of Lyra, and then stroke myself to completion. My fist jerks up and down my cock in aggressive motions until I'm spilling on her mons pubis and open thighs.

As close to coming inside her as I can allow myself.

It's too risky to do so; I'd leave a mess I couldn't guarantee I'd be able to clean.

My ears buzz for seconds after. I'm heaving more rapid breaths into my lungs. I'm dripping sweat, and my heavy-lidded, almost drunken gaze rakes over Lyra and her limp body.

Still so asleep. Yet even more beautiful than before now that she's covered in my cum. On another beat of greed and recklessness, I bend forward and kiss her on the mouth.

Much harder this time.

Though she doesn't kiss me in return, the sweet taste of her lips makes it worth it.

I spend the next twenty minutes covering my tracks. Cleaning Lyra up. Putting her panties on. Fixing her sheets. Caressing her cheek and wishing her good night.

I almost decide to return to the closet, where I'll be able to watch her sleep some more.

In the wake of my orgasm, a sliver of logic has returned, and begs me to go. I've taken enough chances for one night.

If I head home, I'll still be able to catch two or three hours of sleep before it's time to turn up at the practice. Though it's tempting to call in and let Horschman and the rest of the staff handle everything yet again.

I emerge from the narrow alley between Lyra's warehouse

apartment complex and the squat building next-door. My car's parked across the street. I make it to the sidewalk and then stop short when I realize I won't be driving myself home.

A limo is waiting for me. The rear door swings open and the Owner speaks from his cushy seat in the back.

"Get in."

19. KADEN

BLACK MILK - MASSIVE ATTACK

"S ince it seems I have little choice."

I oblige the Owner's request and slide into the back of the limo. The driver up front presses the gas and we sail down the otherwise empty street.

We ride in silence like this.

The limo journeys from the terrible borough where Lyra lives to better, less crime-riddled parts of Easton.

I sit bored and resort to scrolling through my phone. The Owner, donning his gold-plated bauta mask in the shape of an owl, reaches forward and presses a button. The panel before us splits open and reveals a minibar. He gestures to the selection.

"No thank you."

"Drink."

I glower to myself, though I'm in plain sight of him. After intense sex with Lyra and hours of spying, the only thing I desire at the moment is a few hours of shuteye. A late-night excursion with the Owner in the backseat of a limousine, where we consume alcoholic beverages sounds far less appealing.

I forgo the alcohol altogether and opt for a bottled Slvenbaldi.

He sips his usual. Whiskey, straight. Warm, no ice.

The amber liquid slips through the opening under his bauta mask. His fathomless black eyes are on me as my gaze is on him.

The Owner intimidates many. Many bend to his will due to his unnerving presence alone. His quiet disposition and constant stare—all from beneath the mask he wears every moment of his life—make people uncomfortable.

Rich and powerful and weak and poor alike.

I'm an exception.

While the Owner is far from my favorite person, I do not fear him. I fear no one. I fear nothing.

Though, admittedly, the Owner is perhaps the last person I'd intentionally infuriate.

Mostly due to the longstanding complications it'd cause.

"Your time is up," he says after minutes of silence. We've now crossed into upper Easton territory, reflected in the sleek, modern buildings and clean streets. "You were at her residence. She is still alive."

I square my jaw from how hard I grit my teeth. "It would help if I were not being micromanaged every other second."

"You have had the freedom to do as you please. It has been weeks."

"I am earning her trust."

"Trust is not needed for what you have to do."

"It is if it's to be an accident," I snap, my agitation mounting. It sharpens my tone and curls my fists in my lap. "You may think because of the illicit activity I sometimes take part in that I eliminate my prey without thought. That couldn't be further from the truth—I often spend weeks, sometimes months stalking them. I'm a hunter and they are my game. I do not go in for the kill until it is the right time to do so."

"The right time to do so has passed. Your instruction was clear. You are to dispose of her." He sets down his glass of whiskey and sits, composed, opposite me, as though he's a statue on a monument. His posture is rigid and straight, his hands relaxed in his lap. The mask he wears disguises him, however, I sense the same can be said of his face.

Strangely enough, it is the huge, black eyes of his owl mask carrying the most emotion.

Cold indifference. Watchful scrutiny. Endless authority.

He sees all. He controls all. He wins all.

The unspoken truth of the Midnight Society. The unspoken truth of my life from the time I was a kid.

The moment I was reborn in blood...

I tear my gaze away and look out the window. "I will take care of it. I have given you my word I will."

"You will be given one more chance. If you fail, it is not only she that will suffer."

"Your threats fall on deaf ears. You know I do not respond to them."

"This time, you will."

"Where are we going?" I snap, my fists tight.

The Owner doesn't provide an answer. The chauffeur drives on. We drive for so long, I begin questioning if we're headed outside of the city.

Until we pull up outside the Winchester. The valet opens our doors, and the Owner leads the way inside. My teeth remain gritted as I follow.

The night sky has eased from deep plum to an opalescent blend of lilacs and cobalts. The forecast claimed we wouldn't see much sun. With summer over, the weather will soon turn drearier.

It reflects the mood entering the Winchester.

We come to a formal dining room where a fanciful breakfast has been set and a table of guests have already gathered.

Celeste is who I notice first. How can I not when she's sitting with her sharp chin at a defiant angle and bony shoulders poised. Some delicate lace dress drapes her, the pearly color clashing hideously with her pallid complexion. Her delusion wins out, and her lips, painted a red so dark they're almost black, form into a smile.

I want to throttle her.

A current of near-blinding anger surges through me. It's staring me in the face.

Celeste told. That's what her smirk says. The devious glint in her eyes.

"Take your seat," the Owner directs.

I do so. Not in the first empty chair as he seems to imply, but after walking around to the other side. The chair that's unoccupied next to Celeste.

No one seems to notice nor care what's happening. They're too self-involved to pick up on the rapidly rising tension in the room.

If the Owner does, he leaves us be. He sits at the head of table and launches into a slow, composed explanation about the breakfast. He brought us here to clarify recent misunderstandings among club members.

"A bit unusual," admits Mr. Vanderson. He gives off a perturbed sound he hopes sounds like an easygoing chuckle. "But I can always do with a grand breakfast—and the Winchester's is grand."

"Yes," agrees Mr. Newton, glancing at the Owner. "Thank you for inviting us."

"Thank you, indeed." Celeste only wants me to hear her. No one else catches the murmur of her slithery voice.

Similarly, no one catches my hand gripping her thigh under the table. My hand is large enough and her thigh slender enough that I'm able to grab onto it whole. I clamp down until I'm crushing her limb and she winces.

"Ow," she breathes. "Baby. You're... hurting me."

"I know. I will do so much worse soon."

"Mmm. I like the sound of that."

My lips barely move. "You will live to regret what you've done here. Actually, you won't live at all."

"Don't be mean."

I give another brutal squeeze of her thigh and she yelps.

"I will break it."

"I love when you touch me."

"Why?" I grit out, picking up a glass of freshly squeezed grapefruit juice with my free hand. I pretend to sip from it as I demand answers. "Why did you do it?"

"She shouldn't live. Those are orders."

"Excuse us," I say loudly, suddenly.

Every head at the table, engrossed in chatter about the Easton stock market and current events, snaps in mine and Celeste's direction. I rise up and lift Celeste along with me by the elbow. She winces at how roughly I do, though no one cares enough to question.

"Okay," Mr. Newton says, pushing his square-shaped glasses up his nose. "But you may miss out on the Winchester's famed Halloumi and Zucchini Frittata. I've been saving room."

Celeste protests the entire trip from the formal dining room to the first available parlor we find. I yank the door open and fling her inside. Considering she weighs a hundred and ten pounds at most, the strength at which I do causes her to fall over.

I do not care. I stride up to where she's crumpled on the floor and drag her up by her bony arm.

She gets off on this. On my reprimands. On my rough treatment. As I wring and shake her and growl in her face, she only softens in my grasp. A dreamy expression passes over her, and she claws at me as if to embrace.

I shove her away from me in disgust. "Do you really believe what you did will do you any favors?"

"Baby—"

"Call me baby one more time, Celeste, and I will snap your wrist like a twig. Do not test me."

"*Kaden*," she corrects herself in a gentle, delirious coo. She steps toward me as if I haven't just shoved her away. "I was following club rules. The prostitute is to die. You've heard the Owner. Instead, you've brought her into your home. You threw me out days before."

"You fucking crazy bitch," I rage. "That's because I didn't want you there! I don't want you period!"

"She hurt Klein."

"I don't give a fuck."

"She's poor. And *Black*."

I advance toward her, my expression so dark and murderous, a flicker of fear finally bleeds onto Celeste's gaunt face. She tries to step back, but it's too late—I wrench her closer by the wrist and then do what I did earlier.

I crush her. My grip tightens on her wrist to the point of severe pain.

She screams and wiggles her body to escape me. It's useless. Her weak attempts futile.

I only squeeze harder, twisting her wrist. "How many warnings have I given you? Yet you insist on being a lunatic. You attempt to degrade Lyra for something as irrational as the color of her skin. Yet you are a drug-addicted whore. Lyra has infinitely more worth than you will ever possibly dream, you deluded bitch."

Tears fill her eyes, and she begins swatting at me.

I release her. I do it so suddenly, and she's so erratic, that she loses her balance and falls on her ass. She remains where she is, her long, bony legs bent at odd angles and tears and mascara streaked down her cheeks.

"I have gone easy on you, Celeste. But I will not tolerate your interference. The next time you do, I will run you through with my sharpest blade. You mean nothing to me. Less than nothing. Scum on my shoe holds more value. Stay away from me. Stay away from Lyra. Do you understand?"

With a feeble noise, she nods.

It's the most broken I've ever seen her. If I were more human, I'd feel sorry for her. She's that pathetic and lost.

However, it's a necessary evil—it's the only way she'll understand. Should it turn out that she still hasn't learned her lesson, Lyra won't be the next person I eliminate.

Celeste will be.

———

"You will do fine. You are overthinking the situation, which places pressure on yourself."

Lyra exhales a deep sigh that deflates her posture. She's seated at the piano bench on stage at the Velvet Piano. Erma, her manager, has agreed to allow her to practice hours before the bar opens. Though she's off tonight, tomorrow is her audition with Fyodor Kreed.

I've realized it's the culprit for her distant behavior.

Lyra's nervous, racked by imposter syndrome and self-doubt, and when she feels this way, she becomes withdrawn.

A tendency I do not exhibit but that I understand.

I am not capable of imposter syndrome or such high levels of self-depreciation as she is. I have the opposite issue—I think extremely highly of myself at all times.

Lyra believes she is the worst piano player in the world.

As her shoulders slump, I come up from behind and stroke them. "You played Debussy's La Mer with natural finesse."

"My dynamic contrast was off. It wasn't a proper transition."

"It sounded raw to my ears, like you were playing with emotion."

"Maybe that's the problem. For a long time, I was self-taught. My mother was a musician and taught me the basics of things like reading music, but she played the sax. I figured out the piano on my own. Even when I did get lessons and formal training, it wasn't under the best circumstances. My music teacher was very strict. It made me doubt myself."

"You're being hypercritical. You will stop from this point on."

Her brows knit. "But, Kaden, what I'm trying to say—"

"Lyra," I interject, my tone authoritative, "you will stop doubting yourself right now. Do you understand?"

Slowly, reluctantly, she nods.

I palm her smooth, narrow shoulders. "You will recognize you are an accomplished pianist. Your less traditional method of learning has brought you here. Anyone can succeed if taught by the best piano instructors the city has to offer. You made it as far as they have on your own merit."

"But you've gotten me the audition with Fyodor, not my own—"

"Lyra," I growl, squeezing her shoulders, "do we have to play a game for you to understand? Do I have to spank you until your ass is sore before you have confidence in yourself?"

I can hear her smile. "You're always looking for an excuse."

"Then don't give me one. Get up. You've practiced enough."

"The audition is tomorrow."

"Meaning you're already as good as you're going to be. You need fresh air."

We leave the Velvet Piano behind. On our way out, as we pass the spot where I murdered Maximillion, I can't resist glancing over. He had stood right there, spurting out blood with his jaw wide open in horrified shock.

I grin. Soon I'll need to find my next prey.

Though I've told the Owner it'll be Lyra, I still have no plans on fulfilling that promise.

For the time being, she's keeping me entertained. Our interactions are interesting, and I enjoy having sex with her. If the Owner or anyone else in the club has a problem with my defiance, I will figure out what to do when that time comes.

We walk several blocks from the piano bar. The day's pale sun has receded behind storm clouds, and the sky darkens into a gray ceiling. A warm breeze blows against our skin, and though it's not the most refreshing feeling, it's better than a stuffy bar.

Lyra's a bundle of nervous energy beside me, delectable in the top she wears that bears her midriff and the thong she has on underneath her pleated skirt. I know because I spied on her from the app on my phone as she dressed.

Once we make it back to my penthouse, I'll get to see it in person.

"Where are we going?"

"Do we need to be going anywhere?"

She shrugs. "No. But you're the type of guy who always has a plan."

True.

"What can I say? You've inspired me not to."

"You mean I've driven you crazy with my neurosis so you're trying to figure out how you'll shut me up?" She aims a teasing smile up at me.

I stick a hand in my pants pocket and give her comment some thought. "That is precisely what is going on."

"In that case, can I show you the place I usually go when I'm overwhelmed?"

"The way you posed that question, I'm assuming yes is the only acceptable answer."

She hooks her arm into mine and then laughs. "Kaden, you're a mystery."

"That wouldn't be the first time I've heard that."

"Why did you pretend to be someone else?"

"Lyra... we've been over this..."

"Your personality," she clarifies. "When you first met me, you were acting like a different man."

"Is that your way of saying I'm not warm and kind?"

Another short laugh leaves her. "Yes."

"I admire your honesty."

"*But*," she continues, "I like this you more."

"Is that so?"

"Yes. It's more real."

"And the other man you met wasn't? That was my best foot forward."

"I prefer this foot. At least I know what I'm getting. A part of me sensed it—something was off about you."

You have no idea, little lamb. You still don't know.

"You were too perfect," she thinks aloud, frowning. "No one's that good-looking, rich, successful, *and* a good person."

I laugh this time. "Your cynicism is refreshing. Which of those did you eliminate to determine the real me?"

"Take a wild guess."

"I let the elderly go in front of me in lines. I feed strays when I see them. On occasion, I help piano players with crippling self-doubt land career-changing auditions."

"I can't imagine who that last one is about."

"Take a wild guess," I quip, and she shoots me an amused glance.

We walk for so long I'm questioning where she's leading us. We've reached a more desolate pocket of the city, where

corner stores abound and trash scuttles by. I look ahead at the
dead end street and notice the tall iron gates.

"You're taking me to the cemetery?"

She nods. "I used to telework from here."

"That's very... morbid of you."

"Not morbid. Very relaxing. I'll show you."

Lyra's arm stays looped with mine. I allow it for the occasion. It's better than a hand hold. A gesture she hasn't dared
try. She tugs and tugs at me, leading us down narrow pathways
of gravestones and commemorative monuments. Some are
admittedly eerie in the vacancy of the cemetery. Giant angels
of chiseled stone with harps and chunks of their faces missing.

Still, we keep going. We wander past a domed mausoleum
collecting moss and webs spun by spiders. At the far end, we
begin climbing a grassy knoll. On the top sits a giant elm tree
with branches spread out to resemble an umbrella.

A look of contentment lights up Lyra's face when we reach
the top. "See. Isn't it peaceful up here? It's quiet and no one's
ever around."

I stare at her. "There's plenty of places in the city where
you can find the same."

"Yeah, but... the scenery."

"I'm not understanding."

Her face falls, her teeth scraping over her bottom lip.
"Maybe it's because I was an obituary writer..."

"Did your boss ever pay you?"

"Winston? Are you kidding?"

I'll have to pay him a visit...

She plops down in the grass and pats the space next to her.
"Join me?"

I remain standing with both hands in my pockets. "Maybe
next time."

"Okay."

She draws her knees to her chest and folds her arms on top.

Never mind that it affords me a sneak peek of her panties—I'm sure she knows and doesn't care.

At first, I admire the view. Then I take in the whole sight of her. The sadness that's emanating from her in an unmistakable wave.

"Why do you *really* come here?"

"If I told you, you'd think I were weird."

I bite the bullet. Mostly because my curiosity is piqued, and I'll need her trust if she's to open up. I bend down in a stilted move to sit next to her. Being significantly smaller and more flexible, sitting on the grass is more comfortable for her than it is for me. My long legs stretch out in front of me, and I await her confession.

She takes me up on my cue.

"It's like I said. I find it relaxing here. It's like I'm among people I care about. See, I told you. *Weird.*"

"That is what most would consider weird. Yes."

"Do you?"

"Yes. However, that does not make it wrong. Wrong being relative."

"You judged me for dipping my French fries in my milkshake that one time."

"I take that back. Some wrongs are universal."

She smirks. "I'll let you spank me with the crop if you try a French fry in a chocolate shake. It'll change your life."

"Bargaining punishments so that I'll indulge you in your peculiar food habits?"

"Think about it. It's a win for everyone."

I let the amusing moment pass between us. I'll hand it to Lyra—she makes for engaging conversation. Some of the most engaging I've ever experienced. In my superficial world of the rich and powerful elite, conversations predominantly comprise of boasting and listening for your chance to do so.

"How did your mother feel about you playing piano?

Would she have preferred that you play the saxophone like she did?"

Lyra's expression shifts. It freezes into a grimace and her body stiffens. "That's complicated. She ran a tight ship."

"As in?"

"As in... she expected the best of the best. She'd make me play Twinkle Twinkle Little Star 'til my fingers ached. 'Til they bled."

"Perfectionist."

"She demanded of me what she demanded of herself. But the problem was that I was... six? Seven?"

"I thought you started at four?"

"It took a few years before she realized she could turn me into a prodigy."

"Where did you get the piano from? Did you have one in your home?"

She hacks out a laugh that sounds jaded to the ears. "No, Kaden. We didn't have a piano in our one bedroom apartment in Harrisburg. But there was one at the club my mom used to work at. She'd bring me with her."

"What type of club? A nightclub?"

"That's right. It was a jazz nightclub. Kind of like the Velvet Piano."

"Not the best environment for a little girl."

"I found ways to keep myself busy. The piano was one of those ways. When I was a couple years older, she took me to a man who was world famous. He was the most brilliant player. He began to teach me. The only private instructor I've ever had."

"How did your mother know him?"

"The club... maybe. He was very rich. An admirer of hers and she of him."

The manner in which she speaks of her childhood feels

detached. Her tone miserable. I detect no warmth or affection for her mother.

Any research I've done on her past shows Lyra's estranged from her family. Though I haven't been able to dig up many details. Almost as if her mother dropped off the face of the earth.

She doesn't know I know. Which means I'll have to do some more nonchalant probing.

"Where is she now?"

"My mother?" She shrugs.

"You might need her address if you're sending her a Mother's Day card."

"Good thing the last time I gave her one of those I was five. What about your family, Dr. Raskova? You come from money."

"That's about as interesting as my family ties get."

"I'm not letting you off so easily. Tell me more. Brothers? Sisters?"

"Only child. You?"

"One sister."

"Where is she?"

Lyra shrugs again. "Around. So I did some internet sleuthing on the Raskova name."

...that's news to me. When was this? I practically monitor you 24/7.

"Your dad is a billionaire. He's from Russia."

"Those of Russian descent tend to be."

"I couldn't find much info on him. Just a barren autobiography page on some Russian site. The search results didn't even turn up any photos."

"Were you trying to see if my good looks run in the family?"

"Kaden," she says, stretching her legs out like mine. "I'm curious about you. You never talk about yourself."

*That's because I am a man donning a mask. A man hiding
a monster inside.*

"You know enough."

"I could always know more."

"I feel the same about you."

"You know plenty about me."

I angle my body so that I'm partially facing her. My thumb
and forefinger clip her chin and force her gaze. "But I want to
know more. I want to know every weird thought in your head.
Every quirk, habit, and tendency of yours. Tell me all about
yourself."

Her brows raise and she repeats my own words to me.
"You know enough."

I taste her lips. She settles into my kiss without protest. My
arms wrap around her, and I draw her closer until she's up
against my chest, almost in my lap. It's where we reach a stale-
mate for the moment. The taste of warm, sweet lips on mine
and my hand gripping the side of her neck. We kiss because
neither of us wants to divulge another word.

The dark secrets we're hiding. The darker truths we're
keeping from one another.

I know it with certainty. It's easier this way.

20. Lyra
Hearing Damage - Thom Yorke

"**Y**ou."

It's how Fyodor Kreed greets me outside the Easton Opera House. I've been waiting on the top step for over thirty minutes. Several passersby have pointed up at me and conferred with each other with the zeal of gossip queens.

After the first few, I began flipping them off.

Childish? Maybe. But the longer Fyodor left me waiting, the more I went crazy. I picked at my uneven nail beds and tapped my feet—adorned in sleek, red-bottomed pumps Kaden bought me. I checked and double-checked my make up and the high bun I've styled my thick box braids in before starting the neurotic, nervous cycle all over again.

Glancing at the time. Fretting over whether I've been stood up. Burning with embarrassment as yet another person gapes at me as he passes by.

It's drizzling out, and I'm five minutes away from giving up altogether when, finally, Fyodor shows up.

He arrives in a yellow taxicab. His umbrella pops out of the open rear door first. Then he emerges, a slight man with a permanent frown and heavy brow. The eyeglasses perched on his dissatisfied face resemble the thick plexiglass you find in sports arenas.

I sit and watch as he hobbles up the steps one at a time. His hip jerks and his foot kicks out.

It takes him forever to reach the top of the cascading steps leading up to the opera house.

But when he does—he gives me an unimpressed once over and then addresses me not by name.

"You," he spits. "Follow."

So, I listen. I scramble to get up from the spot on the step where I've camped out for almost an hour, and I become his shadow.

He unlocks the grand front doors and then hobbles inside. I lurk after him. He steps onto the elevator. I step onto the elevator.

We ride in tense, unfamiliar silence. He stares ahead at the closed brass doors. I do the same, mimicking him moment to moment.

With the ding, he exits and makes as sharp a left as humanly possible on his short, uneven legs.

"My office," he says. He thrusts an aggressive finger at the open doorway.

I go inside first. Seconds later, I flinch at the loud slam of the door.

His office is a suffocating four walls painted depressive gray and filled with a variety of instruments. In the far corner, as if in afterthought, a puny desk is jammed against the wall. Stacks and stacks of what I'm guessing are musical notes cover the top of it.

In the center of the room, taking the spotlight from every other instrument here is a classic Steinway and Sons Model B circa 1975. Maybe 1976.

I recognize it well. I played on one just like it when my

fingers bled and my mother screamed at me to "respect the composition."

When the only piano instructor I had as a child brought down his cane on me and forced my attention.

Fyodor snaps me out of my dark tour down memory lane. He points another aggressive finger at the piano.

"Sit."

I take a second too long. He limps past me and slaps a hand to the piano bench.

"The bench. Sit."

I drop onto the bench so quickly, my ass makes a smacking noise when it collides. He shuffles his way to the wall directly in front of the Steinway and then uses it as a crutch. He leans against the dreary pewter and looks smaller and more bite-sized than ever.

Yet, even more intimidating. More terrifying. A chihuahua that will bite the hell out of my ankles at the first hint of a mistake.

I get into position. Straightened back. Body toward the front of the bench. Feet flat on the ground. Hands relaxed and fingers parallel to the keys.

It feels so... *unnatural*.

I've always been an outlier. It drove my piano instructor insane when I was a child.

And my mother.

They'd screech at me to sit *properly*.

My mother would make me sit in perfect position for hours.

...'til she drove the point home with tears in my eyes and an aching spine. 'Til *he* shoved my back straight whenever it began to wilt.

The first chance I was able, I played how I wanted to play. Relaxed, borderline slouched, with my fingers everywhere on the keys.

But the music sparked through me. It lived in my bones and nourished my soul. Freed me from the dark pits of my miserable childhood when I let go and trusted the beautiful sounds emitting from the merest stroke of the keys. I became a girl possessed.

By the sounds. By the music.

A mysterious music nymph which suddenly inhabited my body and took me on a shiver-inducing, borderline orgasmic ride through every curled note and deep chord.

Mother hated it. My soul was nourished by it. The magic I created at the stroke of a key.

As Fyodor's hard gaze bears down on me, I try to channel that elusive music nymph. Even with the rigid, unnatural posture, I close my eyes and breathe in and out.

"Play," he directs.

No song instruction. No further guidance on anything.

I play the first song that comes to mind—Claude Debussy's Clair de lune.

I can't stop myself once I get going. I lose the perfect posture and my hands don't hold their technical position.

My fingers move.

They dance across the piano keys in gentle reverence of the romantic, twinkling notes.

I forget Fyodor watches.

My eyes close and I'm whisked away by imaginings of a full moon and dark sea of tiny, glittering stars.

Music has always been a subversive experience for me. As a child, I couldn't articulate my feelings. With my mother screeching at me about posture and key placement, I stuttered over any words I spoke.

Any formal schooling and recitals I had into adulthood were more of the same.

My time at the Velvet Piano is more of the same.

I've spent so much time in my head. So much time doubting, second-guessing, feeling like an imposter unworthy of the keys I sit before.

But, as my fingers take the lead and I play for Fyodor, I'm set free in a way I didn't expect.

I don't even remember to check his reaction. How can I when my eyes are closed and I'm swaying like a dandelion in the wind?

My fingers still and the last note plays. My eyes gently open. I'm dizzy and lost for several seconds.

Silence echoes in the wake of my performance.

I sit up straighter and attempt to settle back into the present. Difficult after going on such a melodic journey.

Fyodor makes no effort to hide his rude, prolonged stare. Still diminutively propped up against the wall, he's not keen on cluing me in to how I did anytime soon.

He makes me wait.

And wait.

He strokes his chin he takes so long. And then—

"*Velikolepnyy.*"

"Um... what?"

"*Velikolepnyy.* Magnificent."

"Oh. Oh! Thank you."

"Kaden was right," he speaks his longest sentence to me yet. It showcases the thick harshness of his Russian accent more than ever.

But I'm more distracted by his wandering gaze.

It slides over me, even as I sit plain at the piano in a conservative black dress. The same type of dress Kaden advised. Though I do wear pumps that can be considered sexy, it's hardly what I was going for.

That doesn't stop Fyodor from doing what skeevy, gross old men do—he gawks at me with unapologetic lechery. He might as well drool, he stares so hard, so lustily.

The air in the room changes.

A prickle of discomfort needles at my spine.

Fyodor pushes off the wall and comes up from behind where I sit.

In that quick of a moment, he's gone from distant and cruel to invading my personal space and leaping over a boundary. He bends over me seated at the bench, and his hot breath tickles my cheek.

"I like how you play." As an afterthought, he adds, "Very much. Very, very good."

"Errr... thanks. Excuse me."

"Hmmm?"

"You're..." I swallow in a gulp. "Please give me some space."

Though I don't glance up to check, an amused smirk crawls across his pallid face—I know because I can *feel* it.

"Why?"

"Why... what?"

"Lyra. Is that your name?" he asks with a feigned air of curiosity. His hand dares come up onto my bare shoulder, resting on the curve of it as if invited.

I shrug off his touch. "Yes. That's my name."

"You play beautifully."

"Thank you. Can you please give me some—"

"*You* are beautiful."

Any gratitude and manners go out the window. I half rise from the piano bench before he grips my shoulders with surprising aggression and shoves me back down. He doesn't let go—if anything, his stubby fingers clamp down harder and hold me still on the bench. He leans closer and presses his cold, slack cheek to mine.

"I will make you a star, Lyra. You will be my muse if you do as I say."

Fyodor groans as he kisses my cheek and squeezes my shoulder.

I attempt to shrug him off to no avail. He refuses to give up, tightening his grip.

A panicked bomb detonates from the deepest part of me. An instinctual reaction waiting in the wings since my encounter at the Midnight Society party, where a guy named Klein Fairchild shoved his dick into my mouth.

But Fyodor's not going down easily. As I dodge his advances and duck out from under him, he anticipates my escape.

His arms come around me, and rather than back off, he doubles down.

"Do not fight me," he coos, nibbling my ear. "What are you afraid of? I told you I will make much of you—"

"Get. Off. Me!"

"Your skin. It's so soft. So dark. Very beautiful."

The groan he releases is grotesque to my ears. I can't take another second, jamming an elbow into his ribs.

Fyodor Kreed goes from practically getting off, caressing my skin, to curling over in pain.

I seize the chance to scramble away.

"Don't ever touch me again!"

I flee. I run away like a frightened woodland creature. Much like the night at the Midnight Society party, where I'd fled barefoot in a wild panic.

In some demented kind of way, this moment is worse; it hurts more.

Here I was, thinking I was on a legit audition, baring my creative soul, and there Fyodor Kreed was, ready to perve. I shove open the grand front doors to the opera house and tumble down the steps at a reckless speed considering my high heels.

In the half hour that's passed, night has fallen, and the drizzle has intensified into sheets of rain.

I don't give a fuck. I slip and slide down the wet sidewalk

in my haste to get away. Fyodor hasn't followed, but you can never be too sure—the night of the Midnight Society party, I ran for almost two miles without stopping.

I'm prepared to do so again. Aching toes and cut up heels of my feet or no aching toes and cut up heels of my feet.

"Lyra! Lyra!"

I almost tumble trying to turn around. I recognize the voice.

Kaden's calling out to me.

As bullets of rain fire away and drench me, he jogs to catch up. He's in his usual neat, white button-down and trousers, though neither are a match for the rain—they dampen and his shirt clings to every hard curve of muscle he possesses.

I stop running and let him overtake me. His arms encircle my body, and he holds me in front of him in considerate scrutiny. His usual waves of shiny, chocolatey hair are drenched and hanging about his face. He shakes several wet strands out of his eyes and pierces me with his lit, dark gaze.

"Where are you going? Why are you running? What happened?"

I gasp at the warm rain pelting down and cling to him. My long fingernails skim his forearms, and my eyes search his for comfort.

He's puzzled—a line appearing between his brows and his lips trending downward. He opens his mouth to question me, then seems to think better of it.

I'm too upset for his police-lineup-styled questioning.

Instead, his palms cup my elbows and I'm pulled snug against his chest. He bends his head and kisses me on the lips. I'm sucked into Kaden's orbit from the first second his lips touch mine. I'm clinging to him and feeling my heart beat against my chest in an emotion I can't describe.

Just that Kaden's here, I'm encircled in his arms, and we're kissing like it's our own language.

Maybe it is.

Butterflies fly free in my stomach. I shiver in the cool rain 'til Kaden clenches an arm about my lower back and yanks me up against him. He forces his tongue into my mouth and takes control. He kisses me and bites me and makes me lose my breath. I'm shuddering within his hold, not from the rain-drops soaking me, but from his kiss soaking my panties.

The second heartbeat that's throbbed to life between my thighs.

"Kaden," I moan between our passionate kisses.

He sucks my lip and grips my ass. "Yes, little lamb?"

I pull away far enough to glance up into his dark, dangerous gaze. "Take me home."

21. LYRA
BOYS LIKE YOU - TANERÉLLE

Kaden tries to dip out once he's walked me up to my apartment. We're both soaked from the rain, dripping puddles in the hallway outside my front door. I rest one hand on the knob and jiggle my ring of keys in the other.

"Coming in?" My eyes glint with insinuation.

He sticks both hands in his wet pants. "You know better than to ask. Your space is not yours."

Anytime I've invited him over, he cites my male roommate as a reason he doesn't want to stay. I haven't been able to tell if it's the truth, or if he feels my apartment's beneath his rich tastes.

Sticking my key in the lock, I say, "That's where you're wrong. Taviar is out for the night... and the next few days. He's visiting family in Lunsbury."

"I'm unclear what that has to do with me."

"I have the whole apartment to myself. Come in. Just this once."

"On the stipulation you tell me what happened at the opera house."

My insides twist into knots, but I agree with a reluctant

nod. Hopefully he'll forget once I've distracted him with a drink... or my titties.

Kaden in my home space feels unnatural. Though Taviar makes a generous enough salary to afford a three bedroom apartment in downtown Easton, he's the farthest thing from sophisticated. Boxes fill up our living room and crinkled movie posters hang on the walls. Most of the furniture you can find at the Shop N' Save for less than a hundred dollars a piece.

In contrast, Kaden exudes riches and refinement. One glance at him and how he presents himself, and you can just *tell* he's loaded. He has the finest of fine tastes.

Suddenly, I'm self-conscious about inviting him in to my warehouse apartment and dragging him into my shitty bedroom with my half broken bed frame and clothes strewn about the floor.

"Sorry for the mess," I mutter. "I'm in the middle of spring cleaning."

"It's October."

"I fell a little behind."

He eyes me with a flash of tepid humor. "I'm sure."

"Would you like something to drink? Or maybe a snack?"

"I'm fine." He glances around my room as if checking for a place to sit that's sufficient enough for him.

"You can sit on my bed... or my computer chair. I'm pretty sure Taviar has a beanbag I can—"

"I'm fine," he repeats.

"Then I'll pour us some drinks! Be right back."

I scurry out of the room in a haste to be a good host. Normally, I refrain from using anything that belongs to Taviar —an unspoken agreement we had along with Jael. But, as the cliché saying goes, desperate times call for desperate measures.

I open the cabinet where Taviar keeps his liquor and mix us some drinks. There's a plastic container of chocolate chip cookies I snag too.

Does Kaden eat cookies, or desserts at all for that matter? I've never once seen him eat a bite of any dessert.

"Jack and Coke," I announce, handing him his drink. I hold up the container of cookies. "And chocolate chip cookies if you like them."

He raises an eyebrow. "Jack and Coke and cookies. And you wonder why I don't come over."

My enthusiasm melts away and I realize I'm still wearing my soggy dress. My glum expression must read on my face, because Kaden reaches for my wrist and pulls me toward him.

"That was sarcasm, Lyra. Thank you for the drink. It's very... hospitable of you."

"If there's anything else you need, just ask. I'm going to change. I wish I had clothes that fit you. Want me to throw your shirt in the dryer?"

"It's Tom Ford."

"Dry clean only, huh? Or do you wear your clothes once and then toss them? I'm sure you can afford to."

I'm teasing him now as I turn my back to him. He gets the hint and reaches up to undo the zipper of my dress. The top portion folds over at my waist and reveals I'm not wearing a bra. As I walk toward the closet, I can practically feel Kaden leering.

His aroused stares are more than welcomed. Creeps like Fyodor Kreed's are not.

I disappear into the closet to find a hoodie and sweats. Kaden proves he won't be distracted for long.

"The opera house. Tell me what went on. Why were you running out crying?"

"Why were you there?"

"I was there to surprise you. I saw you flee Fyodor's office in a panic. He looked puzzled."

I bet he did. The old pervert.

But I don't want to tell Kaden the details. If his reaction

will be anything like how he behaved around Grady that night at the Velvet Piano, it won't be good. A darkness had washed over him that was unsettling. That almost made me want to never see him again.

"It's not important. I'm just glad it's over."

"I take it your performance didn't go well. You let your nerves get the best of you."

I flop onto my bed and stare at him in my computer chair. "Something like that."

"I know when you're lying, little lamb."

"Why do you want to know?"

He takes a careful sip of his Jack and Coke, considering the question. "When the woman you're seeing is in distress, it seems like the correct thing to do is to inquire why."

"Seems like the correct thing?" I fold my legs crisscross style and rest my elbows on my thighs. "Is that your way of saying you're performing at being a good boyfriend—not that you actually are one?"

"I wasn't aware I'm your boyfriend."

I scoff. "We're practically exclusive, Kaden."

"Are we?"

"Would you care if I invited Grady over to fuck me?"

His jaw tenses, his cold eyes flashing in warning. "You will not invite him over for anything... or any other loser you've dated."

"*See*," I say with a smug smirk. "We're exclusive. If we weren't, you wouldn't give a damn who else I was fucking."

"Does that work both ways?"

"If you're asking whether I want you sleeping with that crazy bitch Celeste, absolutely not. I might question your taste if you mess with her again."

He chuckles. "I can't disagree with you on that matter."

"What's the story there, anyway? She calls you *baby* and seems in love with you."

"Celeste lives in a fantasy world. One she refuses to wake up from no matter how many times I deny her. But you are distracting me. The topic was your audition. Tell me what happened with Fyodor."

"Eat a cookie first." I snag one from the container and take an unnecessarily large bite.

Kaden glares. "A cookie."

"Yes. Then I'll tell you. I've never seen you eat a dessert. It's odd as hell."

"You're asking to be punished the next time you come home with me. In fact," he says, glancing around my room, "I'm certain I can get creative with the things you have."

"Spanking by hairbrush? Clothespins for clamps? I have a drawer of vibrators, so no issue there. I usually pull them out to finish the job Grady never does."

We share an amused moment as he finally indulges me and takes a cookie from the plastic container.

"Interesting mask." Kaden gestures to the leather cat mask sitting on my desk. Judging by the subtle twitch of his cheek, I'd guess he doesn't like the cookie, though he eats every bite. Probably some kind of compulsion to finish what he starts.

He's doing what I'm doing as he does so—seeking a distraction.

My cheeks warm watching him pick up the mask. "It's... uh... from a Halloween costume."

"Is that so?"

The stare he pins me with tells me he knows I'm lying. I stubbornly keep up the charade.

"Yes. That's so."

"Maybe I'll make you wear it the next time I fuck you."

"What's stopping you?"

"You say that now. Wait 'til I'm balls deep in that tight ass of yours."

My widening eyes give me away. I lose our impromptu game of chicken. Satisfied, he sips more of his Jack and Coke.

"Your audition with Fyodor."

"I guess I've stalled long enough. It went well. At first. I played Claude Debussy's Clair de lune. He stood back and watched. Then he said I could be his muse."

Kaden's body language shifts. Even if subtly. I have his undivided attention, his long fingers tight around his glass.

"He... um... put his arm around me," I say, looping the drawstring of my hoodie around my finger. "He... he kissed me. I told him to get off me. He claimed he could make me famous. Then I elbowed him in the ribs and took off."

"I see." Kaden swallows, his Adams apple thick and heavy in his throat. He sets down the glass of Jack and Coke with more force than necessary, causing a loud thud.

"Kaden..." I trail off. "Please don't confront him. It's over, and I'd rather forget it."

"You should save your breath. It does nothing to change how I will respond."

"Which is by... what? Beating him up?"

Kaden doesn't answer me. His stone cold, borderline murderous aura emerges. An air of mystery surrounds him as he runs fingers through his chocolatey waves and then slow suspicion drips into his tone.

"I feel... off. What kind of whiskey was that?"

"Regular ol' Jack Daniels. You barely had a glass."

He looks to the container of cookies. "*Those*. What was in them?"

It hits me at once. I gasp and then leap off the bed. "These are probably some weed cookies. Sometimes one of Taviar's friends will bake him some."

Kaden rises to his feet and dwarfs me. "You mean to tell me you fed me cookies laced with marijuana?"

"I... I didn't mean to. I was trying to be a good host."

"I don't get high. I don't do drugs. I don't..." he stops himself and I can see it creeping over him—*his high*.

A laugh bubbles out of me against my will.

The composed and refined Kaden Raskova, stoned. A bleariness develops in his dark gaze, and he threads more fingers through his hair as though desperately trying to control the sensation enveloping him.

"Don't fight it," I say. "Just go with it. The first high's always an experience."

"But you... you had a cookie too... and you're..."

I shrug. "I'm a pothead. My tolerance is higher. It takes two cookies to get me going."

He *laughs*. Kaden Raskova releases a laugh I've never heard out of him—it's borderline ridiculous. It's almost human.

"Something wrong?" I ask.

"I... I feel strange. I feel... funny."

"That's your high. It feels good, right?"

He develops a dazed look about him that's so un-Kaden like, I want to wrap my arms around him and kiss him.

I go for it. I toss my arms over his shoulders and kiss his jaw. "Wait 'til you fuck while you're high."

It's the only hint he needs. He answers my affectionate kiss on his jawline by gripping my torso and lifting me off my feet. My legs instinctually notch at his waist and our mouths seek each other out.

From the first touch of our lips, our kiss is explosive. Deep and devouring. Kaden walks us the few steps it takes to reach my bed and then deposits me onto it. I land with a flounce before I'm consumed again—he's diving forward to recapture my lips and scrabble at my sweatpants.

We wrestle taking off our clothes. The energy bouncing between us spurs on our hurried movements. We twist and jerk 'til he's tossing my hoodie away and I've freed his dick. He reaches for my breasts and pinches my nipple.

He swallows my scream in another hot kiss. Then twists the other.

"For getting me high," he mutters quickly. Cold revenge lives in his tone.

I can't be mad—I did get him high, and I do deserve it. Pain radiates across my breast for every rough tweak he gives.

But I'm also incredibly turned on. My pussy's aching and begging. I'm clenching air in the anticipation leading up to his first thrust.

Kaden's untamed in his passion. We roll over several times. He crushes me under him, pinning me on my stomach. He spears into me and bruises my hips hiking them up. I claw at the sheets and try to keep up.

The sex feels like a fever dream. My high's finally set in. My body percolates with pleasure. I'm hissing and gasping like some kind of feral cat. He contorts me into another shape, finding new ways to bend and stretch me, and then pounds harder into me.

His hands are everywhere. His thrusts brutal and uncompromising. We're wild as we go at each other, our bodies twisted and intertwined. I grapple for him, clawing at his chest and shoulders. I cling to his neck and draw us closer.

Our lips crash together in yet another aggressive, desperate kiss. Our movements don't slow down, but instead grow more furious and fast as we rut away. Our hips clash, and his dick sinks deeper. My pussy squeezes him tighter. He groans out my name and then bites my bottom lip. He flicks my clit. He pinches it to torture me.

A rush of blood floods my sex. I clench shut my eyes and it feels like I'm spinning in a chaotic wave of pain and pleasure.

We've devolved into mindless beings devouring each other, riding our amazing, euphoric high once it crashes over us. My spine arches and my ankles go limp from over his shoulders (he's tossed my legs up against them). I shed tears and babble incoherently as my orgasm destroys me.

My body becomes a tingling wave that I lose myself in.

Kaden grunts and thrusts and comes. Then collapses half on top of me. We lay a sweaty tangled mess of limbs and wrinkled sheets, reeking of our sex. Neither of us move until we have enough strength to make an attempt.

I can barely breathe. Barely *think*.

I glance at Kaden to find him with a wondrous expression on his face. His hair's an uncharacteristically tousled mess and he's folded an arm under his head, staring up at the ceiling.

"So *that's* why people become addicted. That was..."

"Really, really good," I finish, curling against his side.

He's not having it. He grips my wrist and pushes me back 'til he's the one hovering over me. "I haven't forgotten your punishment. Go grab your hairbrush."

"Kaden—"

"Grab. Your. Hairbrush."

Before I even get up to retrieve it, I can already feel the soreness in my ass.

———

"You're walking funny," Imani says the next morning.

I've come through the door of Strictly Pleasures. Imani's on a step stool in front of two sex dolls, dressing them up in the latest shipment of BDSM gear. She takes one look at the limp in my walk and raises an eyebrow.

"Don't ask."

"The sexy Russian doctor again? Remember when I said you needed to fuck him? I didn't mean every hour of every night. Give your coochie a break."

"Tell Kaden that. And I'm pretty sure he wants to... try

the *other* hole soon. He keeps hinting at it. Last night he put a thumb up there."

Imani climbs down from the ladder, giving me her rapt attention. "You going to let him?"

"If it's a punishment—"

"It's always the ones you least expect. I would've never guessed Dr. Prim and Proper is into rough sex."

"I've never been... back there..."

"Easy. Just prepare properly first," she says with a shrug. She walks me down the aisle carrying a vast selection of lube. "It's best if you ease into it over time. Start off slow. Always make sure you're using lube. The last thing you want is a tear. How big is he?"

"Big."

"Bigger than Grady?"

I snort. "Is that a serious question? Bigger *and* thicker."

"Then he'll definitely need to take it slow. Have him eat you out first. Make him work for it."

"Thanks for letting me know what you're into."

A mischievous smirk spreads onto Imani's face. "You know I don't have a fuck buddy right now. But when I do... you best believe he's not getting any cookie 'til he's worked his ass off for it. I expect to come *every* time. Damn sure if he's getting to stick it back there."

"That's the thing. Kaden makes me come. Several times. 'Til this happens." I gesture at my stiff walk as we move over to the shop counter.

Imani waves it off and advises me to use a cold compress on the outside of my panties.

"I never had this problem with Grady."

"That's because Grady had a pinky for a dick that left you unsatisfied." Imani folds her arms in defiance when I shoot her a look. "What?! He did! You told me yourself. You used to finish yourself off after he went to bed."

It's true...

"Grady's very... simple in bed. Almost always the same position. Almost always a few minutes, then we're done. It's routine."

"And Kaden?" Imani's brow arches again.

"Explosive. Terrifying sometimes."

"In a good or bad way?"

I think for a second. "Both."

"So you might actually be done with Grady for real this time."

"He's blocked and hasn't dared come by the Velvet Piano again."

"FYI, he's still keeping tabs. He's stopped by here twice asking about you." Imani senses my dread and then rushes to clarify that she's told him nothing.

We grab coffee from the local Java King when her break time comes, and then go our separate ways. She has to return to Strictly Pleasures. I have more job hunting to do.

Since my audition with Fyodor turned out to be a pervy disaster, I'm back to square one. Searching endlessly for a decent enough job that can supplement the income I used to earn writing obituaries at the *Easton Times*.

The Velvet Piano so far isn't enough to tide me over.

I stop outside a local bakery and check myself out in the glass window. Today I dressed somewhat conservatively in a crop top sweater and high waisted pants. In twenty minutes, I'll be interviewing for a receptionist position at the dental office down the street.

"Lyra Hendrix?"

I drag my gaze away from the bakery shop window and follow the sound.

Two people have walked up to me. One a White man. The other a Black woman. Neither familiar faces.

The man has short, spiky hair that looks freshly cut. He's

sporting the usual middle-aged belly that's the result of one too many beers. In contrast, the woman at his side is tall, toned, and athletic, with box braids twisted into a large bun at the back of her head.

I take a cautious step back at their hard stares. "How do you know my name?"

The man flashes a badge. "We were hoping we could speak to you for a moment. We tried to reach out to your home of record, but we weren't able to reach you. I'm Detective Maloney and this is my partner, Detective Laurent. If you don't mind, we'd like to ask you a few questions in relation to Maximillion Keys's murder."

22. KADEN
KILL FOR YOUR LOVE - LABRINTH

A quarter past seven in the evening, there's a knock on my door. I'm at my minibar prepping the drinks. I'm unsurprised by the knock, though I allow a moment to pass before I make my way over to answer.

With a kitchen towel in hand, I come up to the door and draw it open. "I figured that would be you. Thanks for coming by."

Fyodor Kreed inclines his head in a stiff nod and then steps past the threshold in his argyle sweater and slacks. Rarely one to wear emotion on his sleeve, his countenance rivals mine. He's composed and detached no matter the situation.

"We could have met anywhere," he answers. He wanders the broad, open space of my penthouse with arms folded behind his back.

"That's true. However, I'm not fond of paying upwards of a hundred dollars for drinks at places like the Mint Room. I can make better cocktails at home."

"Vodka is good."

"Amusing coincidence. I was in the middle of making a martini when you knocked. Would you like one?"

Fyodor gives an indifferent sweep of his head. I motion for him to have a seat on my sectional.

"Why did you want to meet?" he asks, settling down as suggested. His arm curls along the back of the sofa and he peers out of one of my many glass walls. The city below has begun to twinkle with nocturnal light. "If this is about that audition, that girl you sent me was no good."

"Is that so?"

"She has stubby fingers. No proper posture. She does not understand how to be poised. I cannot work with such an amateur, regardless of your recommendation."

"I understand." I stroll out from behind the minibar counter and deliver him his martini.

Fyodor accepts, casting a scrutinizing look from under his heavy brow. He dons his suspicion like an invisible cloak. Though it eludes human touch, it lurks as an aura which surrounds him.

He brings the martini glass to his lips but doesn't sip.

I pretend not to notice as I take my seat across from him. "I apologize for sending her. You're right that she's an amateur. I made her a promise and I had to deliver."

"That girl... she was the girl from the recent Midnight Society party. The girl on the stage, yes?"

A stiff splint forms in the side of my neck. I keep my expression vague. "She was at the party, yes."

"I believed so. I recognized her. You have hired her?"

"Not exactly."

"She rebuffed me. I was very polite about it. It was very foolish of her. I can make her a big name in my business."

"You said she was no good."

He shrugs. "Good is... how is it said? Good is *relative*."

I pluck my martini glass off the end table and swallow half of it. It's the best course of action at the moment. Cracks in my facade have begun to form—a violent pulse throbs in my veins and the monster usually buried so deep, claws at my insides.

Demanding to be set free. Demanding to be *unleashed*.

Fyodor is clueless as he sits and stares out my penthouse window. He doesn't notice how the man a few feet away has gradually begun to transform. His earlier suspicion has been assuaged while my true colors bleed through.

My mask has slipped away. I'm no longer a man. The creature I become is something else entirely.

I rise up from my seat and carry my empty martini glass to the minibar.

"So why is it you asked me to meet you?" Fyodor ponders aloud. He's still yet to finish his martini. His sips are small and reserved. "Is this about your father's interest in the opera house? I have heard things. That he is interested in investing."

"Perhaps."

I don't bother fixing a second drink. I unbutton the cuffs of my dress shirt and push both sleeves up to my elbows.

"We would potentially entertain that. He is a big name in the industry. Many would welcome his return," Fyodor says, stroking his overgrown mustache. "It would make sense considering much of our audience are also members and admirers of him."

He goes on discussing the idea of a partnership. I have long ago stopped responding. I disappear down the hall and reappear a few seconds later.

"You should set up a meeting. Your father, yourself, and myself. We can discuss this more. As for me, I must go. I have other plans." Fyodor checks the gold pocket watch he carries with him and then moves to get up. His eyes lift at the same time I present my surprise.

He barely has a chance to attempt an escape. He tries to dodge the inevitable, but it's far too late and I'm far too quick.

"I'm afraid you're not going anywhere."

I swing the meat cleaver as though I'm wielding a sword on the battlefield. In the zero point five seconds it takes for the blunt, deadly blade to make contact, Fyodor's face freezes with terror. His eyes bulge in their sockets, and his mouth opens in a soundless scream.

The meat cleaver connects with his brow. It's a clean strike. The blade slices into him and he tips backward. He lands with a resounding thud. I've let go of the handle and allowed gravity to take its course. The cleaver sticks out of his head. Blood drips from the split in his skull.

It decorates my five hundred thousand dollar, black marble tiles.

I stand over him and admire the sight—yet another most morbid art piece I've created.

Fyodor twitches. He's no longer all the way alive, however, he's not all the way dead either.

Yet.

"I hate to do this to you," I say, reaching forward. I wrestle the blade from where it's lodged deep in his skull. Once removed, I'm given unobstructed access to his gaping wound. The spongy inside of Fyodor's head. "Except I don't hate this at all. You see, you had one use to me—evaluate Lyra Hendrix's pianist abilities and then offer her employment. You were not tasked to be the decrepit perverted fool you turned out to be. In which case, you are the perfect why to satisfy my urge."

I set down the bloody cleaver and then grab him by the ankles.

Fyodor babbles out the only simple word he's capable of. He's partially conscious, partially out. His lids shut half of the way, the whites of his eyes can still be seen.

"Help... help..."

"There will be no help coming," I answer, dragging him across the floor of my living room. "We're only getting started.

I'm not sure yet what I want to do with you. Rest assured, it won't be anything pleasant."

Fyodor's limp body slides along my expensive flooring and creates a gruesome trail of blood from start to finish. I drag him until we reach the door next to the laundry room; the door that leads to my *real* dungeon a floor below.

A different kind of playroom where I usually take my prey.

When Lyra went wandering my penthouse, I wasn't angry because she wound up in the laundry room and discovered a bloody shirt in the hamper. Though that is what I led her to believe. I was angry because she was dangerously close to discovering this room instead.

Using my back to prop the door open, I grip Fyodor by the ankles and then heft him inside. Once he crosses over, the next time he comes out, he'll be in pieces.

I work hours into the night before I take a break from my project. After a steamy shower and change into clean clothes, I walk out into my living room and discover my phone blinking with notifications.

Lyra's texted me. Playful messages that I'm sure she'd like me to respond to.

The first one is simple enough, sent over an hour ago.

> thinking about u 😊

I scroll down to the second message. She's sent a suggestive photo of herself in sheer lingerie that teases her nipples and pussy as she lays in bed and holds her phone up to the mirror on the wall.

The photo is erotic and enticing. The front of my pants feel tighter within seconds.

However, I find the gesture unnecessary.

Lyra, being a Gen Z young woman of her time, believes she must send me these types of photos to keep my interest. The photos are teasing and provocative, and though I am always aroused by the image of her delectable body, I'd prefer she stop.

I'd prefer if she refrain from taking these types of photos altogether.

They draw my thoughts to her Cyber Fans account. Jealousy burns through me when I wonder how many other men she's sent these photos to...

Her Cyber Fans account is an unspoken matter of contempt between us. I've yet to raise the issue, briefly touching on it when I inquired about her leather cat mask. She had tensed up, uncomfortable by my asking, and then changed the subject.

Lyra doesn't know it yet. But she will delete her Cyber Fans account. She will never send another salacious photo to a strange man over the internet again.

A matter I will soon address in my own way.

I text her back a message that's short and to the point.

> I don't need a photo to want to fuck you. I already do.

She replies with a blush smiley emoji. I'll see her tomorrow, and tomorrow I'll make sure not only is she satisfied, more importantly, I am.

With her punishment. With our understanding.

With everything which needs to be addressed.

———

The only individuals I encounter earlier than five in the morning are night shift workers, habitual runners, drunk and strung out partiers, and the occasional early bird employee heading prematurely into the office.

The next morning, as I exit my penthouse building dressed more casually than I usually do in a hoodie and jeans, I don't make it far without noticing something peculiar.

I'm supposed to be on my way across town to the storage locker of supplies I keep. However, as I step onto the sidewalk and head toward the ride share I've ordered (I never take my own vehicle there), I realize I'm not alone.

Across the otherwise slumbering street is an Oldsmobile. Several decades old. Bronze in color. A man seated in the front seat.

He may believe he's being discreet, parked a few buildings down from mine, but I know exactly who he is upon first glance—*what* he is the moment I see him.

I finish my walk up to my ride share car and slide into the backseat.

"Drop off request is for the storage garages on Oakwood Way. Is that still where you're going?" my driver asks from the front seat.

I chance another glance at the police detective watching me from his Oldsmobile and then shake my head.

"Not anymore," I answer. "There's been a change in plans."

23. Lyra
Do You Really Want to Hurt Me? -
Nessa Barrett

Detectives Maloney and Laurent sit me down at Mama's. It's the location I suggested when they came up to me on the street and asked if they could have a word. My job interview at the dental office is no longer on my mind. Both detectives give off a no nonsense vibe that puts me on edge.

We each order coffee and then ask Mama for more time on placing food orders.

"Thank you for agreeing to sit down with us, Ms. Hendrix," says Detective Laurent.

"Sure... I guess. I'm still unclear what this is about?"

"You're familiar with the investigation into Maximillion Keys's murder?"

"Somewhat. I've heard about it at work and in the media."

"And that's all?"

"I didn't know Maximillion well..." I sit with a belly of rippling nerves and stare across the booth table at them.

Detective Maloney has taken to pouring generous amounts of sugar into his coffee. His partner is the opposite— Detective Laurent is razor-focused on me. Her wide-set carob-colored eyes rake over me in quiet, observant study. She's the type to pick up on the most trivial detail.

"According to our records," Maloney says, "you recently worked with him at the Velvet Piano."

"So have the other two dozen people on staff."

"We'll speak to them at a later date. Did Mr. Keys ever mention any issues he was having? Any people he had a contentious relationship with?"

The three of us enter a staring contest. The detectives stare at me in wait for my answer. I stare back trying to sort out where this is going and what the purpose is.

I settle on being upfront and confrontational.

"You already know. Which is why you're asking me. It's no secret Maximillion and I didn't get along well."

Maloney withdraws his phone from the pocket of his shirt and logs some notes. Laurent picks up where his question left off.

"We are aware there was tension between the two of you. But we would like to know if there was anyone else that you know of who he didn't get along with? Any other coworkers? Anyone in his personal life? Any aggressive customers?"

I shake my head. "I'm telling you. I didn't know him well..."

"An eyewitness has come forward," Laurent presses. She slides a photo across the table. "Can you tell us what this was about?"

My gaze drops to the photograph and my nerves go from bad to worse. They intensify into a shaky, nauseous feeling.

I stammer trying to answer.

Detective Laurent has shown me a candid security camera still of myself, Kaden, and Grady at the Velvet Piano. In the photograph, Kaden and Grady glare ominously at each other. I'm in the middle, looking stressed out and confused with my arms up to separate them.

"Uhh... yes," I answer. "Someone was bothering me. So someone else stepped in."

"Can you provide specific names, Ms. Hendrix?"

"What's going on?" I ask. "Am I in trouble? Or either of them? It'd be nice if you provided some context for a change."

"Please just answer the question. This is an active police investi—"

"No thanks. I'd rather not be involved. Enjoy your breakfast, detectives. Order the pancakes. They're amazing. Excuse me."

I flee Mama's diner like it's become a crime scene. Maybe not the best move in the eyes of two police detectives, but I don't give a damn. I didn't agree to become a part of their investigation.

Why would they show me a photo of Kaden's confrontation with Grady? Do they suspect one of them was involved in Maximillion's murder? As far as I know, Kaden and Grady had never met Maximillion; they didn't even know who he was...

I have my answer once I'm riding the escalator off the subway platform and entering the street above. I'm within a block of my apartment building when Grady shows up from around a corner and falls into step beside me.

"You are so fucked up," he scolds. "I'd never do to you what you're doing to me."

"Even if that made sense, I wouldn't care what you have to say. How many times do I have to tell you it's over?"

"Just like that? Ten years of friendship?"

I stare straight ahead and keep walking. He remains at my side and pierces me with a glare. His frustration surrounds me. It's in the heat he's giving off, etched into the tone of his voice, and packed into every bitter step he takes.

My hand slips into my crossbody purse and my fingers wrap around my pepper spray. Grady has never put his hands on me. But he's also never been this deep in his addiction and spiraling this much out of control.

I'll do what I have to do to defend myself.

"Ly," he croaks as we come up on my building. "Will you just slow up? I get it. I've been a screw up. I'm no good. I drag you down. But can't you at least... can't you still talk to me?"

I stop and exhale a sigh, meeting his eyes for the first time. "Every time we try that, it doesn't work. Not anymore, Grady. We're oil and water."

"And you and that dickhead you're dating aren't?! Yeah, I know *ALL* about him! That's the real reason you're cutting me off. You're moving on to somebody rich and fancy and forgetting where you come from! Now that you've used me and pretended to give a shit, you're onto the next one!"

"Fuck off," I growl, my temper emerging. I shove past him and march toward my building.

Grady rushes to follow. The thud of his footsteps sound from behind me.

"I have pepper spray! Come closer and I'm using it."

"Does he really know about you, Ly? Does he know how fucked up you are? I bet he thinks you're some sweet little princess and not the selfish bitch you are! Probably doesn't even know you con men out of money on that Cyber Fans account of yours."

I whip around in a fresh dose of anger. "Stay the fuck away from me!"

"Yeah, that's right. You think this doctor will be your come up. You think you can fool him the way you fooled me. Just remember who knows all the ways you're damaged goods!"

For the briefest second, I'm about to hit him with an equally spiteful low blow, then my temper disappears. Realization pours over me, and I take a step back.

"It was you. You're the informant. You told the detectives

investigating Maximillion's murder that Kaden was starting fights that night?"

Satisfaction shines on Grady's face. "Mr. Doctor's not so perfect, Ly. I'm gonna prove it. Then you're gonna come crying back to me. Like your crazy ass always does. You're such a fucking mess. This time I'm going to make you really grovel for it."

"Stay away from me—stay away from him!" I growl in defense mode, my hand clenched around my pepper spray. I leave him alone on the sidewalk, slamming shut the door leading into my building.

Grady has some fucking audacity. He has some nerve dragging Kaden and I into a *murder* investigation. All out of spite.

But Grady's underestimating me. If he refuses to leave us alone, he'll leave me no choice. I'll have to *make* him.

———

"Hello? Kaden?" I tap my knuckles against the ajar door. I cautiously step into his penthouse and then stop to survey the scene.

His penthouse looks as refined and sterile as usual, like no one *truly* lives here. Crumbs and lint and other signs of imperfection don't exist in Kaden's private abode. The stainless steel appliances in the kitchen shine, and there isn't a smudge to be found on any of the almost 360-degree windows.

He invited me over this evening. But didn't pick me up or greet me at the door.

It's been a couple days since we've seen each other. The most time we've spent apart since we started dating.

He said he's busy with patients, and I've been preoccupied with job interviews and shifts at the Velvet Piano.

Did he forget he invited me over? If so, why would his door be open?

"Kaden?" I call out. My hand gravitates toward my purse to grab my phone and give him a call.

He interrupts me before I can. It echoes from down the hall. "In the playroom."

Though he doesn't say it, I understand what he wants—I'm supposed to join him. I draw a deep breath and then head down the hall. He's requested I bring my leather cat mask with me. He's also yet to finish punishing me from the cookie incident.

My pussy throbs at the thought.

I should be more cautious. Maybe consider if Kaden and I are compatible enough for a long-term relationship. But I find myself unable to even pretend I care the second I'm in his presence. Our chemistry is too hot and the sex too explosive.

He's right when he said I've never been fucked so good.

I've grown addicted to the sex... *and* the punishments.

As I venture down the hall, I'm practically drooling as I imagine what could be next.

"Shut the door."

I do as he says and pull the door closed behind me.

Kaden's standing by the play bench with his arms folded behind his back. He's dressed in his usual uniform—dark pants and a crisp, white buttoned shirt. His head inclines in a gesture at my clothes.

"Strip to your bra and panties."

I obey without question. My purse thumps on the floor as I let go of it and then kick off my sandals. I'm wearing a dress that I easily pull over my head. It crumples to the floor next to my purse. I stand before him only in my panties.

"No bra," I say.

If he enjoys the view, he gives nothing away. He remains composed and issues his next command.

"Where is the mask?"

"In my purse."

"Put it on."

I bend at the waist to pick up my purse and dig the mask out. Kaden's asked about the mask once before. I'd managed to avoid giving him a real answer.

Something tells me he'll be forcing the answer out of me today.

My hands tremble from the thrill and fear that racks through my body. I attach the leather feline mask and then wait for my next order.

"Come here."

I go to him. He cups my chin and plants a kiss on my mouth. He draws away just enough to speak but still close enough that our faces are almost touching.

"You have no idea what you're in store for," he warns. His breath tickles my lips. "Tell me what you've done wrong."

I think fast. "The cookie. It had weed in it."

He begins circling me like a shark in bloody waters. I stand still and feel my heart palpitate.

"What else?"

"Um..." I frown, thinking through the catalogue of our relationship. "I... I went wandering that one time."

"You've been punished for that. What else?"

"I... I don't know."

"What are you wearing?"

"My panties. Oh... *oh*. The mask."

"Do you remember that night in your room?"

"When you asked me about it?"

"Were you truthful in your answer?"

He makes another round circling me. I try to keep him in my line of sight, though it's impossible once he slips behind me.

My fingers connect as I fidget and pick at my nail bed. "No... technically, not."

"What does that mean?"

"I said it was a Halloween costume."

"That's right," he says, coming in front of me. He opens the palm of his hand. Resting in the center are a new pair of nipple clamps.

These look vicious. The teeth sharper, the metal encasing like its own cage. The chain unfurls until it slips over the edge of his palm and dangles midair. This one is several inches longer than the ones we've used in the past.

I gulp staring at them. "I'm sure I know where this is going."

"I'm sure you don't. Tell me what the mask is for."

"Kaden..."

"I won't be asking again."

I breathe out slowly, meeting his dark, cold eyes.

The jig is up. Time to tell him about my side gig.

"Sometimes... sometimes I do cam shows. I have some subscribers that pay to watch me."

"Where?"

"Cyber Fans."

"What's your name?"

"KuteKitty96... but I'm guessing you already know that."

Kaden shifts until he's behind me again. His hands grip my hips, and he presses himself against me. "I did. I saw one of your shows."

My eyes widen. I haven't done a show in over a week. How long has he known?

Kaden knew who I was before we ever bumped into each other at Urban Greenery. He knew who I was almost from the moment he saw me on stage. Not long after his crazy fuck buddy Celeste confronted me at the Midnight Society party.

"W-what did you think?" I stutter out.

He squeezes my hip and pulls me tighter against him. He's hard. His large erection pokes into my tailbone.

"I think no other man should get to see your beautiful tits

except me," he growls. His fingers tweak my nipples and I whine in response. He opens the first clamp and scrapes the teeth along my achy nipple. I hold in my next breath and wait for him to let it close.

But Kaden's all about taking his time. He drags the teeth across my hardening nipple, circling my wider areola. My eyes close and I focus on the scraping sensation. Though fear dwells inside me, a greater impulse of desire overtakes it.

Desire that grows and makes me crave whatever he has planned next.

Close it. Clamp it. Do it.

I almost ask. My lips part to beg, though I bite my tongue.

Kaden must sense my anticipation. He kisses my cheek and then says, "You're not supposed to enjoy this, little lamb. It is a punishment for a reason. This *will* hurt."

I gasp as he shuts the clamp on my first nipple. The intense pressure and sharp squeeze are immediate. I'm not yet oriented when he does the second. It clamps down on my other nipple and I sway in place at the sudden shock of pain.

Kaden's there to hold me steady. He keeps me where I am, a pillar in the flesh. I've lost my breath thanks to the pain throbbing from my breasts. My lungs shudder and I gasp trying to intake air, though it seems I can only focus on the sharp teeth squeezing my nipples.

It's only the beginning.

Kaden's hands sensuously cup my breasts. He gives them a gentle knead, which contrasts cruelly with the clamps, and then he grabs the long chain that dangles in between.

"Now, for the fun part," he whispers against my cheek. "Open your mouth."

I do what he says, but not without first making a whine noise.

He smacks my ass in quick reprimand. "Did I tell you to open your mouth, or did I tell you to whine like a little brat?"

I shake my head, my lips parted.

He pushes a gag into my mouth. It takes me by surprise; I didn't even notice he was holding one. He must've had it behind his back along with the clamps. The ball gag is quickly secured by a leather band and then the long chain hooked onto a loop in the front.

If I move the wrong way, even push on the ball gag too much, the chain will pull, and the teeth of the clamps will sink deeper into my nipples.

My eyes talk for me. I glare at him as saliva quickly gathers in my mouth.

He smirks and thumbs my bottom lip. "Don't be mad, little lamb. You have yourself to blame for this. Isn't that correct?"

I narrow my eyes, though I nod. My breasts ache from the bite of the clamps and my tongue struggles not to push up against the gag.

"Good girl. But your punishment's not over. Take off your panties. Get on the bench. Hands and knees."

Fuck!

An order to get on the bench is never a good sign.

The leather play bench has become a pain in my ass— *literally.*

Something tells me Kaden's about to top himself. He stands back and watches as I fold and bend my limbs into proper position.

I groan around the ball gag. The way my breasts hang only exaggerates the intense pressure of the clamps.

Yet I know I'm wet. I can feel how moist I am, waiting for him to decide what to do next. Once I'm in the position he wants me in, he walks around to the back of the bench. My heart beats faster at the thought that I'm completely on display for him.

It wouldn't surprise me if I turned around and saw his

large erection tented in his pants. I already felt him hardening earlier...

"Do you want me to spank you, little lamb?"

I mumble around the gag. My tongue accidentally pushes against it at the wrong angle, and I trigger a chain reaction—the chain tugs and then the clamps increase their clench around my hard, sensitive nipples.

The throbbing pain begins radiating through me. It mixes with the burning desire that's consuming me and becomes its own kind of sensation. Above simple pain, above simple pleasure. I close my eyes and shudder at how aroused I am.

"I couldn't understand you."

Kaden swats the palm of his hand to my backside. I squeak in sheer surprise. My hands almost slip and give up my position.

His hands knead my flesh. He massages my ass cheeks with his powerful grip and smooths the palm of his hands over the curve of my backside. My eyes slip closed from behind my leather feline mask, and I moan around the ball gag.

I don't even care that it causes more tension on my nipples.

Kaden's hands are on my body. He's touching me all over and it's worth the pain.

His fingers slip under me and find my clit. He rubs me as though in reward.

I mewl from around the gag and push my hips back. I grind against his hand in hopes for more.

His fingers disappear and the palm of his hand returns in a swift smack to my ass.

"Did you really think I'd get you off so soon, little lamb? You haven't been sufficiently punished yet. Here I am, thinking I am dating a woman who is a simple pianist. Yet there you are, logging into your alter ego and flirting with pathetic men on the internet. Do you think that's fair?"

Fuck!

I shake my head and my nipples twinge in pain at the sudden movement.

"I have to be honest," Kaden goes on from behind me. I can't see him, and that scares me more than anything. "Your little cam show was sexy. Very provocative. I can see why men would subscribe. Why do you do it? Is it the male attention?"

I give another side-to-side shake of my head. Nipple pain be damned.

"Is it the exhibitionism?"

Another shake of my head and another twinge of pain in my breasts. I'm dripping spittle at this point. I've pooled so much in my mouth that it's dripped from my chin onto the leather bench below.

Kaden doesn't seem to notice nor care.

"I know," he says coolly. "It's the money. Is that right, little lamb?"

The muffled sound that escapes me is pitiful. It's a mewl that's supposed to communicate *yes*. I had few other choices.

I sense he understands. He just doesn't give a damn.

He smacks another hard hand to my ass. "If you need money, you tell me. It is yours. Under no circumstances are you to ever entertain those men or host another cam show. You are not to entertain any other man but me. Do you understand?"

I shout a desperate, smothered *yes*.

He remains unconvinced.

"I don't think you do. But you will."

A warm, slippery liquid pours over my backside. The feel is jarring at first, then pleasurable as Kaden's hands rub the liquid into my skin. My body arches as he spreads my cheeks and spreads the slippery substance along my rear entrance.

He tests my tight, puckered hole with his thumb.

I produce a startled moan from around my gag. I've

forgotten about the drool, forgotten about the pinch of my nipples. I'm acutely aware of everything going on with my ass.

Something cool and sleek glides over the underside of my thighs and then the curves of my cheeks. I'm certain I can guess what it is even without looking.

"Breathe. Relax your body. Don't fight it."

Those are Kaden's only words before he does it—he begins penetrating me. I gasp at the feel of the plug prodding against my rear entrance. It feels unlike anything I've ever felt before. The strangest intrusion invading my body as he carefully slicks the toy in.

My knees dig into the leather cushion. My spine arches. I've taken to pushing my tongue against the ball gag and causing the chain to pull.

There's resistance. My tiny, puckered hole doesn't want to open up and let more of the plug in. More lube is drizzled onto my ass and the plug, making both slicker. Kaden's patient, applying more pressure against the resistance he encounters.

I'm breathing hard. I've closed my eyes and tried to focus on the other sensations of my body. But it's impossible. I can only focus on what's happening with my ass. My hole stretching around the circumference of the plug can't be put into words.

It doesn't hurt so much as it feels... uncomfortable. The plug brings me a fullness that feels... unnatural.

Kaden persists. He slicks more of it into me 'til it's seated inside. The handle rests between my ass cheeks.

I take a moment to grow used to the heavy feeling. The fullness and the tight fit of an object inserted back there.

It doesn't occur to me that Kaden's studying my reaction. He runs a caressing hand along my naked body and asks me how it feels.

The ball gag disguises my answer, but I'm sure he understands.

Full. Very fucking full.

"Good," he says. "And *now* you'll be spanked."

A throaty noise of protest rises out of me a second before the first spank. Kaden stands behind me and brings down the wooden paddle I've already grown quite familiar with. The wooden surface collides with the softness of my ass cheek.

Pain smarts across my skin. It fires off from my backside, my breasts, the hole that's been plugged.

It's too fucking much.

I drool and shake on the bench and pant for air.

Kaden brings the paddle down on me several times. So many times, I lose count. I have no choice but to surrender to what's being done to me—the cruel clamps squeezing my nipples and the ball gagging me. My pussy throbs in reaction to the plug in my other hole, and my ass stings from the punishing swats of the wooden paddle.

Soon I'm crying out in tune with his movements. I'm gripping the bench and groaning as he brings down the paddle again and then again.

I can come. If I just focus, just concentrate on the tiny kernel of pleasure in the middle of the bursts of pain, I can come.

I close my eyes and focus on how swollen and sensitive my pussy feels. The distant wave of pleasure building in the deepest part of me.

Kaden tosses aside the paddle and spreads my rear cheeks. He teases me with the plug, twisting and twirling it deeper to more moans from me.

Then he kneels down and buries his face in my ass.

Maybe the most surprising turn of events yet. My whole body jerks in my hands and knees position, and my pelvis tilts. My ass lifts to meet him halfway.

Kaden's tongue works magic. It slides along my puckered, stretched hole. Wet and warm, it feels so good it almost chases away the unnatural fullness from the plug.

He moves on. His lips and his teeth nip and nibble at my supple cheeks. His touches, kisses, bites, are worship.

Worship now that he's punished me.

I rest on my hands and knees and savor the wave of pleasure that's unleashed.

His mouth makes it to my pussy, and I'm a goner.

He laps and laves at my pussy from behind. His hands hold my cheeks apart. His tongue flicks my throbbing clit and then pushes inside me.

"Mmmm... mmmm!" I moan from around the gag.

My whole body trembles. I can barely keep upright as his talented mouth tastes me and has my pussy convulsing around his tongue. He squeezes my ass and, if possible, pushes it deeper. He pushes the *plug* deeper.

Pushes me over the edge.

I'm driven to the absolute brink. My body gives in. My pussy erupts. I scream around the ball gag and bow my spine with such an arch that I rip off my own clamps. Blood rushes from my nipples in a burst of pain. A wave of pleasure crashes over the rest of me.

It's dizzying and disorienting. The shake in my limbs becomes too much and I go numb. I collapse on the bench, melting like I've been burned in a flame of hot passion. My arms and legs drape over either side of the bench and my cheek rests against the leather cushion.

All sound is obsolete except for my racing heart.

I'm delirious and out of it even as I come down from my orgasm.

I think... Kaden broke me.

It's a dazed thought in my mind. Vaguely, I'm aware he's cleaning up the scene. He's put the paddle and clamps away.

He eases the plug out of me with a slick pop. His arms enclose around me, and he scoops me up against his chest.

I can do nothing but snuggle closer, feeling almost like I've atoned for my sins.

"How do you feel, little lamb?"

"Exhausted."

He smirks. "Then you've learned your lesson."

24. Kaden
You've Seen the Butcher - Deftones

"You have the distinction of being the only person besides me to sleep in my bed."

Lyra aims a sleepy smile at me. "So you've told me. Don't I feel special?"

You should, little lamb. I was supposed to end you weeks ago.

I prop myself up on my elbow and reach for her left arm. The arm she has her piano keys tattooed on. We both watch my fingers stroke the ink on her dark brown skin.

"What happened with your family, Lyra?" I ask. "You haven't spoken with them in years."

She stills under my touch, immediate tension in her body. "How would you know?"

"You didn't give any details, but you've heavily implied that was the case. Do you not remember?"

"I'm confused why you care."

My fingers trace the outline of one of the keys. "You've said yourself we're in a relationship. You're not fucking anyone else. Neither am I. It stands to reason we would get to know each other better."

Her eyes shrink into a glare. "Then tell me about yours."

"Mine?"

"Your family. You've told me even less. You said you're an only child, but everyone has a family somewhere. Tell me about your father. Tell me about your mother."

I refrain from gritting my teeth, though I'm tempted to do so. Fortunately, I don't give in, remaining cool and indifferent on the outside. I stroke my fingers along the delicate inside of her arm and indulge her request.

"Alright. Though there really isn't much to tell—the Raskova line has all but died from existence. I was born in Saint Petersburg."

"Russia?"

I nod. "That's right. Though we moved to the States at a very young age. I was two... perhaps three. I do not remember much of anything about my birthplace."

"Why did you move? You've always been wealthy, haven't you?"

"My family has been for generations, yes. We have lineage connected to past Russian monarchies. My great grandfather was an advisor to the last czar. He was executed right alongside him at the start of the twentieth century."

She flinches, then scoots her naked body closer to mine. "That's a gruesome history."

"Gruesome would describe my entire family. Anyway, to answer your question, yes. The Raskova name has always carried prestige and wealth along with it. My parents had an affinity for music, like your mother. But my father was also a prominent businessman. He moved to America to expand his business prospects. He felt he would have more opportunity to flourish here rather than deal with the political complications in Russia at the time."

"And you lived in Easton your entire life?"

"No, we lived on a large estate in the Caplan Hills. Secluded almost entirely from civilization to the point it took hours to get there. Including a flight. Our home resembled a castle—my father had it built that way."

"That's... very remote."

"My father is a very withdrawn man. I didn't attend school like most children. School was brought to me. The best tutors money could buy. There was a lot of pressure on me to excel academically. I took it as a challenge and rose to the occasion. Most of my days were spent with books. I had a very... lonely childhood."

She frowns. "That's relatable."

"I didn't mind," I clarify, my hand traveling. It leaves her arm and smooths a path along the curve of her hip. "In fact, I preferred it that way. Children annoyed me. Even when I was a child myself."

"And your mother?"

"As I said, she was a fan of music. She played herself. The violin."

"Is that where your appreciation for music comes from?"

"I began to play the violin because she was brilliant. I'm told my father fell in love with her when she played a violin rendition of Moon River for him."

"She passed away?"

"You could say that," I answer, acutely aware of the tautness in my muscles. I prefer not to think about this subject. "My father was having an affair. She was inconsolable, which led to her taking her own life. Some would say it was the broken heart that did her in."

...that's the clean version.

Lyra studies me for a moment. Her gaze indistinct, though curiosity lives deep in the swirl of earthy brown. I decide to circle back to her.

"You said my childhood being lonely was relatable. Was that the case for yours?"

"I've told you about the piano and how strict my mother was."

"Yes, but surely a girl like you had friends. And your sister."

"No," she answers flatly.

Then she doesn't expound. That's the extent of what she offers.

I arch a brow and pretend I'm still content caressing her naked curves. It seems there is some sort of story she refuses to divulge; I couldn't find much on her family or childhood. Only her grandma.

A seventy-seven-year-old woman named Opal who lives in a fixed income apartment in Old Northam. I might have to explore that lead.

Lyra refuses to budge otherwise.

I meant what I said when I told her I want to know everything about her. I intend on learning everything there is to know about Lyra Hendrix. No stone will remain unturned, no secret buried, or skeleton hidden in closets. My obsession has taken on a life of its own and demanded it of me.

That I fully understand the woman I have become maddeningly fascinated with before I make up my mind how to proceed.

I've stalled long enough. The Owner and the Midnight Society will force my hand any day now.

A decision will have to be made. Either I will go through with my original tasking and do what I promised I would—*end* Lyra—or I will spare her. In which case, I will have to get creative in devising a means for her survival.

However, the question remains: how will Lyra react to the unbridled, grim truth of the matter? How will she react when she learns why I've taken such an interest in her? When I tell her who I am... and *what* I am?

Will she be open to that reality? Will she be willing to

become a part of my dark, deadly world?

Lyra rolls onto her back and stares at the high ceiling in thought. "We're kind of similar when you think about it."

"Care to elaborate?"

"Both lonely kids. Both had a lot of pressure on us. Both had mothers with broken hearts."

Interesting...

"Who broke your mother's heart? Your father?"

"The man who ruined her life... and mine."

"That's quite a title to give someone."

She pushes herself up and crisscrosses her legs. "You want to talk about trust issues? There's a reason I don't let people in. What I saw... tore up my mother. It ruined her. I realized I didn't ever want to be in the same situation. You were confused by what I saw in a guy like Grady? Loyalty. Reliability. As fucked up and unstable as he is, he's a poison I know. Better than the ones I don't. Which is every other man out there."

"A known poison is hardly better than the unknown ones."

"Depends how you look at it," she answers with a shrug. Then she pins me with a stare that can be described as probing and unafraid. "Are you poison, Kaden? Am I going to wind up hurt? Are you going to ruin me?"

That remains a very real possibility, little lamb.

She doesn't realize how the question she's asked provides an answer to the questions I asked—can she handle my truth? Can she handle me?

The real me beneath the mask.

No. She's not strong enough. She's too weak, too gullible. An actual lamb.

I reach up and curl my hand along the side of her neck. The gesture convinces her to return to me. She shifts and lays back down at my side, halfway on my chest.

"I would never do anything you didn't expressly consent to," I say in a soothing tone. I stroke her back and hold her close. "The games we play are just that... games. You understand the difference, don't you?"

Lyra tilts her head back to look me in the eyes. There's a shine in hers. "Of course I do."

I kiss her on the mouth, *almost* feeling sorry for her.

———

I've taken a leave of absence. Horschman protests and threatens to cancel our partnership. He claims he can find another private physician to go into practice with. I tell him to go ahead and fuck himself.

I've never needed the money. I've never needed a stable career.

These are simply things I've done to preoccupy myself between my homicidal escapades.

It's all part of the carefully crafted veneer that I've built. The mask I wear to conceal what I really am from stupid people and society.

With my new abundance of free time, I decide on my next kill. It's time I eliminate Lyra's junkie ex that's begun sniffing around her again.

The loser doesn't realize I know he has; that I'm well aware how he's shown up outside her apartment building and raised his voice at her.

On three separate occasions, I've caught him following her to the Velvet Piano.

Lyra, being oblivious to her surroundings, doesn't know that he does.

It seems Grady has decided he'll simply stalk her if she won't otherwise give him the time of day. The spat they had outside her apartment building revealed he's aware she and I are dating. He must think I won't find out about his preoccupation with her.

What's even more amusing is he seems to think he can go to the authorities and drum up suspicion.

He's reported to the detectives investigating Maximillion's murder that I was angry and irate at the piano bar that night. They've even reached out to Lyra for more information. So far, his accusation is baseless and can't hold water.

Particularly considering I replaced the security footage they're looking for—footage of Maximillion's murder. It doesn't help that I've otherwise never spoken to Keys a day in my life.

In the eyes of the law, Grady looks and sounds like a delusional, drug-addled liar.

However, I cannot risk that he'll continue causing trouble. It's best to remove him from the equation altogether. Something I *meant* to do the night I ended Maximillion instead.

I begin putting the pieces together, sorting out when I'll capture him, what drug I'll give him to make him overdose, and where I'll dump his body to eventually be found.

I'm checking a local map of Stockman, one of the poorer neighborhoods in the city, when the spy app on my phone vibrates.

Lyra's walking home from one of her piano lessons. Grady's waiting for her. I listen in as he confronts her, and she demands he leave her alone or she'll get a restraining order.

"You wouldn't," he says.

"Try me! You're giving me no other choice. I've told you. Leave me the hell alone!"

"That guy is dangerous! You know what happened in his family, right? Has he ever told you, or lemme guess, Mr. Doctor hid that from you?"

"I don't care! Grady, get the fuck out of here, or I'm calling the cops!"

Lyra rushes up the stairs leading into her building. A second goes by where it seems like he's tempted to follow. He edges forward as if about to bound up the stairs after her, then he thinks better of it.

A thick pulse throbs in my neck. My gaze is hard and focused on my phone screen.

Their confrontations are escalating. Each time he becomes more aggressive, more intimidating.

Grady Williams is a dead man.

Tonight.

I switch apps. Instead of the spy app that records and tracks Lyra, I bring up the app I'm using for the cameras I've placed in her bedroom.

She slams shut the door, visibly furious from her confrontation with Grady. Her belongings get discarded on the floor as she shoots toward her desk. She grabs her laptop and then moves to sit on her bed. The second she's able to log on, her fingers fly on the keyboard.

My head tilts to the left in curiosity. "What are you looking up?"

I squint trying to read what's entered into the internet search box.

Raskova family St. Petersburg, Russia

She clicks go, chewing on her lip in wait. A cool sensation blows through me watching her scroll through the search results. She's following up on what Grady told her.

Lyra's investigating me.

A rare, though slight, grin briefly comes to my face. "So my little lamb really does believe it. That I am her poison."

25. LYRA
TIME IS RUNNING OUT - JPOLND

I t's hard to say what's more cause for concern. My lack of prospects at another job, or the fact that my ex friend/fuck buddy believes I'm unaware he's following me everywhere. To my job interviews. My shifts at the Velvet Piano. Even the smaller errands I run. Grady tags along in secret.

The problem is, he's not very discreet.

After a few days, he confronted me outside my apartment building again. I told him if he doesn't stop, I'll be forced to get a restraining order.

He's convinced I've intentionally dropped him in favor of Kaden. "Mr. Doctor" as he calls him. He's gone so far as to insinuate Kaden had something to do with Maximillion's death.

Imani thinks he's gotten too comfortable crossing lines and overstepping my boundaries. That he doesn't respect me when I tell him to back off.

As I make my way to my favorite spot at the cemetery, I can't help thinking she's right. Grady feels like he's known me for so long he doesn't have to take my word seriously. My fault for not putting my foot down sooner.

VEGA

    SIENNE VEGA

I'll have to do better at asserting myself. Something I've always struggled with doing.

The huge elm tree at the top of the grassy knoll welcomes me with long, leafy branches that might as well be open arms. I plop down into the grass and enjoy the view in front of me.

Rows upon rows upon rows of gravestones and the haunting stone monuments of angels that have chipped over time.

In the distance, the outline of big city buildings serves as a backdrop.

A soft sigh soughs out of me and I consider how to proceed.

It wasn't that long ago I came up here to write obituaries. I was broke and struggling, but my life was mundane and predictable. Between my gig at the *Easton Times*, the piano lessons I gave, and my Cyber Fans, I got by. I had enough for my meds *and* my weed. Grady was only an occasional lay, and I spent most of my free time chilling in my room.

So much has changed since then. I can barely register how things snowballed to this point.

Kaden's my boyfriend. I duel at the Velvet Piano. The police are investigating the murder of a former coworker and my drug-addicted ex is stalking me.

That doesn't touch on the other stuff that's happened, like Jael's disappearance and my failed audition at the opera house.

It's my next stop after an hour of deep-thinking on the grassy knoll. I bid farewell to the dead and reenter the world of the living.

Usually, I'd stop by Strictly Pleasures to visit Imani, but I skip that detour and head straight to the opera house. The brilliant domed structure encapsulates me with a bereft sense of longing. I stand outside the cascading steps like a lost puppy and stare up at the landmark.

Kaden has told me he'll help secure me another audition,

though I don't know how he'll pull it off. It can't possibly be with Fyodor. After you elbow a guy in the stomach, relations tend to sour.

I turn away from the building pondering the thought that maybe it's for the best. I hadn't earned my audition based on merit. It was a handout because Kaden was interested in me.

Jael's words from the night of the party at the Winchester float to mind.

Nobody gives a fuck about you playing the piano like some famous dead guy. All the talent in the world doesn't mean squat unless you've got the right connections? Get it?

If she were here, she'd tell me to stop overthinking it. Who helps me doesn't matter so long as I get my foot in the door.

My mother would feel differently—she'd accuse me of being a fraud. Nothing angered her more than someone who cheated their way to the top. Meanwhile, she struggled and toiled for decades, clutching her dulled saxophone she played with a reed that needed replacing.

You little stupid bitch! Why can't you just play like he teaches you to play? Why do you have to ruin everything?

I twitch at the sound of her screeching voice, then chase it away with a shake of my head. She's been invading my thoughts more recently; it doesn't help that Kaden's insisted upon asking about my family.

My hand comes up to my temple and I breathe through the throbbing discomfort in my head. I'm going almost two days off my meds. Another consequence of bringing in less income, which translates to another reminder I'm in no position to turn down any help from Kaden.

I step off the bottom step to the opera house as a pair of musicians do so too. They've come down the steps side by side with their instrument cases in hand. Judging by the slim size, they must play clarinet or flute.

"I can't believe he's missing."

"It's unlike him."

"You said no one's spoken to him in how long?"

"It's been over a week," answers a woman with a blonde bob cut. "Mrs. Kreed has reported it to the police. They're opening a missing persons investigation."

The stubby woman on the left clicks her tongue but says nothing else. The two carry on their way and their conversation fades out of earshot.

I can't bring myself to move. My body's paralyzed midstep as I stare after the female musicians disappearing down the street.

Shock rings through me and leaves me unable to function. I couldn't have heard what I think I did; I must've misunderstood what they were saying.

There's no way...

My feet slowly remember how to work. I take one step and then two before breaking out into what can be called a jogging walk. Everyone else on the sidewalk will have to move. I'm not slowing down.

Several people scold me with irritated looks as they get out of my way.

In a few short weeks, it seems disappearances and murders have become a regular occurrence in my life. Jael dropping off the face of the earth and Maximillion's murder were bad enough. But Fyodor missing too can't be a coincidence.

And then it hits me. I stop in the middle of the crosswalk to disgruntled noises from other pedestrians and a blare of a horn from a car trying to make a right on red.

My head turns left and right, searching him out. He hadn't followed me to the cemetery, and I hadn't seen him coming to the opera house either...

"Grady," I breathe, then I burst into a sprint the rest of the way through the crosswalk.

He doesn't answer his phone when I call. My texts meet

the same fate. I've had him on block for weeks now. Did he put me on block back?

I message Imani and ask her to reach out to him. By the time I'm getting off the subway and turning down the final block to my apartment building, I'm calling his aunt.

"He hasn't been home since him and Russ had that falling out. What's the matter?"

My heart beats hard in my chest but I thank his aunt anyway and hang up.

Grady's been following me for days. Today happens to be the first day he's nowhere to be found.

After Jael's disappearance. After Maximillion's murder. After I've just learned Fyodor has joined the list.

A common thread is emerging, and I can't unsee it.

The last time Grady and I spoke, we were arguing on the stoop to my apartment building. He demanded I look into Kaden. He said Kaden wasn't what he appeared to be. Though I was pissed with him, I'd logged onto my computer, and done some sleuthing online. Not the first time I dug into Kaden's background. I found nothing new.

But something's up.

Something that feels... off. Dark and sinister.

My stomach lurches as I rush up the steps to my apartment and I think about the bloody shirt in Kaden's hamper. His presence at the Midnight Society, and the interest he said he's had for me, which led him to tracking me down.

So many pieces of a puzzle begin to take shape and fit together.

And the picture that begins forming makes me dizzy.

My phone rings in my jean pocket. Kaden's calling.

I blow out a shaky breath and debate whether to answer. If I don't, he'll grow suspicious. I'll have to pretend nothing's up.

"He-hello," I stammer.

"Lyra," he says smoothly. "I'm surprised you answered so quickly."

I give off an unnatural laugh. "Why would you be?"

"You've been busy the past two days."

"Oh. Right. Job interviews."

"Land anything?"

"Um... no. None. Still looking."

"That's a shame. But I have a new connection I think might work. How about we discuss it tonight over dinner?"

The dizziness that's swept me up takes me for another spin. I lean against the wall in my apartment hall and then shake my head as if he can see me.

"Sorry. Tonight's... it's not good. I'm working an extra shift at the piano bar."

"Then how about I come see you? We can have a drink after you perform."

"No!" I answer quickly. "I mean... not a good idea. Erma's getting stricter about the employees having their friends taking up space. I'll call you tomorrow, okay?"

Kaden lets a second of loud silence tick by. "Alright. Good luck on your duel."

The moment we've hung up, I'm letting out a shaky breath, and fretting over what the hell I'm going to do.

26. LYRA
GUILTY OF LOVE - UNLOVED

"Help. I'm in deep shit."

Imani's in the middle of helping a customer. As I storm into the small adult shop, she spares me a quick glance before carrying on her conversation with the mousy woman in front of the handcuffs and restraints section.

That doesn't stop the mousy woman from noticing I'm in frantic need of her help. Nudging her round glasses up her nose, she points me out. "You can help her if you want. She seems to really need it."

Imani flashes a polite smile and assures the woman she can seek her out if she needs anymore help. I know I've pissed her off as she turns away from the customer and snaps at me to follow.

"You do remember I get paid off commissions, right? I had that lady right where I wanted her."

"I'm sorry. But... I didn't know where else to go. I still can't get a hold of Grady."

Imani arches her left brow. "So? Isn't that a good thing? He's been stalking you."

"He's been stalking me and now he's nowhere to be found."

"Ly, you're gonna have to be more specific. What the hell's the issue? I'm not seeing it. You've been wanting the guy to back off. It sounds like he finally has. You *should* be celebrating."

I grip her arm and then take another glimpse around us. The only other person in the shop is the mousy woman and she's admiring a pair of pink furry cuffs. I drop my voice a couple decibels anyway.

"You don't think it's weird that everyone is disappearing or dying off?"

"Everyone as in...?"

"Jael and Maximillion for starters. Then, I overheard that Fyodor Kreed, the guy who I auditioned with at the opera house, has been missing for over a week now!"

"And you can't get a hold of Grady," she says slowly.

"And he's been telling me that Kaden's not who he says he is."

"Wait... let me get this straight. You think Kaden's behind these things?" A perturbed expression blooms across Imani's face and she looks as horrified as I feel on the inside. "But there has to be some other reason you seem to think it's possible? I thought things with Kaden were going well."

"They are. It's just... I don't know... I've been feeling like something is off."

"You did say that."

"He was there the night at the Winchester, Imani. He knew who I was and intentionally bumped into me at Urban Greenery."

Her eyes double in size. "You've never mentioned that part before."

"There're moments where he seems... very... dark. As if

he's keeping some other part of himself hidden. I can't put it into words, but it's scary."

"Girl, what?! Why have you never mentioned this?"

"And then there's the bloody shirt I found in his hamper—"

"I've heard enough. We're calling the police." Imani fishes her iPhone from the pocket of her denim overalls and brings up her call app.

The mousy woman waves goodbye as she walks out the front door, oblivious to our panicked exchange.

"Have a good day!" Imani calls out, faking a smile and waving.

The second we're alone, she darts out from behind the sales counter and locks the door.

"Don't call the police," I say. "Not yet. I don't have any proof."

"Who needs proof? This guy sounds like a psycho. Let the cops get the proof and handle all the rest."

"But what if I'm being paranoid? What if Grady's just on another bender and everything else is a coincidence? He *is* a surgeon—so what if he had blood on his shirt?"

"Who are you trying to convince? Me or you? I'm calling."

"Not yet!" I exclaim, watching her finger hover over the '9' on the number pad. "Just give me a few more hours. Then we'll consider the police. Grady's aunt is supposed to call me back. She was going to reach out to other family to see if they've seen him."

"You like him," Imani says. The perturbed expression deepens on her face. "You *like* this guy, don't you? You're in denial and don't want it to be true."

"I do like him, and I don't want it to be true, but I'll do what I have to do. I shouldn't have come by asking for help. It's too soon when I have no proof."

Imani folds her arms. "You have twenty-four hours. If you

don't go to the authorities, I will. I'm not about to have my bestie join the missing persons list."

———

I promise Imani I'll keep her posted the moment I have an update. We embrace in a sisterly hug—rare considering neither of us are huggers—before I'm on my way.

Grady's aunt hasn't updated me. He's still nowhere to be found.

A few media outlets have begun reporting on Fyodor's disappearance. Other articles detail the latest in Maximillion's murder investigation.

On my way home, I sit in the subway car and scroll through what I find online. My trepidation manifests as a roiling ache in my belly. The findings go from bad to worse the more I search.

The night Maximillion disappeared, Kaden had been at the bar. He had gotten into a spat with Grady. As far as I know, he never encountered Maximillion. But, I had mentioned how overworked I was. I had told him how condescending Maximillion was.

Did he come back after the fact and get into an altercation with him?

Fyodor is a given. The guy harassed me and made a pass. I asked Kaden not to address it with him, but what if he did? He doesn't seem like the type to let slights go. He punishes me no matter how small the infraction. Is he this way with others too?

My spirit is so disturbed I don't notice Detective Maloney until he calls out my name.

"Ms. Hendrix, there you are. I was hoping I'd run into you."

I blink out of my dazed thoughts and stare up at the detective. He's coming down the stoop of my apartment building as if he's just dropped by and tried the door.

"Detective, I've already told you I don't know anything about Maximillion's personal life..."

...and I'm not sure of Kaden's involvement. Yet.

"I have a few more questions, if you don't mind answering them."

"I'm very busy right now. Maybe some other time."

He holds out a small card. "Here's my business card. It has my personal and work number on it. Detective Laurent's number is also on the bottom. Call either one of us the moment you're ready to talk."

For the second time this afternoon, I'm making a promise. The middle-aged detective doesn't hide the steely expression from his face as I accept the card and turn to go. He's plain as day in what he believes—I have some info on Maximillion's murder and the perpetrator that I'm not revealing.

My head hurts, making it impossible to think straight.

I escape into my apartment, tucking his business card into my purse. The lights are off and the afternoon's natural light streams through the open blinds in the window. The silence tells me Taviar's not home (he usually blasts his music when he's home working).

I cross into the kitchen to drink some water and take a dose of my meds.

I've been rationing them even more than usual to stretch them as long as possible. It hasn't been easy considering I'm broke and haven't been able to land another job.

But I can't go any longer. I need a dose, or I'll wind up sicker than I can manage.

The open pill bottle on the counter makes me stop. The cap has been screwed off and several of the pills have spilled out. How did my bottle of pills get knocked over?

Taviar could've done so in a rush. Being as neat as he usually is, I'd imagine he'd fix the mistake.

I pour myself some cool water with my gaze stuck on the open, overturned pill bottle. Something else sticks out to me in my periphery. Down the hall, the bedroom doors are pushed open.

Taviar never leaves his door open, and neither do I.

The roil in my belly deepens. I inhale a reluctant breath and steel myself to go investigate. An inkling tells me I'm not as alone as I thought I was…

Suddenly, the silence in the apartment is ominous and off-putting.

I pass Jael's empty room and the bathroom. Mine comes up next. Anything, or anyone, can be waiting inside.

It could be a trap. Someone luring me.

I stop outside my open door. The person lying on my bed smirks at me.

"Took you long enough," Celeste draws, checking her manicured nails. "I've been waiting well over an hour."

"What are you doing here?"

The willowy woman sits up in a stretch of long limbs. She moves as if desperate to prove her grace, as if there's an imaginary camera snapping away. The pose she strikes with her legs bent and her hands extended behind her feels like she's modeling.

"I wanted to chat," she answers silkily. "Just us girls."

"How did you get into my apartment?"

"Never mind that. Come, sit."

"Get the fuck out of my room. I will call the cops."

She laughs, her eyes closing and mouth opening. Yet another pose. "Silly you. We both know you won't do that. Besides, there's no reason. I'm just here to talk about Kaden. You know—the man you've stolen from me."

"Kaden goes where he wants to go."

The smile drops off her face. The result is a sharp scowl. "We have always had something very special that someone like you wouldn't understand."

"I highly doubt that considering he says the opposite."

"You know nothing." She finally gives up the unbothered charade of model poses on my bed and rises onto her feet.

It's as she stands that I realize what she's wearing—the same T-shirt of Kaden's I had worn the day she dropped by his apartment and she caught us.

I take a step back, dumbfounded by the woman in front of me. If she ever had pants and shoes on, she's ditched them for this confrontation.

"This is the last time I'm telling you to go."

"You don't love him like I love him," she spits, stepping toward me. "You wouldn't dare accept him for the man he truly is. A stupid, boring girl like you from the slums can't begin to make him feel the way I do. You've gotten in over your head. I saw the worry on your face from the window— you're already overwhelmed, and you don't know the half of it."

"You really are a crazy bitch." I pull out my phone.

Celeste remains unfazed. She puts her hands on her narrow waist and says, "Do you want to know the truth about him? I can tell you things about him that will make your skin crawl. The man you think is your perfect Prince Charming is no man at all. He's really a monster. Allow me to show you."

27. KADEN
DESTROY MYSELF JUST FOR YOU - MONTELL FISH

Someday, Lyra will truly grasp the trouble I've gone through for her. I've kept her alive when she was supposed to be six feet under. I've looked out for her and ensured those who have wronged her have been punished. On more than one occasion, I've sought ways to enrich her life.

My methods may be controversial and unconventional; however, they have garnered results. They have put her in a better position than where she started.

She can't possibly begin to understand how fortunate she should feel—how I have demonstrated she is the rarest exception.

Though I'm still sorting out why I have been compelled to spare her in the first place. Where my protective, obsessive instincts as far as she's concerned even come from...

And still, my fascination with her has only grown.

I've gone from monitoring the cameras I have installed in her bedroom to hacking into her computer accounts and sifting through her entire online footprint. I read through her emails and private messages. I look up her search history and browse the collection of photos saved on her laptop.

She's been trying to dig up more information on my family. Search results turned up paltry offerings. The few she did find, she bookmarked. Each one from a finance journal discussing my father's business resume and background. Most of the info included is either incorrect or outdated.

She found even less on me.

I'm not angry she's researching my family and me. Part of human nature is curiosity. However, it does demonstrate Lyra isn't ready for the truth.

It terrifies her to think I'm not the man she hopes I am.

I've always recognized this would be the case. It doesn't deter me from making my decision.

I'm keeping Lyra.

There will be growing pains and challenges to overcome. She'll adjust to what will become her new reality eventually. What other choice will she have?

First, I must tie up loose ends. And by tie up, I mean eliminate the last few roadblocks standing in our way.

Grady is an unbelievably easy catch. Perhaps even easier than Lyra wandering down a crowded street preoccupied on her phone. The twenty-six-year-old man who seems to only own t-shirts with holes in them and happens to be allergic to hair clippers just can't kick his drug habit.

As destitute as he claims to be, he finds a way to scrounge up money for his dealer. They meet on the corner of a poorly lit street located in one of Easton's most crime-riddled areas. I'm lurking in the background, dressed in an inconspicuous hoodie and jeans, waiting out the illegal transaction.

Grady can't wait to get his fix. He barely makes it across the street before giving in. He scrabbles at the plastic baggy he's been given and stuffs two of the pills into his mouth. An immediate euphoric expression rearranges his features.

I step out from the shadows. His eyes connect with mine,

but it's already too late. I've descended on him, jamming my needle into the pulse of his neck.

It happens fast. He goes from full consciousness alight in his gaze to heavy-lidded vacancy that brings him to collapse. I catch him before he does, walking him down the shoddy sidewalk without a single suspicious stare.

It's dark out. Few people are around. The ones who are don't give a damn; they're too strung-out or embroiled in their own criminal activity to spare a glance at the wobbly-legged drug addict getting carried away by a hooded man.

I stuff him into my trunk like luggage and speed off.

It takes him hours to wake up. His head rolls along either shoulder, and he groans out in discomfort. Slowly, his eyes flutter open, and his vision clears. The rigid iron bars of his cell are the first thing he sees.

I'm the second. Just beyond his cell, I'm standing at my workstation in the middle of a thorough scrub down and sanitation.

"Whoa... what the fuck?! You fucking psycho!" he yells. "Where am I? Let me out!"

"Lower your voice."

"What did you do to me? I knew it! You're a fucking— holy shit, what is that?!"

Grady's sneakers scrape against the cement floor and his body thuds against the wall. I don't need to turn around to know why—he's noticed the door hanging open to the industrial-sized freezer in the corner of the room. Fyodor's half disassembled body lays tucked inside.

He loses it. The waste of space ex of Lyra's erupts into wild screams as if he's a toddler that's discovered the boogeyman under his bed.

I still in the middle of my scrubbing and grit my teeth. "Shut up."

"Get me out! Get me out! HELP! SOMEBODY HELP!"

I slam down the sponge and disinfectant and grab the meat cleaver I was about to clean next.

Grady only screams louder as I approach his cell. He shakes his head side to side in pure horror and presses himself against the wall. A wet spot materializes in the crotch of his faded jeans.

"Please.. no... HELP... SOMEBODY!"

"I said shut the fuck up!" I growl with cold menace clenched onto my face. The meat cleaver rests in my hand, ready to strike if I choose to do so.

It's enough to do the trick. Grady whimpers and swallows down his scream. "P-please... dude... I don't want any trouble... just... cool it, alright?"

"No one can hear you. You are in an empty building my family owns, guarded by my security, trapped within sound-proof walls. No one is coming to save you. Just so you know, you're wasting valuable energy when you decide to scream like a banshee. It is in your best interest to get comfortable. You will be here a while."

"Let me go. Please. Let me go."

"I can kill you sooner than I plan to. That is on you. Agitate me enough, and I will." I stride along the perimeter of his cell and take satisfaction in knowing he'll be my next game. I will make the most of this one.

Ending Grady will be sweeter and more satisfying than any of my other recent kills.

"I have an event to attend," I announce, checking the time on my phone. I set down the meat cleaver and head for the passageway. "I'm sure in my absence you will continue to scream like a fool because that's what fools do. However, food and water will not be supplied to you at this accommodation. So, again, you might want to conserve your energy."

Grady proves he's indeed the fool I believe him to be. I

haven't made it up the stairs before he's screaming profanities and demanding I come back down to release him.

After a shower and fresh change of clothes, I head to my next engagement. The Midnight Society is hosting a social hour mixer at the Winchester. Attendance isn't mandatory; however, since Lyra's been avoiding me the past two nights, I've decided to go. I have one purpose in mind.

It's time I draw a line in the sand. The Owner needs to know Lyra will not be dying.

The event has long since started by the time I arrive. Many of the vapid dregs I detest most are in the middle of sipping their martinis and chatting away about whatever inane topics come to mind.

I spy Mr. Newton and Mr. Kimura sneaking off with the girls they have rented from the Midnight Society's Market. The girls twitter like birds as they're led away in their skimpy dresses and lacy black masks. It's the start of what will likely be an orgy long into the night.

Nolan and Klein flag me down from where they hover by the bar. They're polar opposites in how they greet me. Nolan wears his usual pompous grin. Klein appears to have smelled something repugnant if the flare of his nostrils are to be believed.

"Hello, gentlemen," I say. "How's the mixer going?"

"Better now that the real party has arrived," answers Nolan with a chuckle. "What brings the most antisocial member of the club out? The last time you voluntarily showed up to one of these... actually, there was no last time."

"That is because I'd rather saw off my left foot than participate in forced socialization with the likes of the Vandersons."

Nolan winks. "Touché, my friend. I was just telling Kleiny boy here he might have better luck with the ladies tonight."

"Will you shut that trap of yours?" Klein snarls.

I eye the disfigured brunet with cool indifference. "Is that so, Klein? Which woman will you have tonight? The girls from the Market are a sure bet."

"I told him to go for Celeste. Cousin or not, she's just as sure of a thing. Lord knows there isn't a penis in Easton that hasn't been inside at least one of her holes."

Nolan's crude joke finally cracks through Klein's sour mood. He shares a laugh with Nolan. I ignore both. They've pointed out a glaring detail about the mixer that I've happened to miss.

I glance around. "Where *is* Celeste anyway?"

Klein shrugs. "Does anyone really pay attention to where she goes?"

"The girl's probably in the bathroom snorting a line," Nolan says. "That, or fucking one of the waitstaff. I caught her with two at the last event."

"Again," Klein adds.

Nolan sips from his drink with a furrowed brow. "Though I don't think I've seen her tonight. She might've skipped out. She'll be devastated when she learns you attended."

"Where is the Owner?"

"Indulging in a cocktail in the private parlor, of course. Would you like a word?" Nolan asks. His furrowed brow fades and a slow grin comes to his long face. "Don't tell me this is about the prostitute girl. Celeste was telling me how you've fallen in wuv with her."

Klein's bad mood returns. He juxtaposes Nolan's grin with a scowl. "She's supposed to be dead. If you won't do it, I'll hire someone who will."

"I'd say it's best you stay out of the matter, Klein. That is, if you don't want the rest of your genitals lopped off. Excuse me, gentlemen."

I leave them with my gruesome warning hanging in the air. The club security attempts to stop me from entering the private parlor until they recognize who I am. They give an apologetic nod and step aside.

The Owner sits in a tufted armchair made of lush velvet. Despite how comfortable he appears, nursing a drink in one gloved hand, his sense of authority has gone nowhere. The all-black tailored suit and large gold bauta mask in the shape of an owl establish this is no casual affair. He is still acutely tuned into the business of running the club.

"I expected you to come."

"I only did to inform you of what will be happening."

"Sit. Do tell."

I forgo the chair he's offered and decide it's best to rip the bandaid off. No sense making this exchange any longer than it has to be.

"The girl will be kept alive," I say. "She has no real awareness of the club's innerworkings and poses no threat. It does not make sense to bring her harm. Therefore I will not be eliminating her."

"I thought we were clear. There is no choice."

"There is always a choice."

He tilts his head to the side and peers at me with the mask's huge, fathomless black eyes. "You know better than anyone there is no choice in the matter, Kaden. Deep down, you know why she must die. If you will not eliminate her, then we will. Should you attempt to interfere, you will come to regret it."

I stow both hands in my pockets. "I've grown bored of this charade, father. You may hide behind your mask all you like. It may intimidate the others. However, it couldn't amuse me more. I will do as I please, as I always do. The girl lives."

"Disobey the club if you dare. You are operating under the assumption you will receive leniency. You will not."

"I have made up my mind. Leniency couldn't matter less. Honestly, father," I say flippantly, "you're lucky I've played your game this long. This club has grown insufferable. I think I'll show myself out."

He doesn't stop me. He remains seated, his position in the armchair unchanged. His face hidden behind his gold owl mask, he'll never truly give away his hand.

However, I meant what I said. I couldn't care less. The club has been more obligation than a genuine interest, and I've allowed him to believe I'll be his heir for too long. I've known him as the Owner for longer than I've known him as a father. Following in his path was never something I've wanted. Though he's sensed this, it's out in the open now.

I leave the barroom and Winchester Plaza behind.

In a way, it's a burden lifted. There's full transparency regardless of what happens. The Owner is under no pretense that I'll carry out the task he's assigned. I'm aware he'll be coming for Lyra, and maybe myself, to finish the job.

Which means I'll have to speed up my plan.

I drive straight home. Grady will have to be taken care of. The same applies to Fyodor's half disassembled body.

Tomorrow I'll scoop Lyra up, and we'll begin plotting our escape.

The motion-activated lights flicker on in my penthouse. I toss my keys on the credenza and move deeper across the open space.

Then I stop.

Someone has been here.

My gaze remains fixed on the area rug that's been wrinkled in the middle, denoting someone passed through and bunched it up with their clumsy footing. I am meticulous about the most minute details in my home—I'd never leave my rug in such a state.

When I left for the mixer, it was how it should be, flush against the floor.

Grady.

My murderous cloak envelops me, and I proceed forward with my senses on hyper alert. If he should spring out to catch me off guard, he'll receive quite the surprise. I am confident I can more than handle Grady in a physical fight; I will *crush* him.

However, as I turn into the long hall, I discover I'm wrong.

The light in the guest bathroom is on. The sight is no less infuriating. My fists tighten.

Celeste.

I stride toward the door, expecting her hideous smile and idiotic coo of *baby*. The closer I get, the more I slow up.

Water has spilled out of the open bathroom door and onto the hall floor. I come to a stop in the doorway and set sights on the mess.

A massive pool of water that covers the entire floor—*and* the dead naked woman drowned in the bath.

C eleste is dead.

Her arms and legs drape the side of the overflowed bathtub. Her head rests against the back, halfway submerged in the water. Clenched in her pruned fingers is an empty bottle of pills.

I survey the scene for a moment that would likely be considered inhumane. The natural and instant inclination of most human beings would be to rush toward the tub and try to resuscitate her. I'm far less valiant and far more preoccupied with the fact that Celeste used the hour and a half I was gone to commit suicide in my home.

For as erratic and troubled as she's been, it feels out of left field. Our last spat must've pushed her over the edge.

I approach the tub and notice the folded suicide note resting on the nook. She must've placed it there before taking the pills. The letter reads as I expect:

Baby,

All I've ever wanted was to be yours. I would've done anything for you. I would've loved you for what you are. No one else ever will. No one will ever worship you like I have. But you insisted on pushing me away. You loved that girl. You treated her like you should've treated me. You'll regret what you've done.

Celeste

I crumple up the letter and press two fingers to her eyelids, easing them closed. Callous as it may be, the first thought on my mind isn't what Celeste would've hoped it'd be—now I have yet *another* body I'll have to dispose of.

One is more than doable. Two is a handful. Three has exceeded the limit.

I sigh and rub my temples. Leave it to Celeste to inconvenience me in this way.

Grady's still awake in his cell. He perks up at the sound of the door scraping open, then releases a guttural scream at what I drag inside.

"You're a fucking monster! You've killed somebody else, you fucking psychopath!"

At first, I ignore him. I'm too busy tugging Celeste's naked body to the same corner of the freezer where Fyodor's long-dead body resides. I'll most certainly be working through the night. Dusting off my hands, I shoot Grady a scalding glare.

"Lower your voice, or you will jump to the front of the line. Do you understand?"

Grady backs up against the wall and quivers on the spot. "Man... I don't want to die. I don't want to be involved. Let me the fuck out of here."

I ignore him, stacking Celeste's body on top of Fyodor's partially dismembered one.

"I'm talking to you! You can't do this to me. You have to let me go. You... you can't... you fucking psycho."

"You must not realize your words mean nothing." I straighten up and reach into my pocket. My phone has started vibrating. The Caller ID screen reads Lyra. I turn to head for the passageway leading back into the penthouse.

Grady rushes up to the cell bars, gripping them tight, trying to squeeze his face in between. "You can't fucking leave me like this, man. Get back here!"

The dungeon's iron door swings shut with a resounding thud and drowns out the rest of Grady's staunch protests.

I'm much more preoccupied with my incoming call. Lyra rarely calls. She's much more of a texter.

"Lyra," I say when I answer. "I didn't expect to hear from you again tonight. You asked for space."

"I have a confession to make."

Though she can't see me, I lift a scrutinous brow. "Alright. Go on."

"Kaden, I've been..." she sighs in between her words. "I've been investigating you."

I'm aware, little lamb. But I thank you for your honesty.

I feign a sound of mild surprise. "Is that so? Find anything interesting?"

"I found little to nothing. But, Kaden, that's not even close to everything."

"Lyra, what are you trying to say?"

"These detectives have been approaching me. They've been asking questions."

Also already aware.

"Have they? What would these questions be regarding?"

"Maximillion Keys's murder. They received an anonymous tip that you were seen hanging around the club late that night. After it had closed. The tipster was Grady. He's been trying to convince me something's up with you. I... I sort of listened. That's why I started looking into you."

"I've told you, if you have any reservations, you should bring them to me—"

"Celeste stopped by my apartment tonight," she interrupts. "I got home, and she was waiting in my room."

Interesting. That I was not aware of.

I block the irritation from bleeding into my tone. I should've figured Celeste would do her best to sabotage me prior to taking her pitiful life.

"What did she say?"

"Something's wrong with her. Kaden, she's not all there."

I could've told you that.

"She was lying in my bed in your t-shirt, and she told me I'd never accept the real you. Then she offered to tell me the truth."

I crush my phone within my grasp. "Whatever she told you is a lie. She's deranged. You've said so yourself."

"I told her to get out. I didn't want to hear a word she had to say. She left distraught."

...and then came here to kill herself.

"I'm glad you didn't buy into her lies. The next time she shows up, call me immediately. I will handle her. Under no circumstances should you be alone with her."

Though you don't have to worry about her anymore. Considering she's dead.

Lyra's soft breath can be heard on the other side of the phone. The gentle sound stirs something unknown deep inside me. A shiver of a feeling I can't place racks down my spine.

"I've been doing a lot of thinking. We should talk. About our relationship."

"You're off from the piano bar tonight, correct? I'll come pick you up. Perhaps we can do a late dinner."

We hang up in agreement. I scoop my keys up and then waffle last second between the impromptu plans I've made and how I had otherwise intended on spending my evening. I was supposed to get started on clearing out the mounting dead bodies in my dungeon. Not spend the evening with Lyra.

In what can only be called a selfish and reckless decision, I choose to carry on. I head out to my Tesla and drive across the city to Lyra's.

Night has fallen by the time I make it. The streetlights have blinked on, and an aroma of dinner being cooked and prepared is fragrant in the air. I park where I always do, against the curb of the old warehouse building, and make my way up.

The hall outside her apartment is so silent, traces of the TV can be heard.

Lyra answers after my second knock. She's in nothing but her bathrobe, with her thick braids piled on top of her head in a bun.

"You're here fast. Just got out of the shower. I didn't have a chance to finish getting ready."

"I'll wait. Your roommate?"

"Out for the night."

I follow her into her bedroom where I'm treated to the delicious sight of her disrobing. The robe drops to the floor, and she walks to her closet in her bra and panties. I glance at her bed.

"I hope you've changed your sheets if Celeste was laying in them."

She laughs. "Already ahead of you. I was so confused how she got in in the first place."

"She's like a rodent. She'll always find a way."

"So what was it she wanted to tell me?" she calls from the inside of the closet.

I stand casually with both hands in my pockets. "I'm unsure. Knowing Celeste, it could've been anything. She invented an entire relationship. I have slept with her a few times. She took that and decided we were meant to be."

"Black or red?" Lyra emerges from the closet and holds up two dresses.

I step forward, more distracted by the sight of her half naked. Easing the two hangers of dresses out of her hands, I drop a kiss on her mouth, then throat.

"How about nothing at all?"

She giggles and pushes at my chest. "Didn't you say we were going to dinner?"

"Dinner can wait. It's been three days since I've fucked you. In other words, three days too long."

I hold her hips steady, kissing my way along her throat. My lips evoke a tremor out of her. She moans and tips her head back, exposing more of her neck.

I gladly take advantage. My fingers dig into the supple flesh of her hips, and I spread kisses all over her throat. So many I quickly lose count.

Lyra's resistance fades away. She clutches at me, her nails raking down my chest, across my abdomen. I can not only hear the surrender in her sharp breaths, I can feel it in her body—she's melting against me, becoming mine.

She never stopped being mine to begin with.

I will keep her. She will be not only the first person I've spared, but the first person I intentionally hold onto.

By any means necessary.

The Owner will likely make an attempt sometime soon to kill Lyra. He'll send some assassin or hitman or murderous psychopath like me to finish the job. We will be long gone by the time that happens.

Tonight is more than dinner. Tonight Lyra comes with me. She won't know it as we step out for dinner, but she'll be leaving her old life behind.

Once I dispose of the bodies in my dungeon and tie up a few loose ends, we'll leave Easton altogether.

We'll be flying out of the country.

However, first, we can indulge.

We move from the spot next to Lyra's closet toward the bed. I've reached around her back and undone the clasps on her bra. It falls away and her bare breasts spring to freedom. A new treat for my mouth.

I dip my head and tweak her nipple with my teeth. Lyra screams out and sinks her nails into my shoulder.

"Kaden," she breathes. Her chest rises and then falls rapidly as I suck, nibble, and bite. She shudders and struggles for more air. "That feels so... so fucking good! Don't stop. Harder."

I oblige, giving my naughty little lamb another twinge of pain.

"We're just getting started. Take off your panties."

She squirms against me, trying to make my command happen. Her fingers hook into her panties, and she pushes them down.

I curl an arm around her waist and lift her up with zero effort. We join at the mouth again, resuming our heavy kisses, the rest of the way to the bed. We fall in an entanglement of our moving limbs and land with Lyra straddling me. She's attempting to unbutton my shirt and I'm groping her backside.

I'm teasing a finger in her rear hole that's impossibly tight and puckered.

Lyra gasps into my mouth and then rocks against me. Her pussy on the large bulge of my pants. It took little to nothing for my erection to grow so hard and so fast.

What I said is the truth—three days without fucking Lyra is three days too long.

As a result, my dick is hot and volcanic, ready to erupt once it's had a taste of her cunt.

She undoes my pants and grips the length of me. A strangled groan leaves me. I lay back against her bed, for once happy to let her take the lead. She's equally happy to do so—Lyra strokes me and then guides me into herself.

We watch it happen. My dick slipping inside her. Her pussy accepting my thick, engorged length.

I hold her in place against me as she takes me whole. My dick rooted deep. Her slick, tight walls stretching to accommodate me.

She gasps and her breasts sway from the desperate intakes of air her lungs are taking. My free hand slides up her torso, over her breasts, stopping at the base of her throat. It's a command of its own as my other hand bruises her hip.

Gradually, Lyra begins to move. She undulates her hips in a motion that's slow but no less deep and tortuous.

It feels fucking amazing.

Her fluid hips roll. My dick slides in and her walls clamp around me. Then I'm sliding further out, and her hips are crashing down. The cycle begins all over again until we build up to more.

We grow frantic, moving faster, chasing our high. Lyra's hips roll like a tidal wave, and I slam her back toward me.

Back into her slick warmth. The deep clench of her.

I grunt and thrust up. We meet halfway in a violent clash and satisfying friction. I grip her by the ass and then the throat, yanking her to my lips. My tongue pushes into her mouth and explores her taste.

The stimulation grows until I'm moments away from coming. An intense welling of pressure builds from within. It affects every part of my body, tightening my testicles and tingling down my back.

Lyra senses it too. She draws away from my mouth and straddles me, riding me harder. Her hand's snuck down to her pussy. She rubs her clit as her hips dip and roll.

"Fuck, yes, little lamb," I growl through clenched teeth. "Bounce on my cock."

Her lips part in a throaty scream. Her whole body quakes right down to her thighs straddling me.

I watch the marvel of Lyra coming, soaking in my own pleasure. A few more pumps, and I'll be with her. My hands smooth along the curve of her ass and I begin moving her all on my own.

Up and down my cock. Up and down as though she's a vessel to which I'm getting off on.

Lyra lets me as her orgasm flutters through her.

But she changes her mind once she regains some lucidity. She plants a hand on my chest and returns to undulating her hips. She wants to get me off herself—the glint in her dark eyes is playful and mischievous.

Almost... *antagonistic.*

I choke for air. I'm so lost in how good her cunt feels that I don't notice what else is happening.

One second, I'm swimming in wet, hot silk. The next second, the clench is gone. The slickness and heat are no more.

My body tenses and I peer at Lyra with eyes hazy from my near climax.

She's reached over me and grabbed something off her bedside table. A split second later, I discover what—the band of a cold metal handcuff cinches around my wrist. She connects the other cuff to one of the bars on her bed frame.

"Lyra," I growl, my chest heaving. "What in the hell—"

She's crawled over me and handcuffed my other arm so I'm entirely restrained.

It is safe to say, I have never been more shocked in my life. Never have I been more thrown off guard, more confused and at a complete loss.

My brain's foggy from the onslaught of pleasure chemicals that had been invading it up until seconds ago. My body's tense and hot for the same reasons. I haven't come yet. I was mere seconds away.

My dick bobs midair, still fucking hard. Still fucking slick from her juices.

"Lyra! Uncuff me."

She ignores me. She's moved on to something else on the bedside table. My gaze narrows trying to figure out what it is. Some kind of cage device.

She turns it on me, her knees bent at her sides.

"Lyra, take these things off right now!"

"Stay still," she commands.

With careful fingers, she takes my dick in her grasp and lowers the metal-wired device over it. She locks it into place and then eases back on her haunches to admire her work.

A cock cage.

The contraption fits so snugly on my dick, so rigidly, it pinches into me. It makes it downright impossible to come. If I do, it'll be painful.

I stare in shock, still so thrown by what the fuck has happened, I'm unlike myself. I've never been at more of a disadvantage. More outmatched.

"Sorry. But it's time you're punished a little," she says, finally meeting my eyes. "I don't know if I can trust you. I needed a way to keep you in check until I do."

I bare my gritted teeth like an animal. "You will fucking let me go, Lyra."

"I can't be sure. Not yet."

"Let me go... or you *will* be sorry."

She leans close and drops a soft kiss on my lips. "Be patient. I won't be long."

I'm torn between an unparalleled level of rage and shock as she hops off the bed and quickly begins to dress. She slides her crossbody purse over her shoulder and aims a pitying smile at me once at the door.

"Lyra! LYRA!"

The door slams shut behind her. The lock clicks into place.

Little lamb might not be such a lamb after all.

29. Kaden
I feel Like I'm Drowning - Two Feet

I t takes minutes for reality to sink in. I have nothing but time laying handcuffed to the bed. The events of the last hour replay in my mind.

For *once*, I've been outplayed. Lyra invited me into her apartment. She seduced me, *counting* on the fact that I'd been deprived of her for days. The sight of her in that robe... in her bra and panties as it slipped away... she knew what she was doing.

The sex was explosive and engaging. She certainly put forth her best acting. She rode my cock like a professional, treated herself to an orgasm, and then flipped the situation on its head.

The glint in her eye was my clue. She had made up her mind what she was about to do. In that moment, she was a black widow about to feed on the fly trapped in her web.

But the question is why?

As my dick throbs from the confines of the cage and I pull against the handcuffs, I'm left to agonize over this.

She had apologized and said she didn't know if she could

trust me. She wasn't sure about me. What the hell was she talking about!?

What had Celeste told her? Or was this the work of Grady? The police detectives?

I rack my brain. I jerk at the metal cuffs locked onto the bar of her bed. The move proves to cost me more than it helps my situation—the hard pull causes the cage to clench tighter around my dick.

"Argh!" I howl in throbbing pain.

All rationale has left me for the moment. My level of rage and frustration is drowning it out. It's become the only noise I hear as I spiral.

The cage bearing down on me makes me struggle against the cuffs. The cuffs refuse to budge and instead trigger the cage again.

For minutes, I'm stuck in this loop. Trying to muscle my way out of the handcuffs. Roaring in pure fury whenever the cuffs prove unbreakable. Agonizing at the strain on my hard dick that still hasn't had the chance to come.

She might as well have cut it off. That's how torturous the feeling is. I'm suspended in an eternal state of pre-climax. My balls beg in throbbing aches. A soreness develops, warning I'm fit to bust. I'm in need of release.

I need to come. I have to come. It'll hurt. It'll likely bear down harder. Perhaps bite my fucking dick off.

But I need it. I need the release, or I'll lose my mind.

A line of cold sweat breaks out on my temple and trickles down the side of my face. The rest of my body flushes hot.

The contrast makes it difficult to think. That's in addition to the myriad of other fucked up complications about the situation.

I squeeze shut my eyes and urge myself to calm down.

Anger-fueled reactions are for Neanderthals like Grady. Panic-induced meltdowns are for the weak.

I'm better than that. Rarely is escape achieved in these situations when people let their emotions drive them. Usually, it's the opposite. People's emotions do them in during situations like these.

My best bet is to remain calm. Think rationally. Proceed carefully and methodically.

I stare around the room. Lyra's somewhat cleaned up the chaotic mess that her room is usually in. Piles of clothes have been picked up, washed, folded, or hung up. Shoes have been pushed back into the closet where they belong. She's organized the top of her dresser cabinet and her bedside table.

There are plenty of hair accessories on her dresser. If only I could reach one of the clips or pins she has. Though I'd need use of at least one of my hands.

I keep searching. My gaze roves over every inch of the room. My brain spins into overdrive trying to think of a way out of this.

I could take a risk and wait for her return. She'll have to unlock me eventually. Naturally, I'll overpower her—and some severe punishment will be doled out.

Make no mistake, Lyra will not be escaping me under any circumstance.

She still belongs to me; she is still my possession.

While she may have the upper hand in the current moment, it's temporary. I'll be flipping the script at the first opportunity. Ideally, I'd do so before she returns. However, that might not be possible given how I'm restrained.

My clothes are on the edge of the bed. I stretch my body, causing the metal cage to pinch down on my groin, and attempt to hook my foot under my pants leg. If I do so too aggressively, I run the risk of knocking the pair of pants off the edge.

I'm not yet sure what I'll do even if I do pull up my pants. I have a knife in my back pocket. My keys. My *phone*.

With no hands to dial. Perhaps I could attempt to get it into my mouth and fiddle with it that way...

I focus on retrieving the pair of pants first. The rest I'll worry about once that's accomplished.

As I kick up my foot to hook the pants leg over it, the pair is weighed down by the things in my pocket. Instead of pulling it toward me, it's pulled downward off the bed.

"FUCK!" I shout.

My temper threatens to roar back to life until I tamp down on it. That plan was a long shot.

No use fixating on its failure. I'll have to figure something else out. I return to square one, searching the room and thinking hard about what I'll do.

The cage has been locked onto my crotch for so long, it's gone numb. Only a dull throb tortures my poor, still-hard dick.

My motivation becomes the punishment I'll give Lyra not if, but *when* I escape. She's played a good game; the first person to truly beat me for once. That I'll admit.

However, she has no idea the type of hell she's in for. I'm not a man of mercy. I'm a man of cold, cruel retribution, and I intend on collecting the debt Lyra's incurred.

I just have to devise a way out first.

Don't worry, little lamb. You've won this round. But the game is far from over.

30. LYRA
BLOODY MARY - LADY GAGA

My first stop after leaving my apartment is Baldwin Avenue. I pause outside the row of brownstones and survey his front window. The light's on.

Someone's home.

Nerves ripple in my stomach as I tap my knuckles on the door. A dog barks from the other side. The TV mutes and the dog's shushed.

I stand still and wait, peering up at the peephole. I'm sure he's checking to see who's knocked.

Detective Maloney answers the door in his undershirt, clutching a can of beer. It seems to take him another second to realize he's not wearing a proper shirt. I divert my gaze and pretend I haven't noticed.

"Sorry to bother you so late. I... I was hoping to speak to you. It's about the Keys investigation."

"Ms. Hendrix, it is after eight p.m. This is my private residence. I'm not even sure how you found me here, but this is inappropriate—"

"I might have useful info. About Maximillion *and* Fyodor Kreed."

That does the trick. He peers at me cockeyed before caving and opening the door.

"Come in. Mind the dog. He bites."

I step inside his home to clutter overload. I'm far from the neatest person. My room's often a mess, with clothes strewn everywhere and the bed unmade.

But Detective Maloney easily takes the crown. He has two living room sets squeezed into the room. Two big screen TVs. Large plastic containers stacked up to the ceiling, and an assortment of black trash bags gathered in a corner.

The dog he's warned me about is a German Shepherd who glares at me from one of two dog beds reserved for him.

Even the smell of the home seems to be doubled—potpourri notes of lemon zest and thyme clashing with warm, masculine smoke.

My face must reveal how I feel about my surroundings. He walks past me with a gruff chuckle.

"It confuses everybody. I just got married last month. Me and the missus are, uh, having some issues deciding on who's what to keep. We're both stubborn as mules, so you can see where that's got us—two of everything. On the plus side, I have two TVs to watch sports on. On the downside, I keep hitting my damn knee on everything 'cuz it's so crowded in here."

"Right," I answer, standing uncertainly in the middle of the room. "Are we alone?"

"We are. The missus is an RN at Easton General. She's on nights this week."

"Then if you have a moment, maybe we can discuss the case."

"I've discussed the case with you, Ms. Hendrix. You already know what I'm allowed to divulge. We left off requesting that provide what you know."

I draw in a breath, trying to sort out my words.

Maybe I didn't give this enough thought.

I hadn't originally intended on doing what I did with Kaden. After Celeste visited my apartment, I had been conflicted on how to move forward. The woman was unstable. Her visit felt ominous and threatening. She offered to tell me the truth about him.

But how could I trust a woman that had invented a fake relationship?

Celeste wasn't my friend. She wasn't out to help me in any way. Though I knew little of her, it was clear she saw me as a threat for Kaden's affections.

When I called him, I wasn't sure what I was going to do; when he showed up in my apartment and things heated up, I still wasn't sure.

Did I trust him, or was I going to listen to what everyone else around me seemed to be saying?

"Well, Ms. Hendrix?" Detective Maloney asks with his bushy brows raised.

I bring a hand up to my forehead and tune out my intense migraine and rampant thoughts about Kaden. I've already made up my mind.

There's no turning back.

I sit down on the edge of Maloney's second sofa. "Before I give you the information I have, I just need to know something."

He prompts me with another lift of his brows.

"You've honed onto Kaden as your primary suspect, haven't you?"

"Ms. Hendrix, I can't provide unnecessary information in an official police investigation." Maloney pauses long enough to scratch the German Shepherd. He's wandered over to sit between his owner's legs and glare at me like I'm a threat to his owner. Just as my face is falling, Maloney adds, "But what do *you* think?"

His expression says it all—*yes*.

I sigh and rest my hands on my knees. "You must have something on him. I'm guessing from his past?"

"Ms. Hendrix—"

"When I looked into him, I couldn't find much. Except," I say, pinning the detective with a bold stare, "there was an incident when he was younger. A very... gruesome one. It would've made headlines and been investigated by authorities, but his father's money made the whole situation go away. He bought off everyone involved, including the courts and police."

"How did you—"

"I have my sources. That's where your suspicion began, isn't it?"

Maloney scrubs a hand over his unshaven jaw. His other scratches his large, intimidating dog between the ears. He seems to think on whether he should be straight with me.

"I was a rookie at the time. I answered the call. One of the goriest crime scenes I've ever been on. That boy was kneeling in the middle of the room with the knife. He wasn't right in the head then. He can't be right in the head now..."

My stomach roils. "You've been waiting for a chance to land Kaden for years."

"That's right. He's moved suspiciously for a long time. But nothing ever sticks. People disappear around him and nobody bats an eye. Maximillion Keys has been the first case in years where there's a chance we might have something. An actual witness. Potential camera footage. If you have anything that could help, even better. What is it that you know about Fyodor Kreed? Don't tell me Raskova has something to do with his disappearance."

"I think I'd better show you rather than tell you. Can you make a field trip?"

———

It's well past midnight by the time I make it home. I keep my hand inside my purse, my fingers wrapped around my pepper spray. Leaving Kaden handcuffed to my bed was obviously a risk. There's a real chance he's managed to escape.

But it wouldn't matter. I was able to visit Maloney and accomplish what I needed to do.

I flick on the light in the living room and listen for noise in the rest of the apartment. My phone happens to ping with a new message alert. The sudden sound makes me jump, even though it comes from inside my purse. The text is from Detective Laurent.

> I heard from Maloney about the situation.
> On my way.

I text back a quick thank you and head for the hallway. Each step feels like a potential step toward what could be my demise. Either he's going to be restrained where I left him, or I'm going to have an immediate deadly threat on my hands.

Detective Laurent may not make it in time...

The door's still closed like I left it. The light peeks out from the crevice underneath the door. I wrap my hand around the knob and inhale a final, steadying breath.

The bed is vacant. Kaden's things are gone. The handcuffs dangle from the left side of the bent iron bars. He's forced the bar from its frame and freed himself that way.

Something that must've taken extraneous strength, especially given how he was positioned.

How did he possibly manage to get free?

I tighten my hold on my pepper spray and walk deeper into the room.

"Kaden?"

No answer.

It's possible he left. He might've fled the apartment and decided to regroup elsewhere. But I know Kaden too well even after only a few weeks of dating him. He doesn't let things go. He'll be back in some way.

Very soon.

I can't lose focus. I stay put in my room and wait it out. Detective Laurent will show up any moment and then I'll be able to breathe again.

This late at night, with most on the block sound asleep, the silence feels unnerving. Loud and unnatural as I sit alone.

I have no other choice. I have to do this.

A sharp knock draws me out of my thoughts. Someone's at the door.

I get up with my pepper spray and phone in hand.

"Ms. Hendrix?" Detective Laurent calls from the other side. "Open up. I'm here. Is Maloney with you?"

Relief washes over me and I rush for the door. "Thank God you're here."

She's standing with her hands on her hips, a leather jacket around her shoulders, and a tight-lipped look of scrutiny on her face. A look I'm sure she uses often when investigating a crime.

"Well?" she says expectantly. "Is Maloney here? He's stopped answering his phone."

I step aside to let her in, then scream.

Kaden appears out of nowhere. He comes up from behind and slashes Detective Laurent across the throat.

31. Lyra
Closer - Nine Inch Nails

I come to with the unsteady feeling of swaying in place. My body's upright, feet bare and flat on the ground. My arms stretch above my head, bound together by what feels like leather cutting into my wrists.

Seconds pass before my hazy vision clears. My surroundings are more than a little familiar—I'm standing in the middle of Kaden's playroom.

His instruments of pain and pleasure surround me, perched along the shelves and displayed in glass cases. There's the familiar leather play bench we've so often used.

I shiver in fear.

The last thing I remember was letting Detective Laurent into my apartment. Kaden had appeared from behind her and slit her throat. He must've ambushed me before I could even defend myself.

I can't say I'm surprised. I knew there was a chance he'd find a way out and he'd come for me. There'd be hell to pay.

But I at least hoped I'd be able to finish my plan.

I tilt my head back for a look at what's binding me. Thick

leather cuffs snug around my wrists, connected to a chain and hook in the ceiling.

Kaden's brought me into this room at least a dozen times. Not once before have I noticed the different hooks in the ceiling for the setup of all kinds of contraptions, I'm guessing. He's mentioned a sex swing. I hadn't imagined chains to secure an unconscious person against her will being another.

The room's colder than usual. A draft occupies the air and further contributes to my discomfort.

My gaze leaves the ceiling and flicks downward instead. It's no surprise I've been stripped naked—I don't think I've ever spent any time in this room fully clothed.

But it's not the fact that I'm naked that's most concerning to me. It's how my body *feels* that's setting off alarm bells.

My body feels foreign, like it's no longer my own. I've either been transported into someone else's, or I've been through some things I don't remember. Aches plague different parts of me, from my weak knees to the twinge in my wrists from being bound for who knows how long.

The *soreness* between my thighs. The *heaviness* in my rear—

I gasp as I sway in my binds and realize what's going on. A plug has been inserted inside of me. Judging by the fullness it brings me as I become acutely aware of the unnatural sensation, it's a bigger one than the last time.

My heart leaps into my throat. I try to open my mouth and scream, but the only sound I produce is a hoarse grunt. Clearing my throat, I try again.

It's useless calling for help, so instead, I call for Kaden. Why even pretend he's not the one who's done this to me?

The door cracks open and footsteps plod behind me.

"You're up, little lamb."

I'm so relieved he's shown up, my next breath comes out

sputtered. "Kaden... please, I know you're pissed. But I can explain everything. Just unchain me. My arms are aching."

He comes around to stand in front of me. He's changed since the last time I saw him, reverting into his cool, effortless, male model costume.

When I'd walked out of my bedroom, he'd been barking at me, his face reddened and clenched in anger.

The Kaden Raskova before me wears a long-sleeved Henley and dark denim, his loose waves smoothed behind his ears, and his ivory skin as translucent as glass. How's it possible for a man who's more than likely a psychopath to look so good in a moment like this?!

"You want to be set free," he says in a mild tone.

"Please," I chirp.

"Let me ask you this. Do you think you *deserve* to be set free?"

"Kaden—"

"I worked to free myself. Now I think it's your turn to do the same."

"I did what I had to do because I had to look into a few things," I say in haste. The words blending together the faster I talk. "I knew you would be after me. It was to protect myself."

"I have no use for you to talk right now. Time to fix that issue."

He holds up the ball gag that I've become well acquainted with. I open my mouth to protest without realizing I'm helping him along. My mouth open, he pries it wider, and stuffs the gag inside.

"There we go," he says, fastening the band at the back of my head. "I always love the sight of you bound and gagged."

"Kaden!" I yell around the silicone ball filling my mouth. It comes out as nothing more than an incoherent mumble.

"Save the pleading, little lamb. I promise you I am no man of mercy. As you're about to find out. Almost forgot." He digs around in the pocket of his trousers and produces a contraption I've never seen before.

Nipple clamps attached to a chain... and a third clamp which dangles from a longer chain down the center.

They'd be beautiful if they weren't designed to bring me misery. Metal clips that are shaped like a starburst with screws for each point. I can only imagine what they look like when on. How intense they feel once they are.

A sharp shiver runs through me realizing where the third one goes.

Kaden wastes no time clipping them on. First my left breast in a twinge of pain and then the right. His hands grope the pair. His thumbs run over the metal clamps themselves. He stands so close I can feel his body heat. I'm sure he can feel any tremors I make.

Peering into my eyes, he hovers his mouth over mine. "Do you know where the third clamp goes, little lamb?"

For some stupid reason, I actually try to answer. The gag muffles every word.

Kaden laughs and gives my right breast a light tap. "Did I hear that correctly? You think asking me not to is going to stop me? I really thought you were more perceptive than that. You should probably accept you have no say in this situation. I will do what I want, when I want. Actually, I already have. I'm sure you feel the plug in your ass, don't you?"

I fire back with another muffled retort.

Kaden twists my breast as if it's the form of another language—it might as well be as I squirm and whimper at the bite of the clamp.

"If you want to be mouthy, I can find other ways to gag you," he says, his eyes glinting with pure callous delight. "You seem to not understand we have all day. All night. As long as it fucking takes for you to be punished. You're mine, little lamb, and I'm never letting you go. I'm going to keep you, and remake you in my image. My perfect little fuck toy."

"No," I gurgle around the ball. Saliva's pooled in my mouth and made it that much more difficult to speak. "No-no-no!"

"Yes, little lamb, yes."

He reaches between my thighs, his eyes glued to my face, and he does it. He takes the clamp and clips it onto my clit.

"OHHH!"

"How does that feel?"

I couldn't begin to describe it. Just that it numbs all other thoughts from my brain and makes it impossible to think of anything else.

An instant, tortuous throb begins, like any relief I can possibly achieve has been bottled up into my sensitive little nub without any way to escape. Instead, I'm left trapped in between. On the cusp of relief while I suffer at the unforgiving pinch of the metal.

The nipple clamps are nothing compared to this.

He cups my chin and drops a kiss on my cheek. "How does it feel, little lamb? Tell me."

Words escape me, seemingly far out of reach. Between the torturous bite of the clamps and the disconcerting fullness in my rear channel, I'm incapable of speech. Nevermind the gag in my mouth. The intense sensations being inflicted on me not only grip my body but they grip my mind—I'm consumed with thoughts about how tight the clamp feels on my clit, and wondering just what size plug he inserted into me.

I babble more incoherence around my ball gag. Only after do I realize I've started drooling again.

Amusement flickers in Kaden's dark eyes and he steps up to me. He licks at my moist, wide-open lips almost like he can't resist himself, and then swipes the pad of his thumb along the wetness of my mouth and chin.

A second later, I realize why—he's out to torture my clit. His hand finds my pussy and his thumb begins rubbing slow, wet circles on my pinched clit.

My hips buck against his efforts and a growly noise warbles from my throat.

"What's the matter, little lamb? Do you like it when I rub your clit? Does it feel good?"

Yes.

Oh, fuck yes.

I close my eyes and concentrate on the rhythm of my breathing. It's the only thing I have control over. Everything else is happening to me... and I hate that my body's slowly responding to the punishment.

My clit throbs for relief in the most impossible way. It's like being suspended between heaven and hell. The blood flow has been interrupted and I can feel pressure welling up in the nub made up of thousands of nerve-endings.

But nothing happens. Except for the pinch and the pressure and the sensation like I'm so close, so damn close to reaching something I can't even describe.

I make another noise that sounds borderline obscene to my ears. It's the sound of desperation.

Pure, unashamed lust.

I'm trembling in my chains. My nipples ache under the vise of the clamps and a wild fire has lit from within. Even the plug in my ass has started to arouse me, creating a deep need to *truly* be filled.

And not by a cool stainless steel device.

Kaden reads my mind. His dark eyes hook mine and he finishes toying with my pussy. The devilish glint in them sends another chill down my spine.

"You seem to love the clamps. Regardless of your little protests. But how do you feel about the plug, little lamb? Is it too much? I went up two sizes... to better prepare you."

I make a guttural noise that's supposed to serve as an answer.

He laughs and strolls around to the back of me. His large, warm hands grip my waist, and he pushes himself into me from behind. The solidness of his body, the dominating feel of him braced around me, makes my clit throb harder.

I want Kaden to continue. I want him to do as he plans. Finish his punishment. Make me suffer. *Then* make me come.

He bends his head and traces his lips along my jaw. His breathing quickens, deep and harsh, like a precursor to thunder. He's hard, letting his erection prod into me as if it's a weapon he's about to wield.

"You were unconscious," he says silkily into my ear. "But I inserted it anyway. I had my way with you, little lamb. I fucked that sweet pussy of yours... and couldn't resist punishing you with the plug. Do you want to know what I've done? That I've been so unable to resist you, I've had you when you were nothing but a beautiful, sensual woman moaning in her sleep?"

My heart pounds heavily in my chest at his confession. Deep in the core of my being, where my instinct and intuition exist, I'm aware it's the unvarnished truth. I'm aware that some part of me already knew this—there have been times in recent weeks where I was dreaming, though acutely cognizant of pleasure.

I was thrashing and moaning, waking slick between my thighs. Once, I vaguely remember opening my eyes, and in the pitch-black shadows of my bedroom, someone was with me. A guardian angel from the dark side that came out at night and brought me body-tingling pleasure. I had assumed I was dreaming.

Kaden. It was Kaden all along.

He rouses me from my thoughts with a push and pull of the plug. He's gripping the handle and he drags the weighty steel plug back out of my channel before he plunges it in deeper. I can't handle the new kind of torment as my body reacts in a frenzy.

Hips bucking. Toes curling. Arms stretching. Pussy aching. The fire in my belly burning me up from the inside and flushing onto my dark brown skin. Beads of sweat have materialized. One drips between the valley of my clamped breasts.

Kaden twists the plug in and out of me at varying speeds, effectively fucking me with it.

"Let me hear you beg, little lamb," he demands in his usual cool, composed tone. The tone that denotes he's Kaden Raskova and he might as well own the world. "Let me hear you beg for my cock in your ass. That's the only way this ends. I want to hear you cry for it."

"OH!" I shriek when he gives a particularly hard twist of the plug, and it goes deeper than ever.

An aftershock of pleasure vibrates through my body. Pleasure chasing the pain.

Somehow, even with the cloudy mess that my mind's become, I'm able to remember his instructions. I'm so desperate for some kind of payoff that I'm willing to do anything for it. Around the silicone ball gag still lodged inside my mouth, I begin begging.

I plead. I implore. I moan like a wanton slut and tell him how much I want his fat dick to replace the plug in my ass. I want him to fuck my most forbidden hole and fill it up with his cum.

Kaden might not understand a word. My pleading sounds like distorted gibberish to my ears too. But that's beside the point.

The point is that I'm a shuddering, throbbing, aching mess desperate for his dick.

"Music to my ears," he says with a chuckle. He eases the

plug out of me, and I can feel my hole's opened up. I can feel it gradually start to shrink.

The clang of his belt echoes in the playroom. He sheds his clothes and then steps in front of me in naked masculine glory. All chiseled muscles packed onto a tall, imposing frame. He walks with as much power and confidence naked as he does in a twenty thousand dollar suit.

I watch with bated breath as Kaden stops in front of his vast collection of sex toys and devices. He sets down the plug we've used and picks up a bottle of lube.

Kaden smirks disappearing behind me. My gaze shifts to the glass case nearby and I watch him in the reflection. He's about to squirt some of the clear liquid when he pauses.

"Actually," he says with a cruel twist of his mouth, "you don't deserve it."

He tosses the bottle to the floor. I yell in protest despite the fact it's pointless.

This is happening, no matter what I say or do.

With no other warning, no more time to brace for it, Kaden pushes into me. Only the tip at first. My body's already tensed up in a thrumming mixture of fear and thrill. Fear because I'm not sure how I'll handle this; thrill for that very same reason.

Being penetrated back there still feels unnatural... like it's against what my body intends. Yet, as his dick breaches me, the naughtiness of the moment washes over me. The tabooness of what he's about to do only makes me tremor.

My clit throbs harder, more insistently. Another sensation that started off strange that now makes the fire inside me burn hotter.

Kaden encounters slight resistance at my sphincter, but he pushes on. He goes for it, and thrusts the rest of the way in.

My eyes widen and I scream around the ball gag, standing on tiptoe. The lube might've helped to somewhat ease things, but it would've been a struggle regardless. As he forces himself inside, my hole stretches with a dull ache.

To say it's a tight fit would be generous.

I'm sputtering out breaths trying to adjust, trying to circle back to the pleasure I was feeling only seconds ago.

Kaden, however, is in heaven. He groans at the tightness and buries his head in the crook of my neck.

"Fuck, little lamb," he breathes. "Your ass feels so fucking amazing, I just might come right now. Tell me you like how I feel inside you."

I gurgle around the gag, the wires in my brain crisscrossed. I've entered delirium, where I'm so overworked and overwhelmed, I don't know if I'm coming or going.

My body's firing off on all cylinders—so many sensations at once that I'm not sure how much more I can handle without passing out. The teeth gnawing on my nipples almost feel soothing compared to the rest. My pussy clenches on air while my clit throbs with desperate need for relief. Other parts of me ache from exhaustion, like my arms bound above my head, and my mouth from being propped wide open around the ball.

But it's Kaden's cock in my ass that's the focal point.

It's so damn much, I don't know how to process the fullness.

Not that I'm surprised—Kaden inside of me has always been a pussy-breaking experience. Stuffed inside my near-virginal ass, and it's a whole other level.

He begins fucking me. The first few thrusts start at a slow, reasonable pace. He saws in and out of me, leaving his head inside, before repeating the motion.

I sway in my leather binds, my eyes squeezing shut in my search for pleasure. If he'd take the clitoral clamp off, I'd surely come. That would do the trick—I'd be so relieved as my tiny nerve-endings radiated pleasure, I'd be distracted.

Though it's undeserved. As far as Kaden's concerned, I don't get to come.

At least *yet*.

The point of fucking me like this is so that I feel every rough drag of his hips. I do as he picks up speed, as his thrusts dig deeper and become more brutal. If he ever planned to go easy for my first time, he's finished taking that into consideration.

Kaden pumps into me at a hard, unforgiving pace. His long fingers clench my hips, and he ploughs into me, forcing his dick inside my tight hole.

I whine and grunt and do my best to bear it.

The wild fire inside roars to life with flames that burn even hotter than before. It's endless desire and desperation rolled into one that leaves me shuddering and seeking more.

More punishment. More dominance. More of Kaden's cock sinking deeper.

We become a perfect duet of his savage thrusts and grunts and my delirious whimpers as I open up and take it.

Heat sears over my skin. It makes me slick and dewy to the touch. Kaden grips me harder, with bruising fingers, and lifts me off the ground. There's enough slack in the chain that he's able to hold me up at the height he needs. My legs bend at the knee and his arms hook under my thighs.

I'm supported not only by my binds, but by the cruel, dominating man fucking my ass with careless abandon.

He impales me with every inch of his dick, reaching a depth that's so deep it does something to me. Unlocks some new level in the pain/pleasure matrix. My whole body quakes, propped up by his muscled arms as he bounces me on his dick.

Tiny blips of pleasure have begun to pulse through me. I gratefully accept them, so needy and starved that a crumb feels like an entire meal.

Kaden's breathing is ragged. He's losing control. His composure falls away and he fucks into me like a madman.

We've become two creatures so desperate we've spiraled. Nothing in this moment is more important than the intense feelings we're wreaking out of each other's bodies.

"I'm going to come, little lamb," he pants against my neck, his breath warm and arousing. "I'm going to come and fill up your fat ass."

It's a mystery to even me why I continue answering him. But I do—as he pumps into me at a manic pace and warns me of what's to come, I babble another incoherent response.

Then everything I know is turned upside down. I'm blown into pieces.

Kaden grunts as he fucks into me harder and more punishing than ever. He's about to come. Before he does, his hand finds my pussy and he rips the clamp off my clit.

I squeal and squirm at the sudden loss of pressure. Then I'm spinning from the even more sudden rush of blood. It knocks into me at once, restoring true feeling to my clit, and setting off its thousands of nerve endings.

My body is enveloped in a giant wave of paralyzing tingles for several seconds to come. All radiating from my sex to every other part of me.

I've never come so hard. So intensely that I'm questioning reality as everything spins and I see spots before my eyes.

And *still* Kaden fucks me. He fucks my ass so thoroughly, so roughly, that as he finally lets go and sinks deep, I come *again*. His hot seed releases into my rear hole and triggers my spasming pussy into another orgasm.

We're both groaning and shuddering, out of breath and buzzing from what's happened. It takes Kaden a while before he pulls out of me. I'm so spent, most of my weight is held up by the chains; my legs are like jelly and refuse to do any work holding myself up.

I sway precariously left then right and left again.

He dresses first, ensuring he's neat and composed. Then he returns to his authoritative stance in front of me. He unlatches the ball gag and unclenches the nipple clamps, setting both aside.

Just when I think it's over, we're done and I've been sufficiently punished, he proves me wrong. The glint in his eyes tells me so before the words he speaks ever do.

"Don't get so excited yet, little lamb," he says with a twisted grin. "Tonight's punishment is just getting started."

32. Lyra

Kill Bill - SZA

I'm lost when Kaden undoes the leather cuffs and then leads me into his bathroom, where he proceeds to bathe me. I'm lowered into warm, soapy water and told to stay put. He sits on the edge of the tub and runs a loofah over me so calmly I'd think we were two lovers spending a romantic evening together and not in the middle of his revenge games.

I'm being lulled into a false sense of security. That realization makes my heart race when I should be relaxed and enjoying the warm bath. How can I when I know he has something else planned? Another cruel trick up his sleeve.

The only relief I'm brought is from the Epsom salt steeped in the water. After the punishment I've endured, it soothes my aching body.

I meet Kaden's dark gaze, hyperaware he's studying me in his silence. As he gently guides the sudsy loofah down my back, he's drinking in every detail about me in this moment. Details that could very well work against me... like what he plans to do next.

It's clear, despite his silence and his gentle touch, he's livid. He's unbelievably pissed with me.

Fear invades my lungs and comes out as a shaky breath. "Kaden," I say in my softest tone, "can we talk about everything? I promise I can explain."

"I believe I told you to do as I say. That includes not speaking unless instructed to do so. Have I instructed you to do so, little lamb?"

With a sinking heart, I shake my head and then revert into a mute. He finishes bathing me—even reaching between my thighs to wash away evidence of himself—before he wraps a towel around me. I'm dried off, led into his bedroom, and told to stay put.

I do, feeling naked and exposed as he disappears into his obscenely large walk-in closet. He emerges carrying a garment bag that he lays flush onto his bed.

"We have a very important engagement to attend, little lamb," he says. "I'm going to make your biggest life dream come true."

"Kaden, please—"

"Wait until you see this gown. It's quite exquisite. A beautiful garment for a beautiful woman. Come closer, little lamb. We must be leaving soon."

I have no idea what he's talking about. My feet pad over, my reluctance clear. He doesn't seem to care as he turns me to face the huge mirror and then carefully unzips the garment bag.

I'm too curious not to look. My gaze drops to the sleek black bag for a peek at what's inside. A gasp almost finds its way past my lips. I manage to stifle it at the last second, though I'm unable to censor my long stare.

Holy crap.

Kaden removes what has to be the most extravagant gown I've ever laid eyes on. Made of a rare velvet that looks impossibly soft to the touch, the decadent gown flows to the floor like a current of blood-red silk.

Blood-red, a deep and eye-catching hue that seems darkly appropriate considering our circumstances. That's mesmerizing as my gaze travels the length of the dress and takes in the shimmers of gold sewn into the fabric.

Kaden slips the gown over me and zips me into it.

It couldn't fit more perfectly. It's been tailored that way.

I switch my stare to the mirror across from us and drink in the sight of me—the deep, heart-shaped neckline teases my breasts while the straps hang loosely off my shoulders. My mind goes to a twisted fairytale, where I'm a princess about to be captured by the sinister villain seeking to have me.

I already am. Peering into the mirror at our reflection, Kaden glides his fingers along the arc of my neck, then the smooth line of my shoulders. He leans close and takes an inhale as if treasuring my scent.

"You look stunning," he says, spoken as a whisper in my ear. "I'm going to enjoy tonight. But, first, I should get ready too."

I stay where I am as he disappears back into his closet.

It only takes him a couple minutes. He walks out looking like what most women would describe as the perfect man. His loose dark waves of hair are pushed away from his face, and he flashes a smile at me that's somehow both charming and frightening all at once. He's dressed in a custom-tailored tuxedo that highlights his tall and masculine physique.

Especially since I know just what he looks like underneath.

He offers me his arm that I don't hesitate to take. I'll have to play along... at least until he's open enough to listen to reason.

I can explain everything. I can talk him out of whatever cruel punishment he has planned next.

Or so I tell myself.

We leave his bedroom. I throw a glance over my shoulder,

checking that the door next to the laundry room is shut. Has he been down there?

I was so sure it's where he would take me...

The area of his penthouse he punished me for even going near in the past—at the time he claimed it was the laundry room I shouldn't have ventured into, and I was distracted by the discovery of his bloody shirt in the hamper, but I now know that was a lie. He was trying to keep me from that room.

A shiver of fear courses through me thinking about it.

Kaden leads me to his Tesla in the underground garage, ensuring I'm buckled in before he gets behind the wheel himself.

"Where are we going?"

He aims a slight grin at me. "You'll see. You'll get to do what you've always wanted, little lamb. Play for a special audience on the stage you love."

———

The Easton Opera House stands out among the other large buildings on the city street. Moonlight catches in the glass dome, and though in the night it looks dark, there's still a gleam too.

Kaden parks out front and escorts me up the long, cascading steps on his arm. I half protest and point out he's parked once again in a no parking zone.

"My security will handle it."

That's when I notice he's right—a personal valet rushes down to collect his luxury car and move it somewhere more appropriate. Another stands by the house doors and welcomes us inside.

No other attendees are around. We're the only ones.

I glance at him. "Did you rent out the opera house?"

"It's for our use tonight, little lamb," he says mysteriously.

"My security are merely here to assist. Don't for one second think they'll help you if you appeal to them. They are on my payroll, and they take orders from me only. No pleading from you—or anyone else—will convince them otherwise."

I have no clue what the hell he's talking about as he leads me through the marble atrium. I'm sure whatever he has planned will involve me seated at a piano.

But that can't be the end of it. There has to be some twist he'll reveal.

My stomach pits at the thought. I consider pleading with him before I drop the idea. He's still too pissed, too hell bent on making sure I've been punished.

The playroom wasn't enough. Something tells me this is the *real* punishment.

We enter the Grande Stadio to silence and then the added thud of our footsteps. He walks us all the way toward the stage. I survey the hundreds of seats and find them empty.

...until we're closing in on the pit and I realize someone else is here. Someone other than his staff.

Seated in the very front row, gagged and strapped to the chair, is none other than a bloodied and bruised Grady.

My heart drops at the sight, though I don't make an attempt to go to him. I'm clutching onto Kaden's arm, and it'd be pointless. It'd only piss him off even more.

But he notices my shock anyway and takes pleasure in it.

"Yes, little lamb," he says flippantly. "I've invited your junkie loser ex to join us. He's been *dying* to see you."

Grady screams something from behind his gag. He thrashes in his seat, twisting and turning in desperation to free himself. All he's really doing is using up his energy. He chokes out a labored breath and then yells something else.

Hatred and anger are in his glassy, bloodshot eyes.

It's not just for Kaden. It's for *me*.

Kaden seems to notice as he escorts me onto the stage. He

gestures for me to take my seat at the gorgeous Steinway I've played on once—weeks ago, the first night I slept with him—before he rounds on the audience.

On Grady.

"I think your junkie loser ex has something he wants to say, little lamb. Allow me."

I sit uncertainly on the piano bench as Kaden goes down to temporarily lower his gag.

"YOU FUCKING PSYCHOS!" Grady roars the second he's able. His voice goes hoarse from the intensity of his scream. "YOU FUCKING PSYCHOS, RELEASE ME RIGHT NOW!"

"As you can see, he's a little upset," Kaden taunts. "What's the matter, Grady? Are you heartbroken over Lyra? Mad she doesn't want to be with you and that depressingly minuscule penis of yours? Don't give me that look—I've seen what you have, and I must say, you owe Lyra a thank you for putting up with it."

"FUCK YOU!"

"But it goes beyond your inability to properly satisfy her needs in the bedroom," Kaden goes on with an air of arrogance. "It's the fact that a brilliant pianist, a woman as intriguing as Lyra, entertained you for so long. Frankly, you should be kissing the ground she walks on."

"BOTH OF YOU FUCK OFF!" Grady screams. Spittle flies. His face is redder than I've ever seen it. He directs his ire toward me on the stage. "How could you do this to me, Ly? How could you fucking side with him? After everything we've been through!"

I simply stare at him, forcing myself to remain quiet. It'll only make the situation worse to give him a reaction.

Kaden feels the opposite. "What have you been through, Grady?" he mocks. "Tell me. The drug-induced benders? The incessant whining about being a loser? Your continued harassment of her when you stalked her and refused to let her go?"

"I should've known," Grady rants. "I should've known how fucked up you were and that you'd wind up doing some shit like this. I never should've gotten involved with your crazy ass! You've got this psychopath after me! All I did was try to help you. FUCK YOU! FUCK BOTH OF YOU!"

"That's enough of you." Kaden lifts the gag and muffles him once more. He turns to me with his hands in his pockets. "Lyra, it is time for the big performance you've been waiting for. I want you to play Liszt's etude Feux Follets. I want you to keep playing until you grow tired and stop. The moment you do... you'll be saying goodbye."

To who?

The fear inside me intensifies. I shudder out a breath turning to the keyboard. My body shifts into proper position and I set my fingers on the keys despite the way they tremble.

"Begin when you are ready. You might want to pace yourself."

Feux Follets is one of the most difficult piano pieces in existence. Even the most veteran pianists sometimes struggle with the double notes required of the right hand.

Kaden knows exactly what he's doing requesting I play it. All under the threatening guise I'll be saying goodbye the moment I stop.

This is a test. He's grading me somehow, seeing if I'm worthy in some way.

I can tell by how carefully he's watching me. His dark eyes are intent and focused, sharper than I've ever seen them.

You want me to play. I'll play.

A thread of spite unleashes inside me as I decide I'm going to prove myself. I'm going to demonstrate my talent and passion. I'm deserving of passing whatever test it is he's giving me.

As always, my fingers set the tone. They control me, guide me, drawing me into the mindless state I enter whenever I play. I close out everything else and strike the keys with the practiced grace required of a piece like Feux Follets.

Yet, I don't lose sight of its level of difficulty. My fingers sprawl along the ivory keys, touching the naturals, flats, and sharps as necessary.

I don't pay attention to what's going on elsewhere.

Kaden and Grady observe from the audience. Kaden like a monster trapped beneath the human male mask he wears. Grady with the impatient grunts and thrashes of the captive he is.

I ignore them both, filling the cavernous room with whimsical notes that unravel the longer the piece goes on.

It's a chance to flex my prowess. Show I can complete one of the most difficult solos.

And I do.

As I reach the end, I see the finish line. I know I'll succeed.

Kaden interjects by throwing a wrench into the moment. "Again!"

I have almost no time to give it another thought. Striking the final key, I slip straight into an encore. I'm compelled to go faster. Play harder. My fingers speed across the keys as a blur even to my eyes. My eyes that barely even blink the longer I play.

An ache begins in both—my tired eyes and my begging fingers. But I keep playing. I don't miss a single stroke. My right hand does double time keeping up with the changing notes required.

"Again!" Kaden yells when I reach the end a second time.

I roll into another encore. Sweat gathers on my brow. A shakiness develops throughout my body. I'm breathless as I push myself to play harder, stretch myself farther.

Grady yells something from behind his gag. He's yelling at me.

Bad things. Angry things. Hateful things that sound like the many times before, where he's told me he's the only one who'll ever tolerate me. No one else would put up with me. I'm an emotional mess. I'm all alone, and always have been, for a reason.

"AGAIN!" Kaden roars.

Tears spring to my eyes as I start over, barely able to play. Barely able to remember the next key I'm supposed to land.

My fingers do so out of muscle memory only.

Instead of losing myself to the music, I've become distracted by the circumstances. The terrible things Grady's yelling from behind his gag and the fury that seems to be intensifying from Kaden too.

Both men pissed for a different reason.

And then it occurs to me—the epiphany comes on strong and makes me gasp out even while my busy hands continue on the piano keys.

I understand now. I get what's happening and what I'm being tested on. Just why he's doing this and seemingly growing angrier the longer I play.

This performance isn't for Kaden. It's not even for myself.

I throw a quick glance into the audience and realize the inevitable of what I have to do.

Stop playing.

Kaden's standing behind where Grady sits thrashing in his seat. His arms are folded behind his back, holding onto something, with a face sharp and murderous.

He's waiting for me. He's demanding it of me. If I'm to pass the test...

I have to say goodbye.

It happens as I come up on the end of my fifth rendition. Tears flood my cheeks, and my aching fingers thank me. I let the last trilling note echo through the theater and speak for itself.

I'm done. I'm saying goodbye.

For real this time.

A flicker of delight passes in Kaden's dark gaze as he reveals the blunt meat cleaver from behind his back. He raises it up and he brings it down.

Several times, into the base of Grady's skull.

I burst into a mourning cry, rising from the piano bench, and dashing down the steps. Saying goodbye to Grady was a necessary evil to survive and prove myself—I'm aware of it in the back of my mind—but it doesn't make it any easier.

It doesn't make it any less difficult closing that chapter of my life.

I sink to my knees beside his dying body, and I say goodbye as the light leaves his eyes.

33. Kaden
Sigh - Unloved

Lyra sits crumpled in velvet and blood. There's no distinction between the two—the dark red splatters of blood blend perfectly against the lustrous velvet. If not for the meat cleaver sticking out of Grady's head you'd never know he was bleeding out.

He died some seconds ago. His eyes remain open, vacant and witless. Though it's hardly a change from when he was alive.

Lyra's glossy brown eyes flick up at me. A slow track of tears make their way down her cheeks.

It's perhaps an inappropriate time to recognize how beautiful she looks like this, heartbroken and tearful. I'd feel compelled to care if I weren't so pleased with the scene that's unfolded—one step closer to completing what I have planned.

In the atmospheric lighting, Lyra's mahogany complexion matches the lush, decadent opera house surroundings. Her thick, rope-like braids hang down her back, and her blood-soaked, off-the-shoulder gown drapes her svelte body as though she's some modern dark fairytale princess.

Her lips have never been more full and kissable, even

though they're wet with tears. The same tears shining on the soft curve of her cheeks. An urge to lick them off excites me enough that there's an aggressive tug in my loins.

Who says I'm done punishing her?

I'm keeping her—I have all the time in the world to wreak pain, and occasional pleasure, on that addictive body of hers.

I still haven't gotten it out of my head how she grunted and shook in her binds as I fucked her in the ass. The glazed pleasure that came over her face when I latched the nipple clamps on. The one on her clit made her cry out. First in agony, then in the most powerful orgasm of her life as I ripped it off and the circulation returned to her quivering, neglected nub.

Tonight is only the beginning. She has no clue what she's in store for as she sits mourning the drug-addled loser ex of hers. Her heartbreak is my triumph.

"Stand up, little lamb. We have places to be and things to do."

"What about Grady? You can't just leave him here—"

"That's exactly what I'll do. My security will take care of him as instructed. Get up." I make my command through gritted teeth.

It's harsh enough that she obeys. She rises on less-than-steady knees, her long red velvet gown cascading to the floor.

My dark queen.

I smirk. "You played so beautifully tonight. So well under pressure. You will play for me every night from now on."

"I would've done it if you'd asked."

"You'll have little else to do where we're going."

"And where will that be?"

"You'll find out when we get there, little lamb."

It's drizzling on our walk to my Tesla. I escort Lyra to the passenger side and sit her down. She throws daggers at me with her gaze. My only reaction is to think about how I'll have my cock shoved down her throat in the next few hours. Then she can glare all she wants.

We ride to my Primark Tower. My doorman asks no questions as usual as I parade Lyra through the revolving door.

"Have a great evening, Mr. Raskova."

"Believe me, we will."

In the elevator up to my floor, the heat rolls off Lyra. I push her up against the wall and shove down the bust of her gown, exposing her bare breasts for my fondling. She sucks in air as I twist and tweak her nipple and tell her all the ways she now belongs to me.

The elevator dings and I walk her out like this, my grip on her elbow. It's still up in the air what I'll do with Lyra while I clean up the mess in the dungeon. If I'll leave her in one of my contraptions in the playroom as an extra cruel punishment, or if I'll leave her locked in another room.

I could always bring her downstairs with me. Make her help get rid of the bodies.

A bolt of excitement ignites inside me at the thought. It would certainly be a different kind of punishment for Lyra— she'll be my little accomplice dismembering them.

Once inside the penthouse, she wastes no time mouthing off.

"What're we about to do?"

"You'll see."

"You might regret what you've done tonight."

"Am I supposed to be worried, Lyra?" I sneer, walking us through my huge penthouse.

"You've left too many loose ends. You already know the police are investigating you."

I crank the steel door leading into the dungeon open. "Is that your way of telling me you tattled, little lamb? You told the mean detectives on me? Now I'm truly worried."

She shakes her head. "You'll see."

The same glint that had flickered in her gaze when we fucked in her bedroom returns. Even the barest hint of a smirk that blinks in and out on her lips.

My stomach clenches in answer. Only because it feels like, yet again, it's a precursor to something I've overlooked—Lyra has outplayed me once. Has she possibly managed to do so a second time?

Did she really manage to sic the detectives on me? Is that why she's bragging?

In the coming minutes, I have my answer.

I haul her down into the dungeon with me. It's danker and grimier than usual given the recent uptick in bodies I've had come through. The door to what was Grady's cell hangs open. Another thing to scrub clean. I hardly had any time earlier when I collected him; I was in a rush, and I needed to get him to the opera house for Lyra's performance.

I deposit her by my worktable and head over to the freezer. A cold blast smacks into me prying the heavy, industrial-sized door open. I move to go inside and grab Celeste's dead body so we can begin work.

To find the words for the level of shock that encapsulates me would take a lifetime.

It's enough that the air vanishes from my lungs, and for several seconds, I experience vertigo. The cement walls spin around me, the floor itself becoming some kind of carnival ride. Some fucked up Tilt-A-Whirl where I'm trapped and unable to get off.

I stagger a couple steps back and blink several times, daring my eyes to confirm I'm seeing what I'm seeing.

There are supposed to be three bodies lined up inside the freezer.

Maximillion. Fyodor. Celeste.

Instead... there's *four*.

The fourth body with skin pale and blue is none other than Detective Maloney.

I whip around to find Lyra's crept closer. She's watching me, observing my reaction. My mind grinds to a halt and processes no further thought.

The shock's too great.

"You?" I whisper.

The smirk I thought I'd seen moments ago finally brightens to life on her beautiful face. "I did it for you."

34. KADEN
I Was Never There - The Weeknd

"You're messing with my head," I snap, suddenly irate. "This is some kind of mind game of yours!"

"Not a mind game," she answers simply. "Just eliminating the threats. Isn't that what you were doing?"

And then it smacks into me, striking me like a mighty bolt of electricity—*Celeste didn't kill herself.*

A fresh dose of anger wells up inside me. I have no idea what's going on, and I do not like being kept in the dark. I pride myself on always being several steps ahead.

Yet, as I gaze into Lyra's gleaming dark eyes, I realize I'm far behind.

I grit my teeth. "You have exactly a minute to explain to me what in the hell is going on."

She frowns. "I thought you would've been happy I'm doing it. I'm helping you."

"Lyra, I didn't ask for your fucking help! Tell me what's really happening. You didn't possibly... *you* put this detective here?! Celeste?!"

"I hadn't planned on hurting her. But she wasn't going to

stop. Just like the detectives. They weren't going to stop. They were after you," she says, taking a step toward me.

I take one back, staring at her as though she's a monster. As though she's more disturbing than I ever could be.

It's from the profound shock that's taken root inside me. I'm truly at a loss for how to make sense of this turn of events.

"I found a bottle of pills in the bathtub. You used your medications."

"I did," she answers. "She was very easy to manipulate. I agreed to go back with her to your penthouse. She was going to tell me the truth about you. Show me this dungeon. But I already knew. So I took care of her for you. There was a struggle —she tried to put up a fight—but I had it under control."

"The rug. You messed it up."

"I wondered if you'd notice. I force-fed her some of the pills and waited 'til she passed out. Then I dragged her into the bathroom and set the scene."

"You called me afterward and invited me over to your place. I had just gotten home from a Midnight Society event."

"Busy night," she jokes darkly. "You came over fast. I barely had enough time to shower and clean up. But I was being honest with you when I said I wasn't sure what I was going to do. If I was going to tell you everything... or at least try to get the detectives off your back first. That's what you didn't understand. I had to verify what they knew. If what they knew was what I suspected about you.

"It didn't take much convincing. Maloney told me everything I hoped he would. That it was really you. So, I convinced him to come with me by telling him I knew where you kept the dead bodies. I showed him the dungeon. And then... then I took him out too."

The knowledge that Lyra's killed for me—like I've killed for her—further blows my mind. I can't process it no matter how hard I try as I stand opposite her and notice the eager light shining in her eyes as she stares at me.

It's as though a new version of her has emerged. A Lyra I've never even known about.

Gone is the self-depreciating, slightly insecure lamb I've obsessed over.

The woman before me is standing in what she's done. She's *proud* of it.

But... it still doesn't compute. It doesn't add up.

"Why?" I croak, more lost than I've ever been in my life.

The shine in her eyes dims and her frown returns. "Because," she says as though it's the most obvious fact in the world, "I've never gotten the chance to thank you."

"For what? What the hell are you talking about?!"

"For protecting me." She begins stepping toward me again, a softness about her that would be sentimental if it weren't bathed in gruesome circumstance. "The ways you've *always* protected me... you make me feel so special. No one ever has like you do."

"What the fuck are you talking about?! This isn't funny. This isn't a game, Lyra. Stop this charade at once!"

I feel like I'm losing my mind.

That's the only explanation for what's going on. I'm slowly losing my sanity as Lyra flips the script and reveals everything I've known so confidently is up for question.

We're in the middle of a dungeon with a cell in one corner and a freezer of dead bodies in the other. On the table to my right are a variety of devices I've used to dismember countless human bodies. Pools of blood have stained the floor we stand on.

And yet... this moment is the most disturbing moment of all.

As Lyra gazes at me so adoringly, so frank and vulnerable, I feel like I'm dreaming. This can't be real!

"You took the fall, Kaden," she says after a moment of poignant silence. "You took the fall for the murder. For what I did all those years ago. We were only kids... but don't you remember?"

It happens at once.

The shield I've unknowingly erected to hide my past comes falling down. Before my eyes I see the moment in such clarity, you'd think I'd gone backward in time.

It's her beautiful music that often calls to me in the dark halls of our home. I follow the sound, always so ensnared from the first breathtaking note.

I wander for what feels like miles. At first, I do so quietly, hoping to remain unseen so not to spook her. Then I pick up the pace. I trot down the hall with a heart pounding in anticipation.

She's supposed to look up and smile sweetly at me. A shy, pretty smile.

But that wish is only in my dreams—they never let her do anything but play. Instead, tears are often wetting her eyes as she plays again and again and again.

The screams fill the dark air. I stomach them... sometimes. But tonight they've become too much. Too painful and frightening to my ears.

They're hurting her!

They have to be. I sprint down the halls with desperate pants, hoping I make it in time.

...instead, there's blood. Everywhere.

Seeping into the floors. Spreading far and wide 'til it reaches my feet.

And tears. Sobbing.

A small, bloodied little girl sits crumpled in the corner, clutching a knife in her tiny shaking hand. She's bruised and swollen, sporting injuries from what they've done to her.

I look around.

Her mother lays dead in a pool of her own blood. A few feet

off is my father... his cane has fallen from his hand. He's sput-
tering for air, still alive, but just barely due to the deep gashes in
his face.

So. Much. Blood.

I don't know what makes me do it. I don't know what runs
through my head. But as I look back at her bruised, tear-
streaked face, I have to help.

I pry the knife from her shaky fingers and hold it securely in
my own. "Run. RUN!"

She flees. She hops up on her skinny, weak legs and flees
faster than you'd think possible. I kneel down in the puddle of
blood and wait.

I wait until there are flashes of red and blue lights and
sirens whirring from outside the parlor window...

The past fades before my eyes and leaves only the present
behind. Lyra standing before me with teary eyes and a soft
smile.

"It was your music. You were the girl playing," I say
brokenly, my voice hollow. "You were the sound in the halls I
heard. I used to run toward it... and hope for the day you'd
play for me. That you'd just smile at me. But you were always
so upset."

She nods. "I couldn't stand being apart from you any
longer. I had to see you again. So I found a way."

My gaze narrows. "Are you saying..."

Her softness melts away, replaced by an almost catatonic
wave that comes over her. "One of my Cyber Fan subscribers,
Francesco, explained to me he was a wealthy Italian businessman. He wanted to extend an invitation to me to attend the
Midnight Society party. I hoped you would be there. I tried to
meet you... but you were so different. You were so closed off. I
had to get your attention somehow. So I found a way to get
invited on stage."

"You didn't want to be up there."

"You're right. I didn't want to be up there... to suck Klein off. But I knew doing what I did would get your attention. I've never lost sight of you, Kaden. I never forgot you."

"As in... you know? About me?"

She smiles again. "I guess the stalked was also the stalker."

"You were aware I was? That I was stalking you?"

"I was already following you... your whole life. I told you before I had looked you up. I just left out the part about how much. You were rich and powerful and someone. I was poor and invisible and no one. But I still made sure to keep track of you. Kaden Raskova, the boy who saved me... the son of Dmitri Androski Raskova. Sometimes only known as his musical name, Dmitri Androski. World renown pianist, the man my mother loved, and the brilliant man who was my piano instructor.

"I wanted so badly to reach out to you. But you were never within reach," she explains. "After that day, we were separated, and I never saw you again. I returned to my family. We grieved the loss of my mother, but my family couldn't handle my problems. So they gave me up to the system. A part of them... I think... suspected what I had done. The truth of what happened to my mother. I wasn't a normal little girl."

"My father... he abused you."

Her gaze lowers to the floor, a sudden darkness about her. "Every practice. Every time my finger slipped. Every time I made a small mistake. My mother allowed it. She was in love with him, and they believed they could train me into a world-renowned prodigy."

Anger consumes me at the memory of what my father was doing. I had suspected, I had known deep down, and yet I had felt powerless. I hadn't intervened sooner...

Another thought occurs to me and cuts my rising temper short.

"Your medications," I say. "I could never find much on

your medical history. I looked extensively in all the systems. Are they...?"

"For my mental state," she answers, raking her teeth over her bottom lip. "I was too poor growing up to get help. I'm too poor now. I get everything on the black market. Just like my weed dealer. I cope in ways you're not supposed to. It seems you blocked out what happened."

"I did. I erased it from my mind. I convinced myself it was my mother's music I was hearing."

"I do that too... sometimes." She releases a shuddering breath as if dreading the thought of telling me any more. "Other times... I struggle with what's real. I go to the cemetery and visit my friends. My *mom*. I can still hear her sometimes. And others. I invent people. It helps me do things I never would. It gives me courage, like the night of your party. I didn't take my meds and I got high, then I convinced myself to go. Jael was never real. She was just a figment of my imagination that gave me the courage I needed. I know that now."

"Lyra..." I say slowly with a shake of my head. "I don't even know what to say. None of this is what I thought it would be."

Hope shines in her eyes. "You were going to take me away, weren't you? Tonight was going to be the night. Then we can finally be together."

Yes... but that's before I found out... everything.

"We still can," she says, moving toward me. She reaches for my hand, curling her fingers around it. "Don't you see? We have a bond. We always have."

Peering down into her eyes, the core part of me recognizes the truth of her words.

There is a bond between us. There is a mutual obsession. Some kind of innate urge on my end to protect her... and on her end to do the same.

Tonight, Lyra outmatched me. In doing so, she proved *why* she is my match.

Perhaps something I've sensed all along in my stalking of her, though I couldn't put the pieces together.

"Before we do," she says, bewitching me with her dark brown eyes, "there's one last thing I think we should do."

I understand immediately.

With the truth laid out and our connection reestablished, I know Lyra intimately. I know exactly what is on her mind.

"Yes, we should take care of that. It's what I call a loose end."

She smiles. "I meant to that night years ago... but I never got the chance to finish him off. He had been abusing me so long. My mother was so in love with him. I snuck a kitchen knife into my backpack for our lesson. Then I attacked both of them. I wanted them dead, Kaden."

"Neither deserved to keep living for what they did to you."

"He has... he's survived."

"Tonight that changes. Come." I intertwine our fingers in a tight handhold—a first time in my life—and I pull her toward the stairs. It's as we come up to the top that it hits me what's happening. That another wave of disbelief rolls over me. "Lyra," I say, "you're insane."

She smirks at me, squeezing my hand. "Thanks. You too."

35. Lyra
Mad Hatter - Melanie Martinez

It took me a while to realize that it was happening again.

I was caught up in another period of my life where I was spiraling, losing my grip on reality. In the past, it's taken different forms. As a teen girl it manifested in severe emotional outbursts and distress. Those were the years I met Grady, as an unstable ball of misery and insecurity that he fed off for years.

Once I was old enough, I worked hard, juggling multiple jobs, in hopes I could buy meds to treat myself.

I've tried many. I've experimented and researched, failing and succeeding along the way. For a long time, I couldn't keep a friend to save my life. Then Imani came along, and I found the right mix of pills that kept me going. That made me able to function.

But playing the piano has become such a complicated headache. I range from even-keeled as I give piano lessons to a panicked mess when forced to play on my own again. Mom invaded my head and self-doubt ran rampant.

....until Kaden stepped in. Valiant and stoic in ways he didn't even understand as he gave me the confidence I needed.

He helped me rediscover the joy in playing. My passion for the music that flowed from my fingertips.

There were a lot of things he didn't know, like how we're destined to be together.

I knew. Even when I was heavily medicated and in denial, I knew.

I kept tabs on him for years, on and off. Kaden Raskova became as unattainable a dream as playing at the Easton Opera House.

Instead, he reentered my life all on his own. At least he believed he did. He proved that he was the man I always hoped he'd be. The same boy that he had been so many years ago.

He would always look out for me even if he didn't realize why. We would always have a special connection even when we were far apart.

Kaden and I rush out of his penthouse and hop into his Tesla.

The night's halfway over, minutes away from striking midnight. We couldn't care less as we race off down the city streets.

It doesn't take us long before we're coming up on the luxury hotel that is the Winchester. Kaden swings into the valet with an unmistakable air of confidence. It's a trait I've always admired about him; he moves through daily life as though he owns the world. He could if he wanted to, given his family name.

We circle around and meet on the carpeted pathway leading into the ritzy hotel. The valet approaches in recognition of him, but Kaden waves him off as if he couldn't matter less.

"Have it waiting for me in twenty," he orders.

The man fervently nods and then scurries off.

I loop my arm with Kaden's and walk fast at his side. We make for an interesting pair—though we're dressed to the nines, Kaden in his tuxedo and me in the gown from the opera house, we've got blood stains on our clothes. Even on our skin.

Kaden owns it. He strolls into the sparkling marble lobby as though the blood is part of his outfit. I take a page from his book and do the same. I hold my head up high and strut at his side like I'm worthy of being here.

I'm a queen on the arm of a king.

The event being hosted by the Midnight Society teems with life. We cross the lobby and enter a ballroom of masked elites mingling among themselves. Many are so entrenched in their own worlds that they hardly notice us coming through... until they're forced to do so.

We don't blend in. We stand out as we blaze a path across the room. The only two unmasked among a sea of disguised power players.

I clutch Kaden's arm and whisper, "Where would he be?"

"In his private parlor. He never comes down to mingle. He considers himself above it."

We're crossing the cavernous room to the other side when two men step into our path. Both are masked in tuxedos as fine and tailored as Kaden's. Though I can't make out the details of their faces, the one on the left looks eerily familiar.

My stomach knots up and I almost take a step back. Kaden serves as enough support to keep me in place.

Klein Fairchild.

The man who shoved his cock into my mouth in front of a theater full of people.

He obviously recognizes me. How can he not? I'm not wearing a mask like the others.

His cold eyes settle on my face and a sneer develops at the corners of his lips. "Kaden, I see you've brought the prostitute with you. I can't say I'm surprised. Your taste in women has always left something to be desired. But even I thought you'd do better than this—WHAT ARE YOU—STOP!"

He shrieks out in the same kind of panic as he had that night on stage. His eyes bulge and his skin pales.

I snap as quickly as I had that night, coming to the conclusion I have to do what I have to do. A waiter passes by with a tray of silverware and cutlery, and that's when I seize the opportunity. I snatch a knife off the tray, and I rush forward, driving it into his groin area.

The other man at his side leaps back in utter shock and alarm.

Klein drops to his knees, hands clutching the front of his pants where I jammed the knife into him. The panicked scream he releases catches the attention of everyone else in the ballroom.

Kaden grabs me by the wrist and drags me onward, breaking out into a sprint. I hold onto the bloody knife with a laugh bubbling out of me. A sense of exhilaration runs through me.

This is the moment I've been living for. The night I've always dreamed of.

I know it as we flee from the ballroom and make it into another hall. We race up the curving staircase two at a time, my long dress almost slowing us down.

"You really are fucking insane, little lamb!" Kaden grits out. He shoots me a lopsided grin as we reach the top of the stairs. "But, damn if it isn't making me even more obsessed with you. You just might have me beat. Come quickly. We only have a few minutes before security catches up."

I'm grateful Kaden knows exactly where to find him.

We make quick work of the hall. The doors on either side serve as mysterious barriers to the things happening behind them—more than once I hear what sounds like a moan or the lash of what can only be something like a leather crop.

Kaden pulls me along until we reach the last door, then

bursts inside. It takes me another second to digest our surroundings and understand where he's taken me.

We're in a parlor of some kind. A fireplace roars to our left. The entire wall on the far end is comprised of a wide window that offers a scenic view of the hotel courtyard below. My gaze swings to the armchair nearby, finally spotting the man in... an *owl* mask?!

I take half of an uncertain step back. Kaden does the opposite. He moves forward, letting go of my hand, his glare set on the man.

The man sits up straighter in his chair. Though his mask disguises his face, just the subtlest change in his body language tells me he's surprised. He wasn't expecting us.

"What are you doing here?" he asks in a slow monotone.

"Tonight's the night, father. Tonight's the night I finally do what I should've done many years ago," Kaden says.

"You have *her* with you."

"You knew all along, didn't you? *That's* why you were so insistent that I eliminate her. You wanted revenge... for how she disfigured you."

His posture tenses up even more. I can't tell for certain due to his gold-plated mask, but I can feel it—his gaze landing on me. Mr. Raskova, *Androski*, stares straight at me.

His contempt fills the room.

"I should've done it myself," he says. "The girl disappeared. I assumed into whatever impoverished child care system they have set up for vile little girls like her. I confess I didn't expect her to come back in this way. Right into my club where she's proceeded to do what she's always done—cause nothing but trouble. I should've had her eliminated myself.

"You've always been too weak. Even when you've claimed not to be. You took the fall for what the girl did. Had you not been my son, your life would've been ruined. Perhaps I should've let you suffer rather than pay off the authorities. I could've forgotten I ever had a disappointment of a son."

Kaden's jaw clenches. The rest of his face goes eerily blank. His eyes darken 'til they're almost black. "You speak of weakness, father. But I'm not sure there's anything weaker than brutalizing a defenseless little girl for sport."

"It's amusing that my son with an unending appetite to kill people would believe he has the room to criticize me for violence."

"I may be a monster," Kaden admits. "I've done terrible things and offer no apologies for any of it. That's true. And yet you're still infinitely worse. You deserve the fate you eluded that night. I'm here to ensure that this time, there will be no escape."

He sits up straighter in his seat, his deformed face hidden behind his mask, but his anger emanates off him. "You believe you're going to get away with this? My security's right outside the door."

"Lyra," Kaden says in a calm voice. "Hand me your knife. Then lock the door. No one leaves until this is handled once and for all."

I rush to do as Kaden says, his accomplice to the end. I hand over the knife smeared with Klein's blood before scurrying over to lock the door. We're guaranteed the privacy we need in this moment.

No one will be interfering anytime soon.

Kaden clenches the knife within his hand and then advances toward his father...

———

"Do you want to give it a try?" Kaden asks. A slow grin comes to his face as he holds out his hand.

My gaze drops to the bloodied meat cleaver resting in the palm of it. "I've never used one before."

"Perfect time to learn. He's still breathing. All the more suffering."

I wrap my hands tightly around the wooden handle, a beat of excitement in my veins, and then I take my swing. The smooth, curved blade comes down into the gaped wound on his chest. I've swung so hard that I can't even pull the blade out—it's lodged deep into his chest cavern.

Mr. Raskova barely produces a grunt of pain. His head's turned to the side, his skin cold and pale. He's holding onto his life by a thread.

Kaden gives an impressed nod and then takes the wooden handle of the meat cleaver from me. "Sometimes it requires some muscle. If you get it in there deep enough, it can be difficult to pull out. Allow me."

He pries the cleaver free with a hard tug and then glances at his father's pained face. "What do you say? Is it time to put him out of his misery? Do you want to do the honors or should I?"

I smirk at him. "Go ahead. I've gotten my revenge."

Wielding the cleaver like a true expert, Kaden ends it with a final blow. This time he leaves the blade stuck in his skull. He's barely let go of the handle before I'm tossing my arms around him and pressing a deep kiss onto his lips.

"Little lamb, do you know what you're starting?" he groans as I run fingers through his hair and notch my legs around his hips.

But I can't control myself. The moment couldn't feel more celebratory. More of a reunion between the two of us as we tie up loose ends and embark on a new journey together.

It doesn't matter that we're in the middle of a dungeon with dead bodies, some still bleeding on Kaden's table and others dismembered in his industrial-sized freezer. If anything they're symbols of how deep our bond is.

How our bond has linked us even when we didn't realize it was.

Kaden kisses me and then pins me against the nearest wall. We make the most of each other, tearing at clothes and shuddering at how good we can make the other feel. When my orgasm does slam into me, it's a dizzying wave that leaves me with a satisfied smile.

Kaden's no different. He nuzzles my face and takes his time letting go. He's just as obsessed with me. Just as endlessly devoted.

"Let's finish this up," he says, thumbing my cheek. "Then... we can finally begin our lives together."

36. KADEN
(You Made It Feel Like) Home - Trent Reznor and Atticus Ross

1 MONTH LATER...

"More champagne, Mr. Androski?"

I look up at the sound of my name and then give a nod to the flight attendant. He fills up my flute as he inquires if I'm in need of anything else. I decline and return to the newspaper I'm reading.

It's amazing that forty thousand feet up in the air seems to be the only place I've had a chance to catch up on reading about current events.

The past few weeks have been that busy. The headline on the front page of the *Easton Times* should be alarming. Instead, it makes me grin as I reach for my flute of champagne and take a sip.

Lyra Hendrix, 24, the Latest Victim of Wanted Serial Killer Kaden Raskova

So much for ever returning to Easton—or America at all, for that matter.

The city of Easton is currently worked up into a frenzy over me. I've been revealed to be a monstrous serial killer who has murdered dozens over the years. People like Maximillion Keys and Fyodor Kreed were tips of the iceberg.

Once the light was shed on me, the long list of other murders I've committed over the years was unraveled. Authorities are still finding chopped bodies buried strategically throughout the city. They're still connecting the dots of unsolved missing persons cases and linking them to me.

After I murdered my father in the most bloody, gruesome fashion, I escaped. I was able to flee from the city unscathed.

There was no time to waste.

Any moment police would track me down and slap handcuffs on me.

Surprisingly, my fatal mistake didn't come from murdering my father. It wasn't even the bodies I had in my penthouse.

It was the police detective. I had slit the throat of Detective Sloan Laurent in the hall of Lyra's apartment building, then quickly dragged her inside to store her in her closet.

The woman should've been dead. I normally make sure my victims are. I had been in such a rush to get Lyra back to my place, I hadn't checked. The detective had survived; she lay bleeding out in Lyra's closet but she managed to call 911.

She's the one that survived and helped piece together everything. If she hadn't survived, I would've gotten away with it.

The name Kaden Raskova wouldn't have gone down in Easton history as the deadliest serial killer in existence.

Such is life.

By the time she was well enough to speak and help authorities, I was long gone.

I had taken a private jet out of the country. Much like the jet I am flying in now as I set off to another discreet location.

I look around my luxury accommodations and sip more champagne.

The future is entirely up in the air. I could meet a karmic ending sometime soon (though I believe in no such thing). Authorities could find a way to track me down in another country and attempt to force me back to the States.

A more violent, murderous serial killer than me could decide I'm their next target. They could kill me just as easily as I have killed so many times.

But none of these things worry me. I have never lived my life plagued by normal human concerns. Death doesn't scare me, even now.

Nothing does.

However, as I fold the newspaper, and lock eyes with the woman approaching, I can't help letting the grin on my face spread.

Lyra matches me, like always, and returns my grin. She's in a knitted sweater dress that hugs her body's every female curve, with her rope-like braids hanging long down her back.

In the past, I may have preferred to live my life as a loner. A man on his own with no care or regard for any other human being on this planet. For the most part, I still feel that way.

Except for Lyra.

I've discovered that sometimes it is better to have a companion. Particularly when that companion is as brilliant and neurotic as you are.

She takes the seat next to mine. Her hand seeks me out, slipping her fingers between mine, and leaning over the armrest dividing us.

"Enjoying yourself?" I ask.

She hums in answer. "But I'll enjoy myself more when we're back on solid ground."

"One more hour at most. Then we'll be home. For the foreseeable future."

"I saw what you were reading. They have my photo on the front page."

"You're famous."

"For all the wrong reasons."

"That makes two of us," I say, unfurling the paper in my lap. "You're dead to the world, little lamb. I'm a murderer to the world. It's the way things had to be so we can start over. You understand why."

She nods and gives my hand a squeeze. "But I wish you didn't have to. What if they track you down?"

"Where we're going, it's unlikely," I answer. "No extradition treaty. We'll be living in a remote enough area. In the unlikely chance they do, so what? No one lasts forever. We will be no different."

"I love your realism."

"It's necessary... so we can make the most of every day we have. Your hand is healing up nicely."

She looks down at the hand that's not clutching mine. A large scar heals across the palm of her hand. A severe gash that I caused at the height of our escape plan. We had murdered my father and dismembered the bodies as time dwindled.

I knew it was inevitable the police would trace what was happening back to me... and Lyra.

So I killed her.

I cut her with my knife. I did so using my surgical expertise, with great care, and let her blood drip onto the floor.

We staged a struggle. I even left the murder weapon with my prints and her blood.

Her belongings were left untouched in her apartment. Her phone abandoned. All means of communication cut between her and the few people who knew her.

As far as the police are concerned, her body is still missing, like many of my other victims. But Lyra Hendrix as the world knew her is dead.

It's a sacrifice that's asked a lot of her—she didn't get to say goodbye to her best friend, Imani, and she had to leave her life behind on the spot. She's been forced to take on a new identity much in the same manner I have.

Sacrifices she's said she's willing to make.

"I wonder if they'll ever stop looking for you," she says, peering out the window. We're soaring among the morning clouds, on a fast track to our next destination. "I wonder what everyone thinks."

"I can tell you that. The people in my world have moved on. They have returned to their vapid conversations and existence without a single care... except for when they were photographed mourning at my father's funeral. The others who knew you, I'm afraid are likely the same. Perhaps except for your friend. The city may be in a panic over a loose serial killer, but make no mistake, the world at large has moved on. That is human nature. People will continue living their lives."

"And so will we." A small smile lights up her face.

I drop a kiss onto her lips, unable to resist. "And so will we... as it should be."

"I love you, Kaden."

I stroke my fingers along the inside of her forearm, where her special piano keys tattoo is inked onto her brown skin. My deep affection for Lyra may be what most would call unhealthy and morbid but it's what a man like me is capable of.

A love that's dark and twisted; a love that's violent and obsessive but no less deep in its own unique way. It's something no one else understands and no one else needs to understand.

"I love you too, little lamb."

Author's Note: Thank you for taking this dark journey with me! I appreciate every reader and would love it even more if you took a quick second to drop me a review/rating. 🖤

You can also preorder book 2 in the series, **Cruel Pleasures**. Turn the page for the cover and blurb!

CRUEL DELIGHTS PLAYLIST

1. High Alone - Sevdaliza

2. Get Into It (Yuh) - Doja Cat

3. Biting Down - Lorde

4. Moth to a Flame - The Weeknd & Swedish House Mafia

5. Inertia Creeps - Massive Attack

6. Cyber Sex - Doja Cat

7. Nobody Gets Me - SZA

8. Atmosphere - Joy Division

9. Strange Effect - Unloved & Raven Violet

10. Kill of the Night - Gin Wigmore

11. Love Language - SZA

12. Careful - Lucky Daye

13. Bad Guy - Billie Eilish

14. Girl is A Gun - Halsey

15. I Want it All - Cameron Grey

16. Obsessed - Zandros & Limi

17. Eyes Don't Lie - Isabel LaRosa

18. Sweet Dreams (Are Made Of This) - Emily Browning

19. Black Milk - Massive Attack

20. Hearing Damage - Thom Yorke

21. Boys Like You · Tanerélle

22. Kill For Your Love - Labrinth

23. Do You Really Want to Hurt Me? - Nessa Barrett

24. You've Seen the Butcher - Deftones

25. Time is Running Out - JPOLND

26. Guilty of Love - Unloved

27. Destroy Myself Just for You - Montell Fish

28. Ends & Begins - Labrinth

29. I feel Like I'm Drowning - Two Feet

30. Bloody Mary - Lady Gaga

31. Closer - Nine Inch Nails

32. Kill Bill - SZA

33. Sigh - Unloved

34. I Was Never There - The Weeknd

35. Mad Hatter - Melanie Martinez

36. (You Made It Feel Like) Home - Trent Reznor and Atticus Ross

Listen to the playlist here on Spotify!

A dark and twisted story about obsession that blurs the lines between what's real and what's fantasy...

Have you ever felt like you were going insane?
I have. The day my best friend disappeared and the world pretended she was dead.
I'm just about the only one who cares that she's gone.
It becomes clear I have to take matters into my own hands.
I have to infiltrate the secret society that's behind her disappearance.

But the Midnight Society is no normal club.

It's a society where your darkest fantasy comes true.

Soon, I find myself in the middle of a sick and twisted game.

The prize of two men as mysterious as they are sexy, competing to be victor.

Their obsession they'll do anything to have.

And I discover the answers I'm seeking might be too disturbing to be real.

PREORDER NOW

STAY CONNECTED

Let's keep in touch!

Join my reader group and follow me on social media below.
♥

Also by Sienne Vega

The Capo and the Ballerina

Book 1 - Vicious Impulses

Book 2 - Brutal Impulses (Coming March 2024)

City of Sinners Series

Book 1 - King of Vegas

Book 2 - Queen of Hearts

Book 3 - Kingdom of Sin

Book 4 - Heart of Sin (Louis & Tasha Novella)

City of Sinners Special Edition Boxset

Gangsters & Roses Series

Book 0 - Forbidden Roses

Book 1 - Wicked Roses

Book 2 - Twisted Roses

Book 3 - Savage Roses

Book 4 - Devious Roses

Book 5 - Ruthless Roses

Gangsters & Roses Special Edition Boxset

The Steel Kings MC Series

Book 1 - Kings Have No Mercy

Book 2 - Kings Don't Break

Book 3 - Kings Fear No One (Coming August 2024)

The Midnight Society

Book 1 - Cruel Delights

Book 2 - Cruel Pleasures (Coming May 2024)

Seattle Wolves

Book 1 - Break the Ice (Coming February 2024)

Savage Bloodline

Caesar DeLuca (Coming June 2024)

Novellas

Shared by the Capo

Or scan the QR code below for a direct link to my books!

ABOUT THE AUTHOR

Sienne has a thing for dark and brooding alphas and the women who love them. She enjoys writing stories where lines are blurred, and the romance is dark and delicious. In her spare time, she unwinds with a nice glass of wine and Netflix binge.